THE NUDE

THE NUDE

A HISTORICAL ROMANCE

DOROTHY MCFALLS

FIVE STAR

A part of Gale, Cengage Learning

GALE
CENGAGE Learning

Detroit • New York • San Francisco • New Haven, Conn • Waterville, Maine • London

GALE
CENGAGE Learning

Copyright © 2009 by Dorothy McFalls.
Five Star Publishing, a part of Gale, Cengage Learning.

LIBRARY OF CONGRESS CATALOGING-IN-PUBLICATION DATA

McFalls, Dorothy.
    The nude : a historical romance / by Dorothy McFalls. — 1st ed.
        p. cm.
    ISBN-13: 978-1-59414-767-8 (alk. paper)
    ISBN-10: 1-59414-767-1 (alk. paper)
    1. Painters—Fiction. I. Title.
PS3613.C4383N83 2009
813'.6—dc22   2009001227

First Edition. First Printing: May 2009.
Published in 2009 in conjunction with Tekno Books.

Printed in the United States of America
1 2 3 4 5 6 7 13 12 11 10 09

To Jim
This story has always been for you, my personal hero.
And to my father, Robert Dollar McFalls
You were my best champion with my writing.
I miss you dearly.

ACKNOWLEDGEMENTS

Writing a book can be a solitary and sometimes lonely endeavor. But like any passion in life, it's rarely accomplished without outside support. My family has provided never-ending encouragement as I chased my dream of writing fiction, believing in me even when I forgot to believe in myself. My online buddies, especially Tracy Anne Warren and Mallary Mitchell, have let me share in their writing triumphs, which lately have been many. Can I be you when I grow up?

And I can't say enough about my critique group partners: Nina Bruhns, Kieran Kramer, Vicki Sweatman, and Judy Watts. They are a group of talented writers who are unfailingly honest, cheerfully supportive, and quite simply a great group of friends. The next bottle of wine is on me.

Finally, my loyal readers, your emails and notes have touched my heart and have never failed to make me smile. I hope this book does the same for you. Bless you.

PROLOGUE

London. May 1814

He'd finally lost his sanity. There was simply no other way to explain it. His breathing quickened as a lone tallow taper sputtered, the bright orange flame turning smoky. Dionysus tore his gaze from his work long enough to search the cluttered workshop—the floor littered with discarded brushes and paints—for a replacement.

"Sir?" a servant called after tapping on the door. "Sir? Please, will you eat today?"

Dionysus, too absorbed in his work, lit a new taper and returned his attentions to the canvas. His heart thundered in his chest. He lifted his brush and pulled it slowly across the canvas—tracing the gentle curve of a thigh.

Her thigh.

He'd only seen her briefly at the Baneshire's ball. She was a widow, one of the grand matrons of the *ton* had whispered, after taking notice of his overlong stare. He could not, no matter how hard he tried, lift his eyes from the beautiful creature dancing—nay—floating like a gossamer faery across the glassy ballroom floor.

"She's my niece," the Earl of Baneshire had told him when asked. "Her husband died on a battlefield in France, poor thing. Left her without a *sou*. It appears his estate was mortgaged to the hilt." The earl paused to watch his niece curtsy to the man she'd been dancing with as the set came to a close. "She's just now out of mourning clothes. It warms my heart to see her in something other than widow's weeds. I could introduce her to you."

Dionysus's heart had been hammering, like now. His palms had grown moist and his mouth dry.

Could it be her? Could it really be her?

"No, no, thank you," he'd said with a bow. He didn't even ask her name before finding a footman, before demanding his carriage sought and his cloak retrieved. No matter what, he could not stay.

He could not.

That very evening he'd locked himself in his workshop, trying desperately to exorcise the demon that had stolen his sanity. He'd tossed aside six canvases before finally finding the right strokes and the right shades of pigment to create a portrait of the woman.

He held his breath, lightly tinting the tips of her breasts with a delicate paint prepared from powdered garnets. Her deep eyes from crushed sapphires. Her full lips from the dust of rubies.

As he stepped back, a wave of dizziness overtook him. He reached out to steady himself against a small worktable. He'd missed too many meals, lost too many nights of sleep. Pulling a shaky hand through his hair, he stared at the image in front of him.

It was perfect.

She was perfect.

Now that the work was finally finished and his obsession drained away, he could see what he'd done for what it was—madness.

Unable to lift his eyes from the painting, he sank to his knees. What had he been thinking? What had he created?

No one could ever see it.

No one.

But to destroy it, to deface the perfect image of *her*, would surely be echoed by the destruction of his soul.

His strength gone, Dionysus curled up at the base of his easel and fell asleep with her perfect ruby lips smiling down on him.

CHAPTER ONE

"You must come!"

The breathless demand sailed into the tiny parlor where Elsbeth sat alone. Not a moment later the parlor door came crashing open. Elsbeth glanced up from her embroidery work, and frowned. What excitement had caused her cousins to forget, yet again, that they were gentlewomen and well beyond the reckless age of sixteen?

"The exhibition promises to be the grandest event this week! You simply must want to come," Olivia shouted as she dashed into the parlor. Lauretta, the younger of Elsbeth's cousins, came trailing closely behind. The two ladies crowded around Elsbeth's overstuffed chair.

"Papa already said we could attend, but only if *you* agree to chaperone," Olivia said in an overeager tone. She tugged on Elsbeth's sleeve, nearly ripping the tender pale-blue muslin.

Their exuberance brought a bitter pang to Elsbeth's chest. They were both so innocent, so excitable. She paused, trying to remember what it truly felt like to be so mindlessly happy . . .

No matter, such foolishness only led to trouble.

She pried her cousin's fingers from her arm. "I fear I'm suffering from another headache." She set aside her embroidery—a table runner she'd been trying to finish for the past three months—and reached for the tea tray. A delicate Wedgwood cup clattered against the saucer in her hand while her conscience battled a silent war.

Her uncle, the generous Lord Baneshire, had invited her to come live with his family after her husband's death. Although her options had been severely limited, she'd accepted his charity only after he'd agreed she could serve as chaperone to his two daughters for the Season.

She shouldn't be shirking her duty to her uncle. Not after all he'd provided. It shouldn't matter that the thought of mingling with the gosspy ladies of the *ton* frightened her all the way down to her trembling toes.

No, that wasn't precisely correct. It wasn't society she was afraid of facing—but herself. How could she live with herself when nearly everything that passed her lips felt like naught but a lie?

"La, you've suffered from a headache for the past week," Lauretta said with a long sigh.

"Ever since Mama's and Papa's ball," Olivia finished.

Ever since the ball. All gathered had praised her for her strength of character. And they praised her husband for his heroism.

Elsbeth winced, and thought just how undeserving they were of those praises. But she'd accepted their words, agreed with them even though she felt by no means strong. And her husband . . . She shuddered at the thought of him; her husband was certainly no hero. He'd been just a man . . . a man foolish enough to be shot by a Frenchman a mere six months after purchasing his commission.

Thank the Lord.

"Yes," she agreed, yet another lie forming on her tongue. "I haven't been well since the ball."

Her gaze strayed to the new pile of invitations that had arrived in the morning post. Her husband's dead hero status—a by-product of a brutal war—had made her a curio, a much sought after one at that.

14

Despite the *ton*'s eagerness to include her at their entertainments, Elsbeth had discovered she was unready to face the *beau monde* and continue the charade. She planned to pen gracious refusals, delaying her full return to Society for at least another week.

As if a week could change the truth.

"Ask your Aunt Violet if you're so anxious. She should enjoy the frivolities of such an art exhibition."

The younger ladies drew long faces.

"But—but—" Lauretta sputtered.

Olivia swooped down beside Elsbeth's chair. "But you're ever so good at puzzles," she said, her hazel eyes coming alive with color. "Shouldn't you want to attend the art exhibition? Shouldn't you want the chance to discover the true identity of Dionysus?"

Olivia inched closer. "Imagine, all those fantastic paintings. They say a nobleman paints them. But no one knows who. His identity is more carefully guarded than Sir Walter Scott and his Waverley novels."

"Wouldn't it be grand if Dionysus were my Donald?" Lauretta whispered. "Wouldn't it simply be grand?"

Sir Donald Gilforth was a fine young gentleman perfectly suited to the mild Lauretta, and dull. Exceedingly so. He couldn't possibly be this mysterious Dionysus, this new artist fueling the gossips.

Elsbeth sighed. She *was* curious about the paintings. She would like to see for herself if—

A sharp pain struck her heart.

Dionysus couldn't be—

"Elly," Olivia whined, using a pet name that set Elsbeth's teeth on edge. "Please, please, please, come with us."

"We don't want Aunt Violet to come," Lauretta said. "She never allows—"

15

"Ah—she doesn't give us the company you do," Olivia quickly said, sending her younger sister a quelling glance.

"I understand very well why you prefer me over Aunt Violet. I allow you and Lauretta to disappear with your beaus unescorted. She does not."

Lauretta and Olivia both lowered their pretty heads. Tears sparkled in their eyes. It was the lowest trick in their arsenal. She hated to disappoint the lovely girls. Olivia, the elder of the two, had recently turned one-and-twenty, and Lord Baneshire was beginning to openly despair that she'd ever settle on a man long enough to marry. Lauretta, on the other hand, at merely eighteen was lost in love.

Elsbeth reached over to pat Lauretta's hand. "Will Sir Donald Gilforth be in attendance?"

"Oh yes, he's promised to explain the finer points of the paintings."

"Truly?" Elsbeth said, and felt the tug of a rare smile. Lauretta was something of an artistic genius and could tell Sir Donald volumes more about the paintings than he could possibly think to tell her.

"If I refuse, you will no doubt badger me the entire afternoon. At least at the art exhibition your attentions will be on something other than me."

Both of her cousins remembered their manners long enough to thank her politely before dashing away like unschooled hoydens.

The carriage rocked and swayed while the horses' hooves clopped a steady beat on the pavement as they approached Montagu House, which housed the British Museum. It was located in the middle of the affluent residential neighborhood of Bloomsbury. Having visited its exhibits several times with Lauretta in the past few weeks, Elsbeth knew the building well. And she usually enjoyed the museum. But unlike her regular visits, this event turned out to be a quite a crush. She should have known it would be. Hadn't Olivia warned her?

Her cousins led the way into the special exhibition room, their eyes wide. The three of them squeezed their way past a throng of young gentlemen and a pair of giggly young ladies with their stone-faced chaperone, stopping in the first unclaimed niche adjacent to a small painting framed with ornately carved mahogany.

The work—a lush landscape of deep purples and greens—depicted the vast expanse of the Yorkshire moors with vibrant colors and bold, broad brushstrokes.

"It's lovely," Olivia breathed.

"It makes me uneasy," Lauretta said with a shiver.

It's him. Elsbeth gripped her golden locket. Her heart thumped heavily in her chest. *It's him.* She now had a name—although a false one—to put with his work.

Dionysus.

She felt herself being pulled into the scene he'd created. The desolate, uninhabited moors appeared to extend far past the horizon, as if nothing else in the world could possibly exist. The painting evoked so sharp a pang of loneliness that it threatened to bow her in half.

She barely had time to recover before Sir Donald approached, bedecked in the most outrageous pink and yellow striped waistcoat decorated with a half-dozen shiny watch fobs. He greeted them politely, flashing his teeth.

"Lady Mercer," he said, touching her arm.

Elsbeth shuddered.

"If you would but allow me to escort Lady Lauretta over to a particular painting. It's the pinnacle of blending color and light and realism, and I wish to point out to her its less obvious merits."

Elsbeth warned Lauretta not to stray far, and watched Sir Donald as he led her cousin to a large painting filled with crimson and violet shades.

"Did you see those silly watch fobs he wears?" Olivia whispered, after Sir Donald was out of earshot. "I say, that large one is the most—"

"Not now, Olivia," Elsbeth said tightly. Severin, the fifth Baron Ames was fast approaching and there was absolutely no possible way she could make a graceful escape.

"Oooo, look," Olivia had noticed him, too. She latched onto Elsbeth's arm. "Lord Ames is ever so handsome. Please, Elsbeth. You know him. Please, introduce me."

Introducing Lord Ames to her innocent, young cousin was one of the last things she wished to do. Unfortunately, Olivia curtsied to Lord Ames before Elsbeth could stop her.

Ames was a powerful man with dark hair and a clever gleam to his eyes. Elsbeth prayed for strength as she stepped in between her cousin and this wicked rake, for he'd been friends with the late Earl of Mercer—her husband.

In his favor though, Ames had, on certain occasions, actually stood up for her. Foolish man.

Even so, rude or not, she refused to give Olivia an introduction. Olivia, not one to be thwarted, blurted out her own name while batting her long eyelashes.

Ames didn't appear the least bit shocked by Olivia's outrageous behavior. He flashed a playful smile.

"My dear ladies," he purred as he bowed in their direction. He then lavished Olivia with the most outrageous compliments: inquiring after her dressmaker, praising Olivia's skills in selecting the most refined fabrics, and suggesting Olivia's complexion rivaled the moon in its beauty.

Much to Elsbeth's vexation, Olivia drank it all in. Blushing, the young woman started babbling on and on about some silly fluff of a bonnet she'd spotted in a shop window. Ames crossed his arms over his broad chest and appeared to be utterly enthralled by the conversation.

"Lady Mercer?" a soft voice from behind startled Elsbeth. She turned her back on the wicked Lord Ames long enough to come face-to-face with a beautiful woman dressed in a shimmering gold gown.

"Ah, it is Lady Mercer," a second woman said. Several heads turned and before Elsbeth knew what was happening, she was surrounded by the very people from which she'd been trying to hide. They were closing in on her, pressing her with questions.

She backed away, murmuring her answers—lies, mostly—and berating herself for being such a coward. One bold woman pressed more doggedly than the rest, insisting that Lord Mercer deserved a medal for his sacrifice while tut-tutting over the debts he'd accumulated before his untimely death.

It was really too much to take.

She pried the woman's hand from her sleeve, only to have another take her place. She was trapped. And she had no choice but to smile, and pretend, and play the dutiful wife who had loved her husband.

Damnation.

Severin, Baron Ames, listened with only half an ear as young Lady Olivia twittered on and on about a dress she planned to wear to Almack's that week. He smiled and nodded at the appropriate intervals, but his attentions kept straying to Lady Mercer.

Offering his arm to Lady Olivia, he edged closer to where Lady Mercer stood, trapped by the worst of the town tabbies. He stepped closer still, but the din in the large room was too loud for him to hear a thing. He fought an urge to toss himself in front of those swarming vultures. Lady Mercer had suffered enough.

Once, several years ago, he'd overstepped his bounds and tried to rescue her from her bounder of a husband only to be rewarded with a sharp tongue-lashing from her for his efforts.

Lady Mercer was a cold woman. He watched as her deep blue eyes hardened. She was strong, much stronger than her willowy form would lead one to believe. But he knew better.

She would never allow a man to rescue her.

He smiled down at Lady Olivia and patted her hand. "And kid boots to match the dress, you say? Splendid, simply splendid," he said absently, checking his battered pocket watch. It was past time for the circus to begin. With one final glance in Lady Mercer's direction, he gave a shrug.

She wouldn't welcome his assistance anyway, he assured himself.

"See that painting in the front of the room covered with the heavy sheet?" he asked, interrupting Lady Olivia's excited nattering. "It's time for the unveiling."

Just minutes before the doors had opened to the public; Severin's assistant had delivered the extra painting wrapped tightly in brown paper. His hands already full with last minute arrangements, Severin hadn't taken the time to think about the painting, much less inspect it. But its existence had given him an idea. The added drama of unveiling a new work would only intensify the *ton*'s interest in the artist, increasing his demand and, hopefully, the prices of his paintings.

Not that Dionysus needed the money. He didn't need to be selling the paintings at all. Why he felt the need to offer his paintings for purchase—or to keep his identity hidden—Severin could only guess.

True, the man was a powerful member in the House of Lords and confidant to the Regent himself, but that shouldn't be a reason to hide his talent. But who was he to question the man's motives?

Unlike Dionysus, Severin sorely needed the funds and was more than thankful for the sixty percent commission he earned from each painting sold. For far too many years, he lived off the generosity of wealthy friends, putting up with more than he should. He still thanked God he made that fortuitous acquaintance of Dionysus last year. He wouldn't be alive otherwise . . .

"Ooo, this is ever so exciting," Lady Olivia breathed and latched tightly onto his arm. Her eyes were alive with color as she accompanied him up to the front of the exhibition room.

His first instinct had been to return the noisy young beauty to Lady Mercer. But, he sighed, he needed to keep up his appearance as fashionable rogue by escorting a different, yet equally, beautiful woman on his arm at every event.

The crowd parted to let him pass to the tiny stage where the veiled painting sat on a wooden easel. At Severin's prodding, the room quieted to excited whispers, and the crowd slowly closed ranks around him.

His gaze swept across the crowd. He heaved a sigh of relief when he saw that Lady Mercer had extracted herself from the gossips' clutches and had found a place in the crowd beside Lady Olivia's younger sister, Lady Lauretta, and the young lady's suitor, Sir Donald Gilforth.

Lady Olivia waved from the stage to her sister, who quickly returned the gesture.

"It is my great pleasure to unveil Dionysus's most recent work," Severin spoke in a voice loud enough to reach the far corners of the room. "I have it on the best authority that this painting is, by far, Dionysus's finest yet. And, I am sure, will command a steep price."

He grabbed a handful of the sheet.

The room took a collective breath.

"I give you—" With a grand sweep of his arm, he uncovered the painting the crowd had waited breathlessly to see "—*The Nude.*"

Elsbeth swayed, her vision blurring. If not for Lauretta's steadying hand, she might have collapsed.

The throng pressed forward to get a better look, closing in on the little space afforded to Elsbeth and her cousin. Her gaze flew back to the painting. Perhaps she'd been mistaken.

She wasn't.

Lord Ames stood frozen still clutching that sheet Elsbeth prayed he'd toss back onto the painting.

"Why Elly," Olivia blurted loud enough for half of London to hear. "That's you!"

Roaming eyes tore themselves from the painting to search out the lady it portrayed.

A heavy blush stung Elsbeth's cheeks and heat quickly spread down her chest. Those around her glowered at her, judging her, damning her. She would have died, simply died if not for Lauretta's tight hold on her hand.

"Is this some kind of punishment?" she muttered, closing her eyes. If only she could pinch them closed long enough for the fervor to die down. But such a scandal would outlast any effort on her part to hide. And worse, the scandal could tarnish the spotless Baneshire name. Olivia and Lauretta, two prime specimens on display in the Marriage Mart, deserved better than to be ruined by something done to her.

She drew a deep breath and forced herself to face the crowded room. She couldn't forestall the scandal, but she could take steps to endure the brunt of it, and protect her cousins from the irreparable damage that could befall their futures.

Lord Baneshire had trusted her after all.

Freeing her hand from Lauretta's strong grasp, she pushed

her way to the front of the room. The gentlemen in the audience glared, while the ladies turned their backs to her as she made her way to the steps of the stage.

"This was done without my permission or knowledge," she forced from behind clenched teeth. After taking one last look at the painting, her blush deepening, she ripped the sheet from Lord Ames's hand and tossed it back over the accursed painting.

"How could you?" she said, and slapped Ames across the cheek. The sound of flesh striking flesh echoed within the now eerily silent room.

CHAPTER TWO

Nigel Purbeck, the sixth Marquess of Edgeware, liked the sharp sting of a damp ocean breeze against his face. It made him feel alive. With a shift of his thighs, he urged his dappled gray stallion, Zeus, into a hard run along a trail that paralleled the low cliffs. The crimson morning light glinted off the turbulent waves. The sight of it made Nigel's heart race. It had been many months since he'd witnessed such an inspiring sight. London, where he made his home for most of the year, was dank and smoky and not at all as wildly beautiful as the landscape surrounding his Dorset estate.

Zeus flicked his ear and stubbornly tugged on the reins, pulling his head in the direction of the estate's main house, Purbeck Manor. Its worn rock and marble walls rose up on a knoll in the distance behind a line of storm-beaten, half-dead palm trees his father had imported from Italy ages ago.

Zeus pulled harder to the right and danced in his step, bobbing his head.

"Easy," Nigel soothed.

The large horse was willful and notoriously difficult to handle. Only Nigel and the estate's head groom could consistently manage his bouts of bad temper. Under Nigel's patient care, the stallion rarely showed his temper, almost never demanded to get his own way like he was doing on this damp, spring morning. The stallion snorted and yanked on the reins, fighting with a ferocity Nigel hadn't seen in years.

"Easy, boy," he said, and reached out to pat the horse's broad neck. "We'll head home." He let Zeus turn back toward the manor while he tightened his thighs over the stallion's broad back, hoping to regain some control.

Zeus immediately screamed and reared up. While pulling up on its powerful hind legs, the horse twisted his long, sleek neck back toward his own shoulder, and nipped the back of Nigel's outstretched hand.

Nigel cradled his bleeding hand while leaning forward, desperate to keep his seat, but Zeus had other ideas. The great beast landed with a thud and kicked up with his hind legs, sending Nigel sailing over the top of his stallion's head.

There was nothing he could do to protect himself. His head hit the pebbly ground first. Dazed and wondering if death would soon be upon him, he landed flat on his back, staring up into the sun-kissed morning sky.

Zounds, this was not the way he imagined he'd die. He'd hoped to live at least a few more years than his father had been able to eke out. In fact, he'd rather hoped he'd live to be a very old man. At least live long enough to find a woman to love.

With the sound of approaching hoof beats thundering in his ears, he raised his head. A sharp pain struck him, and his eyesight blurred.

Damn, he thought as darkness enveloped him. *Damn and blast.*

"Lord-a-mercy! What havey-cavey is this?" Joshua peered down on the bloodied and crumpled body sprawled out on the wet grass and shook his head. No one in the tiny village of Purbeck ever expected the Marquess to gain his thirtieth year. His father hadn't accomplished such a feat. Nor had his grandfather. And his lordship, on the dawning months of nine-and-twenty, was growing close to surprising the members of the village.

"Who's his heir?" the stranger standing next to Joshua asked. He was a messenger dressed in full livery who'd recently arrived on horseback, demanding to see the Marquess without delay. His mount was still blowing hard. "Considering the urgency I was told to treat this task, I believe this message should go to his lordship's heir straightaway."

"Aye," Joshua agreed. "His lordship was a bachelor. He produced no children, least none that weren't bastards." He shrugged. "His uncle, Lord Purbeck, is his lordship's heir. God save him."

"Take me to him. I was given orders that this letter be given the highest priority."

The messenger's cold demand momentarily stunned Joshua. He tilted his head, still staring down at the immobile body that once was his master. "His lordship was a good man, he was. Always treated his servants kindly." Joshua dragged his cap from his head and clutched it against his chest. "He will be sorely missed, he will. God deliver him."

The corpse moaned.

Both men jumped back as Lord Edgeware, eyes still tightly sealed, slowly sat up.

"The devil!" Joshua shouted.

"Don't be too quick to deliver me up to the devil, Joshua," Edgeware said. "I have yet a few more breaths in these lungs."

Nigel's head menaced him. The pain, sharp and unmerciful, tried to draw him back to unconsciousness, but he wouldn't allow it. By sheer force of will, he pried his eyes open.

"You're alive, m'lord!" Joshua, his head groom, cried.

"Of course, I'm alive. I hope you planned to have me checked over more carefully before sending for a casket maker."

Joshua stumbled a step back and looked as pale as if being forced to stand before the devil himself. "F-forgive me, m'lord.

It-it's just that everyone expects you to—"

"I'm soaking wet," Nigel mused aloud. "Did you douse me with water?" He pulled a handkerchief from his coat and wiped the liquid from his brow and looked at it.

He puzzled over the ruddy cloth until his sluggish mind realized what he was seeing. Water shouldn't stain a handkerchief. But blood did. Goodly amounts of it, which was never a good thing.

"Help me stand." He reached out to Joshua while fighting a wave of panic. "Damn man, don't just stand there gawking. I will bleed to death if you don't help me."

With some effort, Joshua and the messenger helped Nigel get his wobbly legs underneath him. Joshua fastened Nigel's cravat tightly around the crown of his bleeding head and had tucked several handkerchiefs against the wound for good measure.

"That should staunch the flow, m'lord," he said, drawing a deep breath. His groom's senses seemed to be returning. Joshua jammed his cap back on top of his head and turned to the messenger. "Go fetch a litter to carry his lordship back to the manor."

"Wait, I'll ride back. I'm not dead yet. I refuse to be transported as if I were."

"But, m'lord, your head."

"Damn my head. I want to have a look at Zeus. He tossed me as if I were a bee in a woman's bonnet and I want to know why." He quickly spotted his ill-mannered stallion happily feasting on wildflowers no more than a few yards away.

Joshua offered his shoulder for support. Leaning heavily on him, Nigel limped over to inspect his horse. Every muscle in Nigel's body screamed with pain. He needed to get into a tub of hot water before his muscles tightened into a set of impossibly stiff knots. But first he was determined to tend to Zeus. It had been years since he'd seen his horse panic so forcefully.

There had to be a reason.

"Gads, m'lord," Joshua exclaimed, when they lifted the saddle and blanket from the horse's flank. A metal burr was embedded in Zeus's tender skin.

"The harder I tried to control him, the deeper I drove this cursed thing into his back. Zounds, how did this happen? Who saddled him this morning?"

"I did, m'lord. You know I did, m'lord. No one else would dare touch your horse." Joshua grew pale.

"Then how did this happen?" A new wave of dizziness hit Nigel as fresh anger made his blood race. A trickle of blood ran down his cheek. He rounded on his groom. "How did this happen?"

"I-I don't know, m'lord. You know I take great care with the blanket and saddle. I check the blanket for burrs every time, m'lord. You know that." His ruddy cheek bloomed red with anger. "Someone purposefully injured Zeus."

"A chilling thought." Nigel accepted Joshua's innocence for the moment. His groom sung to the estate's horses and treated them as if they were his children. He wouldn't harm a horse as a means to kill a man. But if not Joshua, then who? Who would be interested in his death?

"My lord," the messenger stepped forward. "Begging your pardon. But my master insisted I not hesitate to deliver this note to your hands. I am to await a reply." The lanky messenger held out a folded piece of foolscap.

"Joshua, take care of Zeus. I'll ride Hera back to the manor." Nigel stumbled a step. "In a moment."

He took the message and studied the red, wax seal. The seal, a growling beast surrounded by a circle of flowers, was a mark he quickly recognized.

Matters had to be dire for Severin to contact him. Nigel peeled back the wax and opened the letter.

Lord Edgeware, it read, *a certain situation in London requires your immediate attention. I dare not explain more. But I must impress on you the urgency in which this is written. I only pray you make every effort to attend to this catastrophe with utmost haste.* The message had been signed with an elaborate letter "A".

Nigel blinked several times as his vision swam in and out of focus. The timing of this new crisis could not be any worse. He swore an oath beneath his breath as he crumpled the foolscap clutched in his bloodied hand. He knew he could not ignore the plea for help. Severin would not write without desperate cause. There could only be one reason he'd send this note.

Dionysus.

CHAPTER THREE

Lord Baneshire ground his jaw as he paced the green-hued parlor, the muscles in his reddened cheeks visibly straining. A day after the scandal and his anger had still not cooled.

Word of the scandalous painting had reached the Baneshire household even before Elsbeth could usher Olivia and Lauretta into the carriage and rush home. Lord Baneshire, grim-faced, had waited for them at the front door. His arms crossed and his legs spread wide, he made quite a menacing picture. He'd taken one look at the three girls and pointed the way to their bedrooms. They had silently obeyed.

Late the next morning, the earl summoned Elsbeth and her cousins into the front parlor. Elsbeth sat primly in her favorite chair. An uncomfortable calm filled her as she watched her uncle pace.

Lord Baneshire had every right to be angry. His family was a model of propriety. Such a scandal wouldn't only mortify him and harm his children's chances at finding husbands, but it would also touch his political career. A career in which he took great pride.

She should have never accepted his invitation to live with them. She should have known her dream of returning to London and settling into a quiet, unassuming life had never been possible in the first place.

"Strumpets pose for artists," he said without altering his stride. "Whores pose for artists."

"The children, my lord," Lady Baneshire, paler than usual, scolded softly with a quick glance in the direction of Olivia and Lauretta who sat huddled together on a small sofa, their heads lowered.

"When did you do this?" he shouted with a great wave of his arm. "You were supposedly observing a period of mourning this past year. Or did this happen before your husband's death? Were you unfaithful? Were you seeing another man while he was fighting—dying—for our Mother England? That's what the gossips will think, you know. Is it true?"

He stopped pacing to tower over Elsbeth.

She clasped her hands in her lap, squeezing them tightly together to keep from trembling. She reminded herself she'd never seen him strike anyone, but then again she'd never seen him so angry, his cheeks so red.

Surely, he wouldn't strike her.

"You must tell me who this—this Dionysus is," he demanded. "I will call the cove out if I have to."

"Nooo," Lady Baneshire wailed.

He waved away his wife's distress. "He will do the right thing by you. I will insist upon it. He will marry you if that is what society demands."

"Marriage?" Elsbeth's head turned icy cold at the horrifying thought. The green urns sitting on shelves in the alcove swam in and out of view. "I cannot marry." Lord Baneshire appeared to have floated away.

Elsbeth drew a fortifying breath and straightened her shoulders. All she could seem to think about at that moment was the first time her husband had flown into a rage. He'd tossed her onto his bed, twisted her long hair in his hand, ripped at her gown, and—

"No! I *will not* marry again!" *Never again.*

Her uncle crouched down beside her chair. "You will if I

"Then why, Elsbeth? Why did you do this?"

To that she had no answer her uncle would be willing to believe. She had lied too well for too long to expect him to believe the truth now.

Dionysus lit a solitary candle before turning the brass key in the cellar door's heavy lock. He used his shoulder to jar the swollen door from the rotting jam and then raised the candle, shedding a flickering light into the cavernous space. Not enough light for someone unfamiliar with the uneven stairway. Yet he knew each stone step well. With a quick stride he nearly flew down the last steps. He'd come, not to paint, but to gaze on his latest work— his obsession—his madness.

Her smiling lips, her haunting eyes, her golden hair were forever imprinted in his mind. Those delicate features, perfection in the form of womanhood.

And still he didn't know her name.

She was the Earl of Baneshire's niece. But Baneshire came from a rather large family, and so did his wife. She could be the daughter of any number of the respected families populating the *ton.*

She'd been married and must have loved her husband dearly. The pain shadowed in those eyes could only be borne from great suffering. Terrible sadness.

Dionysus knew such pain. If only she could peer into his eyes, she'd recognize a fellow, suffering creature. And perhaps, her soft, upstanding gaze could heal.

He closed his eyes and drew a deep breath. The lovely image of her—the one he called Perfection—swirled into view.

A flash of a memory.

Nearly a decade ago he was a young man just completing his studies at Oxford, tall and lanky, still shy and uncertain of his own power. When the weather was pleasant, he would escape

34

Merton College just as the sun-rose and hide among the trees near the Iffley water mill, trying to capture in oil and canvas the elusive slant of light of the sun's golden rays as they skidded off the mill pond's glassy surface. With the wooded hills and lush pastures forming a gentle bucolic backdrop, he once believed he'd never find another subject that could keep his artistic attentions so enthralled.

But that was before *she* walked into the scene.

A young woman still dressed for the schoolroom, she'd gathered her wide skirts into her hands and dashed across the grassy field. Two matrons, one clearly a lady aunt or mother, chased after the child. The girl's golden locks tumbled free from the pins and flowed freely in the gentle breeze.

His breath caught in his throat. It took no great feat of artistic talent to recognize the budding woman, hovering oh so near to sweet ripeness, in the schoolgirl. Given a year or two, she would be married.

He gulped at the thought and swung away with those uncomfortably long arms of his and crashed into his easel. His paints and brushes scattered onto the dew-moistened grass.

"Damn and blast," he muttered as he dipped to his knees and started gathering up his mess, all the while praying the women wouldn't spot him, praying that if they did, they wouldn't come over to speak to him.

If that young beauty came over and turned her sapphire gaze toward him . . . His heart hammered painfully enough in his chest at the mere thought of speaking to her.

He glanced up. The girl was still sprinting across the field, her long legs carrying her as gracefully as a young doe. She waved a bouquet of yellow flowers in the air and danced circles in front of her harried-faced guardians.

"So this is where you sneak off to every morning, Pole." Hubert, a thick bully who lived for the day he'd be able to take his father's title, punched Dionysus in the arm with such force the paintbrushes tumbled to the ground again.

Dionysus rose. He wiped at the grass stains on his breeches and maneuvered himself in front of the painting he'd been laboring over. "Leave off, Hubert. A man's entitled to some time away."

Hubert tossed back his head and boomed a laugh. "What are you trying to hide there, Pole?" He pushed Dionysus aside with a meaty paw and crossed his arms as he studied the painting.

Dionysus gasped when he saw it himself. In the center of the unfinished landscape the beginnings of the dancing schoolgirl's face had appeared. His hand, without his mind's permission, had captured but a fraction of her beauty.

Hubert looked out over the field and quickly spotted the sensuous phantasm. She was laying out a blanket among a throng of wildflowers. His lips quirked up into a grin.

"I didn't realize you indulged in, in—what would your uncle call it?—in a female's talent, Pole," he said as his gaze remained trained on the young woman. He licked his wide lips. "I certainly can't fault you in your choice of subjects, though. Zounds, that chit would make a man of my ilk a mighty fine wife." His grin grew by wolfish proportions.

"I-I can't imagine what you mean. I only paint landscapes. The child intruded into my work, that is all," he protested, though Hubert's interest had already been turned.

"Child? She's sixteen, if not a day," Hubert said, and snatched the wet painting from the easel.

"Hand that back!"

"If you don't want your uncle learning of this frivolous pursuit of yours, you'll do as I demand," Hubert said.

His uncle's efforts to forcefully mold Dionysus into a hard, no-nonsense man—the exact opposite of his dreamy father— were common knowledge at Merton College. The blood drained away from his head at the thought of pricking his uncle's ire. He backed down and stood unmanned, silently cursing his bloody weaknesses and his wretched fear of his uncle, as he watched Hubert swagger toward the bevy of women, the wet painting swinging in his paws.

More than eight years later, his heart still thundered, his breath still fled at the thought of speaking to the lovely angel Hubert had so boldly approached that spring morning. But he didn't need to speak to her, for he now possessed the painting. He crossed the dimly lit workroom to his pile of discarded canvases where he'd hidden it away from anyone's eyes but his.

Tossing the canvases aside, one by one his muscles grew taut, eager to drink in the view of her rose-petal lips and her creamy body.

He lifted the last of the canvases and stared at the bare, stone floor. "What trickery is this?" he whispered, dragging both his hands through his hair. He tugged at the strands until his scalp burned. "Where is she?"

His mind raced, his chest constricted, frightened to consider the possibilities. His painting—the proof of his madness was gone.

Someone must have found it.

Taken it.

It had taken only two days for the *ton*'s censure to fall on the entire Baneshire household, confirming Elsbeth's worst fears. Because of her position as chaperone to Baneshire's daughters, not one member of the *ton* dared send an invitation for fear of her inadvertent attendance. And yesterday, Sir Donald Gilforth had paid a call to Lauretta. She'd been expecting him to propose marriage. But instead, he coldly broke off their relationship, announcing that in light of Elsbeth's scandal, he needed to think of his unmarried sisters' reputations. And that he didn't dare let his name continue to be associated with theirs. Elsbeth decided right then and there that something drastic had to be done to remedy this disaster. And soon.

Early in the afternoon the very next next day, Elsbeth hastily departured from the Baneshire town house. None of the servants raised an eyebrow or questioned the wisdom of her venturing out alone on foot with only her oilskin cape for protection from the freezing rain.

She curled icy fingers into a pair of tight fists. Dionysus, whoever that rogue turned out to be, would soon regret the day he sought to ruin her. He would pay for the humiliation he'd served her while hiding like a coward in the night. She hadn't lied to her uncle. She didn't know Dionysus's true identity . . . but she knew someone who might.

A cold wind whipped a stinging rain against her face. She tugged at her cape, pulling the fabric close to her body. Trying to ignore the water soaking through her thinly soled half boots, she marched down the street, head lowered, toward what surely would be considered improper behavior.

She was about to visit a bachelor in his home.

If her reputation were not already in tatters and Lauretta's heart not already smashed to pieces, she would have never considered such an outrageous course of action.

"What is it now, Graves?" Severin asked his butler who'd appeared once again in the doorway. The baron had spent the afternoon sequestered behind closed doors in his shabby study, working desperately to keep one step ahead of his creditors. The constant patter of rain against the windowpane confirmed that the weather outside continued to be dreadful. For a day when any sane man or woman should be huddling beside a blazing fire, he couldn't imagine why his study was becoming as busy as a fashionable tearoom.

"There is a woman demanding entrance, my lord," Graves announced in a tone that made Severin wonder if his butler had recently gotten a whiff of some truly awful scent.

"Send her in," he said, without glancing up from the piles of ledgers on his desk.

"But-but, my lord," Graves stammered in a most uncommon manner. "The lady is unescorted. I shall send her away."

"Send her away? *An unescorted woman?* Graves, I am shocked. You know I have a reputation to keep. By all means send the woman directly up—and be sure the neighborhood witnesses my thoroughly debauched behavior."

"Very good, my lord," Graves said flatly.

A few moments later the doors to the study again slid open. Severin set down his pen and waited to see who his mysterious visitor could be. The dowager Lady Buckley had been making bold passes of late and had hinted that she was looking for a new lover. Would she be so brash as to appear on his doorstep in the middle of the day? Her coffers were overflowing and her face still lovely. He could dearly make use of such a combination.

He sat forward in his leather chair and watched as a slender figure, still cloaked, entered the room. A heavy hood shadowed her face. Water dripped from her hem, staining his bright red Axminster rug, a rug he could ill-afford to have ruined.

"Graves!" he shouted. "Graves! Where is your head? Take the lady's cloak straightaway. And fetch a pot of tea."

The butler returned, his back ramrod straight. "Aye, my lord."

Severin took to his feet and crossed the room while the lady allowed Graves to help her shed her sodden cloak. "Please," he said, and let a seductive smile curl his lips. "Stand with me by the fire. I daresay your bones must be chilled through and through."

She turned toward him. There was no matching smile in

sight. The heat in her gaze damned well burned him.

Severin's rakish grin froze on his face. Shock—that was what had done this to him.

What in blazes was *she* doing here? The Marquess of Edgeware, after blistering Severin's ears for having displayed the scandalous painting without his knowledge or permission, had promised to set things right. Dionysus was, after all, Edgeware's responsibility. Severin had spent more money than he could afford already when he'd dispatched a messenger to the Marquess of Edgeware's estate a few hours after the unfortunate unveiling. Severin's responsibility had ended there. Or so he'd hoped.

"Lady Mercer, this-this is indeed a surprise." He motioned again to the fire. "Please, take a moment to warm yourself."

The bright peacock and white striped promenade dress made from the thinnest muslin fabric complemented her winter-pinked cheeks and rosy lips. Her golden hair, swept up away from her slender neck, formed a halo of silky curls on the top of her head.

"This is by no means a social call." She drew a deep breath and straightened her shoulders. "I am here on an important matter of business."

"Indeed," he said.

He leaned against the hearth and watched her slender fingers tug at the damp woolen gloves, struggling to peel them off. After a few moments, she gave up and with a huff turned her attentions instead to the contents of the rather plain reticule hanging from her wrist.

Severin stepped forward, concerned she was about to produce a revolver.

"Actually, two matters of business," she said, as she retrieved a silken purse from the reticule. "I don't possess a great fortune. And I cannot take an advance in my quarterly income without my uncle's knowledge."

She swallowed hard and cleared her throat. "I wish to purchase the painting." A blush brightened her cheeks. "The painting of me."

"I'm sorry, my lady, but that would be quite impossible."

"I am more than willing to pay your price." There was a compelling strength in her tone. But when she held up the silk sack, clearly heavy with coins, he saw that her fingers were shaking. "You *must* sell it to me."

Fearing she was on the verge of collapse, Severin rushed to her side and led her to a chair near the fire. He kept a tight grasp on her damp hands as he freed the silk coin purse from her fingers and laid it on her lap. "I am sorry, but the painting is no longer available."

"Oh dear," she whispered. "I hadn't considered that possibility."

She looked up quickly. "Provide me the name of the buyer. I must have the painting. I simply must. Certainly you can understand why."

Severin returned to the large fireplace. "Forgive me," he said. He kept his back to her, unable to face the anger that darkened her sparkling blue eyes. "I gave my word as a gentleman that I would never reveal the buyer's name."

The room fell silent for many minutes save for the occasional crackle from the fire burning behind the grate. Slowly he turned to find her gaze set upon him and her mouth drawn to a thin line.

"You had two matters of business? Perhaps I'll be able to assist you with the second?"

Lady Mercer blinked.

He held his breath, bracing for her patience to come to a quick end.

"If you gave your word . . ." she said finally with a sigh. She rose from her chair. "Dionysus." A sharp fire flared anew in her eyes. "Tell me, Lord Ames, who is he?"

His mouth dropped open. "You don't know?"

Her slender body trembled, but this time it looked as if womanly rage, not fear, shook her.

"No. No, why should I know him? Tell me, Lord Ames. You are his sponsor. Tell me, who is he?" She shook her bag of coins. "I can pay for the information. I must . . . I must find him and demand that he answer for what he's done to me . . . and to the Baneshire family."

Severin stood torn between rushing to comfort her and fleeing to the far side of the room to take cover from the fury he was, no doubt, about to cause. "Forgive me, my lady. As much as this too pains me, I have sworn an oath of secrecy to the artist. I cannot help you."

He had sworn an oath?

"Very well," Elsbeth said while silently cursing her own foolishness. Why had she expected answers from him? Just because he'd been kind to her once? She should have expected nothing, for despite the kindness he'd shown her years ago, he'd also been a friend of her husband's. And that fact alone should have been enough to warn her not to expect any goodness from the likes of him. "With or without your help, I *will* find him."

With her shoulders squared, she marched out the door.

"If there is ever anything else I can do—" he called after her. She didn't wait to hear the rest of *that* empty offer.

What a simpering fool he must think her to be. He was probably laughing behind his hand right now. Ames's butler quickly helped her with her cloak and ushered her back out into the worst of the cold, wet weather. She took one last look at his town house.

The rogue, along with his cronies, knew exactly what they

were doing when they chose to display that horrid painting. Her cheeks burned with a deep blush from the memory of seeing the image of herself spread out like a wanton, naked and unashamed, on a crimson sofa. The details were startling. How could Dionysus know her so intimately? Not even her husband had seen her in such a willing pose. *Never, ever, had she been so comfortable with her body to so abandon her modesty.*

She stifled a sneeze.

What a fine fettle this afternoon was turning out to be. And her folly was about to reward her with a terrible head cold. "My family would probably be better off if I contracted a lung affliction and died."

She sneezed again.

"God bless you, my lady." An unmistakably masculine gloved hand pressed a crisp handkerchief into her soggy palm. "The weather is wicked enough to kill the stoutest of creatures. Whatever is a delicate bird like yourself doing tempting the fates so?"

The stranger stood so close she could feel the heat rise from him. His hand captured her elbow, sending every muscle tightening in her. Her nervous fingers dabbed at her nose with the man's handkerchief while her mind raced at a frantic, almost unmanageable rate. She shivered and thought how foolish it was for her to leave the Baneshire home without a maid. The London streets weren't safe for ladies, even widows. The men of the city seemed to prowl upon them like hounds on the hunt for foxes.

She dabbed the handkerchief to her nose again, stifling another sneeze. The foreign scent of him was strong on the warm cloth, a spicy mix of almonds and sage—a scent she'd imagine wafting out of a Dionysus painting. It sent her gaze sailing to his face.

Large, black eyes overflowing with questions, stared back

from down a sharp, aristocratic nose. His sun-kissed brows, raised slightly at the corners, drew her attention, as did the wisps of hair escaping from the confines of his hat. He pursed his lips with amusement but kept his thoughts to himself. Rain dripped from the rim of a highly polished beaver hat and beaded upon the shoulders of a long, black greatcoat.

He was the devil, she thought, fueling her courage to try and jerk out of his grasp.

His grip on her elbow tightened, and he pulled her closer. "We must not delay getting you out of this weather." He hastened her forward using brute force.

She planted her feet, struggling against his quickened stride. But his muscles were stronger than her resolve. Her feet tangled beneath her legs and she stumbled, sending her tumbling into his solid chest.

A surge of panic struck her and she fought him. "If you don't unhand me, sir, I will scream."

"I beg you, don't." He faltered a step. She followed his gaze as he peered up and down the unusually deserted Queen Street. "I don't wish to draw undue attention."

A loud enough shout would rouse servants to the door, despite the cold weather and heavy rains.

The pressure of his hand on her arm burned through the layers of her clothing, reminding her not to trust her safety to a man. The hard gleam in his eyes betrayed his determination. He would not let her go without a fight.

But considering the frustrations she suffered earlier in the day, she was only too ready to provide him with a royal battle. She tossed back her head, the hood of her cape sliding away, and opened her mouth to let out a scream guaranteed to stir the most sedentary of beings.

A warm, dry gloved hand swiftly pressed against her mouth. "I sincerely apologize, my lady. But in the interest of protecting your reputation, I cannot allow you to alarm the good people residing on this street." He bustled her toward a waiting carriage as if she were nothing more than an extra piece of baggage.

Two enormous horses, dark as midnight, stood before the black unmarked carriage, waiting to carry her into the depths of hell, or worse—to this man's personal bedchamber.

A finely appointed footman, dressed in green livery, tipped his hat to her as if she were a willing guest and swept the carriage door open. Ignoring her struggles, the stranger lifted her and tossed her unceremoniously into the carriage's darkened interior.

He climbed in behind her, filling the small space with his full frame. Without a word of apology, he dropped down on the upholstered bench across from her, trapping her legs between his thighs and then rapped on the roof with his fist. The carriage jerked into motion, tossing her against the carriage's leather squab.

"It is good to escape that dratted rain, wouldn't you say so, my lady?" He had the audacity to lean back and stretch his arms out along the back of the bench as if abducting helpless ladies was a common practice. "I despise the interior of carriages. Too cramped and airless for my liking, but on a day like today I gladly make allowances."

She clasped her hands together in front of her. "Sir." Her teeth chattered with the word. "Are we acquainted? For I don't recall you being introduced to me at Lord Baneshire's ball, and I cannot imagine where else I would have met you." She struggled to draw a calming breath. "Are you a friend of my deceased husband?"

"You're shivering." He reached toward her legs.

She squealed and drew her feet up from the floor.

He gave her a puzzled look but kept his hand beneath her

bench. "Here," he said. He grabbed her ankles and set her feet on a heated brick. "That should warm you." He then produced a blanket from underneath his own bench and draped it over her legs.

It wasn't the cold that was making her shiver so; her heart fluttered wildly in her throat. She'd been abducted. Why ever would he want to kidnap her? Her husband's inheritance wouldn't buy a loaf of bread, much less warrant a ransom.

"W-what do you want from me?"

Instead of answering, he leaned forward in the seat. "I know all about Dionysus's painting," he said softly.

Chapter Four

"Dionysus?" Elsbeth's anger heated the entire compartment. "Dionysus!"

She curled her tiny hands into a pair of tight fists and shook them at him. "I have no idea why he'd wish to ruin me. I don't even know the man. And—and if you think I'm the kind of woman portrayed in that painting, you are sorely mistaken. I am a God-fearing woman, chaste and faithful. Society may believe me fallen, but I *assure* you, *sir*, my morals are above reproach. I will fight you to my death if need be."

The stranger laughed. The hearty sound filled the carriage as he tossed off his top hat and gave his head a good shake. "My dear lady," he said. "I'm not looking to steal your virtue, but to restore it."

She regarded him with grave caution. "Who are you?"

He sobered. His dark eyes flashed from the shadows. She wished she could see his face more clearly. She considered herself fairly competent at reading a man's intentions— especially the depraved ones.

"Forgive me, my lady. The company of the gentler species is foreign to me." He inclined his head a notch. "Allow me to present myself. I am Edgeware. And you are correct. We have yet to be introduced."

"Edgeware? *The* Marquess of Edgeware?" She couldn't believe she'd heard him correctly. Edgeware was a well-known name. A powerful political figure. The matrons of the *ton* all

47

clamored for his attendance at the most elite of events. More often than not, he'd disappoint the poor women, refusing all but a select few engagements to attend every year.

A powerful recluse.

A mysterious bachelor.

"I would have acted sooner, but I only recently learned of your predicament." He settled back in his seat again. "And unfortunately I have other pressing matters also requiring my attentions."

"Predicament?" she cried. "Predicament? That's a blasted understatement! I, sir, have been ruined, utterly ruined. And even so I would be able to survive this scandal if it only affected me. But my cousins are suffering every bit as much." She closed her eyes and remembered the tears glistening on Lauretta's cheeks after Sir Donald had stomped on her heart. "More so."

She drew a breath and straightened. "For them, I intend to find this—this Dionysus. I intend to expose him, to force him to answer for what he's done. If you can help me, I implore that you do."

Her abductor tugged at his gloves. "I will help restore your reputation," he said, crisply. "However, I cannot allow you to act against Dionysus."

"*Why?* Why would you help me? I don't even know you." A prickle of unease crept down her spine. In her experience, gentlemen, despite their supposed code of honor, rarely acted without expecting a sharp payment in return for their troubles.

Only one man, her uncle, had ever treated her with unfailing kindness. She winced, imagining how he must now be regretting his invitation to have her live with his family.

"True, I do not know you." He leaned forward. The interior lantern illuminated his face. His haunting eyes latched onto hers. "I do know, however, that you've been wronged. And though I cannot discuss this matter much further, I can tell you that I bare the brunt of responsibility for Dionysus and his actions. I am his keeper, of sorts. You have nothing to worry about with me." He reached out and stroked her cheek. A tremor of alarm shot through her when his touch sparked a pleasing tingle that spiraled through her chest. Startled, she pulled away as sharply as if he had stung her.

"I will set things right for you." He sunk back into the shadows of the carriage. "But understand, too, I'll do what I must to protect Dionysus from your efforts to expose him."

He rapped on the roof.

The carriage, Elsbeth was shaken to notice, had already drawn to a halt. A cloaked footman, damp from the pouring rain, swung open the door. She peered out the opening and recognized the highly ornate front door to the Baneshire town house only a few feet away.

"Thank you for the carriage ride," she said as she scooted across the bench.

"I am hosting a house party next week at my country home in Dorset. Attend the party, my lady." His deep voice rumbled in the darkness. "I'll accept no excuse for your absence."

With a quick nod and a silent vow that she'd do well to avoid any and all events involving the Marquess, she dashed through the rain and inside the town house. After depositing her dripping oilskin cape with Tallford, Baneshire's grim-faced butler, she hurried up the stairs despite Olivia's attempts to delay her. Elsbeth managed to make it up to her room without missing a stride.

"Imagine that," she said to her empty bedchamber as she leaned against the door. "He expects me to attend a house party." Her heart raced and a fresh rush of heat burned her cheeks.

She may have escaped his carriage, but she feared the abduction was far from over.

She'd barely a moment to hatch an excuse for getting out of the invitation before a light knock sounded at the door. Elsbeth jumped. "Go away, Olivia."

The door eased opened. Molly, Elsbeth's rather unconventional lady's maid, one of the very few reminders of her life with her dead husband, backed into the room with a tea tray in her arms.

"Beg pardon, milady," Molly drawled in her less-than-perfect English. "Tallford said you'd be needin' a pot o' tea?"

"Yes, thank you Molly. I would also appreciate a hand changing into a dry gown."

"Gracious, milady." Molly closed the door after her and rushed to set the tray down. She tugged at Elsbeth's damp gown like a nervous mother hen. "We must get this off you before you catch your death. You should have rang for me right away."

Elsbeth allowed Molly to fuss over her. Soon she was dressed in a serviceable wool gown that was not only warm but also extremely comfortable.

It was not at all the thing a fashionable woman would dare wear. Her late husband would have claimed she looked as dowdy as a washerwoman. She smoothed out the deeply creased skirt while Molly reluctantly excused herself from the chamber. Once again alone, she pressed her ear to the door, straining as she listened for evidence of her cousins lurking in the hall.

This afternoon, she heard blessedly few sounds. A creak here, and a moaning floorboard there. Alone, and after surviving such an adventure in the dreary cold, she felt as if she could finally breathe easily.

Before she realized what she was doing, she knelt beside her bed. The day she'd moved into this chamber she had shoved a carefully wrapped package underneath it.

Her hand quickly found the flat package wrapped in a length

of pink and white fabric. She sat on the bed and brushed a layer of dust from its surface. A pink ribbon criss-crossed the package. It was a ribbon she'd worn in her hair when she was still a young woman as silly and carefree as her cousins. She pulled one end of the ribbon. The knot loosened and the fabric slipped away.

With a heavy heart she picked up the stiff canvas and ran her finger over the beautiful oil painting. At one time she owned many such works.

In a fit of rage she had destroyed them all—all except this one.

Why had this small painting survived? The work of art, not much larger than a sheet of foolscap, gave life to a simple scene. The artist must have stretched out flat on his stomach in the midst of a field of wildflowers to capture such an intimate perspective of the deep purple and bright yellow flowers waving in the soft summer breeze.

In the forefront, a single white daisy leaned forward, almost reaching out from the canvas, so close it must have tickled the artist's nose.

A mist of tears clouded Elsbeth's vision. She blinked, hoping to hold back the memories and the pain. The life, the freedom, the unbridled happiness in the painting pricked her heart like a broken promise.

Fields of wildflowers were long gone from her life.

She could scarcely remember the love she'd once felt toward the creator of the painting. The feeling had changed, become twisted, and transformed into something ugly.

Even so, she still appreciated the passion in the artist's bold brush strokes. She'd never seen any other artist work the same way, plying the paints so heavily on the canvas, but at the same time evoking a light, sometimes playful effect. Nor had she ever seen a painter reveal so much of the deep longing that must be hidden in the artist's heart.

She'd never again seen such a painting . . . not until Dionysus. Why was he so determined to torment her? Damn the man to Hades and back. *Who was he?*

Were the years of pain and horror she'd suffered living with her husband not enough? Was the artist determined to deny her even a moment of peace? A glimmering chance for happiness? She raised her hand, poised to tear the aging material and destroy the last remaining evidence of her ability to love.

Her arm, hanging in the air, froze.

"I can't." She tossed the painting aside and collapsed on the middle of her bed.

"I can't," she sobbed.

Nigel lifted the neatly folded handkerchief Lady Mercer had left on the empty bench as the carriage pulled away from the Grosvenor Square town house.

"Well, well," he said. The damp scent of lilacs and orange blossoms lingered with his cologne on the soft linen. "She's not quite the wilting flower I'd expected."

In fact, after meeting her, he decided she was much more a mystery now than when she was just a beautiful figure sculpted on canvas.

A canvas now safely locked away in his private vault.

Her fiery spirit was delightfully intriguing. It pained him that he'd have to block her efforts for revenge. He would much rather be fighting battles for the lady than waging one against her.

He could easily crush her. But destruction was the last thing on his mind.

Perhaps . . . perhaps . . .

Perhaps he wouldn't wage a war against Lady Mercer after all. Perhaps he could bend her will to suit his own purposes.

He smiled at the prospect. Seduction wouldn't be simple. He wasn't a fool. The young widow had frozen like a terrified doe when he touched her. Her warm skin had cooled to ice under his fingertips.

But her feelings didn't signify. Nigel relished challenges, the more impossible the better. And never did he meet a proper unwed lady who wasn't either moon-eyed or near to swooning in his presence.

Disdain—now that was a novel experience. Terrifyingly so.

The carriage pulled to a halt and the door swung open.

He took one more whiff of the sweetly scented handkerchief before jamming the cloth into his coat pocket and leapt from the carriage with the confidence of a man prepared to take on the herculean task of holding up the world.

The game was on. He'd seduce Lady Mercer—she was a widow after all—save her reputation while distracting her; until he destroyed all evidence of Dionysus's existence.

CHAPTER FIVE

Molly pulled back the curtains, sending an overly bright beam of sunlight streaming into the large bedroom. Elsbeth groaned and buried her head within the soft folds of her down pillow.

"No use 'iding, milady," Molly drawled. "Lord Baneshire is already calling for ye to meet 'im in 'is breakfast room. An invitation 'ad been delivered yesterday. To a party, milady." She hummed an unrecognizable tune as she bustled noisily about the room.

"You're dropping your H's again."

"Forgive me, milady. It's just the excitement 'as me tongue slippin'," She bobbed a curtsy and blushed. "*Here* is a pretty gown, milady." She'd tossed open the wardrobe and quickly produced a bright pink morning gown. The intense color made Elsbeth draw in her breath.

After a year of donning black gowns, the array of brightly colored gowns her uncle had insisted she have made still surprised her.

Molly laid the gown across the foot of the bed, then stood back and smiled. "I pronounced me ach's nice an' clear that time, I did."

"Yes, Molly, you did. You are a gem." Molly, the youngest daughter of the Mercer's smithy, was by no means trained as a lady's maid. Mercer's housekeeper, Mrs. Brucket, gasped and sputtered so much when Elsbeth brought the sturdy young woman into the house, everyone present feared the poor housekeeper was suffering from a fit of apoplexy.

"I will have to inform his lordship about this," Mrs. Brucket had threatened once she'd caught her breath. A knowing gleam had darkened her eyes. The housekeeper's threat did nothing to deter Elsbeth even if the threat of her husband's anger had given her reason to pause.

The danger of not acting was simply too great.

Georgette, the lady's maid originally assigned to her, had been much more interested in pleasing Lord Mercer than attending to any of Elsbeth's needs. Georgette's seductive presence, jealous rages, and seemingly innocent lapses in memory proved to be a dangerous combination.

After the girl had created a situation where Elsbeth was "discovered" by Lord Mercer alone in her bedchamber with one of the estate's footmen—the consequences Elsbeth shuddered to remember—she knew, for her own safety's sake, that Georgette had to go.

Molly, a plain girl, strong and silent, became her saving grace. The younger woman, proud of her new position, had quickly assumed the role of Elsbeth's keeper. Together they persevered against Lord Mercer . . . and his violent rages. She doubted she'd have been able to survive without her lady's maid's unbreakable cheerfulness, strength, and friendship.

"Well?" Molly scoffed. "Are ye planning on commentin' on the gown or no?"

Elsbeth shook her head to clear away those shadowy memories. "Yes, of course, that pink gown should suit." Not that she could fathom what manner of dress she should choose to tell her uncle of her plans to refuse Lord Edgeware's summons to attend his house party.

Less than a quarter hour later, she made her way downstairs and paused in the doorway of the breakfast room. The stormy weather had broken sometime during the night, and the sun poured into the windows filling even the corners of the room with a warm light.

And that was where she found *him*—the demon himself dressed in gentleman's finery—standing in front of the sideboard, grinning from behind sparkling onyx eyes, and spooning a serving of eggs onto his plate as if he were in his own home.

It wasn't by the farthest stretch of one's imagination a decent hour to be visiting. How dare he make such a breach of etiquette and enter her home?

And what in blazes had he said to Lord Baneshire?

"Good morning, Elsbeth," her uncle said. He was clearly beside himself with excitement. "Please, join us." He motioned toward the empty chair next to his wife. Even her wan cheeks held a blush of color as she smiled upon the gentleman who looked too young to be a marquess.

Elsbeth felt no need to be taken in by Edgeware's dashing looks, which were a good deal more striking in this morning's bright sunlight than in the dim light of the dreary day before. He was too handsome by half, and by the arrogant way he held himself he knew the havoc his stunning good looks could do to a lady's knees.

He turned toward her. His expression became serious as he gazed at her for a moment with a smoldering under-look that made her think of dark carnal desires. Repressed desires.

Her breath caught deep in her chest.

Lord Baneshire missed their sinfully improper albeit silent exchange as he rose from the table. "Edgeware, please allow me to present my niece, Elsbeth, the dowager Countess of Mercer."

"My lady," he said smoothly, "the Earl of Mercer was your husband? My sympathies."

She blinked twice, still feeling somewhat unbalanced and uncertain of the feelings his simmering gaze was provoking.

Purposefully provoking, no doubt.

"What are you doing here?" she demanded.

"Elsbeth!" her uncle gasped, his brows rising sharply.

"I beg your forgiveness, Uncle, Lord Edgeware," she said, carefully avoiding the Marquess's gaze. The tingling that spread through her belly must have been sparked by those seductive eyes of his. She stared at her satiny kid slippers instead. "I meant no insult. It is just that I'm unaccustomed to receiving guests so early in the morning, and in the breakfast room. Is this a new London custom I've not yet been made aware?"

A tense silence followed her less than sincere apology. She dared to chance a peek. The dark lord, as she was beginning to think of him, tilted his head and stared at her in the most aggrieving manner.

She tried again to decipher his expression. Amusement? Did he think of her and of her predicament as nothing more than a silly joke? A diversion to relieve a case of ennui?

"I was speaking with your uncle about my upcoming house party. I wanted him to understand that the invitation I'd issued yesterday was presented with the most heartfelt feelings of goodwill." A smile curled his pursed lips, drawing her attention to them. "Please, do join us in the discussion."

Her heart sputtered despite her efforts to hold rein over her control. Running from the room was beginning to look like a reasonable course of action. She didn't want to gaze at his lips or remember the gentle way his hand had caressed her cheek in the carriage the day before. And she certainly did not wish to remember the pleasant dream his wicked self had marched into and made even more pleasant with fantasies of gallantry.

This marquess, no matter how refined, no matter how handsome, was willingly aiding Dionysus. No matter what, she could not overlook that fact. She simply couldn't let her defenses be swayed. She grasped the doorframe and held her ground, remaining a step outside the breakfast room.

At least she hadn't yet run away.

"Lord Edgeware." Her tone could have frozen the flames licking the coals behind the grate in the fireplace. She stiffened her shoulders, finding her body trembling from just the thought of speaking against a man's wishes, especially a man whose broad shoulders looked ready to burst through the material of his fashionably tight coat.

She gulped. Truly, she was a widow now, and though a poor relation, no longer beholden to any man. "Lord Edgeware," she tried again before her conviction waned. In her experience men didn't take well to having their wishes thwarted. Her gaze strayed to the rosette plasterwork on the ceiling. "I do thank you for inviting the Baneshire family and myself to your house party. I'm sure the attentions you're giving Olivia and Lauretta will restore them to the positions in Society they so dearly deserve."

She swallowed hard and hurried on. "And I am glad to see you here, in the breakfast parlor. For, my lord, it will save me the trouble of penning a note. Though I have given the matter a great deal of thought, I feel I must refuse your invitation. My presence will only remind the *ton* of the perfidy they believe true of me and will surely further taint how they view my cousins."

Edgeware stood in the center of the room clutching the breakfast plate in his powerful hands and just stared at her.

"Elsbeth," Lady Baneshire spoke in her gentle tone, "are you certain you are taking the wisest course of action?"

"The wisest course of action?" Edgeware said, his tone rising. "What she has suggested must be the most damnably idiotic notion I have ever heard." He dropped his plate on the table with a loud clatter and took two broad steps toward her.

God protect her, the dark lord was going to attack her, here, in the Baneshire breakfast parlor! She crossed her arms in front of her chest and with a small cry of alarm backed away. Before she could gain any great distance, his hand shot out and clamped down around her arm, effectively trapping her.

"I'll not have this conversation with you cowering in the doorway, looking like a frightened rabbit ready to bolt . . . my lady." He pulled a chair out from the table and sat her unceremoniously into it. With his hand still trapping her arm, he dropped into the seat next to her.

"I cannot imagine what has gotten into our Elsbeth," her uncle said, his complexion suddenly as pale as the white linen tablecloth.

"She is obviously suffering from a breakdown of nerves." Edgeware's unbreakable black gaze threatened to singe her. "The strain, the suffering from society's censure must be taking a terrible toll. But you need not fear the outcome of the house party, my lady."

Both Elsbeth's aunt and uncle heartily, and loudly, agreed, both launching into lengthy speeches.

Edgeware chuckled. "It appears I've created some discord here," he said, not sounding a whit sorry for it. Instead, he leaned in close and lowered his voice so she could barely hear him above her aunt and uncle's excited speeches. "As I have already explained, I fully intend to restore your reputation . . . with or without your cooperation, by the way. Besides, I find I enjoy your company."

She tried with little success to ignore him and, for that matter, to ignore the arguments her aunt and uncle were quickly offering up as reasons why she ought to agree to attend the blasted house party. And she found it impossible to ignore the warm hand still curling around her arm.

A man as self-important as Edgeware, a man so like her husband, could easily lose his temper and justify harming her.

Though his grasp was surprisingly gentle, she dared not trust the dark lord. His eyes were as black as the devil's heart.

She was barely able to stifle the whimper that tried to escape her quivering lips.

Lady Mercer stared, fixated on his hand, the hand gripping her slender arm. Her sapphire eyes turned as hard as the gems they resembled. A look of outrage tightened the fine features of her slender face, rushing away the wariness that had frozen her expression a moment before.

Nigel had to admit his actions bordered on the outrageous. But if he hadn't grabbed her when he did, she would have dashed from the room, creating an impossible scene that may have trapped him into withdrawing the invitation to the house party altogether.

No, he could not allow that. Besides, he despised nasty, emotional scenes. They served no purpose other than to play havoc with his digestive system.

Lady Mercer brought her gaze up to meet his eyes. "Do what you must to serve whatever twisted version of justice you are seeking, but understand this. I vow I won't stop until I've uncovered that demon you hide. Dionysus will not be allowed to continue his charade," she whispered. A fire sparked between them as a deep flush deepened the pink of her cheeks.

"Your eyes, my dear lady," he said, finding himself becoming trapped by her stinging gaze, almost seduced by them. Dionysus's efforts to capture the life in her vivid blue eyes were but pale imitations when compared to the real things.

"What about my eyes?"

"They are not quite a deep blue, are they? But there is an unusual quality that darkens them. That shade of blue is far from what I'd consider dark," he said, and let his hand slip from her arm. "I believe they are almost a Sardinian blue. But not quite. Like you, they are quite unique. A treasure."

Lady Mercer—no, he could not think of her by that cursed name—to him she was simply Elsbeth, and Elsbeth, pretty as a spring flower, didn't smile at his compliment.

"Do you not like your eyes?" he asked. "Perhaps you wish they were a pretty shade of green, like emeralds?"

Elsbeth stiffened her shoulders and sat ramrod straight in the chair. "I, sir, am not at all displeased with the color of my eyes. It is your commenting on them that offends me," she said, no longer whispering.

"Indeed?" He sat back in his chair. Most young women were trained to be coy, not straightforward. And she had come back with her set-down as quickly as a seasoned society matron. "Do you care to tell me why?"

Before she could answer, her uncle broke into their conversation.

"What nonsense is this?" he asked. "We were discussing the house party. How ever, Elsbeth, did you manage to stray from the topic?"

Elsbeth glared at Nigel, sputtering with frustration. "I-I-he—"

"No matter," Baneshire said smoothly. "I can quickly settle this matter of the house party."

That caught Nigel's attention.

"Lady Baneshire and I have been more than pleased with your service as lady's companion to my daughters, Elsbeth." Baneshire smiled as he spoke, but Nigel recognized an undercurrent of tension in the man's voice. "And of course you will never be turned away. You may feel free to stay with us as long as you wish."

"Thank you," she said. She lowered her head and appeared to be very interested in the intricate stitching on the tablecloth.

"I remember when you first came to us, you insisted on making yourself useful. You were the one who begged to assume the duties of Olivia and Lauretta's companion and chaperone. Do you wish to continue in that role?"

"Of course I do. I just don't—"

"Splendid." Baneshire clapped his hands once. "Then it is settled. You will accept Edgeware's generous invitation to his house party and allow his irreproachable reputation to repair yours."

"I will have Tallford send for Madame Bossier this afternoon," Lady Baneshire said. She, too, was clearly delighted. "Olivia, Lauretta, and, of course you, my dear, will simply have to order a new wardrobe."

At that, Elsbeth glanced up from the tablecloth with more than a little degree of alarm. "I beg you, Aunt. Please do not go to any bother for me. I am in no need of a new wardrobe. I have barely worn any of the dresses ordered for the Season. They should be sufficient for a country house party."

"No, my dear," Lady Baneshire's voice was gentle but firm. "As you already know, a house party requires a very specific wardrobe."

"Surely my gowns will do." There was an edge of panic in Elsbeth voice. Nigel wondered at it.

"No, they won't do."

Her chin tightened. Nigel could only guess why the thought of ordering a new wardrobe would overset a young lady's nerves. Money, or rather a shortage of it, was most likely at root of her worries.

"Baneshire," he said, rising from the table. He gave Elsbeth a warm smile. "I thank you for a delicious breakfast." Of which he did not eat a bite. A shame, really. The pastries did look very tasty. "Unfortunately, I have another engagement I cannot delay."

Actually, he didn't have any waiting engagements that morning. He had cleared his schedule so he could focus all his attentions on repairing this delicate flower's reputation. The reason for the lie was that he suddenly needed a moment alone with Elsbeth, and he would not get one while lounging in the breakfast parlor.

Baneshire rose from his chair and took Nigel's hand, thanking him again for inviting them to his house party.

"I am indeed sorry to hear that your health prevents you from attending, Lady Baneshire," Nigel said as he bowed over the lady's limp hand. "It was certainly a pleasure seeing you again."

He purposefully ignored Elsbeth and started toward the door. Baneshire, naturally, followed with the intention of walking his guest to the entranceway.

"Lady Mercer." He paused at the threshold and turned to face her as if she were an afterthought.

She looked so untouched in her perfection. He couldn't picture that this slender beauty had lived as another man's wife for nearly six years. The thought of her engaged in any sort of carnal act was staggering.

He quickly cleared his throat. "Perhaps Lady Mercer would be kind enough to show me to the front door?" He posed the question to Baneshire instead of Elsbeth who would have deftly rejected him.

Her uncle appeared delighted. He stepped back, giving Elsbeth ample room to take Nigel's arm and no room to refuse.

She wrinkled her gentle, blond brows and frowned deeply, hesitating a long moment before touching his sleeve. "My lord," she said briskly, "the front entry is this way."

Within a few steps they were alone in the hall. He stopped and turned abruptly to her. Her sapphire eyes darted beyond his shoulder, to the ceiling, to his feet, and after a lifetime of breathless moments and a long shuddering on her part, stilled to gaze on his face. He rewarded her with a smile.

"Very good, my lady. I don't believe you met my eyes once in the breakfast parlor. A lady of your standing has certainly been trained better."

Her gaze hardened, and thanks to his rebuke she appeared to have grown all the more determined to hold his gaze.

"What do you want from me?" she asked with a huff.

Splendid. The question surprised him, of course. From what he'd heard from Severin, he'd expected to be singed by her tongue. But the fact that she hadn't burned him to a crisp made what he wanted to accomplish today seem even more accessible.

He peeled off a glove and held out his hand.

Elsbeth, slightly alarmed, flicked a glance at his open palm before locking her gaze with his again. "I don't understand."

"Place your hand in mine, Lady Mercer."

Both her hands closed into fists. "Why?"

At least she had left room for negotiation.

He glanced up and down the hall. There were no servants about. They were still quite alone, though in a busy London town house he could only expect to remain so for longer than a mere moment or two.

He gave her a blazing smile; one he knew could melt even the most jaded woman's knees. "I promise not to scandalize you. And I also vow that you have no cause to fear me. Please, place your hand in mine. To indulge in a lengthy discussion of why a man would wish to touch a woman's hand would only destroy the effect, do you not think?"

"I don't see this as necessary, my lord."

"Indeed, it is not necessary at all." He kept holding his hand out like a beggar, waiting. This was foolish. She was definitely planning on spurning him. But in spite of his misgivings he did not let his smile waver. "I will not force you."

At least she had spent the past several moments looking only upon his face. That was something.

Chilly fingers brushed his palm. He closed his hand around hers. She flinched but kept her hand within his. Her skin was as cool as the purbeck marble mined from his cliffs. With the pad of his thumb he began tracing a broad circle on the back of her hand.

"Is this so very terrible?" he asked.

"I have experienced worse things." Her chin lifted a good inch and her lips thinned.

Touching her and believing her to be his, if only for a fleeting moment, filled him with a surprising amount of satisfaction.

It was an experience he definitely intended to have repeated and . . . soon.

"I'm glad to know I do not completely repulse you." He lowered her hand, and released it.

Her eyelashes fluttered as she lost her composure for a moment. A deep blush rose to her cheeks. "The door, my lord," she said with a grand gesture.

"Just a moment." He held back from touching her arm. She was as skittish as a kitten when it came to being touched. "Take this." He held out a banknote he'd fished from his pocket for her. He'd intended to use the note along with several others to pay Severin for his services, but he suspected Elsbeth needed the money even more desperately. "Use it to purchase your gowns."

"What is this?" She eyed the banknote as if she thought it might bite her. Her sapphire eyes then flashed to his face. "I will not accept charity." Her eyes grew even wider. He spied a touch of fear in them as she stumbled back a step and stared at the hand that had touched his. "I may be a destitute widow, but I am no doxy whose favor you can purchase."

Nigel laughed. "No, my lady, I never thought you to be a doxy. You are a treasure, and this is a payment."

Her nose wrinkled delightfully as she stared at him with some confusion. He fought a very strong urge to kiss her heart-shaped lips.

"A payment? A payment for what?"

"For the painting, of course. If Dionysus received money for selling *The Nude,* why ever shouldn't you share in his bounty? You have certainly suffered its existence."

She stared at the banknote again, this time with more curiosity than caution. "Two hundred pounds? Are you sure that is the sum of money the painting had been sold for?"

"*The Nude* didn't sell for two hundred pounds," he said, a pleased smile spread across his face. She listened to him so eagerly. "The painting was commanding a price more than twice that." He didn't tell her that since he took possession of the painting, it never actually sold. If she knew the truth of the matter, she wouldn't accept the money. "But since you merely acted as the muse to prompt Dionysus to paint the piece, I didn't think you deserved to keep the full price of the work."

"Indeed?" she sniffed. He suspected she was about to demand more money from him before she caught herself and pushed the money into a fold of her skirt.

He quickly accepted the victory, small that it may have been, and offered her his arm. She took it much more readily this time and politely led him to the door.

Being a poor relation must be a terribly trying experience for a proud woman. She seemed uncomfortable with the charity the Baneshires no doubt freely gave to her. And the Season's obligations and events were expensive enough; they were surely straining Elsbeth's nerves.

Nigel vowed to change all that.

For Elsbeth, a woman far more interesting than a seductive image on a canvas, deserved everything he could give her.

CHAPTER SIX

"Attend the house party, my lady," Edgeware said with an imperial air. Before Elsbeth had a chance to respond he signaled his intention to leave with a bow. It was a grand gesture full of romantic flourish, yet tempered with a teasing grin. He then turned on his heel and sauntered away.

She watched, feeling more than a little stunned, as he departed down the long hallway. She should call out to him. She should rebuke him. But the words simply wouldn't come.

She pressed her hand to her mouth. Her skin still felt warm from Edgeware's strong but gentle touch. Like a lover's caress, his heat spread from the tips of her fingers to her tingling lips.

"No," she whispered as tears pooled in her eyes. Even though her feelings were in turmoil, even though her belly quivered with both excitement and fear, she would not lose herself to her emotions.

And yet, it had been so long, so very long since she'd felt this way. For the first time in more years than she cared to count, she could feel a slight stirring in her heart. This was Edgeware's doing, of course. He'd blown into her life like a maelstrom. Or like a brave knight atop a white horse with his bold promises to save her. What woman wouldn't find herself falling prey to his charms?

Not her. She was no longer a bright-eyed virgin, naively believing in fairytales. Though she didn't fully understand his motives, she knew exactly what Edgeware was doing. She recognized his heated glances and pretty words for what they were. She also recognized the way her own treacherous body was responding. There was no question in her mind at all about what was happening.

He was trying to seduce her.

And, Heaven help her, she was tempted, oh so dearly tempted to let him.

Nigel sipped his brandy and peered over the top of the *Gazette* he was reading. White's was crowded with the influential men of the *beau monde*, many enjoying the warmth of the blazing fires while London suffered from yet another day of chilly rains. His appearance at the gentleman's club created a minor disturbance. A self-acknowledged recluse, he rarely graced the private rooms of White's. But despite how much he hated drawing attention to himself, some matters needed to be handled in full view of the public.

"Have you lost your marbles, Edgeware? You have the matrons of the *ton* all twittering." Mr. George Waver, Sir Justin Waver's second son and Nigel's neighbor in Dorset, plopped down in an adjacent leather chair.

Nigel set his crystal snifter on the small round table between them. He'd nursed the brandy for close to an hour, waiting for George to arrive.

"It's rare when I'm not the topic of gossip and speculation," he said wryly.

"But it's so out of your nature to be the one creating the gossip, to—I hesitate to say it—to *entertain*." George threw his legs over the arm of the chair and crossed his ankles. "Do you realize how much entertaining you'll be responsible for with a house party? Guests linger, you must know, for longer than the week."

"No one will linger. I'll make certain of that."

George shook his head. "For someone who has never hosted a party, you're certainly jumping into this endeavor with both feet. May I inquire what the blazes you're up to?"

Nigel chuckled. He never imagined he could surprise George, the founder of a large, though often beleaguered, shipping company. He lifted a manicured finger to his lips. "You may find the house party's purpose even more shocking than the fact that I'm hosting it, I'm afraid. But it is one of the reasons I've asked you to meet me."

George lurched forward and swung his feet to the floor. "Really?" His sky-blue eyes sparkled. "It involves danger? And you need me to watch your back?"

"Danger of another kind, George. And, yes, I do need you to watch my back." He paused for the sheer joy of watching his friend squirm in his seat. "I'm setting out to restore Lady Mercer to the good graces of society."

"Lady Mercer? *The Nude?*"

Nigel clenched his teeth. "Yes, Lady Mercer. She's suffered a great wrong and I intend to make reparations. I hope I can count on your assistance in ensuring my guests treat her with the highest degree of respect."

"I say she's just as guilty as your Dionysus. If she didn't want to be sneered at like some rantipole, she should have never taken up with the artist. She's no better than any common light skirt—"

"No!" He reached over and caught George by his coat's collar. "She had no knowledge of the painting. She's had no contact with Dionysus. She is an innocent in this affair."

"Very well, Edgeware." George's expression darkened. "Release me before you attract the attention of every damned gentleman in the club."

Nigel let go of George and tried to straighten his friend's crumpled lapel. "Can I count on your support?"

"Of course you have my support. You always do. I will kiss her hand and speak pretty words to her. And I will use my influence to sway my friends to do the same." He frowned. "But Edgeware, Lady Mercer? Are you certain of her innocence? I mean, she *was* married to that bastard Mercer, after all."

Nigel shuddered at the thought. Before a few days ago he hadn't known of the Earl of Mercer's marriage to Elsbeth. Sure, he'd known that the dastardly earl had married. All of the *beau monde* pitied his poor, nearly invisible wife. But Elsbeth? That delicate flower married to a monster? Worse, he suspected that the marriage was, at least in some part, Dionysus's fault.

"The lady is above reproach," he said.

"Even so, I cannot believe your sponsorship at a house party will repair the damage done by the painting. Over half the *beau monde* turned up at the exhibition."

"If one party is not enough, I will have more. I have a duty to fulfill."

"What is this connection to Dionysus? Is he a bastard sibling?"

"You know I cannot tell you, George."

"I don't know anything." The matter had grown to be a sticking point between the two men. "Pardon me, I'm going to fetch a brandy."

Nigel returned his attentions to the paper he'd been reading. But his mind wouldn't focus on its articles. Instead, he spent the time alone cursing himself for not trusting his closest friend with this secret and cursing Dionysus for ruining Elsbeth's reputation.

"I'm glad to see you've finally decided to make a presence for yourself in Society, my boy. It took you long enough."

Nigel glanced up from the paper. Lord Charles Purbeck's thick lips were pursed with the same sour expression he seemed to always wear. "Good morning, Uncle. I didn't realize you made a regular haunt of White's. I would have suspected Brookes's more to your political tastes." He motioned to the empty chair beside him. "Please take a seat, sir."

"Brookes's. White's. Bah! I keep membership in all the clubs, just as you should, boy. Wise men keep close tabs on both sides of the political fence." His uncle settled in the chair and dug his hand into an interior pocket of his coat. "You cannot imagine the pleasure and surprise I felt when I received notice of your upcoming house party. I hope you have invited the right sort." A strange gleam grew in Uncle Charles's eyes. He pulled a slip of paper from his pocket. "It's not too late to amend the invitation list."

Nigel accepted the paper and unfolded it. He quickly read the names of three of the most influential families of the *ton*. Luckily, the families had been invited. His efforts to secure Lady Mercer's return to society would be a waste of time without the cooperation of powerful families.

"These families boast some of the most eligible young women on the Marriage Mart. I would most assuredly approve of such a match for you, boy."

Nigel fought an urge to bury his head in his hands. His uncle despised such behavior, deeming any show of emotion to be below their class. "I'm not yet in search of a wife. This is nothing more than a simple house party," he said very calmly, though the panic welling deep within him was anything but calm. His uncle had played the role of matchmaker four times. Each time ending in utter disaster.

"Bah!" Uncle Charles leaned forward and thumped Nigel on the chest. "It's past time you to beget an heir, boy. You have a duty to your title, to our family line. And don't think I haven't heard of your accident at the estate. You're lucky to be alive after being thrown from a horse like that."

"But I am alive. And I fully intend to enjoy living a bit longer before I shackle myself to some simpering milksop or fishwife."

"Nonsense! You only need to stay with a wife long enough to get her with child. An heir and a spare. That's all that's required of you. Find a wife who enjoys the country and keep her at the estate while you continue to pursue your business here in London. Nothing needs to change in your life. Nothing at all. You can even keep your doxies, and after your wife has produced your brood, she can do the same." Uncle Charles sighed and smiled. "That's how it went between your aunt and myself."

And look how happy their lives had been. Nigel remembered grimly a terrifying summer morning. He was probably no older than six or seven at the time. He entered the breakfast parlor just as his aunt tossed a pretty blue and white flowered butter dish at Uncle Charles. Uncle Charles had ducked and the dish had shattered against the door mere inches above Nigel's head.

"I'll consider the notion of marriage, Uncle." It took much less energy to agree with the man who'd raised him than to engage in what would inevitably turn into a vehement argument.

As much as his uncle resented the truth of it, Nigel's hands were now firmly on the reins of his fortune, his title, his estate, and yes, even his life. He doubted the world had ever experienced such a battle of wills such as the one he'd waged to wrest control from his well-intentioned uncle.

Charles had made his home at Purbeck Manor shortly after the death of Nigel's father, which bestowed the title of the sixth Marquess of Edgeware on Nigel's head at the tender age of three. Lady Purbeck, and their infant son, Charlie, naturally accompanied him in this move.

"See that you do, boy. Life, especially yours, is too short to delay on such important matters as begetting an heir." Charles heaved out of the chair and bustled away, leaving Nigel to wonder if his uncle knew how his recent brush with death had not been an accident.

"Gawd, Edgeware, you look as if you need this brandy more than me. Your jaw's as long as an old nag's." George returned, chipper as ever. It was a wonder how George never held a grudge for long.

Nigel waved away his friend's comment with a negligent flip of his wrist. "Just a brief encounter with my uncle, who was only too happy to provide recommendations of whom to invite to my humble house party."

"Sounds like you'll be sleeping guests in shifts at Purbeck. I don't remember the old place having enough bedchambers to house the bulk of London."

"It doesn't, and I have been a trifle more exclusive than that in my invitations." He leaned forward in his chair. George, though projecting his usual lazy demeanor, was acting anything but normal. The deep lines underscoring his eyes hinted at several nights of lost sleep. "I know what my worries are. Why do you require a brandy fortifier?"

George flustered for a moment, a most unusual behavior for the businessman. "I? Did I say something was wrong?" He swallowed nearly half his drink. "You must be mistaken."

"Come now," Nigel urged.

"Just a bit of trouble with the shipping business. Nothing that wouldn't bore the ears off a true aristocrat such as yourself." George took another sip. "By-the-bye, I want to thank you for involving my mother with this grand event of yours. She's bubbling over with excitement, chattering on and on about how delighted she is to have been asked to play hostess at your house party."

"I'm only too pleased she'd agreed. With a household filled with men, I required the services of a respectable matron to fill the role." He let the matter of George's business problems fade to the background, though he wasn't quite ready to let the matter drop completely. If his friend needed assistance, he wanted to help.

"Let me ask you an impertinent question, Edgeware." George's natural smile returned. "Why a house party? A series of balls hosted by yourself and some of your most powerful friends would do just as well in repairing Lady Mercer's good name."

"Time," Nigel muttered. "I'm short of it. I was at Purbeck when Lady Mercer's disaster erupted." He glanced around the room to make sure no one could overhear them. "No one other than my head groom knows this," he said. "I expect you'll be able to keep your mouth shut regarding what I am about to tell you."

"Have you ever known my lips to run unfettered?"

"No, I haven't. And don't pick up the habit now. A few days ago I was riding the borders of the estate in search of fresh evidence of smuggling operations when Zeus bolted. He tossed me headlong to the ground."

"*Zounds*, you're lucky to be alive! That stallion of yours is a mammoth."

"That's not the half of it. I took a pretty bad crack on the head and suffer from various pains ever since."

"Zounds," George breathed through his teeth.

"It wasn't Zeus's fault. Someone placed a metal burr beneath his saddle. My weight caused him considerable pain."

"A murder attempt? You cannot be serious."

"Considering how I was mistaken for dead for several minutes after the accident, I have to be serious about this." Nigel pulled a hand through his hair. "Since I can't imagine having any enemies among the locals in the village, I'm wondering if I hadn't stumbled into the middle of a crime ring. Smuggling is growing again in the area. You've been to your estate in Dorset recently. Have you heard any talk about illegal activities?"

George paled. "Gad no. If I had, I would have come straight to you. You're the highest ranking landowner in the village, after all."

Nigel eyed his friend carefully. There was something in the way George's mouth twitched and in the tone of his quick answer that didn't sit right.

"Of course you would," he said slowly. "Why wouldn't you?"

"There *is* no reason I wouldn't, so put that out of your mind," George said a little too vehemently. "So you're sitting on pins, anxious to get back to your problems at Purbeck? Certainly you're not actually considering conducting an investigation while a house party is underway in your own home?"

"That is precisely what I'm planning."

"And you suspect an attempt against your life is connected to some errant smuggling operation?" George paled further.

"What else am I to think?"

"Then you must not return. Not with the confusion of a house party. There will be too many new faces on the estate for you to properly protect yourself. Not only the guests, but you'll have to bring in extra servants to care for all those demanding sops residing under your roof."

"I know, I know all that. But I can't let this trouble with Lady Mercer simmer. I have a responsibility to take care of Dionysus's messes. You know that."

"No, I don't know that. And what good will you serve Dionysus if you are bloody well dead?"

"Don't get flustered, George. I have a plan all worked out. But I do need help. If your business can spare you for the week, I would be delighted if you attended my party as an honored guest."

"You can always rely on me." George laughed then, though it lacked its usual warmth. "Another adventure, eh Edgeware? What a change this will be. I'm usually the one who's dragging you down into stews. It'll be a treat to be pulled up into the bright world of high society."

"Don't put yourself down. Your family is perfectly accepted in the *ton.*"

This time when George laughed, the rumbling sound was genuine. He stood and drained the last of his brandy. "I work for my fortune; you inherited yours. There's a world of difference in that statement, Edgeware. A damned world of difference."

CHAPTER SEVEN

A gentle breeze rustled through the crisp, brown fronds hanging limply from the ailing palms encircling Purbeck Manor in the southeastern end of Dorset. Despite the ill-chosen tree species, the manor house itself was impressive in both size and architectural style. Adorned with the local Purbeck white marble, a stone commonly found on many of the estates and homes in the region, there was nothing common about Purbeck Manor. The pale marble blocks that had been quarried from the estate grounds had been finely polished and intricately carved in the 17th century to form fanciful details such as sweeping arched lintels and spiraling columns. The work had been directed by an ancestor Nigel had always thought of as a bit mad.

Who else but a madman would have built such a sprawling manor? Fashioned to mimic a palatial Italian villa, the colossal structure held no less than ten guest apartments, a master suite, a grand ballroom, and an adjoining dining room with a table large enough to seat fifty people. Why anyone would willingly want to feed and entertain so many had been beyond Nigel's understanding until now.

Fashionably dressed for the upcoming country affair in a long coat and tailored breeches, he stood outside the front entrance and leaned against one of the fifteen marble columns flanking the front exterior while a line of carriages rolled up the lane and past the estate's neatly-scythed front lawn.

The first of the guests were arriving as scheduled. The plan promised to be a challenge. But Nigel felt ready. He had to be, for Elsbeth's sake. His thoughts strayed to that steely flower. Her strength had startled him. She refused to be cowed. And her determination to expose Dionysus appeared unbendable. Yes, he'd do well to restore her reputation before she could unravel the mystery behind Dionysus.

If only he didn't have other distractions—like an attempted murder—to deal with. He was going to need all his concentration to seduce Elsbeth in order to keep her mind off Dionysus. He was contemplating the delightful task of enticing the intriguing lady into his bed when the hair on the back of his neck rose.

He caught a glimpse of movement in the dark grove just north of the manor.

Damnation, what now? His nerves were frayed to begin with. The entire household was excited and noisy and in his way. He could hear Lady Waver, George's mother, rushing about, giving last-minute instructions to the servants. Certainly his imagination was joining in the excitement, creating villains where none existed and seeing shadows of men in the home wood. His nerves must surely be undone.

But again, out the corner of his eye, he fancied he saw a clear outline of a man. His senses alert, Nigel gazed out into the dark grove.

An unmistakable pair of eyes flashed from within the shadows of the wood. Someone was definitely out there watching him.

"Lady Waver!" he called out. He paced the portico, eager to track the intruder. A round woman with bright eyes and flushed cheeks joined him on the front steps.

"Ah, carriages are approaching," she said cheerfully. "The house will soon be filled with activity."

If he went through the house and out the back way, he might be able to sneak up on whoever was hiding in the woods.

Perhaps those eyes belonged to the cove who'd put that burr in Zeus's saddle.

"My lord?" Lady Waver said, her cheerful smile fading. "Is something wrong?"

"Yes." He started toward the front door. "Please greet the incoming guests and give them my apologies."

Lady Waver caught his arm. "My lord!" she cried. "You don't plan to greet them yourself? Surely your guests are expecting—"

He slipped free from her grasp and gave a brisk bow. "I trust you will manage well enough without me, madam."

The guests would have to make do without him. He had a shadow to catch.

Nigel returned from his search of the woods to find that the carriages had already emptied of their passengers. Other than the ripped piece of wool he'd found hanging on a tree branch, there were no other signs to suggest there had been an intruder on the property, no other evidence to prove he hadn't imagined his being watched.

Just to be safe, he sent Guthrie, a rather burly footman, to thoroughly search the woods and report anything suspicious.

Perhaps he should also find George and—

"I will not have it!" a round tone sang out just as he entered the front hall.

Damn and blast. The guests.

Nigel forced a grin and forged forward, prepared to play the friendly host.

Lady Waver stood in the middle of the entrance hall, her face red as a cherry. "But—but Lady Dashborough, you cannot mean to *leave.*" She waved her stout hands in the air while blocking the path of three ladies who were trying to push their way out the front door.

Nigel drew a deep breath. He'd expected trouble, and though the prospect of confronting the formidable Lady Dashborough frayed his nerves, he was not unprepared.

"Ladies," he said, as he strode quickly across the hall to greet the unhappy women.

Lady Dashborough was the first to turn around. "Lord Edgeware, how dare you?" She punctuated each word and then thrust her chin in the air. "We are leaving."

"Leaving?" he echoed. He leaned against an interior column and let a crooked grin form. "Why ever for, my lady? You've only just arrived." He knew the picture he created, the untamed bachelor with a gleaming smile.

Lady Dashborough, still a beautiful woman in her own right and one of the most influential gossips in the *ton,* stepped toward him. Her hunched shoulders relaxed a good three inches.

"There has to be a mistake," she said, her voice softening to almost a whisper. "Your hostess has shown that Mercer creature to one of your guest rooms. We cannot be expected to consort with a woman of . . . of . . . *that sort.* I cannot imagine how the Baneshires manage to allow *that thing* to live in their home, much less allow it to act as chaperone for their daughters. I, for one, would have swiftly kicked it out and let it fend for itself in the stews where it assuredly belongs."

Nigel gave a quick nod to Lady Dashborough's two daughters before taking the grand lady's hand in his. "I am sure you would have done just that. I can understand why you'd feel offended by her presence." He led her to the far end of the hall and lowered his voice. "But then if Lady Mercer knew of the secret liaisons you and a certain married duke, a married duke who has openly sworn his devotion to his lovely wife, have been carrying on for nigh three years now, she might feel just as offended to be included on the same guest list as you."

Lady Dashborough sucked in a great deal of air. "I have never broadcast that relationship. There is no scandal."

"No?" he said smoothly. "No, I suppose not. At least, there won't be one as long as a certain influential wife of a certain duke remains ignorant."

"Are you threatening me, Edgeware?"

Nigel loathed both threats and confrontations. But since the success of the week depended on the guests actually staying for the house party, he was forced to play the clever bastard.

"Yes, my lady, I believe I am."

George had been right. His friend had spent the previous week gathering all sorts of nasty bits of information against the invited guests from a variety of underworld sources. Nigel had protested but was now glad George hadn't listened.

"Shall I have Lady Waver show you and your daughters to the guest chambers I've selected specifically for you?"

Lady Dashborough smiled through tight lips and her voice sounded strained. "Yes, my lord, that would please me."

He gave a deep bow. "Until this evening then, my lady."

The first crisis of many, no doubt, had been quite smoothly handled. Satisfied, he turned his mind to Elsbeth. Lady Dashborough was not the type of woman to keep her dislikes silent. If she and the Baneshire family had arrived at the estate at the same time, he could only suppose that Elsbeth was upstairs licking her wounds and planning her escape.

He stopped a footman who was descending the grand stairs. "Is Lady Mercer settled in the chamber I've selected for her?" he asked, thinking to invite her and her cousins into the red parlor to take an early tea. Women often required extra attention and reassurances when faced with a difficult situation. He doubted Elsbeth was any different.

"No, my lord," the footman said.

"She is not?" Had she run off so quickly?

"Lady Mercer had asked for directions to the gardens. I

showed her the way myself, my lord. And then a few minutes later, I showed Lady Olivia the same path."

"Very good," he said, and raced back down the stairs and out the back door into the estate's private gardens.

The soft scent of daffodils greeted him. Beyond the yew hedges, he heard the whisper of voices and the rustle of skirts. Steeling himself for the worst—namely, a river of tears—he straightened his coat and began a brave march forward.

"Ho there!" George's voice carried across a grassy field.

Nigel waited for George to trot across the field. "What detective work have you been pursuing today?" he asked.

"Me?" George shrugged. "Nothing, really. Just a brisk trot around the grounds."

"Looking for evidence, perhaps?" Nigel pulled out the scrap of material he'd found in the woods and handed it to George. "Something like this?"

George studied the woolen fabric.

"I believe someone was stalking in the woods, watching me. He eluded me when I went in pursuit but not without tearing his cloak."

"Strange," George said, giving the cloth even more attention. "I spoke to Charlie on the wooded path between our houses a few minutes ago. He arrived this morning with three young friends. They are looking to invade your house party."

"Charlie?" He was surprised to hear that his cousin, the younger Charles Purbeck, would leave the excitement of the London Season for what promised to be a staid country gathering.

"He's set up at the dowager cottage."

"Fine. I'll send a footman to invite him and his friends to dinner. The younger women will be grateful for the company of men closer to their age."

George frowned. "Are you not the least concerned that Charlie or one of his friends might be wearing a torn cloak?"

Nigel considered the idea and quickly dismissed it. "Charlie's harmless."

George frowned, not looking at all convinced.

"Granted, Charlie has an uncommon talent for mischief," Nigel conceeded. "But I assure you, he would never do anything to harm me. We were raised together. We survived his father's rages together. We're as close as brothers."

"Of course you are," George shook his head and smiled. "I've been working in the shipping business too long, I suppose. I no longer trust anyone."

"I'm sure that's not true. Anyhow, I don't have time to worry about this now. I'm tending to a fire on our other front." He explained the situation and was more than a little relieved when George followed him into the gardens. His friend had a certain way with women, handling the fairer sex with a rogue smile and a smooth tongue.

Without too much searching they found Elsbeth and Olivia in the folly, a sham ruin celebrating the goddess Athena. The round Greek temple sat in the midst of one of the garden's many ponds.

"My ladies," Nigel said, as they crossed the arched bridge and joined the women in the shelter of the marble stone structure. "Please allow me to introduce my friend and neighbor, Mr. George Waver."

Olivia stepped forward. Her smile rivaled the sun reflecting off the pond. Elsbeth stayed behind her cousin. Her features remained as still as the stone ruin. At least her sapphire eyes, though hard and wary, were clear. No evidence to suggest she'd been weeping. Perhaps Lady Dashborough's complaints had not reached her ears.

George greeted the women using his extraordinary charm and began to recount a silly adventure Nigel and George had shared as lads. "We were convinced the head gardener was a French spy and had set out to uncover the truth," he said and then launched into his tale with vivid descriptions.

George's presence seemed to put the young Lady Olivia immediately at ease. Elsbeth was more reserved in her reaction. Her wary gaze, Nigel noticed, kept straying away from George and in his direction. Nigel crossed his arms in front of him, hoping to strike a languid pose.

What was she thinking? What did she find so unpleasant about him that she would have to regard him so?

George must have noticed Elsbeth's odd behavior for he stopped mid-story. "Lady Olivia, would you care to stroll the bulb garden with me? The flowers are near their peak, and the light is perfect for viewing."

Olivia quickly agreed and latched onto George's proffered arm. "I will see you at dinner, my lady," George said, giving a departing bow to Elsbeth, who had stepped forward to join in the stroll. "And do not worry after your young cousin. I will have her back to the house in a trice."

"Very well," Elsbeth said with a sigh. "I will be waiting for you in our apartment, Olivia." Her gaze stayed fixed upon the departing couple until they disappeared around the corner of the path. She then turned to Nigel.

"Why do you stare at me so?" she asked in a harsh whisper.

"I?" He was quite taken aback at the charge. He took a step toward her. "It was *you* who was staring at *me*. Not that I mind the attention, mind you. At least you are finally taking notice of me."

"Absurd. Simply, absurd," she said, as she backed away from him until she'd pressed herself up against one of the far columns.

This was beyond strange. No woman had ever feared him before.

"Is it so terribly frightening to find yourself alone with me?"

He braved a second step forward. Pursuit of a woman was foreign to him. He was much more used to the role of hapless prey than aggressive predator. And aggressive predator was unquestionably the role he filled now. He purposefully stood between Elsbeth and her escape, making damned sure there was no danger of her fleeing. There could be no seduction if she refused to remain in his presence for more than a moment or two.

"I am not afraid," she whispered. Her lips quivered ever so slightly as she pressed herself more firmly against the far stone column.

"You believe I will attack you?" Certainly she didn't think he'd—

"A-attack me?" she breathed.

Ah, she did.

Her gaze shifted toward the bridge, the only way out of the ruin, and back to where he stood blocking the way.

"I promise that you are safe with me," he said as he stepped to one side, careful to keep his distance while opening up her escape route. "I spoke with Lady Dashborough. Lady Waver mentioned that she arrived the same time as you. I hope she—"

"Did she leave?" Elsbeth asked before he could explain. "She told me she planned to leave."

"I'm sure Lady Dashborough told you a good many things she now regrets." He couldn't help but chuckle as he remembered how easily the good Lady Dashborough came into line. "She would not dream of leaving *my* house party."

The news didn't seem to cheer Elsbeth in the least. "This bodes to be a very long week."

"And pleasant, I hope. I am pleased you decided to attend."

"You gave me no choice! You conspired to set my own family against me!"

Despite her fierce scowl he couldn't help but take heart from her sparking anger. Where she was standing, at the far end of the ruin, the sunlight streamed in and bathed her in the most ethereal light. She could have been the warrior, Athena, returned to earth as lithe as a deer and as strong as a lioness.

A sudden surge of lust nearly stole Nigel's breath. He wanted this goddess to come to life, this picture of perfection, but he had no idea how to win her. The goddess standing in his garden was as real as the water in the ponds. She would be staying in his home and sleeping in one of his beds. The thought was staggering.

"You're doing it again," she said.

"Doing what?"

"Staring at me *like that*." She clutched the locket at her throat. "Like you're hungry. It makes me uneasy."

Well hell, that was the last thing he wanted to do. "I only wished to speak with you. I was curious to know how you fared after your encounter with Lady Dashborough." His voice was purposefully neutral, though he felt anything but neutral toward her and the whole bloody situation.

"I'm fine. Lady Olivia has convinced me that my uncle would be most upset if I showed up at their London town house a few days after leaving."

"That is a—what did you say? Baneshire is in London?" Her uncle, a very well respected member of the *ton*, was to play a large role in the reformation of Elsbeth's good name.

"He sends his regrets. He had every intention of attending. But at the last minute found it impossible to leave Lady Baneshire alone. She's been gravely ill for some time now, you must know. He insisted we come, though. He sent an army of footmen with us to guard the carriage."

The unplanned change of topic worked well to smooth the worry lines from Elsbeth's brow. Her tone strengthened and turned quite clipped and frosty. If only the change in topic would do the same for Nigel, and his lust for her could be so easily forgotten.

"Lord Baneshire will be missed." He took a step toward her. He caught a whiff of her perfume, a sweet orange scent in the cool breeze.

"Stroll with me in the gardens," he said, and instantly cursed himself for sounded imperious. He had rather hoped his invitation would have sounded as accommodating as George's had when he invited Olivia to accompany him through the gardens.

"I should return to the guest chamber, my lord. I am still in my carriage dress."

True, she was dressed in a heavy dark blue gown, suitable for traveling. There was a smudge of dust on her cheek, a tiny matching hat sat askew on the top of her head, and a few pins were coming loose, letting the random blond strands of hair escape from the tight styling.

"Very well," he said, but he was not ready to leave her company. He tilted his head and smiled at her. "Perhaps you can do one thing for me before you take your leave?"

Her gloved hand shot out. "You wish to touch my hand again, I suppose." Sapphire blue eyes smoldered from behind her steady lashes.

"Please Elsbeth," he said. He drew off his hat and tossed it aside so he could drag his hand through his hair. This was going to be a very long week indeed. "You have no need to feel a duty to placate me. And I promise you there is no reason to fear me. The only two things I will insist upon is that you accept my assistance in restoring your reputation, and that you do not attempt to uncover Dionysus's identity."

She closed her palm and lowered her hand. For a moment her brows furrowed. "I don't know . . ."

What she didn't know, Nigel wasn't sure. "I had hoped, though, to persuade you to agree to a chaste kiss." Of course he had pictured the kiss blooming into something daringly passionate.

She appeared scandalized by his admission. "I would not enjoy it."

"A challenge, then?" He stepped away from her. She looked ready to dive over the railing and into the pond to escape his wicked presence. "Now you will certainly have to agree to permit me to brush my lips with yours. For if you don't, I will forever believe you find me lacking."

With a look of outrage, Elsbeth charged toward the bridge. Nigel's heart dropped as he watched her go. Skirts raised, she made haste over the wooden planks and down several feet of the garden trail.

And then, much to Nigel's astonishment, she stopped.

"How chaste a kiss?" she inquired over her shoulder.

"Our lips would touch."

She took several more steps down the path before stopping again. "For how long?"

"For as long as you desire."

She stayed frozen in the middle of the path with her back to him for several moments. Nigel was wise enough not to pursue her. Instead he held his breath while she considered the request, convinced she'd refuse. But like a skittish wren lured to a bowl of seeds, she slowly turned around.

"I will not enjoy it," she said, but closed her eyes and puckered her lips.

As light as the spring breeze in the air, Nigel made a jaunty trail to her. Elsbeth stood stiff with her eyes tightly sealed. He didn't dare wrap his arms around her for fear she might bolt again. So he leaned in close until his lips were a whisper from hers. "I will kiss you now," he said softly.

He brushed his lips against her mouth. She stood unmoving, unresponsive. And yet, his desire grew. He flicked his tongue over her puckered lips hoping to soften them, praying he could draw her out.

She gasped, perhaps to protest. No matter, he took advantage of the opening and suckled her lower lip.

Instead of pulling away, she leaned in closer, her mouth drinking in the attention as if starving. She pressed a hand against his chest and returned his kiss passion for passion.

Nigel groaned.

Suddenly, she pulled back. "That is not the kind of kiss we had agreed to." Her whole face was flushed, her breathing hitched.

"Did you not enjoy it?" he asked, knowing full well that he was the very devil for teasing her.

"Certainly not!" She turned on her heels and held out her arm. "I would thank you to escort me back to the house now."

He gratefully placed his forearm under hers. At least she'd not run away. She was a proud woman and strong. He could admire that. "I must practice then, my lady. For a kiss should be most enjoyable for both parties. Perhaps you will give me pointers?" He said seriously, though a smile played upon his lips. He guided her back to the house while she remained silent.

"Your lips are most exquisite," he said just before leaving her at the base of the grand staircase, knowing it would scandalize her. "I won't be able to think of anything other than your sweet taste upon my mouth for the rest of the day."

CHAPTER EIGHT

Elsbeth stood off to one side of the drawing room door and watched the ladies taking afternoon tea with the gentlemen gathered within. Everyone appeared so at ease. They visited and laughed freely with each other.

Her heart shuddered.

She'd never experienced such familiarity with her husband and his friends. Men, loud and often brash, simply could not be trusted. They needed to be watched as carefully as one would watch a thief around the household's best silver.

She felt much more comfortable around the servants. That was where she had spent the afternoon, questioning the servants about Dionysus. Though they had expressed honest concern, every single one she'd questioned was either too loyal to the Marquess, or they truly didn't know Dionysus's secret identity.

She tended to think that it was the latter, that the servants simply did not know. The secret was that deep.

"Dreadful, isn't it?" a voice whispered in her ear, startling the wits out of her. She nearly jumped to the ceiling before she whirled around with such speed that her feet jumbled beneath her, tossing her directly into his chest.

His chest.

She felt his muscles ripple from beneath the layers of his clothing. Or was that just her overactive imagination at work? And that kiss in the garden. She couldn't seem to keep from thinking about it. Or wondering if there would be a second one.

Those unruly thoughts frightened and excited her all at once. She shouldn't be having such thoughts about a man, especially not about a man who could turn her legs to jelly with the twitch of his lips.

Edgeware smiled down on her as he very gently set her back on her feet. "I didn't mean to frighten you," he said softly.

Her face heated from embarrassment . . . and from that other emotion she was unwilling to acknowledge. She was forever making herself look the fool around him.

She quickly gathered her composure and turned a hard glare toward the devilishly handsome lord.

"What do you mean by saying I am dreadful?" she asked.

"Not you, dove." His gaze flicked toward the drawing room. "*Them*. I despise such gatherings. One feels obligated to be in a perpetually cheerful mood and such obligations tend to irritate my nerves by half."

He looked so miserable, so utterly put out, she couldn't help but smile. Surely he was jesting. A man of his position and wealth must thrive on social gatherings.

"We must go in, you know," he said. "My fortifiers—brandy, sherry, and port—are all on that sideboard . . ." He sighed. "On the far side of the drawing room."

"Poor man." His behavior was so unlike her late husband's. Lord Mercer would have never bemoaned the location of his brandy. Instead he'd have plowed into the room, poured a snifter full, and ignored the guests if that was what he chose to do.

"I have a duty to my guests," Edgeware said and heaved another deep sigh. "Perhaps if you stay close to me, we'll both survive the ordeal."

He wasn't jesting. He was actually dreading this evening more than she. And he was looking to *her* to be his strength.

Amazing.

"If you smile like that all evening, I won't notice anyone in the room but you," he said. A wolfish gleam appeared in his black gaze. His eyes shimmered with a brooding hunger, the same erotic and almost tempting hunger he'd used against her defenses that afternoon in the garden. And just like in the garden, she couldn't run away. Not from him . . . or herself.

"Thank you, my lord. But I have no need of support. I am perfectly capable of enjoying an evening with my peers." This time when she turned, she did so with careful precision. Head held high, she marched into the drawing room. Alone. The laughter and giddy chatter abruptly came to a halt. All eyes turned to her.

She *did* need his support, damn his teasing ways.

She didn't want to face his guests alone. She didn't want to face them at all. They *knew*. Because of that horrid painting, they now *knew*. She could read it in their disapproving gazes. They knew she'd been unfaithful to her husband, the royal hero who'd bravely given his life in battle. Though she hadn't taken comfort in another man's arms in his absence—as some now believed—she *had* broken her marriage vows.

She'd denied the truth to her uncle. Denied it to herself, too. She hadn't been a faithful wife. She'd withheld herself from him in the worst possible ways. A wife was bound by duty to love and honor her husband, no matter the hardships. And she'd done neither. The day word of his death reached her ears, she'd breathed a sigh of relief for being released from him, a man she despised.

Somehow Dionysus had seen through her stiff upper lip and silent nods. Somehow he knew of the dishonor lurking in her heart and was determined to reveal her secret to the world.

She had to stop him before he dealt another blow to her and her family's reputation. There were too many secrets hidden beneath the pain. Society would forever shun her if they ever learned the full truth of her marriage.

With a brave smile that was anything but real, she stepped toward her cousins, who were, unfortunately, sitting on a sofa next to Lady Dashborough's two daughters. Just as she was about to politely greet the lovely quartette of ladies, her gaze landed on a large painting hanging above her cousins' heads.

And she froze.

Varying shades of purples and crimson had been blended to create a stunning sunset. The paint nearly glowed. The artist's short bush strokes and heavy use of paint struck Elsbeth immediately.

Dionysus had painted the scene.

Even here, far away from the frivolities of London, he plagued her, underscoring the urgency of her task. Naturally, she'd expected it to be the case since Edgeware had baldly admitted to being Dionysus's keeper. But even so, her heart wasn't prepared to soak in the heartrending landscape.

A man, alone, with only his back visible stood on a rocky outcropping, a cape fluttering in the harsh wind. Other than the rocks and the vast expanse of the sunset, the landscape was barren. Utterly barren.

The raw despair bared in that scene threatened to rip open her heart. How could this be the same artist who wished to ruin her? How could he display such depths of feeling while being cold enough to seek to destroy her bruised and broken heart?

"Elly," Olivia said loudly, saving Elsbeth from being completely absorbed into Dionysus's painting. "I was afraid that you were determined to hide upstairs for the entire week."

The younger of Lady Dashborough's two daughters, a creamy-skinned beauty with soft auburn hair, sniffed haughtily. "One could only have hoped."

"That new gown looks lovely on you, Elsbeth," Lauretta said on the heels of the snide comment.

"Yes," Lady Dashborough's elder daughter said. "The silver

threads are simply stunning."

Elsbeth held her breath, waiting for the young woman to follow up the compliment with a snide remark of her own. The woman merely batted her pretty long eyelashes and stared up at Elsbeth with a look akin to reverence.

"Thank you," Elsbeth said finally. Shock kept her from saying anything more.

Besides, her attention was drawn back to the painting. It was a self-portrait of course, a man utterly alone in a harsh environment. His shoulders sagged, drawn down with exhaustion from bearing too great a weight for far too long. She recognized his anguish, knew such pain only too well. Here, in the middle of this drawing room, she felt just as alone.

"Lady Sara, Lady Constance, please permit me to introduce my cousin." Olivia jumped up from the sofa and pulled her arm around Elsbeth.

"There is no need," the younger of the daughters said. She rose from the sofa and walked away.

"I am Sara," the elder Dashborough said. "Please forgive my sister. She is . . . insecure." Sara edged closer to Elsbeth. "But I am fascinated by you. I would dearly enjoy talking to you sometime this week."

"I would be only too happy to—"

"Please excuse me, ladies." Lord Edgeware appeared at Elsbeth's side and deftly captured her arm. "Allow me to introduce Lady Mercer to the other guests before the three of you monopolize all her attentions." He gave the women such a charming, dimpled smile it would have been impossible to object.

"A pretty splattering of colors, do you not agree?" he said, not sparing even a passing glance toward the painting she could not seem to ignore. The dark lord stood too close to her. His spicy masculine scent left her breathless, her mind muddled. "I thought it matched the décor of this room."

Pretty? She shivered and forced herself to turn away from the haunting image. He couldn't even *begin* to understand how Dionysus's lonely images could sting her heart.

Just standing next to Edgeware and looking at the "splattering of colors" made her miss the soft emotions she'd long ago abandoned. *Gracious,* she needed to regain control. Allowing her foolish heart such freedom would prove dangerous.

It always did.

"Don't run from me again," Edgeware whispered as they strolled across the room, his voice an intimate caress on her ear, making it all the more difficult to steel her nerves against the softening of her resolve.

"Forgive me, my lord," she said, her voice as sharp as a fishwife's.

"Just don't do it again," he replied smoothly. "I would hate to wrack my brain once more in order to come up with a fresh excuse to lure you back to my side."

She bit her tongue, stopping herself before she told him that spending the evening in his company was one of the very last things she wished to do. A lie, if there was ever one, too. Perversely, like Dionysus's paintings, Edgeware fascinated her.

So, with a smile forming on her lips, she allowed herself to be introduced to the crowded room. Every now and again she caught her gaze straying back to Dionysus's painting and would have to forcibly return her wandering attentions to the guests being introduced.

Not all present that evening were staying at the house. Some were Edgeware's neighbors. And not all of the faces were unfamiliar to her. Lord Ames had the decency to blush as he rubbed his cheek in memory of the slap she had given him the day of the exhibition.

The famous "Beau" Brummel, the arbiter of taste and refinement, bowed over her hand and complimented her silver sheath of a gown. Stunned by his acceptance, she just barely murmured her gratitude. Mr. Brummel and Edgeware paid her no heed as they talked amicably about courtly affairs.

Lady Cowper, one of the patronesses of Almack's and a powerful figure in her own right, greeted Elsbeth with cool civility before turning her charm toward Edgeware. "I have pulled myself away from London during the height of the Season with the sole purpose to recruit you into our ranks, Edgeware. Whenever will you join Almack's?" She swatted him with her fan. "There are so few eligible, handsome faces attending lately."

Lady Cowper's husband, the Fifth Earl of Cowper, was on the other side of the room, talking politics with several of Edgeware's neighbors.

Much to Elsbeth's surprise, other than Lady Dashborough's youngest daughter, no one insulted her or tried to spurn her company. Even Lady Dashborough apologized for her earlier behavior. Apparently the Marquess's social influence hadn't been overstated.

After the introductions, she wasn't given the chance to return to her cousins or to disappear into a corner where she could ponder her unsettling reaction to either Dionysus's painting or the way the dark lord made her heart race. Instead, she was persuaded, rather doggedly, to partner Edgeware in a game of Whist, a game she was, luckily, able to play with a great deal of skill and confidence. After a while, she found that the evening promised to be a bit better than the utter disaster she'd initially imagined. And much to her surprise, many of her giggles were even genuine.

Did she realize the effect she had on men when she let her eyes sparkle so?

Nigel supposed not, since no accompanying coy smile tugged

on her artfully shaped lips. Nor did she sneak glances with the other men at the table to read their reactions. Her behavior was as straightforward and honest as a sunrise. The only fleeting glances she'd sneak were toward that damned painting on the wall.

He cursed his decision to hang that dratted painting in his drawing room. She was clearly repulsed—frightened even—by it, though her gaze seemed drawn to it.

George and Severin, the whist team Nigel and Elsbeth were pitting their wits against, were playing a sharp hand while talking incessantly about the most nonsensical topics. Elsbeth laughed prettily at a jest George made before laying down the queen of hearts—exactly the card Nigel had been waiting for.

"I'm tempted to smuggle you into the worst of London's gaming rooms," he leaned forward and said as he played his turn, winning the fifth consecutive game point. "I'd say your skills would win me a fortune several times over."

"Then you simply must let *me* have her," Severin said. "I could make better use of the lady's skills than you ever could, Edgeware."

Severin made the comment in such a lilting manner that no one would have taken him seriously. They were joking, having a bit of fun with the compliments. From the way the color drained from Elsbeth's face, one would have thought they'd been contemplating selling her into slavery.

"I say," Severin said, mirroring her distress. " 'Tis a little jest, that's all. Truly, nothing to get the vapors over."

Elsbeth murmured something unintelligible. Since it was her turn again, she drew a card from her stack and dropped it on the pile without even looking at it. Her play stunned Nigel. The card she'd tossed down hadn't followed the suit of the trick being played nor did it trump the highest card on the table. In fact, she'd revoked. A move only a novice player would make.

According to the rules, they'd be penalized three points. Not that he cared about the points. It was her reaction that had him worried.

He tried to get her attention, to ask her what was wrong, but she refused to look up from the tabletop.

"Lady Mercer?" he asked softly. "Are you unwell?"

She blinked up at him for a silent moment before flicking a glance toward the drawing room door. At least she wasn't sneaking another look at that accursed painting. Her slender hand reached up and clutched the locket hanging around her neck. The color in her cheeks faded further and her lips tightened when her gaze returned again to the drawing room door.

Something was terribly wrong.

Nigel rose as he followed her gaze. Charlie, followed by three of his friends, was strolling into the room like a group of well-groomed roosters.

"Nigel!" his cousin called out. "Surprise!"

Devils and demons, Elsbeth cursed. She should have suspected a handsome demon like Lord Edgeware would be mixed up with a devil like Charlie.

"Lady Mercer." Edgeware had somehow slipped from his chair and made his way to her side without her notice. He placed a steadying hand around her arm and urged her to her feet. "Lady Mercer, allow me to present my cousin, Mr. Charles Purbeck."

She stared into Charlie's dead eyes. A chill direct from hell sailed through her. Charlie and her husband had been two parts of a very close trio. The third, a Captain Pime, was still on the continent with the British army. When the three men had stayed at the estate, she'd felt as if she was their main prey. And it was Charlie, always Charlie, who'd mercilessly tease her husband about his lack of heirs. It was a topic that was a source of endless tension in their marriage, made worse by Charlie. While the men would drink in the parlor after supper, Charlie would whisper in her husband's ear. She never knew exactly what he was saying to Hubert. But the result was always the same. Her husband's face would turn a ruddy red and his eyes would harden every time he'd glance in her direction. And then, later—

Charlie took her hand with brash familiarity, caressing her fingertips before lifting her hand to his lips for a tender kiss.

"Elly," he said. The nickname grated her nerves, and he knew it. He also knew how improper it was for him to be addressing her so intimately. "Elly, my dear, it is ever so good to see you again."

He paused and licked his lips. "With the rumors of your indiscretion flying, I'd been worried about you. I'm glad to see you have found safety under my cousin's . . . um . . . protection. I look forward to renewing our acquaintance this week." His gaze held a wealth of promises that churned her stomach. Before she could tell him that she wanted to do nothing of the sort, he turned his back and greeted Lord Ames.

"Severin," he said, and gave Ames a good pound on the arm. "Good to see you, man. We've missed you in our group. What with the war and all, our numbers have been dwindling. We need you back at our tables to help fill in the void, and our pockets."

Charlie's friends all laughed at the joke.

Edgeware frowned. "Now Charlie—"

"Don't get your indignation all twisted about, cousin. Severin knows I'm just having a bit of fun."

At his expense, Elsbeth thought, remembering only too well the times she'd been the target of Charlie's inappropriate humor . . . and worse, much worse once her husband and his friends had gotten deep into their cups. She moved to escape the drawing room and bumped into Edgeware's chest.

He wrapped a comforting arm around her waist. "Easy," he whispered. "There is nothing to fear here."

She longed to believe him. But with Charlie in the room, she had reason enough to doubt her safety.

"Donald?"

Elsbeth glanced up at the sound of Lauretta's voice. Sure enough, the fickle-hearted Sir Donald Gilforth stood beside Charlie, his fingers playing with a large crested fob hanging from his waistcoat pocket. How could she have missed him before? She was becoming careless, and with so many gentlemen about, that could prove dangerous.

Sir Donald stared blankly ahead as Lauretta rushed up to greet him. Elsbeth's heart stopped. She pulled away from Edgeware just as Lauretta, with eyes bright and a pretty smile pursed on her satiny lips, stepped happily into what promised to be a crushing scene.

"Lord Edgeware," Lady Waver bustled up and latched onto the Marquess's arm. "Dinner is ready to be served."

"Splendid," said Charlie while capturing Elsbeth's hand. "Please allow me to escort you to the dining room, Elly." She had no time to refuse him. Not when there was a more pressing matter worrying her.

Lauretta's fragile heart.

"Donald, it is wonderful to see you," Lauretta was saying, her pink cheeks glowing.

"Yes," Sir Donald said vaguely, no longer looking in Lauretta's direction but at someone beyond her shoulder. "Excuse me, my lady." He brushed past Lauretta and made a beeline to Lady Dashborough's youngest daughter, the lovely Lady Constance.

"Oh dear," Elsbeth muttered, and tried to hurry over to comfort her cousin. But Charlie held her back, squeezing her hand so hard she feared her bones might snap.

"Come along, Elly. Dawdling is so very unbecoming." For a moment he sounded exactly like her dead husband, and she suddenly felt as helpless as a rag doll, unable to do anything other than obey. She might have let Charlie lead her away from her cousin and into the dining room if Edgeware hadn't stepped into their path.

Anger smoldered deep within the brooding dark lord's eyes. With a smooth motion, he freed her hand from Charlie's crushing grip. "George has already claimed the right to escort Lady Mercer this evening," he said.

George had done nothing of the sort.

But no matter, she was grateful for the lie.

George gave a little start, shook his head, and stepped forward. "Of course, I don't know where my mind is."

"I would have escorted you myself," Edgeware quickly explained. "But Lady Waver would never forgive me if I were to ignore the convention of personally escorting the highest ranking lady into the dining room. I am the host, after all, and Lady Waver has graciously agreed to play hostess since this household has been woefully without one for over a decade. I will not upset her."

"I wouldn't expect you to," Elsbeth said, perplexed.

"And Mr. Waver will be crushed if a lady were to turn him away at the last moment." Edgeware spoke so gently, so calmly. His voice soothed her raw nerves, and she was so very glad to accept his friend's proffered arm.

Oh dear. Once free from Charlie, her concerns returned to Lauretta. The girl stood in the middle of the room, alone as a lost lamb. Tears were just starting to well up in her eyes as she stared, disbelieving, after her beloved Donald.

Olivia, Elsbeth saw, would be no help. She had attached herself to the illustrious "Beau" Brummel, certainly a coup of enormous proportions.

Elsbeth squeezed her eyes shut. She needed to take care of her cousin. As chaperone, Lauretta's welfare was her duty and no one else's.

"Mr. Waver," she said and swallowed deeply. There was no hope for it. She'd have to feed herself to the lion in order to keep Lauretta from being stranded and brokenhearted in the middle of the drawing room. "I hope you'll forgive me for crushing your spirit," she said, "but, you see—" she cleared her throat "—I did not realize Charlie would be here. And since he was a dear friend of my late husband's, I feel compelled to accept his company." That didn't quite come out as graciously as she'd intended. "Lady Lauretta is without a companion, sir."

George followed her pleading glance and nodded, understanding her purpose. "Yes, of course. I see Lady Lauretta is waiting for me."

Edgeware, unfortunately, didn't seem to follow the byplay occurring between Lauretta and Donald or notice the young lady's budding tears. His brows darkened as he stared daggers at Elsbeth. "Forgive me for presuming, Lady Mercer," he said tightly and stormed over to where Lady Waver was waiting.

Halfway through the meal, food Elsbeth scarcely touched, Charlie leaned over and spoke in a low voice just loud enough for her ears. "I don't know how you tricked your way into this house party. I'm truly surprised to find you under my cousin's roof. I'd have thought that glorious nude painting would have transformed you into a social pariah." He took a bite of the roast pheasant on his plate. "No matter, Elly. I don't even care that you've attracted my cousin's attentions. You're still the most beautiful woman in all of England."

He chewed and swallowed. "And I would dearly like to renew our acquaintance and take it to a deeper, more intimate level. Before this house party is over, Elly, I will have you in my bed."

CHAPTER NINE

No! She had told him emphatically, no! And he'd laughed.

That night, Elsbeth tossed in her bed, unable to sleep. Charlie had made himself only too clear. He wanted her. He'd tried time and again to convince her husband to share her. For the most part, Hubert had resisted. And she had *always* resisted. She wanted nothing to do with Charlie. Ever.

She stared into the darkness while listening to the light snores of her two cousins in the adjoining room, and worried.

Though Charlie had been one of her husband's closest friends, almost always accompanying Hubert when he'd return from London after the Season, he certainly wasn't her friend. Charlie used to sip his brandy and smile as he watched Hubert take his angers and frustrations out on her. It was as if he enjoyed seeing her cower, as if he enjoyed seeing her humiliated and suffering.

Elsbeth winced as the dark memories swirled through her head. They pricked like tiny infected wounds. She fought to push them away, crying softly into her pillow.

Charlie was back in her life, again. Why? What could he possibly gain from tormenting her?

With nothing at all resolved and an ocean of unease thrashing through her body, she finally slipped into a troubled slumber just as dawn sparked on the horizon. Morning sunlight streamed down tinting a wide field of wildflowers an eerie purple shade. She rubbed her eyes, wondering just how she came to be in this place. And still dressed in her nightrail.

She couldn't remember leaving her bed. She turned around, searching for Purbeck Manor or, for that matter, any sign of civilization. The field of wildflowers stretched out for as far as she could see.

"Elsbeth," a voice called out to her.

"I am here!" she called back, feeling a trifle unsettled since she had no idea where "here" was.

A warm hand closed around hers. "I've been dying, waiting for you." The soft voice caressed the back of her neck.

Dionysus? Her heart tripped at the thought of meeting him at long last. He would explain himself, would explain how he loved her and had never meant to cause her pain. She simply knew he would.

Spinning around, anxious to meet the only man she had ever let into her heart, she stepped into Lord Edgeware's embrace. His dark, brooding gaze sought hers as he dragged a finger seductively across her lower lip.

A deep longing—one that surely matched the hunger in the dark lord's eyes—contracted in her chest.

"You?" she whispered.

He kissed her then, his lips brushing lightly over hers, demanding nothing.

She breathed in his scent, an unforgettable mix of almonds and sage. Embracing it, she pressed her face into his chest.

"Trust your broken heart, little dove."

His hands traveled down the length of her body, tracing the gentle curve of her hips. This was what she wanted. What she longed for. She was comfortable with him, here, among Dionysus's wildflowers . . . until a sharp cackle of laughter broke the spell.

She peered over Edgeware's shoulder to see Charlie leaning back, laughing his pretty blond-haired head off.

"You can't have him, Elly." Charlie raised the pistol clutched in his hand. *"No one can."*

The pistol popped.

Elsbeth bolted upright in bed. Sucking in air, barely able to catch her own breath, she peered around the darkened room. Olivia and Lauretta were both still in the other room sleeping soundly.

Good gracious, Elsbeth thought, *whatever could that dream mean?* Had she really imaged herself losing herself so completely within Lord Edgeware's arms? Never had her nerves been so overset to produce such a dream. Never had she felt so . . .

How did she feel?

Her jangling nerves and leaping pulse made her think of fear. But no, fear had never warmed her like an oven. Fear was a cold emotion with the power to freeze her from the inside out until she was sure death would come. Whatever she was feeling wasn't fear.

She tossed aside the heavy blankets and swung her feet to the floor. The first light of dawn was streaming across the horizon. There was no possible way she would be sinking back to sleep any time soon, so she might as well start the day. Better be up and moving than worrying over an emotion she had no time to be feeling. She had things to do, and a long morning walk was just what she needed to clear her head. She needed to plan.

And Dionysus needed to be found.

Curse him! Curse his heartrending paintings!

They'd made her feel as hot as an oven . . . once . . . a long, long time ago.

Nigel stood on a rise of the Purbeck Cliff that wasn't more than several hundred yards from his estate's manor house. He gazed out over the ocean. It was early. The morning light was still dim and lightly dusted with fog. Reds and pinks streaked across the sky, as the first signs of dawn broke through the darkness overhead.

His thoughts weren't on the brilliant brushstrokes of colors, or on the way the waves crashed on the beach below him. There was no room in his head for such thoughts when it was tightly latched to figuring out how to seduce Elsbeth.

She was so unlike the beautiful woman portrayed in Dionysus's painting. There was a stubbornness, a fire in her, that he ached to understand. What in blazes made her so different from every eligible miss in England? Why had she spurned his attentions last night and yet accepted Charlie's? But even with Charlie, she'd shied away from even the most innocent of touches. Her behavior reminded him of his stallion. Zeus had been like that once, wincing away from the slightest touch as if expecting a blow. She acted as if she were protecting herself from the abuse she feared she might suffer at the whim of any man.

His insides churned at the thought. No, he had to be mistaken. She was overly proud. Pride did terrible things to one's behavior. He'd witnessed the truth of that firsthand.

It had to be pride, not abuse.

Still, he shivered.

"I was hoping you would wander this way," Nigel said, when he heard the crunch of leaves scattered in the field behind him.

"You were?" George asked as he strode up from behind. He sounded surprised.

"I saw you crossing the lawn earlier. I suppose you were on the lookout for intruders?"

George's gaze tripped nervously across the landscape. "Yes, yes, I was searching."

"And?"

George shook his head. "And nothing. All has been quiet."

"I don't believe so. Follow me." Nigel led George down a

narrow, hazardous trail that brought them down to the beach far below the cliff's ledge. They stood side-by-side in the sand for a moment before Nigel kicked a charred log, stirring the ashes of a recently doused fire. "I'd say whoever used my beach last night unloaded a ship's cargo."

"Cargo, Edgeware? You don't actually believe smugglers came onto your property, do you?" There was a shiver in George's voice. "To flaunt such a crime beneath your nose would be beyond bold."

"True. But take a look at these footprints and where they're leading."

Rumors of smugglers were common in the region. Many families bolstered their incomes on the illegal trade. Even so, Nigel was outraged that someone in the village might commit such a crime on *his* property.

"Damn it. I had several footmen on watch last night. Why didn't they see a blasted thing?"

"There was no moon, Edgeware. And with a fog rolling in, we have no way of knowing what happened on the beach last night. Smuggling is only one explanation, and not even the most likely. I'd rather guess that a band of gypsies was passing through."

"I pray that is the answer," he said, unconvinced. He scanned the white cliffs searching for more clues. After the weather cleared, he'd send men to scour the area. The chalky cliffs were peppered with caves, both natural and from the quarrying of the purbeck marble. Those caves would serve as excellent hiding places and storage areas.

In the distance, he spotted a shadow moving along the cliff's ridge. He cupped his hands over his brow and watched the figure crouch down out of view.

"I say, what's that about?" George asked. But George was pointing toward the trail, not the top of the cliff.

Nigel followed his friend's extended arm.

"It couldn't be—" *But it was.*

"What in blazes is she doing?" George asked. He must have recognized her too.

Elsbeth was waving her arms and running down the hazardous trail to the beach much too fast. If she tripped she'd fall to her death. Rocks skittered off the steep edge as she lost her footing and slid several feet before catching herself. Nigel's heart stilled in his chest as he breathlessly watched.

He was too far away and unable to do anything but watch.

"Look out!" her voice carried over the roar of the waves.

Look out? He was about to shout those same words to her.

She stumbled again. Her arms flailed as she slid over more rocks. The dark cape she wore flapped in the foggy ocean breeze.

This time both Nigel and George charged forward. She was halfway down the trail, and there was no way either man could hope to get close enough in time to catch her if she were to fall, but that didn't seem to matter. They had to do something. Running toward her, Nigel sprinted ahead of George.

Before either of them could reach her, the sand beneath their feet jumped and the air exploded with a loud crash from behind that whomped the breath from Nigel's lungs.

Sand and rock shards rained down the side of the cliff. He raised his arms over his head to protect himself from the falling rocks. He turned back toward the place on the beach where he had come from.

He was shocked at what he saw. A three-foot tall boulder that hadn't been on the beach a moment before sat half-buried in the sand. Nigel and George had been standing in that very spot a few moments earlier. If Elsbeth's reckless charge down to the beach hadn't compelled the two men to rush toward her, one or both of them would have been crushed. Nigel turned back toward the trail. He froze where he stood, stunned.

Elsbeth, still running toward them, stumbled into his outstretched arms.

"Are you injured?" she asked, out of breath. She ran her hands up and down his chest and arms as if searching for injuries.

"Am I?" He stood utterly still while she continued to caress his chest, his arms, his legs. The front of her body was pressed against him. She didn't seem to notice. A wicked smile captured his lips. She could touch him however she wished. He wouldn't complain. "I should ask you the very same question. Are you injured, my dove?"

"Of course she isn't injured and neither are we," George said irritably.

Nigel mentally shook himself. He took Elsbeth's hands in his own and stepped a proper distance away.

"What were you thinking blazing down the trail like that? You're lucky you didn't break that lovely neck of yours," he scolded.

Elsbeth straightened her shoulders. He watched as her soft, vulnerable expression hardened into that damnable stiff shell he was beginning to know too well. She drew back, breaking away from his touch.

"A boulder crashed down onto the beach, my lord. Or perhaps you didn't notice. The wretched thing nearly smashed you and Mr. Waver into the ground."

"You were trying to warn us?" Nigel gazed up at the spot high on the cliff where the boulder must have sat just moments before. It was very near the spot where he'd seen a shadowy figure moving around.

"I saw the boulder rocking. And then I spotted the two of you. I thought you might be in danger." She drew a sharp breath, her sapphire blue eyes sparkled in the morning light.

"Obviously my instincts were correct. That boulder would have killed you."

Nigel nodded. Over time, rocks shifted, boulders tumbled from the cliffs. But in this instance, with the past attempt on his life, he found it impossible to believe the boulder's fall was anything but natural.

"There must be a connection," he said to George.

He turned to Elsbeth. She did appear to be fit and safe, despite that harrowing charge down the trail. She could have fallen to her death! But, thankfully, she'd managed to keep her feet underneath her.

He watched her as she strolled over to the boulder. She ran her slender hand along its rough surface. There was nary a limp in her gait or any other evidence that her sliding plunge down the cliff wall had caused her any harm.

"George, please escort Lady Mercer back to the manor."

"And what will you do?" George demanded.

"I think I'll have a look around." Nigel gave a quick glance in Elsbeth's direction. He didn't want his guests, especially not Elsbeth, to know anything about the dangerous situation he was trying to keep under control. "I want to see if there are any other loose boulders preparing to fall."

"Did you see anyone else on the top of the cliff, Lady Mercer?" George asked, concern in his expression. "Anyone at all?"

"No. I was surprised to see the two of you, in fact. The house was so silent I thought I was the only one up and about this early."

Nigel eyed the top of the cliff again. Elsbeth had been wandering along its edge alone with a killer out there. The number of mishaps that could have happened was staggering.

"George," he said, his panic rising, "take Elsbeth back to the manor. Now! Before anything else happens."

"No. I have more experience around . . . um . . . loose

boulders than you, Edgeware. And besides, the welfare of your guests must take precedence over any attempts . . . um . . . freak accidents."

Of course George was right. Nigel offered Elsbeth his arm, which she accepted much more readily than the day before. He led her back up the trail.

"Is it you or Mr. Waver whose life is in danger?" she asked once they reached the top of the cliff, and out of earshot of George.

"I cannot imagine what you mean."

"Someone was trying to kill one of you, or is it both? I saw the boulder move. I may not have seen anyone, but I'm convinced someone must have forced it over the edge." She heaved a deep sigh. "I suppose I should have chased after the villain."

"It was simply an accident, dove."

She stopped suddenly in the middle of the path. "It's Dionysus, isn't it? He's mad, isn't he? Of course he's mad. He's an artist, and since you're his keeper, he's striking out at you."

He caressed the deep crease that had formed between her brows. "Dionysus is perhaps a bit mad. And I have already told you I am his keeper, of sorts." He paused, wondering what exactly he was planning to tell her.

In light of the havoc Dionysus's existence had caused her, he knew he owed her the truth. But how would she react? His finger strayed from her troubled brow to trace the gentle curve of her chin. She stiffened but didn't quail from his touch as she had before.

If he kept to his original plan, he'd need to continue playing these seductive games to keep her distracted and away from the truth. It was a plan that offered some pleasing prospects.

He smiled wryly. "I'm not in any danger." He leaned forward, his lips carefully seeking hers. "Unless . . ."

Her scent, a fresh bouquet of lilacs and orange blossoms, filled his senses. "Unless," he whispered, "I am in danger of losing my heart to you."

Elsbeth closed her eyes and leaned into his kiss, accepting the tingling surge of heat his lips sent spiraling through her chest, down her body, centering firmly between her thighs. Heavens above, last night's dream sprung to life!

She laid her hand against his chest. His kisses demanded nothing. They were merely gentle pleas, urging her to respond, tempting her to give over to him everything she had to offer.

Their tongues touched.

She pulled back suddenly.

"No," she whispered against his mouth. The heat of the moment left her breathless and wanting. His warm hand cupped her cheek. Instinctively, she reached up and caressed the hard plains of his jaw. "No," she said, protesting her own reaction, not his. "We mustn't. I—I cannot."

Stumbling a few steps backwards helped give her the distance she needed to weaken the spell he seemed to have woven around her. The magic must have come from those black eyes of his. He stared at her, wide-eyed and looking just about as dazed as she felt.

His chest heaved as if he couldn't catch his breath. "Elsbeth," he breathed her name and pulled her close again. His lips felt hot against hers. She sought his kisses and welcomed his whispering caresses. "I-I didn't know that this could be so—"

"Nigel!" Charlie's voice carried across the trail, effectively throwing a pail of cold water over the whole smoldering situation.

Elsbeth was grateful. Charlie, the devil himself, had saved her from forgetting herself and the painful lessons she'd learned about men and love—at least their protestations of an ability to possess such a tender emotion. How in Heaven's name had she gotten to the point of wanting to let Edgeware ease his way into her heart?

Charlie grabbed Edgeware's shoulders. "I just spoke to George. He told me what happened. Gad, it makes me shiver to think the horrible death you would have suffered if our Elly hadn't happened along. You are unharmed, aren't you? Oh, cousin, please tell me you are unharmed!"

"Don't get yourself worked up, Charlie. Of course I am well. It was a freak accident. Nothing to worry over."

"Not worry? How could I not worry? Wouldn't you fret after me if I'd been the one in danger? Sometimes I feel as if you are my keeper, Nige," Charlie said, and smiled a deep smile that narrowed his eyes. Elsbeth had seen that look of sheer satisfaction on him before and knew to be wary of it. Charlie was plotting.

"Please excuse me, my lord," she said with a bowed head, wishing to escape the men and, more importantly, her tender feelings that were threatening to betray her. "I believe I should head up to the manor house after all this excitement."

Charlie latched onto her arm. "I'll escort you, Elly."

Edgeware stepped into their path and peeled Charlie from her arm. "It's vastly improper for you to address Lady Mercer in such a familiar manner," he said.

"Hubert, her dear late husband, and I were very close. Weren't we Elly?"

"Yes, they were close," she conceded. Charlie had been close to her husband, and he had said it himself: he thought of Lord Edgeware as his keeper.

Charlie? She felt the blood drain from her cheeks.

"Almost like brothers, I'd say. Or like you and I, Nige." Charlie laughed and patted Elsbeth's hand. It was all she could do to keep herself from bursting into tears.

Could it be true?

The air seemed suddenly too thick to breathe. "Please excuse me," she murmured before picking up her skirts and darting back toward Edgeware's sprawling estate house.

What if Charlie was the link?

Charlie knew both her husband and Lord Edgeware, and with his love of high-stakes gambling he was certainly greedy enough to wish his own cousin dead. With Edgeware out of the way, the title and control of the money would go to his uncle and eventually to Charlie.

And wasn't Edgeware responsible for Charlie? As head of the family, Edgeware would naturally be considered his cousin's keeper, of sorts.

She dug her nails into her palms, determined to keep a level head. *Please, please no. Let me be wrong.* But how could she be wrong? As harsh as it seemed, this was most likely the truth she'd traveled all the way to Dorset to learn.

Charlie was Dionysus.

Of course she needed proof. There was no need to give up all hope until she knew without doubt that Charlie was in fact Dionysus. No need at all.

Dionysus would pay for his sins, of that she was certain. Perhaps it would be easier, knowing the rogue was naught but a devil and someone she couldn't have—*should never have*—loved.

"Come now, Elly." Charlie caught up to her and grabbed hold of her hand. She jerked it away, giving the bounder cause to have a good laugh at her expense. "Now, now, don't be this way."

She took a moment to search Charlie's face, looking for a clue, a glimmer of Dionysus's passion, his pain, his genius. She found nothing but emptiness. She saw nothing but mischief in his scheming eyes.

"I'm sure Hubert would want the two of us to remain close,"

114

he said, and flashed a toothy grin. "He and I shared everything, did we not?"

"Not everything. And it-it is unkind of you to remind me of such things, sir," she snapped just as Lord Edgeware caught up to them. "My husband is *dead!*"

Thank the good Lord!

Chapter Ten

Nigel paced his study. The ladies were in the far field, holding an archery competition, and the gentlemen had left for the afternoon on a hunting excursion. He'd claimed an urgent estate matter demanded his immediate attention and had sent Charlie with the men in his place to serve as a guide.

What a blasted lie. He couldn't concentrate on even the simplest of his estate's concerns even if he'd wanted to.

Elsbeth. She'd filled his mind, overwhelmed him in a way no woman had ever done before.

What was he to do? He'd barely begun the game of seduction. He'd petted her, paid her lovely complements, and kissed her. That last kiss had been his downfall, turning his desire into a creature stronger than simple lust.

This was no longer about seduction. He wanted to bed her; that was certain. But he also wanted more. This need ran much deeper than wanting to win her or own her like he owned his estate, or how he owned his horses. He wanted her every breath to be for his sake.

What madness was this?

And worse, he didn't know how to reach her. Her dedication to her departed husband, that bounder Lord Mercer, was visible. She'd paled, nearly swooned, at the mention of his name. *I can't,* she'd told him after pulling away from his kiss. Her husband was dead, and yet she believed herself unfaithful?

Nigel poured himself a second glass of brandy. "I can't

compete with a dead bastard. How he won her heart, how he'd won such devotion, I will never understand."

Before rushing off to the Peninsular War, Lord Mercer had made quite a reputation for himself. Debauchery, gambling, rumors of brutality and cruelty would rush through the *ton* whenever the young earl happened to be in London.

To Nigel's knowledge, little was known of Lady Mercer. Though he shunned the parties and the clubs, he kept abreast of the activities and rumors flaring within that tight circle of High Flyers. If Lady Mercer had ever visited London with her bounder of a husband, tongues would have surely wagged, and Nigel would have inevitably heard about it. Which possibly meant that Elsbeth had no idea of the true character of the man she'd married.

A light knock on the door jarred him out of his thoughts.

"Come," he called, after swallowing a healthy dose of his drink.

George entered and closed the door behind him.

"I thought you went hunting with the rest of the men," Nigel said.

"Begged off. Never had a taste for the sport. Besides, I've been meaning to catch a private word with you. But what with the morning's excitement and your obligations as host, there hasn't been an opportunity."

Nigel shrugged as he offered George a drink.

"No, thank you," George said. He took a chair by the fire. "Stop pacing and sit, Edgeware. I won't talk to you otherwise."

Nigel sank into the leather chair next to George's. "I'm listening."

George steepled his fingers in front of his pursed lips and stared at Nigel for several long minutes. "I have been wondering about Lady Mercer," he said at last.

"What about her?" She was the last person Nigel wanted to

talk about. Not with George, and not now.

"I know you too well. We've been friends since before your father died. I've seen that obsessive look in your eyes before, though never for a woman."

"I cannot imagine what you're talking about. I have engineered this house party for no other reason than to repair her reputation. It's only natural I show an interest in her activities."

"Indeed?" George said wryly. "And if I were to pursue the lady's attentions? She is a stunning beauty, is she not? That long blond hair of hers, the delicate structure, and those crystal blue eyes are quite memorable. Yes, Edgeware, I do believe I should try to win her favor. What do you think?"

Nigel's jaw tightened. "Go ahead, though I'd recommend you pursue an heiress for a wife. What, with the volatility of your shipping business, I'd think a woman who could fill your coffers would suit you much better than the penniless Lady Mercer."

"I wasn't suggesting I was looking for a wife."

Nigel slowly rose from his chair and walked back over to his liquor cabinet. George was bluffing. He had to be bluffing. His friend couldn't possibly be suggesting he'd take Elsbeth for a mistress.

"Before you shoot me, Edgeware, let me just say I noticed—as I'm sure every bloody person in the drawing room did last night—that your gaze never left Lady Mercer and that you scowled all through dinner while you were forced to watch your cousin flirt with her."

"As I already explained, my attention to her is more than warranted. I fear she might inadvertently thwart my efforts to repair her reputation," Nigel said.

"So you're afraid her morals are indeed as warped as her husband's were purported to be?"

"No, damn it! Not that. Just—just she doesn't feel comfortable here. And I have to keep a close watch on her because she has vowed mischief. She's determined to expose Dionysus."

"She is?" George perked up. "Perhaps I should help her. That cove takes advantage of your protection. He deserves to be exposed and ridiculed. What hold does he have over you, anyhow?"

"Enough," Nigel said. "Enough that his destruction would be mine as well."

George lapsed back into silence. The tension in the room was palatable. Nigel hated this wall building between them.

"Tell me—" Nigel hoped to turn the subject "—did you find anything of interest on the beach?"

"No, nothing of import. Did you see anyone when you escorted Lady Mercer back to the house?"

"Just Charlie." Nigel saw red for a moment as he remembered the familiar way his cousin had behaved toward Elsbeth, taking her arm, speaking too freely with her, shamelessly calling her *Elly.* "But Charlie's harmless," he said. But for the first time in his life, he questioned just how harmless his younger cousin really was.

"Then, I suppose we need to dig deeper," George said as he rose from the chair. "I won't waste any more of your time." He paused at the door. "Just indulge me once more and answer this question—When this week is over, will you be able to set aside your affection for Lady Mercer and return to your hermit-like lifestyle?"

Nigel tried to imagine his life returning to normalcy. Would he be tempted to attend the horrendous balls if he thought he'd have a chance to dance with Elsbeth? Would he be tempted to accept invitations to those dratted teas if there was the hope he'd have a chance to sit next to her and speak with her for a moment or two? Would he be able to return to his lonely life?

"Honestly? I don't know."

At that very moment on a far field, the ladies had all gathered to partake in a friendly archery competition. With the pressing puzzle of Dionysus and what appeared to be an attack on Lord Edgeware, Elsbeth had claimed a headache and had excused herself from the excitement. Lady Waver had graciously volunteered to chaperone Olivia and Lauretta to the field so the girls wouldn't miss out on the fun. Even more surprisingly, Lady Cowper had cheerfully joined in, volunteering to watch over the young ladies as well. It seemed that Edgeware's efforts were beginning to change the *beau monde*'s opinion of her and her cousins.

Which was amazing, simply amazing.

Perhaps he wasn't quite the villain she initially believed him to be. If he were a rotter like Charlie and her husband, certainly he wouldn't have come to her defense after Dionysus's painting went public. Which meant there had to be a good heart hidden somewhere inside the dark lord's seductively broad chest, making what she was determined to do all the more difficult.

She tightened a gray cashmere shawl around her shoulders and followed one of Edgeware's footmen into the manor's dank buttery, a small storeroom off the kitchen where bottles of wine and other liquors were stored on shelves and casks of ale were stacked against the walls.

She was dressed in a gown purchased specifically for the house party. The fashionable pale pink walking dress with a muslin skirt flowed with almost indecent ease. Madame Bossier must have made a mistake with the design. Nearly all of her new gowns revealed far too much skin and seemed too sheer, hinting only too well at the shape hidden beneath the material. She gave her shawl another tug.

"I do beg your pardon," she called out to the servant she was following, "but may I trouble you for a moment of your time?"

The footman, a giant of a man, stopped and turned toward her. His heavy brows furrowed and his thick lips sank into a deep frown. "Yes, m'lady?" he growled.

"What is your name?" she asked, briskly. This one footman, she'd noticed, tended to skulk through the halls at the most unusual hours and listen in on conversations he had no business hearing.

"Guthrie," he said, the creases in his brow deepened. "What can I do for you? I'm busy."

"Well, Guthrie," she said slowly. "With the number of guests at the house party I can imagine you are sorely overtaxed. If you will allow me to take but a moment, I have a question for you."

"I don't see how I could—" he started to say when Elsbeth raised her hand.

"You appear to be a clever chap. I've noticed you have the opportunity to see things that go on in this house that perhaps his lordship wouldn't want you to know about."

"I don't know what you—"

She raised her gloved hand again. "I would be willing to pay a pretty coin for some information."

"How pretty a coin, ma'am?"

"A gold sovereign." She held out the heavy coin. His muddy brown eyes lit up at the sight of it. "Two, if you can provide proof of what you know."

He wiped his hand on his trousers several times and looked eager to snatch the coin out of her grasp. "What do you need to know, ma'am?"

"The Marquess is protecting a gentleman. This gentleman may be his cousin or friend. Whoever he is, he hides behind the name Dionysus. Have you ever heard anyone refer to this man?"

"Dial . . . nay . . . what-sus, ma'am?"

"Dio-ny-sus," she pronounced with care. "He is an artist. I believe he might be Mr. Charles Purbeck."

Guthrie guffawed at that. It was a crackly, rumbling sound. "Mr. Purbeck an artist?" He laughed some more. "I ain't heard anyone use a fancy Dial . . . ny . . . sus name around here. And Mr. Purbeck ain't ever expressed an interest in art, not like his lordship. I was a young lad and so was his lordship when I first came to work in this house. I'd been told his mother breathed her last a few days after his lordship was born. And his father, too, dropped short when the lordship was just a young tot, no more than three or four. It's common knowledge in the village that the Edgeware men leave this world at a young age."

Elsbeth gasped. "The family is prone to sickness?"

"Nay, my lady. Duels, fox hunting, carriage races, and the like are to blame. Shortly after his father's death, the lordship's uncle moved into the household with his wife and son in order to care for the estates and to mold his lordship into a sober and rather grim gentleman like himself, or so I've been told. I came to work here years later." The footman sighed. "Hadn't been here for much longer than a fortnight when I watched his lordship's uncle fly into a rage and toss all of the Marquess's artwork into the parlor's fireplace. He then dragged his lordship by the scruff of his hair out to the barn and horsewhipped the lad something fierce."

"So the Marquess is something of an artist?" she mused. It would be so easy to believe Edgeware, with his expressive but dark and foreboding eyes, brooding moods, and impossibly romantic notions of being a knight-in-shining-armor, was her devil, Dionysus. But that would be quite impossible. How could a man be his own keeper?

She chewed her bottom lip, thinking. *No . . . no, it would be* quite *impossible. The bounder had to be Charlie.*

"There has been an attempt against the Marquess's life. Do

you know anything about this?" she asked, determined to stay focused on the puzzle she needed to unravel.

"Aye, ma'am. His lordship was nearly killed when someone slipped a metal spur under his horse's saddle a little more than a week ago."

So the boulder hadn't been the first attempt on Edgeware's life? Elsbeth struggled to keep her surprise hidden. "And who do you think was behind this dastardly trick? Was Mr. Purbeck in residence at the time?"

"He was, ma'am," he said, his eyes growing wide. "Are you suggesting Mr. Purbeck had something to do with—?"

"That is quite enough. Guthrie, return to your duties." Edgeware, looking as dashing as a carefree London Corinthian in a pair of tight fawn-colored pantaloons, gleaming white waistcoat, and hunter green riding coat appeared in the buttery doorway . . . glowering.

"Yes, m'lord, of course m'lord." Guthrie gave one last yearning glance at the sovereign Elsbeth still held in her hand before he hoisted a cask of ale onto his broad shoulder and hurried from the room.

"Pray excuse me," Elsbeth said, as if she hadn't just been caught asking one of Edgeware's servants questions concerning him. "I should attend to my cousins."

When she tried to sidestep him and slip out the door, he blocked her and drew the door closed behind him. She hadn't noticed before how dark the room was. There was a heavy coating of dust on the arched window at the far end of the room, and with the door closed, very little light seeped into the chilly interior. Lord Edgeware's expression was completely hidden in the shadows. She heard, rather than saw, the material of his clothes rustle as he crossed his arms in front of his chest.

"I will not kiss you again," she said with considerable more bravado than she was feeling. "And it is highly improper for you to be alone with me in here . . . with the door closed."

"Indeed?" he said.

The silence that followed had a dangerous air attached to it.

"Move out of the way, sir," she said, giving him a healthy shove with the hopes of getting to the door before something truly shocking happened. It wasn't exactly that she didn't trust him. After this morning she wasn't sure how things stood between them. And worse, she feared she shouldn't dare trust herself around him. In a panic, she gave him a second shove when the first failed to move him.

It was for naught. She might as well have been trying to dislodge a stone wall.

"I must ask that this stop, Elsbeth," he said, just as she put her shoulder into pushing him.

"I would stop if you stepped out of my way."

"Not this," he said, capturing her hands before she could shove against him again. "Interrogating my servants."

"My lord, I would never—"

"Come now, Elsbeth." He lifted her hands to his lips and gently kissed her knuckles. "Your unrelenting questions of my staff is creating quite a havoc belowstairs. Many of my people are worried that you wish to do me harm." His teeth flashed white in the dim light as he smiled at the thought. "Naturally, I'm not the least bit concerned, for I know my secret is safe. But for my servants' sake, you must stop. I rather pride myself on my ability to keep those in my employ happy."

"I don't know what to say." Her cheeks prickled from a sudden rush of heat.

"Say you will leave my servants in peace."

They were standing so very close she could almost feel the length of him pressed against the front of her all too thin skirt.

"Trust me to handle this matter for you, *Elsbeth.*"

"Trust?" She'd misplaced her trust once before and had

ended up trapped in an abusive marriage. "I do appreciate what you've done for my cousins. Several of the ladies present have promised to issue invitations to them for upcoming teas and balls after we return to London. For that, you have won my regard."

"But do you trust that I would never purposefully do anything to harm you?"

Did she dare trust him? He'd been honest with her about so many things, even warning her of his intention the very first time he'd kissed her. But what did she know of men? She'd done a miserable job judging her husband's character before their marriage.

"I would like to trust you," was the best she could offer. "However, I cannot and will not trust Dionysus, especially considering how it appears that he is not only trying to ruin me, but that he has tried to kill you even before this morning."

"Dionysus is not trying to kill me," he insisted, but she didn't let that stop her.

She raised her voice to be sure that he listened. "He has ruined my life twice already. If you cannot control him, why should I trust that he won't harm either you or I again?"

Edgeware didn't seem to have a ready answer for her.

"My lord?" she asked. He was still holding her hands and standing a hairsbreadth from her in the midst of a tense silence that seemed to go on for an eternity. "This is highly improper. We shouldn't be alone together in this room. I implore you let me go—"

"Twice?" he asked.

"What?" She tried to twist her hands free, but he only tightened his hold.

"You said he ruined your life twice." He sounded angry. "Your marriage to Lord Mercer was the first time?"

Her reputation couldn't stand being caught in the dark lord's clutches like this. She didn't trust his servants to keep quiet about what they might suppose she was doing alone with him.

"Let go of me," she demanded, in not quite a shout.

"No. Explain it to me, what exactly did Dionysus do to you?"

She twisted again, her hands burning from his unbreakable hold. Tears sprang to her eyes.

"What did he do to you, dammit?" He gave her a little shake. "You need to trust me, to tell me what happened."

"The paintings," she cried. "He gave me paintings."

"The paintings."

"Every one more beautiful than the last. They made my heart ache. They made me love him. But they weren't from him. Or rather, Lord Mercer gave Dionysus's paintings to me as if they were his own." She drew an unsteady breath. "Don't you see? They conspired together. They lied to me. Tricked me. I would have never married Lord Mercer if it hadn't been for those cursed paintings."

Edgeware's hands turned cold. "You were unhappy in your marriage?"

"I wish I had never met the bounder," she confessed for the first time in her life. Perhaps it was because of the darkness. Or perhaps it was because the way he held her so very close made her want to bare her heart to him. "He was a monster. He didn't have a drop of kindness in his blood. And I became just like him—a monster of another sort—the day I celebrated his death."

"I didn't know." He pulled her into his arms and cradled her against his strong chest as she lost her battle holding back the tears.

For too long she had kept this secret, pretending her marriage was everything it was supposed to be. The pain she'd held at bay ripped through her. If not for Edgeware's strength, she would have surely been torn apart by the years of pent up grief and anger swelling within her. In that terrible moment, her dark lord was her rock. Though he held himself stiff, unbending, she felt safe.

"Forgive me," she said as soon as she was able to pull herself together and ease out of his embrace. "You must think me evil to bewail what many would say was a fortunate marriage. Please forget I said anything. I am overly tired." She dabbed at her nose with the handkerchief she'd retrieved from a sleeve and skirted around him. He didn't make a move when she tossed open the door. "I do apologize."

"Don't—" he said with his back to her.

She didn't wait to hear what he had to say. She fled like a thief in the night from the kitchens, glancing over her shoulder only once to see him standing in the buttery doorway. Such naked longing was reflected in his eyes that it stole her breath.

She'd been wrong about him yet again. Though she'd feared his strength, he hadn't used it against her just now. Instead, he'd wrapped his power around her like a magical cloak. Unlike any gentleman she had ever known, he seemed desperate to help her.

An hour later, Elsbeth joined her cousins on the archery field. The sun was shining bright enough to have completely burned away the morning fog. In a lush part of the field, the ladies had gathered, dressed in their most fashionable promenade gowns, which Elsbeth thought was impracticable attire for demonstrating their skills.

When newly out of the schoolroom, she'd enjoyed archery matches, mainly because her skills were unmatched with the neighboring ladies. But despite the pleasant weather and the excitement of the friendly competition, she found it nearly impossible to enjoy herself. She toyed with the long wooden bow in her hand, plucking the taut string while her thoughts tumbled through the morning's events and her shocking confession to Lord Edgeware about her unhappy marriage. Part of her was mortified and wished she could take back her words. Another part of her wished she had told him the full truth of her marriage. Edgeware had made her feel safe. Confiding her secrets had been easy. Perhaps too easy.

"Elly, pray pay attention. We are all waiting for you to take your shot," Olivia said and pointed toward the round, straw-stuffed target.

The young ladies were watching her. Their elder chaperones had also turned their heads to watch from the wicker chairs that had been set off to one side. They were all looking at her . . . and a few were smiling.

Lauretta, Elsbeth noticed, was standing next to Lady Cowper, and the two women were chatting amicably. Only Lady Dashborough and her younger daughter, Lady Constance, appeared less than pleased with Elsbeth's presence on the archery field.

Elsbeth drew an arrow from a leather quiver hanging on a wooded stake. She stroked the feathered end before setting it on the bow. The target had been placed at a distance generally reserved for the gentlemen. As a result, several of the ladies' arrows had fallen short and stuck out of the ground like pins in a cushion. The few that had struck their goal had completely missed the center of the target.

As she drew back the string, the ladies all grew silent save for a giggle here and there. Though such consideration hadn't been given to any of the other participants, Elsbeth wasn't surprised. She understood only too well how closely her every action was being watched and judged. Because of that, she took her time as she aimed—praying that time hadn't erased her abilities. She raised the bow higher to compensate for the longer distance. Holding her breath, she released the string.

With a thunk her arrow pierced the target very close to the

center. Not a heartbeat later a second arrow sailed past her so closely that its breeze teased the ribbons on her bonnet. That errant arrow landed with an even louder thunk as it pierced the center of the target, hugging the spot Elsbeth's arrow had already taken.

The ladies cheered with delight.

Elsbeth blinked, unable to take her eyes off that second arrow. She certainly wasn't cheering when she turned around to see which young lady had played such a reckless trick. She hoped their hostess, Lady Waver, would have some stern words with whoever the young lady turned out to be.

Their hostess had risen from her wicker chair, but her mood was as bright as the sky. She was clapping and beaming a smile as genteel as the rest of the matrons. Elsbeth's searching gaze quickly brought her face-to-face with the cause for their excitement.

Edgeware leaned upon his bow as if it were a fashionable walking stick. The smug expression on his lips told her all she needed to know—he'd purposefully sent his arrow whizzing past her and was confoundingly proud of himself for it, too.

"Ladies, I see the archery competition has been a resounding success," he said. His rich voice hummed through Elsbeth's body as if it were an intimate caress. Her cursed knees were on the verge of turning to jelly. "Naturally, I come prepared to present a reward to the victor."

He produced a simple white daisy. Holding the bloom out toward Elsbeth, he went down onto one knee, making him look as valiant as the Robin Hood his green riding jacket had made him resemble.

"For your favor, my lady," he said softly.

The ladies on the field all sighed with delight. Elsbeth couldn't seem to breathe as she accepted the prize. She lifted the soft bloom to her nose and drank in its mild, sweet scent.

"And a stroll," he said. That wolfish gleam returned to darken his eyes.

"A stroll?" She didn't want to be alone with him, not with her heart all twisted up with no small measure of confusion.

"In the gardens." He rose to his feet and offered his arm.

"I am sorry, but I cannot," she said, backing away. Why in blazes was he trying to get her alone again?

"My lord, if Lady Mercer is unable, I will gladly take her place," Lady Constance said as she rushed over to them, stopping just short of latching onto his arm. She, too, must have sensed the spark of disapproval in him. After taking a long look at his stony expression and raised brow, her coy smile froze on her lips.

"I have a duty as chaperone to my cousins, sir. I cannot leave them," Elsbeth quickly explained, hoping to soothe his bruised pride.

He shook his head. "I am sorry, my lady, but the prize must go to the victor." With delicate grace, he lifted the daisy she was in danger of crushing between her fingers and threaded its stem through the ribbon of her bonnet. "Lady Waver," he called without looking away. Those hard, hungry eyes gnawed at her resolve. But how could she survive spending any time alone with him after having confessed to him her deepest shame?

"Yes, Edgeware?" Lady Waver called back.

"Would you be so kind to watch over Lady Mercer's charges for half an hour while she strolls the gardens with me?"

"Of course, Lord Edgeware. Baneshire's daughters are such lovely company, it would be a pleasure."

He held out his arm again. "Any other objections, my lady?"

With her chin raised and her lips held firmly in place, she accepted his arm. A walk in the gardens wouldn't be a terrible thing, she told herself. His manner reminded her of a playful pup's. Certainly, her confession hadn't shocked him. Certainly, he hadn't sought her out just to scold her or condemn her for not having loved her husband. Still, she was uncertain.

What was a lady to do when one of the most elusive bachelors of the *beau monde* showed an interest in her, romantically tucking ribbons into her bonnet? What defense could a lady possibly use to guard her heart against such a man? A man who now knew her deepest secret? She couldn't seem to stop her heart from racing as he led her through the arched entranceway that led into a tidy, privet-hedge labyrinth.

"There is a surprise at the center," he promised, his voice deepening a degree.

"I won't kiss you again," she said a bit too tartly.

"As I have said before—" he patted her hand "—I won't press you to do anything you don't wish to do. I won't even mention a certain matter that might cause you pain."

"You won't?" she asked, suddenly wishing she hadn't renewed her vow not to kiss him.

"I don't want you to get the wrong impression or to think of me as the worst sort of cad, Elsbeth. I want you to feel completely safe around me. I want you to trust me."

He stopped in the middle of the path. "You may not believe this, but I do need you to know that Dionysus has never done anything to purposefully harm you." He pressed a finger against her lips when she started to argue. "What appears to be his plotting against you were, both times, situations that were beyond his control. In fact, it tears at his heart to think that he has caused you harm. You must believe that."

"I believe you plan to do everything in your power to protect me," she said, for Edgeware did truly appear to be a good man. Perhaps, like herself, he was too trusting, blindly believing Dionysus's lies.

"Good," he said. "I am glad."

"But I will never again trust Dionysus, and neither should you."

"I assure you, I trust him no more than I trust myself, which sometimes isn't very much." He smiled ruefully when she backed away from him. "Don't be alarmed, dove. You're safe with me." He led her down a twisting path through the labyrinth. The hedge walls extended several feet over her head and were so thick that she could barely see daylight through them. She glanced around, realizing just how isolated they were. Such a vulnerable situation should have left her trembling.

Oddly, she felt safe. And it was the dark lord's doing.

He'd been so careful as he eased his way past her defenses. She closed her eyes and lost herself for a moment in the feelings of longing swelling deep within her.

She wanted to trust him completely. She truly did. She wanted to love—

"Please," she said, and opened her eyes. Very slowly she reached out to him and slipped her hand into his. It was a heady feeling to have her hand nestled within his strong grasp and her fingers entwined with his.

"About misplaced trust," he said as they strolled. "I have had some stern words with my cousin, Mr. Purbeck. He will no longer treat you with disrespect."

"Thank you," she said.

"Nor will I treat you shabbily. My initial intention for the week had been to seduce you. I had thought I would use my charms to distract you from searching for Dionysus."

"I know," she said, unable to think of any other way to respond to such a bald declaration.

"You do?"

She nodded. "I'm not an innocent taking her first turn on the Marriage Mart. I do know something of men and their intentions."

"I suppose you must." He sighed. "I had planned to . . . but after that kiss this morning, and our . . . um . . . discussion this afternoon, I have changed my mind. Seducing you in order to bend your will would prove too complicated. There is a strong attraction between us, pulling at us. I know you feel it.

"And the last thing I want to do is violate your trust. So know this, Elsbeth, if I am lucky enough to succeed in seducing you, it will be for one singular reason. I will do it solely because I want you to be with me." He paused long enough for Elsbeth to catch her breath. "Ah, we have reached the center of the labyrinth. I've been told that this was my father's favorite place."

At the center of the maze was a round clearing. A smooth marble urn seated in an oval fountain sprayed water up at least ten feet into the air. Edgeware lingered there, watching the water dance in the sunlight.

"The secret—" he said, directing Elsbeth toward a second path on the other side of the clearing. Unlike the rest of the hedge-lined trail, the path was straight and short. Within a few short steps, she found herself in the middle of an open, geometric garden from which the manor house and archery field could be easily reached. "—is revealed. We spiraled around and around to find the prize when we might have taken a short, direct route instead. But tell me, if we had taken the easier path, would finding the hidden jewel have been as satisfying?"

She wanted to touch him. Even now, even after he'd declared his intention of seducing her, she wasn't frightened . . . she was fascinated.

He was a mystery, a puzzle as complicated as one of Dionysus's paintings with layer upon layer of depth waiting to be discovered—a secret prize she ached to unravel.

"Tonight is the ball," he reminded her, lifting her hand and placing a reverent kiss on the top of her knuckles. "Perhaps you will save me a dance? Perhaps a waltz?"

Ninny, that her soft heart was turning her into, had her nodding her agreement and eagerly looking forward to the coming evening and the prospect of losing herself all over again to his seductive spell.

CHAPTER ELEVEN

"Lauretta, why ever aren't you dressed?" Olivia scolded. She sounded surprisingly like Elsbeth, even to Elsbeth's ears. But she ruined the stern image when she impatiently stomped her pretty foot. "Lord Edgeware's ball is starting. I can already hear the guests arriving downstairs."

Lauretta, dressed in the same gown she'd worn that afternoon, slumped on her bed, her chin cradled in her hands. "I have one of Elsbeth's famous headaches."

"Oh, pooh! Papa would never permit this. Elly, you aren't going to allow her to hide up here, are you?"

Elsbeth emerged from the dressing room where Molly, her lady's maid, had been fussing over her. She'd listened to her two cousins with only half an ear as she'd gazed at herself in the mirror. The gown, made from the sheerest pale purple muslin she'd ever seen, was cut very low. Nearly indecently so. Surely the modiste had made a mistake.

"Oh, Elly," Olivia exclaimed, "you look ever so lovely. That gown is so much more fashionable than the ones you ordered for the season. It fits you much better too."

"I feel like I am in danger of falling out of it," Elsbeth muttered.

"You do look lovely," Lauretta said rather sedately.

"Why, thank you." She frowned at the long face Lauretta wore. "But you, my dear cousin, will not look lovely coming to the ball in that gown. You need to make a grand appearance, dazzling everyone present. You need to show Sir Donald—and everyone else—his actions have not affected you in the least."

Lauretta gave Elsbeth a desperate look.

"It needn't be true," she said as she selected a white gown for her cousin to wear. "It simply needs to be believed." She took Lauretta's hands in her own. "Trust me, this is for the best."

With Molly and Olivia's help, it didn't take long for Elsbeth to tuck Lauretta into her gown, fix up her hair, and lure her to the ball.

The guests, dressed in their most fashionable attire, lined the sides of the ballroom, chatting animatedly. Edgeware had reportedly invited gentry from as far away as a quarter day's ride to Purbeck. Elsbeth guessed further by the number who had already arrived.

Shiny silk ribbons dyed to represent Edgeware's family colors, dark green and rich lavender, floated across the ceiling and spiraled toward the grand chandelier in the center of the room. Matching drapes billowed in the breeze in front of the half-dozen arching double doors that had been opened to keep the room from becoming overheated. Palms potted in ceramic urns overflowing with exotic orchids marked the edges of the dance floor. Musicians dressed all in white stood at the ready on the far end of the room.

"For a man who has never hosted a ball, the Marquess certainly knows how to create a fairytale scene," Olivia said.

Elsbeth nodded in agreement. The decorations made her feel slightly unhinged, almost as if she'd stumbled into one of Dionysus's colorful paintings. "I have never seen such a wondrous spectacle. And look, there's a miniature fountain at the edge of the dance floor."

Lauretta followed along as quiet as a stone beside them, her shoulders hunched and her head bowed. The poor child was destined to have a miserable evening if circumstances didn't quickly turn.

"Oh," Olivia sighed, as her cheeks grew flushed. "There is Lord Edgeware dressed all in black. And I believe he is looking this way. He looks so formidable, don't you agree, Elly?"

"I haven't taken the time to notice," Elsbeth lied. She had, in fact, sought him out the moment they'd stepped into the ballroom. And she thought the dark lord looked disturbingly dashing tonight.

What the devil was wrong with her? She gave herself a stern mental shake. In no way should she allow her feelings to grow for him. Even if his easy manner seemed to draw her like a moth to a flame, she shouldn't risk losing herself to his seductive charm. He was a man, naught but a man.

"Ladies." Edgeware had wasted no time crossing the room to personally greet them. He gave a grand bow and, blast him, looked as elegant as a prince. "Please allow me to reserve a dance with each of you beauties in turn."

He gave Lauretta a second look, and frowned. "What's this?" he said, gently lifting the unhappy girl's chin. "I cannot allow such a gloomy face at my ball."

"I simply can't muster a happier feeling, my lord. Perhaps I should—"

"Do not speak nonsense, my beautiful lady. You've only stepped foot in the ballroom. How can you possibly know how the night will turn out?" He was scolding her, of that Elsbeth was certain. But his tone was so light, so playful that even the sensitive Lauretta's grim expression appeared to lighten.

"But-but, my lord," she sputtered. "You don't understand. You couldn't possibly know—"

"That Sir Donald has broken your heart? Yes, I do believe your father had mentioned something of that matter to me when we were discussing this house party." He caressed the girl's chin as an uncle would, before releasing it. "Just say the word, my lady, and I will ban Sir Donald from ever stepping foot in my house again."

Lauretta gave a start. More than a little distressed she waved her satiny-gloved hands in the air. "No, my lord, I beg that you don't punish him." She swallowed hard. "I-I couldn't . . . I mean, he-um-he-he—"

"Ah. I understand only too well," Edgeware said. "Please grant me the pleasure of this first set, then." His smile brightened again as he extended his hand to her with a grand gesture. "I promise Sir Donald will rethink his earlier foolishness after seeing his competition tonight."

Elsbeth watched with a pang in her heart as her dark lord led Lauretta away. It was foolish, really, that she should feel jealous of her cousin. She didn't want Edgeware's attentions, truly she didn't. Hang it all, she didn't want him smiling at her like he'd smiled at Lauretta. And she really didn't want him to remind her of that morning's passionate kiss . . . or whisper any more shocking promises of seduction.

"Wouldn't it be grand if Lauretta went home to father engaged to Lord Edgeware?" Olivia said dreamily.

"Don't be ridiculous. Edgeware wouldn't propose without talking to your father first," Elsbeth snapped.

Olivia giggled. "Oh Elly! I didn't realize that you—"

"Now you *are* being ridiculous, Olivia. Come now." She latched her arm with her cousin's. "Let's step away from the entrance."

"Am I being silly? The Marquess gallantly presented you a flower this afternoon and placed it in your hair as well!"

"Please, Olivia," Elsbeth said, not quite able to fight off the tender memories.

"I do believe you are blushing, Elly. Oh la, there is nothing to be embarrassed about. He is an eligible bachelor, is he not? Ah, Mr. Waver, how do you do?"

George Waver inclined his head and smiled. "Good evening ladies. Please allow me to present to you Reverend Sirius Waver." The handsome young man with features strikingly similar to Mr. Waver's tugged nervously on his waistcoat. "Siruis is my younger brother as well as the local vicar," Mr. Waver added with considerable fondness, which only seemed to make the vicar look more uncomfortable.

Mr. Waver hurried on, presenting Elsbeth and Olivia and detailing their family connections, Elsbeth puzzled over the young vicar's agitation until she noticed how pink his cheeks had become when George Waver had spoken Olivia's name. Once the introductions were completed, Mr. Waver turned and gave his brother a nod.

"L-lady Olivia." Reverend Waver cleared his throat a couple of times. "Lady Olivia, I would be honored to lead you in the first set. That is, if you haven't already accepted an invitation from another gentleman. Which in that case, I'd hardly expect you to agree to dance with me."

Olivia giggled, her pink cheeks brightening even before she latched on to his arm.

"And would you, Lady Mercer," Mr. Waver asked, "be available to dance the first set with me?"

"No, I'm afraid she would not," Charlie said, nudging Mr. Waver out of the way. "The first set is beginning and *Lady Mercer* has promised it to me," he said, using her proper title for the first time since they'd been reaquainted. But despite that courtesy, he took possession of her arm as if he owned it.

"Perhaps later, then?" Mr. Waver said with a frown.

"Yes, later would be nice," Elsbeth said. She allowed Charlie to tow her along with him, even though the thought of being with him made her whole body tremble with fear. This was no time for cowardice. If Charlie was indeed Dionysus, she needed to gather evidence in order to expose him. Besides, she reminded herself, she had no reason to be frightened of Charlie. He wouldn't dare harm her in the middle of a crowded ballroom.

The small orchestra began playing a minuet, the traditional opening set. The dancers lined up, waiting for their turn to whirl down the line with their partners. Lauretta, looking worlds livelier, was the first to dance in front of the other guests. She turned toward Edgeware for the lead-in. They did a right-hand turn, a left-hand turn, and then a two-hand turn before starting the sequence again until they had glided to the end of the line. Edgeware had given Lauretta a wonderful gift. By choosing her to partner him in the opening dance of the ball, every man present would now look at her in a new light.

Charlie kept Elsbeth by his side as he lagged back in the line of guests. "I know who you are," she said, in hopes of tricking him into a confession, "and what you're up to."

"You do?" he said and raised a brow.

"Of course I do."

He snarled at her confidence. "You've won my cousin as a champion and it makes you grow bold. He turned on me this afternoon because of you," he whispered with a ragged breath in her ear.

Elsbeth tried to pull away, but Charlie only clamped down on her arm. "No," she said, feeling a tremor of alarm. "No, you have no power over me."

"I may not. But be warned." Fire flashed in his eyes. "I won't let you come between me and my cousin."

"And I won't let you harm him!" she spat with a passion loud enough that several heads turned. But she didn't regret a word, realizing suddenly she would fight to protect Edgeware from this bounder. She simply could not let Dionysus ruin anyone else's life. Especially not Edgeware's.

Charlie's face bloomed red. He glanced around, smiling

benignly. "Very well," he said though his lips were pulled tightly into a sharp grin. "Very well," he said again and stalked off.

As Elsbeth watched him retreat, her bravery wavered. She feared her little act of rebellion would not go unpunished.

Severin prowled the ballroom, keeping a keen eye peeled for scheming young ladies that might be lurking behind a potted palm or a Doric column. He pulled a handkerchief from his pocket and dabbed at his heated brow. Edgeware's welcoming ball was brimming with young, innocent, unmarried ladies all hoping to put the matrimonial hook into some poor, unsuspecting sot.

What was a poor rogue to do? He'd danced with most of the young chits at least once. Several of the approving papas had approached him in conversation, prodding him for information about his state of affairs and intentions.

"There you are, my lord," a tender voice said just as a silken fan swatted his arm, sending Severin nearly leaping out of his skin.

He turned around and stood chest-to-chest with Lady Dashborough's more than ample bosom. She stepped closer, brushing up against him. "My word," she said, a sly grin adding a new dimension to her pretty features, "you are jumpy tonight."

"Am I?" he asked, taking a step back. "I suppose I am." Lady Dashborough's youngest, Lady Constance, had been shamelessly pursuing him all evening. He prayed her mama wasn't planning to plead a case for her. He simply wasn't interested in naive young ladies . . . or marriage.

"I've heard rumors that you are especially skilled at pleasing women, Lord Ames." She placed her hand on his arm, letting her fingers stray to his bare wrist. "These young girls populating this ball must surely bore you."

Severin let out the breath he was holding. "I have a great

admiration for experience and knowledge, as I am sure you understand."

"Yes," she purred. "I, too, feel the same way." She traced a gentle circle over the sensitive skin on the underside of his wrist. Her gaze strayed to her diamond bracelet as it brushed against his skin. "I also generously reward talent and skill."

That diamond bracelet could pay his living expenses for a month. Her offer was becoming very tempting indeed. "I see." He ran his tongue over his lower lip as if tasting a succulent fruit. "A midnight rendezvous? A sharing of experiences?"

"Yes, my lord. I would enjoy that." She slipped a key into his hand. "Midnight, then."

He discreetly pocketed her key. "Would you care to dance?" he asked, offering her his arm.

She gave him a calculating glare. "I think not," she said, and then turned and sashayed away.

Severin leaned against one of the Doric columns he'd been hiding behind and smiled as he watched her dress sway around her full hips as she walked. A relationship with the wealthy Lady Dashborough could prove most lucrative.

"Oh Sir Donald, you are so very funny." He heard Lady Constance's high-pitched voice and cringed. The young woman's sweet laugh tinkled in the air. He peeked around the column and watched as Sir Donald maneuvered Constance toward the terrace. The young man took her hand and raised it to his lips, turning her palm up. He nudged her glove and kissed her bare skin. "You, my love, must be the most beautiful woman in all of England. The other ladies present tonight all look like wilted flowers compared to you."

A woman gave a strangled cry from the opposite side of the column. She then charged into Severin, nearly knocking him over.

"Do pardon me," he called irritably after her as she raced

across the ballroom and up the staircase.

Who in blazes was that gel? Lady Lauretta?

Severin remembered then—he'd seen Lady Lauretta and Sir Donald together at Dionysus's now infamous art exhibition. What had that silly Lady Olivia said to him about the pair?

Oh dear . . . the Baneshire family had been expecting an engagement announcement before the end of the Season. Who could tell what mischief a broken-hearted girl could find for herself when in such a state? Concerned, he followed Lady Lauretta through the darkened hallways of the maze-like Purbeck Manor. Her virginal white dress appeared to glow in the gloom. She looked more like an ethereal specter than a woman in solid form. Her light whimpers and stifled sobs made the hair on the back of his neck stand on end.

He picked up his pace and turned a corner only to confront an empty hallway. Not easily discouraged, he systematically opened doors in the hall, peeking into the dark rooms.

A clock somewhere within the house began chiming. Severin slowed his step as he counted the hour.

It was midnight and Lady Dashborough, wearing a very expensive diamond bracelet, was in her chamber waiting for him. He should go to her and leave Lady Lauretta to her grief. But as he opened one last door he heard a muffled sob. With a sigh, he pulled out his handkerchief and smoothed it in his hand. Lady Lauretta was in desperate need of a few kind words and gentle reassurance. And, it appeared, he was the only one around to give that to her.

"Please, my lady, do not cry over that bounder," he said softly. "No man is worth those lovely tears." He crossed the threshold into the narrow portrait gallery and closed the door behind him.

CHAPTER TWELVE

Elsbeth wrung her hands until they stung. Nothing was amiss, she assured herself. Just because Lauretta was absent from the ballroom and Charlie, also unaccounted for, had stalked away from her earlier in a thundering rage shouldn't mean that she needed to disintegrate into a leaky watering pot while stranded in the middle of the dance floor.

But what if Charlie had lured Lauretta away? What if—?

She shook her head. Fretting never solved a crisis, real or imagined. What she needed was action. And help.

She quickly found Olivia sequestered in a corner with the illustrious Beau Brummell, discussing—of all things—the troubles of importing fashionable fabrics from France because of that troublesome war.

"Olivia," she said as she pried her cousin from the sofa's plush cushion, "go straight up to our apartment and see if Lauretta has hied herself off to bed."

"But-but I'm—" Olivia twisted out of Elsbeth's grasp so she could turn her gentle, albeit shocked, expression back toward Brummell.

"Heed me, Olivia, and do as you are told."

Olivia paled a degree. "Is something wrong?"

"*Wrong?*" Elsbeth squeaked. "Of course not. Why would you ask such a question?" No matter what, she couldn't let the other guests suspect that Lauretta might be alone with a gentleman; she couldn't let another scandal darken the Baneshire door.

Olivia turned and stared at Elsbeth, her eyes grew wide. "Oh dear," she said and then uttered a polite excuse to Beau Brummell before rushing from the ballroom.

Elsbeth wondered what her cousin had read in her frozen expression. No, she shook her head and forced a brittle smile. She could not lose herself to paralyzing fear, not now. Things were different when it was just her, and she could collapse like a simpering rag doll after her husband flew into one of his heartless rages. But now Lauretta and Olivia both depended on her, and Lord Baneshire, foolish man, had entrusted her with his children's safety.

Charlie. And Dionysus. Or were they two names for the same man? Damn her husband, damn his friends. They seemed to always be at the root of her troubles. Even now when, by all rights, she should be free from them.

Until death, the marriage vow had proclaimed, not beyond.

"Pardon me." She reached out and latched onto the arm of a rather flustered Lady Dashborough as the lady rushed by. "Have you seen Charlie . . . um, I mean Mr. Charles Purbeck, the younger Purbeck, I mean."

"Men!" Lady Dashborough exclaimed, as she shook off Elsbeth's hold. "This blasted ball has misplaced more men than I care to acknowledge. If you happen upon Lord Ames, you can tell him that *he* needn't come looking for *me*. Good evening."

"What was that all about?" a deep voice whispered in Elsbeth's ear, sending her senses reeling into a dizzying spin. She dug her fingers into her palms and walked away from the spicy scent she now associated with Lord Edgeware. He was one complication more than she could handle at the moment.

Two iron-willed hands curled around her arms and twirled her around until she was forced to stare into his shimmering black eyes. Fear tickled the back of her throat.

"Elsbeth?"

"You are not a man I must bow to," she said sharply. There were too many men haunting her life already. She didn't need another. "You have no hold on me. You don't own me, my lord. You cannot hurt me."

His frown deepened. "I merely hoped to assist you. Forgive me if I have offended," he said softly. At that, she could only blink. He'd done it again. By acting in the complete opposite manner than she was accustomed from a man, he'd thrown her and the whole ghastly situation off balance.

"Lauretta is not in the bedchamber. I cannot imagine where she has disappeared to," Olivia blurted out as she hurried over to them, which Elsbeth dearly wished she hadn't. She was hoping to keep Lauretta's disappearance private.

"Am I interrupting something?" Olivia asked, as her gaze landed on Edgeware's hands and how they were trapping Elsbeth's arms.

"Not exactly," Edgeware said and cleared his throat. He let his hold slip away, leaving Elsbeth feeling cold, as if she missed his touch. Which didn't make any sense, and was completely beside the point. She needed to find Lauretta, not fall under this man's spell. He was, after all, the one who assisted a bounder like Dionysus and a villain like Charlie.

Lawks, it had to be Charlie behind Lauretta's disappearance! He was punishing her. She was certain of it.

"Charlie," she said, her gaze frantically searching the ballroom for a glimpse of that devil. "Where is he? Don't try to protect him, Edgeware."

The doors leading out to the gardens were open. She gathered up her skirt and started toward them. Any number of unspeakable horrors could befall an unsuspecting young lady in an unlit garden. Lord help her, Charlie would pay dearly if he harmed her sweet, innocent Lauretta.

"What's going on?" she heard Edgeware ask from behind her.

"Lauretta's gone missing," Olivia replied. "Elly must be worried my fool sister has gone and done something rash. She believed herself in love with that milksop Sir Donald, you must know."

Edgeware grunted. "And what has Charlie to do with this?"

A shiver traveled up Elsbeth's spine. The worrying edge in Edgeware's voice and the undeniable fact that he was determined to follow along continued to unsettle her.

"I cannot imagine why she's searching for Mr. Purbeck. Perhaps he has seen Lauretta?"

"Doubtful. Our most accommodating hostess, Lady Waver, wished to accompany her daughter home. I sent Charlie to escort them in my carriage. He's been gone for a little over an hour and I don't expect he'll return before for least another quarter hour."

Elsbeth stopped abruptly and turned back around. Her eyes sparkled with an angry brilliance rivaling the purest blue sapphires as she stared fixedly at Nigel. "If not Charlie, then who has stolen my Lauretta?" she demanded.

Stolen Lauretta? She'd suspected Charlie, harmless Charlie, of debauchery? But why? Charlie had claimed to be so chummy with her—like brother and sister. Could these accusations of abduction be sparked by a growing romantic attachment?

By a womanish jealously?

"Well?" she pressed. "This is your house party, Edgeware. Whom should I suspect?"

He mentally ticked off the names of the male guests in his head. Sir Donald had been seen leading the lovely Lady Constance into the gardens. George and his brother were still in the ballroom. Severin was—for the life of him, Nigel could not remember the last time he'd seen Severin.

"Severin, what are you up to?"

"Lord Ames?" Elsbeth gasped, and looked ready to throw daggers.

Damnation, he must have said the last aloud.

"I assure you, Lord Ames is as trustworthy as they come." She didn't appear convinced. Wringing her hands again, she made a beeline toward the stairs that led toward the center of the house.

Nigel gave instructions to a nearby footman before following after her. Soon, nearly half the manor's staff were discretely searching the serpentine halls for Lady Lauretta and Lord Ames.

It would only be a matter of time before one or both of them would be found. Nigel caught up to Elsbeth and told her just that. Even so, she insisted on forging ahead with her own search. In the shadowy light of Purbeck Manor's back staircase, they formed an unspoken partnership. Together they searched, methodically opening doors along a rather long and dimly lit hallway. With each step, Elsbeth's shoulders bound up tighter and tighter.

"She'll soon be found, and she will be found safe," he said. "I promise that."

She released the door handle she was holding and chewed her bottom lip. She tilted her head up toward him. "I know you don't mean me any harm. I mean—" she said and stopped, frowning. "The Baneshire family doesn't need another scandal. If this were to get out—"

"No one will ever learn of this." He crossed the hallway and drew her into his arms. "I won't allow it."

He felt her muscles loosen as she snuggled against his chest. Her arms tentatively reached around him until she was holding onto him as if for dear life.

"I should never allow myself to feel safe while alone in a hallway with a man," she whispered against his neck. "But with you, I do."

"You are *painfully* safe with me," he said with a groan. For all the world he wanted to kiss her, but he held back. Men frightened her. That he was beginning to understand only too well . . . and it was beginning to appear as if her unhappy marriage to the Earl of Mercer was at the root of that fear.

She gazed up at him and, with a halting motion, ran the tips of her fingers along the side of his face. "You're different from the others, I think. You're rather like a pleasant dream on the verge of wakefulness, not quite understood yet comforting." She blinked back a bright sheen of tears that had flooded her eyes. "If only I could just wake up into a dream and know that Lauretta is safely tucked into her bed and that my social ruin and . . . and . . . my marriage were nothing more than ghastly figments of an overactive imagination."

What she needed more than his passion or his lust was his strength. So he tightened his arms around her. "I'm right here. And you can trust that I'll do everything in my power to make your life whole again."

Holding her near and not acting on his desires was torture. She was too real, too close. She broke through all his carefully laid barriers, and this time he couldn't ignore it. He covered her mouth with his and fed her the strength of his longing . . . and Dionysus's longing. The erotic energy that had been nipping between them swirled into a liquid heat, rising up through them as their lips mated.

She pressed her body against the length of him, molding to him. Her soft lips parted at the pressure of his tongue and she moaned when he slowly explored past her lips.

He guided her until she was pressed up against a wall. He planted his hands on the plaster just above her head to keep his hands from roaming over her body. As difficult as it proved to be, he kept a tight rein over his desires, afraid he might frighten her flaring passion away.

And it was passion, as alive and hot as his own, that answered his exploring kisses. She nipped his bottom lip. Dear Lord, who was this woman in his arms? She was nothing like the feminine ideal of perfection that had lingered in his dreams for nearly a decade. This woman was real.

"I wouldn't dare trade this moment for even the sweetest dream in the world," he whispered. Immediately he knew he'd made a tactical mistake. She peeled her lips from his. The passion that had been so real a moment ago was gone.

"Lauretta." She wiggled away from the wall. The dreamy passion in her eyes had been replaced with panic. "We have to find her."

"Of course." His lower half was screaming for him not to give up so easily. He was being ruled by lust and had started this seduction in the hallway even though he'd known finding Lauretta was their priority. "As I already promised," he said tightly. They continued down the rather quiet, narrow corridor, each resuming the task of opening doors on either side. "I won't ignore this attraction between us."

"Later, we will discuss this—" Elsbeth gasped. "Lauretta!"

Nigel peered over her shoulder into his portrait gallery in time to see Severin pull away from Lauretta and jump to his feet. Even in the yellowy light, Nigel could see how the young woman's lips were as swollen as Elsbeth's and her cheeks brightened from Severin's skilled kisses.

"Severin?" he said, his temper building in concert with Elsbeth's agitation. "Do you care to explain yourself?"

"Do not speak," Elsbeth said, throwing her arms wide. "I cannot bear to hear your voice." She paused just long enough to scowl at Nigel. "Or yours, my lord."

Severin backed quickly away while Elsbeth approached as assuredly as a harridan with a weapon. Without another word, she snatched Lauretta up from the small bench in the middle of the gallery and bustled her out the door.

Nigel followed until Elsbeth turned a corner. He then returned to the gallery and closed the door behind him.

"So, Severin." He crossed his arms in front of his chest. "Tell me. Do your tastes now run toward young innocent maidens?"

Severin, intelligent man, seemed to sense the danger he faced and took a step back. "Really, Edgeware, this isn't what you think. We were merely discussing art and artists."

Elsbeth paced her bedchamber. A silvery moon sent a chilling beam through the floor-to-ceiling window. She'd sent Olivia and Lauretta to their beds in the adjoining room without allowing Lauretta to explain herself or her actions.

She didn't care to know, for whatever had happened, which didn't appear to extend beyond a few kisses, was not nearly as bad as what could have happened. And what could have happened was what had Elsbeth worried.

Charlie, Dionysus, and Lord Ames, they were all dangerous in their own way. And, as was proved tonight, they were dangerous not only to herself but also to those closest to her. Attending this house party without the protection of her uncle was beyond foolhardy. She couldn't protect Olivia or Lauretta from those men. She should have never thought she could. Years of marriage should have taught her better.

When, in the past six years, had she ever proven she could protect herself from the men in her life? *When?*

Even now, even after Edgeware had boldly declared for a second time his intention of seducing her, she felt her resolve slipping. His words, his touch, his blasted presence was driving her out of her mind. Only an hour ago, he'd nearly brought her to her knees with wanting him, and she hadn't a clue how he'd managed it. Something about him made her feel young and innocent again, as if the child who'd once blindly fallen in love with Dionysus's paintings had miraculously sprang back to life.

She stopped her pacing and stood at the window, gazing out into the darkness. A shadow crossed in front of a row of trees. She frowned.

There were too many intrigues going on in this accursed place, too many opportunities for mischief.

She should leave. That's what she needed to do, escape. At first light she planned to see that Olivia and Lauretta's belongings were packed up. By mid-morning they should be well on their way back to London. Her fingers involuntarily curled around the oval locket hanging around her neck. But she hadn't needed the reminder.

Dionysus.

He was still out there. And despite Edgeware's assurances, he was still a threat to the Baneshire family.

Tonight.

She lit a candle and pulled a wrapper on over her thin nightrail. Tonight, she would have her proof.

CHAPTER THIRTEEN

Sleep would be impossible. Nigel wasn't even going to try. He shrugged off his evening coat and tore at the knot of his cravat until it fell free. Damnation! He flexed his stiff hand before undoing the buttons on his waistcoat. He'd punched Severin for no better reason than for causing a moment of embarrassment in front of Elsbeth—his paragon of perfection.

A sudden urge to paint overcame him. But he couldn't give in to it, not while the house was bursting with guests. He wandered to the window, instead, and pressed his sore fist against the pane. Being so near her and yet so distant, was tearing holes into his sanity.

What the bloody hell?

In the moonlight, he watched as a shadowy figure darted from the garden path toward the cliffs.

Now there was a problem he knew exactly how to handle. He retrieved his pistol from a small wooden box sitting atop his dressing table. Come morning, he'd have one less problem.

Elsbeth eased the door to Lord Edgeware's study open and held a small candle aloft as she poked her head into the room.

There was a stillness. A safe, undeniably empty, stillness.

She slipped inside, nudging the door closed behind her with the toe of her slipper. A few embers smoldered behind the fire grate casting a deep red glow into the room. She went straight to a large oak desk that was in front of a bank of windows and gave the top drawer a tug.

It didn't budge. The whole desk had been locked up nice and tight. Not even a scrap of paper had been left sitting out on its shiny top. Undeterred, she set the candle on the floor near a keyhole and fiddled in her hair a moment, quickly finding a pin. Her husband had once snatched a hairpin from her hair and had used it to open the household liquor cabinet after she had hidden away its key. He'd made it look so easy, his fingers nimbly working the mechanism until a faint snap had signaled his success.

She felt fairly confident she could copy her late husband's actions. After all, he'd never really been all that clever.

Crouching down behind the desk, she slipped the pin into the lock and fiddled with it, with absolutely no idea what she should expect to happen.

"Gracious," she muttered aloud and sat back on her heels. "This is harder than it looks."

The door swung open. She moved fast, snuffing the candle as she dove behind the desk.

"Come out from there." Edgeware's voice tore through the room. She remained perfectly still, praying he'd just leave. "I know someone is in here. I saw the candlelight from under the door and I heard your voice." Edgeware sighed. "If you don't show yourself, I vow you won't leave this room unscathed."

"Pray don't hurt me," she said very quietly as she rose from her hiding place.

"Elsbeth?"

"Though you have every right to—"

"What in the world—?"

"—do whatever you choose. You caught me in the act. I was breaking into your desk." She cast a soulful glance down at her hairpin still sticking out of the lock.

"You were robbing me?"

"Not very well, mind you. Perhaps if I had more time. You see, it had looked so easy when my husband had—"

"Money?" He stepped into the room and passed in front of a moonlit glass-paned door. His shirt was open at the chest and he was wearing a dressing gown instead of his coat. "Are you in need of money?"

"You see, he had once picked a lock with a hairpin and . . . *what?*"

"I said—" he took another step toward her so that only the desk stood between them "—are you in need of money? You have but to ask. I am your servant in this and in anything else you desire."

"*Money?* You thought I would rob you?"

He leaned over the desk and stared at the lock she'd been working. "Why else would you want to pry open the drawer that holds my strongbox?"

"Certainly not to rob you!"

Edgeware smiled at that. "Then why?"

She fought an urge to scream. "Because of Dionysus, blast it all! Because I need to know who he is! I need to know why he torments me. Why does he wish to ruin my life?"

His smile faded and his eyes grew dark, as dark and frightening as the bleakest of nights. "As I have already told you, he has never wished you harm, Elsbeth. I swear it."

"That tells me nothing." She bent down and plucked the hairpin from the lock and the unlit candle from the floor.

Edgeware circled the desk, blocking her escape. He spread his arms wide. "Then, I fear, I can tell you nothing."

Oh, how she wished he would confide in her. No matter how hard she fought it, she felt drawn to him. They would make a good team. Together they could stop Dionysus from ruining any more lives. And, perhaps, they could share more kisses.

She quickly turned away and caught sight of a small marble

status bathed in a pale beam of moonlight. The statue, sitting atop a round pillar in the far corner of the room, was of Dionysus, the Greek god of wine and ecstasy. The lithe figure reclined against a marble rock outcropping, his head thrown back, a lyre about to slip from his fingers. A diamond tear sparkled on the stone god's cheek.

Dionysus, a myth known for his eternal pursuit of life's pleasures, was a tragic figure really. Like Edgeware, Dionysus's mother had died at his birth. Elsbeth had forgotten, until that moment, the stories her governess had read to her about the god. A god who'd not been accepted in either the realm of Olympus, or in the world of mortals.

"A mystic wanderer doomed. All whom he loved was destined to share in his tragic fate," she mouthed, trying to remember something she'd once read. Something important, but then a hand caressed her jaw, turning her face back toward Edgeware until she was trapped in his penetrating gaze.

"I only seek to restore your reputation," he said. "I will do everything in my power to protect you and your relatives from the sharp tongues wagging through the *ton*. Beyond that, I-I—"

He faltered, seemingly at a loss for words. He closed the distance between them. His warm hand, the hand still cupping her cheek, traced a line slowly across her jaw until his fingers could curl around the nape of her neck.

She felt her senses flee. She licked her lips, and her eyelids grew heavy with desire for this mysteriously gentle man.

"Oh hell, Elsbeth," he whispered a moment before he kissed her. Her passion reawakened from the madness they'd shared in the hallway just a few hours ago. It stirred a dormant part of her heart. A lonely, aching need she could no longer deny.

She leaned into his chest and snaked her arms around his waist as she parted her lips. Her mind was surprisingly silent. She couldn't think; she could only feel. She could only drink in how his touch, his caress brought life to her most intimate parts.

He helped her push away his shirt and she rained kisses on his bare chest, quickly becoming drunk from his sweet scent, that welcome mix of almonds and sage. His hands explored her body. He was slow and patient with her as he pushed away her wrapper to trace her shape through the thin nightrail she wore beneath. With a satisfied sigh, she reached out for him, feeling desperate to touch him. His muscles were taut, his skin smooth.

This was like a dream, a distant dream she'd long forgotten. "Yes," she whispered, instinctively knowing how the scene was to play out, and knowing not to fear it.

Agile fingers unlaced the top of her nightrail and bared her breasts. Each round globe felt particularly heavy and wanton. He dipped his head and took a nipple between his teeth, suckling until she thought she might cry out. A vibrating heat filled her chest and spread low in her belly and high in her legs.

With his thigh he gently pushed her legs apart.

"Elsbeth, I have waited too long for this." His smoldering gaze spoke to her in a way only Dionysus's paintings had ever done. She longed to ease his suffering. And ease her own aching need as well.

He pushed her skirt up while fumbling with the front of his trousers. "This isn't how it's supposed to happen, dove," he said between deep kisses where their tongues were given the chance to play. "There should be flowers, music . . . at least a bed." His fingers parted her nether curls. His touch was warm and gentle with her delicate flesh.

"Relax," he whispered, stroking her deeply between her legs until she thought she might melt into nothing at his feet. "Just feel."

Her breathing hitched. Awareness of her body—of how he was stroking her, touching her in her most delicate of places— exploded with a flash of bright colors. Her budding heat pulled and strained against his touch in such a pleasing manner she opened her legs wider. And then desire took over. She traced her finger down his chest and daringly reached into his unfastened trousers to caress him.

Slowly, he withdrew from her until only his lips touched hers, breaking the contact she had learned to crave.

"The door," he whispered and gave her a quick kiss. He was only gone a moment. But it felt like a lifetime. He hurried across the room and pushed the door closed. He then fumbled with the key in the lock. But before he could turn it, the wretched key slipped out of his hand, bounced across the oriental carpet and disappeared under the heavy desk. She'd never seen him look so harassed. He drew a ragged breath. He'd probably come to the same conclusion she had. They'd have a devil of a time finding the key in the dim moonlight.

"Everyone is abed." She reached out to him. "Surely, we are safe."

With him, she felt uncommonly safe. His body was trembling with need by the time he pulled her back into his arms. She grabbed his shoulders and held on to him, silently begging for him to give her more.

He answered by positioning the wide tip of his manhood at her opening and pushing deep into her with one smooth stroke. She'd always been small, tight. Her body stretched to accommodate him. Though he was stretching her to her limit, she welcomed his fullness, a swelling of sensations more fantastic than before. A fullness that felt natural.

The tip of his tongue eased her mouth open, urging her to breathe. He pulled out and pressed back in again, moving slowly and rhythmically massaging her sensitive flesh.

"Oh my," Elsbeth moaned. It had never been quite like this. She had never even dreamed . . .

His motions grew more urgent. He filled her over and over

until she was sure she could take no more. She cried out, her muscles trembling as she rode wave after wave of pleasure until she sank into his arms, feeling more relaxed than ever and unable to catch her breath.

He kissed her forehead, her nose, her chin, and then slipped from between her legs. "Next time," he whispered, sounding as breathless as she, "we should definitely have a bed nearby."

The mere thought of repeating that miracle set her legs quivering anew. Her eyes slipped closed as she held on to his strong shoulders and waited to wake up from what had to have been her most vivid dream ever.

His lips found hers again and she lost herself in his touch. Her life would never be the same again. Nothing would ever be the same, nothing would ever be so—

An angry fist knocked sharply against the study's heavy wooden door. "Lord Edgeware!" a woman shouted. "La, I hope you're in there. This is really most unacceptable. There is a man lurking outside the—" Lady Dashborough pushed open the study's door and gasped. "What-what-what is the meaning of this?"

Chapter Fourteen

With his hand inside her wrapper, cupping her breast, his other hand tangled in her hair, and her nightrail hiked up about her waist there was no hope of pretending that what they'd just been caught doing was anything other than what it looked like.

Elsbeth jerked free of Edgeware's embrace, pushed her skirt down, and pulled her wrapper closed as priggishly as possible. Still, her cheeks flamed the moment her gaze met the sharp scrutiny of Lady Dashborough, who had a brightly lit four-stem candelabrum held high over her head.

What a pretty pair they must have made. Her, dressed in her flimsy nightclothes with only a sheer wrapper for coverage. Edgeware, dressed without a coat or cravat, his shirt open, nearly torn off, revealing a goodly portion of his chest. And—Elsbeth's blush grew hotter—his trousers hung open, unbuttoned. Yes, what a pretty gossip they had just handed to Lady Dashborough.

"My lord," the good matron said after a sharp intake of air, "not only are suspicious men roaming your grounds. There is this. You must now understand why I was worried about letting my daughters cavort with such a . . . such a . . . hoyden." She waved her arm in the general direction of Elsbeth. "Or has she woven her wiles so tightly around you that you're blinded to the beast she truly is?"

Edgeware appeared to be having a bit of trouble gaining his

wits. He cleared his throat several times while setting his clothes to right.

"My lady—" he implored only to be interrupted.

"I demand, Lord Edgeware, yes, demand, that you remove this thing from your house first thing in the morning. I would say sooner, but I am a charitable lady with charitable feelings toward the ladies Olivia and Lauretta. What damage their association with such an immoral—"

"My lady," Edgeware nearly shouted, "you do not understand the situation!"

Elsbeth's jittery attentions snapped toward him. How could he expect to convince Lady Dashborough that she was mistaken in what she had clearly seen?

"Not understand?" Lady Dashborough's chin shot up toward the ceiling. "How can that be possible? What I saw was a woman with a history of questionable morals using her charms to ignite your lust."

Edgeware chuckled nervously. "You see, my lady. This is where you are mistaken. It is my charm that has won the rather proper Lady Mercer over. For, I'm delighted to announce that—" he cleared his throat and gave Elsbeth a blazing smile "—the enchanting lady has just agreed to be my wife. What you saw was my expression of gratitude for her acceptance to my suit."

Wife? The room began to spin. "But I must never marry again." What was the dark lord doing? Why was he stealing away her freedom? What possible use could he have for her?

He didn't know.

"Elsbeth?"

He surely didn't know.

"Elsbeth? Breathe, my little dove."

Two strong arms supported her.

"Sit her in this chair, my lord. She looks ready to faint. Your charms have overwhelmed her, no doubt. You are a very charming man," Lady Dashborough said.

Elsbeth sank into a leather chair and cradled her dizzy head in her hands. A warm hand rubbed her back heartily.

This was foolish, and she never accounted herself acting a fool. She drew in a deep breath and slowly straightened her spine. She had to blink several times to clear away the blurriness.

"I say," Lady Dashborough quickly spoke up, "I would imagine any respectable young lady would be overwhelmed by your suit, Edgeware. Your interests undoubtedly have near to killed a woman of Lady Mercer's standing." She clicked her tongue.

Elsbeth, feeling as if she was plodding through a murky dream, turned her head away from Lady Dashborough's pained smile to focus on the hand now covering hers. She blinked.

"You cannot mean . . . I mean, my lord, surely you were jesting." She drew a steadying breath. "And such a thing to jest about."

He didn't know. How could she possibly tell him?

"Lady Dashborough," she said, her voice strong and clear. She rose from the chair. "Lord Edgeware is jesting. There is no engagement, only an indiscretion as you first suspected. I assure you, it was not planned."

A sly smile spread on the lovely matron's face. "Of course. How could I have thought otherwise? The *ton* will be very interested to know how the leopard has failed to change her spots." She raised her hand. "No, Lord Edgeware, don't you dare ply me with your threats. I'm willing to weather a minor scandal to protect others from this beast."

"Threats?" Elsbeth asked.

"Threats?" Edgeware sounded perfectly innocent. "I cannot imagine to what you are referring. As for the engagement, I vow it is true." He grabbed Elsbeth's hand and cradled it against his chest. "My sweet dove, you cannot insist it be kept secret. You see, Lady Dashborough, her family is not yet aware of the arrangement. And then there is the matter of the marriage settlement and solicitors to be consulted. Of course, she insists she speak with her uncle before a formal announcement is made."

"I see," Lady Dashborough said, eyeing them both far too closely.

"Lord Edgeware—" Elsbeth began, ready to present him with a royal scolding. She had no desire to be party to his fiction.

"Hush, my dove," he pressed a finger to her lips—lips that felt shamefully swollen—before she could utter her first protest. "She is adamant about the secrecy, I am afraid."

"No, my dear," Lady Dashborough said. Her eyes flashed in the candlelight. "This will not do. You cannot expect to suppress the news of the Marquess's engagement. He is much too important. This move will come as a great shock to the matrons who have been busily grooming their daughters for him." With that, Lady Dashborough took up her candelabrum and swept from the room.

"Sir!" Elsbeth rounded on the dark lord, her tiny fists pressing painfully against her hips. "What have you done?"

What had he done indeed?

Nigel's insides stirred with an unsettling mix of delight and terror. Certainly what he had just done would be very difficult to undo.

"I believe you should consider yourself engaged, madam," he said, his words clipped and sharp. Anger against himself boiled over onto Elsbeth. "I have told you this several times before. I am prepared to do anything . . . *anything* to restore you and your relatives' reputations in the eyes of society."

"I never asked for this kind of help. Gracious, I believe I would rather seek the assistance of a footpad."

"That can be arranged!" he shouted and charged from the room, muttering curses against Elsbeth, the rigid society they lived in and its damned rules, and himself.

Especially himself.

CHAPTER FIFTEEN

"You did what?"

Nigel was lounging against a brick wall with his arms crossed against his chest. He kicked a pebble lying in the middle of the walk, sending it skittering across the slate stones. The day promised to be a warm one.

He'd spent the morning with George, searching the grounds for intruders. After his surprise engagement the night before, he'd forgotten, until that morning, all about the shadowy figure both he and Lady Dashborough had seen prowling the grounds. By that time, no traces of mischief could be found. And even though his life depended on catching that bold, nameless interloper, he had a devil of a time keeping his mind on such matters.

"I believe you heard me," he said, snarling.

"Yes, yes, I heard you." George waved a hand in the air. "I just don't understand why. Why tie yourself to Lady Mercer? Certainly you've heard the rumors about her. Her reputation was teetering on a sharp edge even before Dionysus's painting of her emerged. Lord Mercer was a depraved maniac, and many believe his wife picked up several of his worst habits. Society matrons were inviting her to their teas and parties to see for themselves what kind of mad woman he'd created."

Doubt flickered in Nigel's mind. Hadn't Elsbeth admitted to learning how to pick a lock from her husband? What else had Mercer taught his innocent dove? It was a disturbing enough thought to imagine Elsbeth having anything to do with the brute. He especially shied away from picturing her learning the secrets of the marriage bed from him. The image roiled his stomach.

"It was the only way I could think to protect her from that viper Lady Dashborough."

"Blast it all, Edgeware, I never took you for a fool, but this . . . this is unbelievable. Lady Mercer is not your responsibility. What she and that rogue Dionysus did . . . well, that was her decision. Her responsibility. It's not as if she's some young innocent too stupid to know her own mind."

Nigel pushed up from the wall he'd been leaning against. "That is quite enough," he said, and stalked down the daisy-lined path back toward the manor.

"Damn and blast, Edgeware," George called after him, "don't run away from your friends. You'll doubtlessly need all the help you can get to not muck this up!"

"Elly, why ever didn't you tell us?" Olivia, trailed by a beaming Lauretta, rushed into the bedchamber and hugged Elsbeth where she sat at her dressing table, busily pulling her hair into a severe topknot.

"We're ever so happy for you," Lauretta said.

Elsbeth batted her cousin's arms away. "The rumor of our engagement is a mistake, a horrid mistake. I have no intention of marrying Lord Edgeware or anyone else for that matter."

"I don't understand," Lauretta said.

"I mean . . ." Oh, why couldn't there be just one happy ending for her? But no, her heart had been betrayed once and she had vowed long ago to protect that tender organ from further damage. Even if it meant being doomed to live each day with Edgeware's passion seared onto her soul while still keeping him out of her life. "I mean I will not marry," she said very softly.

He would be relieved. No man would wish to be forced into a marriage, especially not a confirmed bachelor like Edgeware. "I cannot marry anyone. And when the Marquess learns the truth of the matter, he will most assuredly agree."

Olivia sank down onto a little bench beside the dressing table and pried Elsbeth's fingers from the locket she was clutching. "You mean . . . ?" Her cousin blushed. "Surely, he won't hold that against you."

"Whatever do you mean, Olivia?" Lauretta asked.

Olivia's blush deepened. "Never you mind." With a sharp tug, she pulled Elsbeth to her feet. "And what in blazes do you have on, Elly?"

Elsbeth briefly glanced at the dark gray gown. The material was heavy and the drab color did terrible things to her complexion, making her skin look dreadfully pale and splotchy.

"It is a suitable gown for a woman of my status. Half-mourning, I believe, is very proper."

"Papa and Mama have both told you that you are too young to mourn a husband for the rest of your life. You *need* to remarry."

"If *I* were to get such a marriage proposal, you would find me dressed in my happiest, brightest, yellow gown," Lauretta said wistfully. Poor heart-broken Lauretta. No wonder she'd fallen prey to the dastardly Lord Ames so easily.

Olivia, flitting from man to man, leading the hapless gentlemen on a merry chase while guarding her heart, would be a good role model for her sister to follow.

"We have no time to dawdle," Elsbeth said, her fingers nervously pushing the unruly strands of hair that had fallen from her topknot back into place. "Your maids should be along any minute to help with the packing."

"Packing?" both Lauretta and Olivia cried.

"Packing." Elsbeth said firmly. "There is too much going on

at this house party that I do not approve. We, girls, are to be on the road back to London by noon."

Elsbeth turned a deaf ear to her cousin's cries of protests. She had another matter to settle before they could leave. "I will return shortly. I have put off confronting Lord Edgeware and his misguided idea of marriage for quite long enough."

"Have you gone and lost your bloody mind?"

"Good morning Uncle Charles," Nigel said as his uncle stormed into Nigel's study and slammed the door closed behind him. Nigel had been standing at the glass-paneled door, looking out into the housekeeper's small physic garden. Pale lavender flowers waved at him in the warm morning breeze. "Pleasant morning, is it not? I believe I'll take a ride. Would you care to join me?"

"Do not try to turn the subject, my boy."

"I had not realized a subject had been raised. Pray tell me, to what were we speaking?"

"You're trying my anger, boy. I have no patience for your pale attempts at humor this morning. Not after hearing how you plan to tie yourself to that harridan."

"You speak of Lady Mercer?"

"She is most unsuitable for a marchioness."

"Unsuitable?" He raised a brow at that. "She was once married to an earl."

"Exactly! You should marry a virgin! Not a woman with such loose morals that you'd never know if her child was yours or not."

Nigel closed his eyes and drew a slow, steady breath. Arguing with his uncle rarely accomplished anything. He unclasped his hands and flexed his numb fingers. His uncle no longer had a hold on his future. And though he had every right to express his opinion, his uncle's thoughts were just that, opinions.

And those opinions weren't going to change his mind . . . at least, not where Elsbeth was concerned.

"Uncle Charles," he said as he turned around. A tremor of anger hardened his voice. "I appreciate your concern. But my mind is quite set." He knew he was playing with a very hot fire. His uncle could be a brutal man. But he had to stand up for himself or else risk losing control over his own affairs once again. "Lady Mercer is going to become my wife."

"Gracious, Father, I could hear your voice all the way down the hall," Charlie said as he slipped into the study, closing the door behind him.

"My brother, your father, entrusted me with your care. He entrusted me to see that the family name continued to be respected." Uncle Charles said a bit more sedately now that young Charlie was in the room. He glanced briefly at his son and gave him a quick smile. "Nigel, I cannot believe you would willingly disgrace our title by breeding your sons on an inferior woman. There are plenty of pretty, young ladies more suitable for the task."

"Father," Charlie said quietly, his gaze trained on Nigel. "I don't believe my cousin understands the truth of the matter."

"I understand everything I need to know. There is no woman better suited to the position of marchioness than Lady Mercer." He turned back to look out into the garden, wishing his uncle and cousin would simply disappear, knowing they would not.

"I agree with you, Nige," Charlie said. "A man would have to search long and hard to find the equal to our Elly."

He cringed at Charlie's familiarity with Elsbeth's name. "She is Lady Mercer to you."

"My pardon, Nige . . . No, Father," Charlie said quickly, "hear me out. As much as I love her, I cannot recommend *Lady Mercer* for marriage."

The muscles in Nigel's shoulders tightened. He wasn't about

to let anyone, especially not Charlie who appeared to know far too much about Elsbeth's personal life, speak against her.

"Sit down, Nige," Charlie said gravely.

Nigel refused, not wanting to abandon his spot at the window, the very spot where he and Elsbeth had shared an intimate and completely life-changing moment. He would fight to the death to protect that exquisite memory. "You won't change my mind."

Charlie's confidence seemed to waver. "This is something Elly would not wish you to know. But if you confront her with this, I'd wager she would not lie to you."

"Yes?" Nothing Charlie could say would change his determination to marry Elsbeth.

"You see." Charlie lowered his voice. "Despite Elly's good attributes, she is quite—"

Elsbeth stood outside Edgeware's study. A footman had directed her here, claiming she'd be able to find his lordship within. She raised her hand to knock when she heard voices.

Several voices.

She hesitated. Perhaps she shouldn't interrupt. What she had to discuss with Edgeware was very personal. She would die— simply die—if he demanded she blurt out in front of others her very logical reason they could not be married.

She stepped away from the door. She'd come back later . . . when he was alone.

Later? How much later? She needed to get her cousins on their way back to London without delay. The ride to London would take nearly two days. She didn't wish to waste the morning waiting for Edgeware to find himself unencumbered by guests.

He would simply have to make time for her now. She would demand he see her in private. This sham of an engagement was of his making. Indeed, she shouldn't be the one to be inconvenienced.

Her fist hammered out three sharp raps on the wooden door.

The sound of voices on the other side abruptly stopped. She held her breath and waited. An eternity seemed to pass before the door swung open.

Edgeware stood not a foot from her, his dark eyes glittering with anger. He was a demon. She'd not been mistaken about him so many days ago when he'd forced her out of the freezing rains and into his carriage. He was a demon fresh from hell, sent to earth to punish her for her unfaithful heart.

"I wish to have a word with you," she said. Her voice sounded tight and unnaturally high. She quickly cleared her throat. "What I mean, my lord, is I *demand* to have a word with you. In private. Now."

His formidable features softened a touch before he glanced over his shoulder. She followed his gaze and set eyes on the two Charles Purbecks, both the younger and the elder, who were frowning sharply at her.

"Please do excuse me. I believe I have heard quite enough," he said to his relatives and turned back to Elsbeth. A strange light sparkled in his eyes as he stared down on her, assessing her. "If you care to follow me, my lady," he said, "I know of a place where you may speak to me privately."

She readily accepted his hand, more than a little anxious to get this difficult situation behind her as soon as possible.

"What a practical gown," he said as they strolled out into the estate's vast gardens. "The color isn't quite right for your fair complexion, but the fabric must be soft and sturdy." His gaze was still trained on the path before them. "Such a gown would be useful to a marchioness. The running of an efficient household, as you must know, involves much more than ordering servants about from a chaise in the parlor."

She gave a curt nod. Though she agreed with him on the involvement required of the lady of an estate, she wasn't at all comfortable with how he believed her becoming *his* marchioness was such a certainty.

"Pray tell me, my lord," she asked after they had walked quite a distance, passing neatly manicured beds that flowed into a more natural pasture of elegant flowers, and worked their way through a rather nasty patch of flowering brambles. "Where are you taking me?"

The dark home wood loomed just ahead. The shadowed forest promised to be too ominous for her nerves. She would never tempt her fate by agreeing to accompany a man into such a secluded location. Even with a man she felt as safe with as Edgeware.

"Why, my lady," he said, matching her formal tone, "you wished to seek out privacy. As you must already know, one must travel far and sacrifice much in order to find such an illusive treasure."

He skipped over a root that had pushed up onto the path.

"This is quite far enough. I don't wish to go into the woods with you, sir. I will not."

"And you needn't venture into the dangerous wilderness, my lady. Come, we are nearly there." He took her hand and led her off the slate path and through a field of tall grasses. The ground sloped down. Soon, she heard the melodic tinkling of water.

At the edge of the tall grass stood a grand oak tree, its branches so massive the lower limbs hovered mere inches above the ground. A pebbly brook meandered around the base of the oak's great trunk. Light streamed through the oak branches, making Elsbeth feel as if she were being showered by sunbeams.

Edgeware pulled out a handkerchief and gave the cloth an elaborate shake before he carefully placed it on one of the tree's low-slung branches. "Please, do sit," he said.

The branch gently rocked under her weight. The height was no different than a bench and just as comfortable, which made her uneasy. She hadn't accompanied Edgeware deep into his garden for pleasure, and comfort was the last thing she desired.

"Now, what did you wish to speak to me about?" He had stepped back to the edge of the grass and stood there watching her. That strange look still making his eyes glitter. "I have never before brought another soul to this place . . . my place. I daresay no one else knows of its existence."

The clearing, the small area beneath the large oak, was indeed an Eden. A cricket chirped and several toads answered. It felt almost as if she'd stepped into one of Dionysus's landscapes.

Oh, how that painter, that monster, had damaged her heart. If only Edgeware was willing to point the way to the mysterious bastard. She might even be willing to marry the dark lord in exchange for Dionysus's name.

Blinking away the mist in her eyes, she steeled herself to the task she had set before herself. "My lord—"

"Nigel," he interrupted. "I believe, under the circumstances, you should call me Nigel."

Of course she couldn't bring herself to do so. "Yes," she drawled. She stood. "I cannot marry you." Before he could protest, she raised her hand. "I cannot marry you or anyone else for that matter. Even if I wished it, marriage to me would not be fair to you."

"Not fair? What do you mean?" He paled—frighteningly—several shades.

"Please, sir, I beg you hear me out."

"Nothing you can say will convince me to withdraw my proposal. And do not forget, your reputation—"

"Please, my lord," she said sharply. Her cheeks flamed. Admitting the truth aloud was proving harder than she initially imagined.

"Nothing you can tell me will change my—"

"I was married for nearly six years," she said more loudly than she intended. Edgeware was startled into silence. "Six long years, I was married to the Earl of Mercer." She swallowed hard. "There were no children, my lord. In six years, there were no children born."

"I don't see—"

"He wasn't a monk—"

A sharp pop ricocheted through the dark woods. Edgeware leapt toward her.

"My God. Someone is shooting at us." He took her hand in his and tugged her arm. "We aren't safe. Not even here."

Elsbeth, too shocked to move, held her place. She could barely think. She looked down to where she'd instinctively covered the harsh stinging in her side and peeled her hand away.

Blood. Bright, warm blood stained her palm.

CHAPTER SIXTEEN

"Jenkins!" Nigel called for his butler, quite surprised he had any air left in his lungs. Every breath strained from the exertion it had taken to run with Elsbeth cradled in his arms all the way back to Purbeck Manor.

Damn it, he should have never taken her to such a secluded place. He should have never led her so far away from the main house, not when someone was plotting to kill him.

She was going to die.

"Jenkins!" he shouted again.

She'd fainted in his arms when he began the mad dash across the fields and through the flowered gardens, taking the most direct path and not minding the delicate blooms crushed under his boot as he charged back to the house. She still hadn't stirred. Her delicate features were drawn and ashen . . . almost lifeless.

Taking the stairs two at a time, he continued to call for his mysteriously absent butler.

"What is the matter, Edgeware?" Severin dashed up the stairs from out of nowhere and easily matched Nigel's stride.

"Shot," he managed.

"Zounds! Many of the men are out hunting. Must have been a stray bullet. Poor Lady Mercer. Has a doctor been fetched?"

"No." Nigel kicked open the door to Elsbeth's bedchamber. "Jenkins!" he shouted again. "My damned butler has gone missing."

Elsbeth moaned when he lowered her onto the bed. The

pained sound twisted inside him, tightening like a vise around his throbbing heart.

"Go down to the stable and find Joshua. Tell him what has happened. Have him ride into town and fetch Doctor Pryor . . . and the vicar."

Severin muttered a curse and was gone.

Nigel, too concerned after Elsbeth's health to give a whit about proprietary, slipped a knife from his boot and sliced open her sturdy gown. That gray color was not good for her anyhow. Which was a silly thought, seeing how there was a chance she might not live to scold him for ruining her dress.

She would live. She would *have* to live. He simply couldn't lose her now.

He peeled back the last layer of clothing, a thin chemise that had been white at one time but was now stained red. Blood oozed slowly from an ugly hole in her side. It was blood she couldn't afford to lose.

He quickly searched the room and found a clean cloth neatly folded in the washbasin. He grabbed it and firmly pressed the cloth against the wound.

"Milord!" a woman screeched from the doorway. A short, stocky dark-haired maid stood frozen at the entrance to the bedchamber. Her face was as pale as Elsbeth's.

"Come help me," he ordered. "She is your mistress?"

The maid nodded but remained at the threshold like a terri-fied rabbit. Her behavior was beyond strange. He would have to instruct Elsbeth to scold her maid.

If she lived.

No, he mustn't think like that. She would survive this. She would soon become his wife.

The cloth pressed against the bullet wound was quickly becoming saturated with Elsbeth's blood. "Bring me some fresh linens," he ordered.

"What have you done to her?" the maid shouted. She charged fully into the room when she saw the fresh blood. She wrapped her hands around Nigel's neck and tried to pull him away from the bed. "What have you done to my ladyship?"

"Stop this foolishness," he ordered, prying her sturdy fingers from his flesh. The tiny maid was much stronger than she looked. "Do as I say, woman, and find me some clean linens."

"Lord Ames told me Elly's been hurt," Lady Olivia cried as she rushed through the doorway. She pushed the maid out of her way and made a hasty path to the bed.

"What has happened?" Lady Lauretta demanded as she followed in her sister's path. "What did Lord Ames say?" She took one look at Elsbeth and stopped in the middle of the room. Her hands flew to her lips.

"Catch Lady Lauretta," Nigel ordered of the maid.

The maid, thankfully, had regained enough of her wits to grab Lauretta's arms just as Lauretta began to sink. Using brute strength, she heaved Lauretta into a small chair near the door.

"The linens," he reminded the maid. Even he recognized the panic in his voice. "I'll need a stack of them. And then fetch a kettle of hot water from the kitchen."

"Yes, of course, milord," she murmured. Lifting her skirts, she ran from the room.

"What has happened?" Lady Olivia whispered as she sat carefully on the edge of the bed and cradled Elsbeth's hand in her own.

In the fewest number of words possible, Nigel explained the situation.

"Struck by a stray bullet just like my husband," Elsbeth whispered. Her voice sounded rusty as she choked on a laugh. "Fitting."

Nigel squeezed her hand. Her eyes had barely opened. "Elsbeth?"

Dorothy McFalls

She didn't answer him.

Some time later, the maid returned and took a position beside Nigel. "She's in pain," she said quietly and pressed a small vial of laudanum into his palm.

He gave a nod and carefully measured a few drops of the drug into the glass of water the maid held in her other hand, took the glass, and guided it to Elsbeth's lips.

"Am I to die?" Elsbeth asked after greedily drinking a goodly portion of the water. There was no emotion in the question. Am I to die?—she had asked as if inquiring whether the cook intended to serve peas or carrots for supper that evening.

He held her hand even more tightly. "No darling, I will not allow it. You are forbidden to do anything of the sort."

Elsbeth chuckled, sounding weaker with each passing moment. "I don't believe you can bully death into submission . . . Nigel. You are not so very terrifying."

"Where is that damned doctor? Jenkins!" he shouted. Everyone in the room jumped.

Still, no butler appeared.

"I'm not afraid to die, mind you," she said, scaring the very breath from his chest. "But my side hurts like the devil, and I'm afraid that it may never stop hurting."

Damn and blast that Jenkins! The lazy sot will be out on his ear before the day's end, he vowed. And Joshua, what in bloody hell was taking him so long to fetch Doctor Pryor? Were all his servants unfaithful sots?

He was about to go out of his head with worry when Doctor Pryor, an elderly gentleman with a pear-shaped figure, finally ambled into the room.

"Heard there's been an accident," he said and then hummed a tuneless note. "Let me have a look. Can't be as bad as you think, my lord." He unceremoniously pushed both the maid and Nigel out of his way and then started humming again.

"Lord Ames," Lady Lauretta cried as Severin came rushing into the room. She rose from her swoon in the chair and was quickly at Severin's side, petting the side of his face. "What happened to your eye? It's nearly swollen shut." She frowned in Nigel's direction.

There was a purple shadow rimming the underside of Severin's left eye, true. But considering her cousin suffered a much greater mishap than coming in contact with Nigel's fist, her concern seemed woefully overdone.

Severin did nothing to discourage Lady Lauretta. He let the poor girl make a fool of herself as she caressed his face and ran her hands up and down his chest in a most inappropriate manner. Nigel was about to step in and separate the two—Elsbeth would want him to act on her behalf and protect her young cousin from disreputable rakes like Severin—but he was diverted by the arrival of George's brother, Sirius.

Doctor Pryor glanced up from Elsbeth for only a moment. "Ah, Reverend Waver, I enjoyed Sunday's sermon as always. The thought of taking one loaf and making many in our own lives really gave me something to contemplate. You must come by and join my wife and I for dinner some time this week. She's been after me to invite you."

"Vicar." Nigel took Sirius's hand in greeting. "Thank you for coming."

"We're not in need of his services today, my lord," Doctor Pryor said. "This young lady has suffered only a flesh wound. The bullet has passed through her side without much damage. As long as we can stave off infection, she'll be traipsing through the countryside in no time."

"I am glad to hear I'm not needed after all. Lord Edgeware," Sirius said with a bow and started toward the door.

Nigel caught his arm. "Wait, Vicar. But you are needed."

Sirius smiled in that ethereal way of his. "Yes?"

"I insist you perform the marriage ceremony for Lady Mercer and myself. Now. You must marry us right now."

His words shocked the room into silence.

Only Sirius seemed to take the demand in good stride. "I understand you're upset over this accident. The lady—" he gave a nod in the direction of the bed "—she is your intended?"

"Yes." He supposed he would have to submit to answering a few of the vicar's questions before he could reasonably expect to proceed with the business of marriage.

"I sympathize with your concern, Edgeware, but I don't see the need for such haste. Have the banns even been read?"

"No, but—"

"Doctor Pryor, is the young woman in any danger of succumbing to her injuries?"

"No, Reverend. We'll have to keep an eye out for fever and infection. But that won't happen for a day or two."

Sirius's smile deepened. "Now there, see. You have no need to rush."

"But the danger of infection—" Nigel became suddenly very aware of the other people in the room. He led the vicar out into the hallway. His heart began pounding as he realized no one was going to turn his course. "Something might happen. Even Doctor Pryor admits he cannot be assured of her recovery." He swallowed hard. "If something were to happen, if she were to . . . were to . . . I would want her to have my name."

Sirius patted him on the shoulder. "Very well. I suppose I could petition the bishop for a special license after the ceremony. Perhaps he will agree with the urgency of the situation."

Several minutes later Doctor Pryor banned everyone from the room, even Nigel, whom he claimed was hovering far too close. Elsbeth's cousins left with Severin, saying they would wait in the drawing room. Nigel hesitated at the door. He knew he should follow the ladies to make sure they were properly chaperoned and to make sure the rest of the guests were being properly looked after. But the neatly stacked boxes just outside the door stopped him.

Damnation. Elsbeth had been planning to leave him? She hadn't been willing to give him the chance to prove to her how much he wanted this marriage? She hadn't been willing to listen to what he might say?

He suddenly needed to be alone.

He made it halfway down the hall when a small voice called out, "Milord?"

He turned. The stout maid who'd hovered with him at Elsbeth's bedside marched toward him. "Yes?" he asked.

"You plan to marry my ladyship?"

"Yes, I do."

The maid wrinkled her nose with displeasure. "My ladyship didn't seem at all pleased by your suit. She was most upset this morning, she was, fidgeting with everything in sight."

"She has yet to become accustomed to the idea." He turned to continue down the hall, but the maid would not let him leave just yet.

"She doesn't need another blooming man," she hissed. "She is 'appier now. She is 'appier without a bloomin' husband. An' I am 'appier without 'aving to nurse my ladyship back to 'ealth."

He peeled her hand from his sleeve. "The gunshot wound was an accident."

"You 'aven't taken my meaning, milord." She hesitated. "Lord Mercer—" she lowered her voice "—'e was a monster, 'e was. My lady doesn't need another man like 'im."

Nigel's heart stopped beating. "Another man like him?" he asked slowly.

"He liked to hurt her somethin' fierce, milord, and far too often. And 'e'd not let me call a surgeon. 'E'd sooner let 'er die than 'elp 'er, 'e'd said."

Mercer had better be in hell.

"Go back to your lady." His voice trembled with rage. Damn the false mask of Dionysus. Damn his own failings. He should join Lord Mercer in hell. He should suffer for her marriage to that bastard and the pain he'd unwittingly led *his* beautiful little dove into.

"Milord?" The maid's eyes nearly popped out of her head.

"Go!" he ordered, his sanity threatening to crumble. "Help the doctor make her comfortable. I will return to the bedchamber in an hour with the vicar. Do not doubt this. I will marry your lady today."

Elsbeth's vision swam in and out of focus. She blinked; her eyelids felt as thick as a wool blanket. Her body didn't feel at all steady. One arm seemed too long, the other too short.

Edgeware was there, caressing her hand.

She furrowed her brows—at least she thought that was what she had done. Edgeware was dressed in a highly ornate light blue coat. She couldn't fathom why he would be dressed in such finery. His cravat cascaded in a multitude of starched waves. And he looked very, very serious.

Too serious.

Oh . . . dear. Was she drooling?

They had plied her with laudanum. That was a certainty. As a child she'd once fallen ill with a terrible fever. The doctor had kept pouring the opium concoction down her gullet while bleeding her dry.

She was lucky she had not died.

Unlike now. She must be dying from that silly, stray bullet. Why else would the local vicar be standing beside Nigel, incanting some terribly formal-sounding ceremony? Though she couldn't seem to make her drowsy mind concentrate on his words for more than a sentence or two, she could tell by his tone that he was performing a ceremony.

". . . charge you both, as ye will answer at the dreadful day of judgment when the secrets of all hearts shall be disclosed, that if either of you know any impediment, why ye may not be lawfully joined together . . ." his droning words trailed away.

Wait a blessed minute!

The vicar was asking a question . . . an important question. She really needed to tell him what she had unsuccessfully tried to confess to Nigel earlier under that sprawling oak.

My, that tree was enormous.

No, if those men were discussing the wedding engagement, she really needed to stay sharp.

"I cannot marry Lord Edgeware," she said. They must have understood her words, which was saying something since she could barely understand her slurred speech herself.

Edgeware sent her a quelling look that really disrupted her concentration. He gently squeezed her hand. His touch comforted her.

The vicar, who was the image of George, placed his hand on her arm and gentled his expression. "What are you saying, my dear?"

"I cannot marry. I-I tried to explain to him already this morning."

"You *cannot?* But I thought—" He turned to Edgeware. "The-the lady is unwilling?"

"She is confused, Vicar. Please proceed."

But the vicar didn't seem at all pleased. He gently shook her arm, rousing her from another batch of wandering thoughts. "Speak, my lady."

The room shifted and swam around. But she was determined.

There was no need to be embarrassed, she told herself. The only other people in the room, at least visible to her, were Molly and Doctor Pryor . . . nice man.

Wait, what did she need to say?

"I am barren," she blurted out.

"I . . . see . . ." The vicar drew out those two words. At least it sounded like he had drawn them out. But in her drugged state, she couldn't be too certain of anything.

Edgeware bent down and kissed her on the cheek.

"It doesn't matter," she could have sworn she heard him say.

Nigel lurked in the butler's pantry, the tiny room that served as a corridor between the kitchen and the dining hall. The hall just beyond the door echoed with voices. The guests at the house party were undoubtedly dissecting every tidbit of information they knew regarding the "hunting mishap" while waiting for their host to arrive and supper to be served.

In no way did he want to join his guests gathered in there, but it was beyond rude—though forgivable considering the circumstances—that he hadn't attended to them earlier. As host, he should have sought them out and offered reassuring words.

He had not.

And now he had to face them—those vultures—with the knowledge that they had already filled those nosey heads of theirs with a plethora of servant gossip.

He took a sip from the glass in his hand and gave a nod to the two footmen who had arrived with bottles of Nigel's best wine.

"Good evening," he said in a booming voice as he stepped into the dining hall. "Supper will be served in a trice. But first, I would like to raise our glasses in a toast." He paused, giving time for the footmen to make their way around the table to fill the spiral-stemmed crystal goblets.

The room fell silent. All eyes turned to Nigel. George appeared especially perplexed and perhaps a bit out of favor with his friend at the moment.

"What the bloody hell is this nonsense about?" Uncle Charles muttered as Nigel took his place at the head of the table next to him.

Nigel raised his glass and gave all his guests a smile to placate them. They followed, lifting their wine goblets in the air, with a variety of confused emotions coloring their faces.

"I wish to offer a toast to my new bride, who because of the accident this morning sadly cannot join us tonight."

"Bride?" nearly every guest at the table echoed.

"Elsbeth, the former dowager Lady Mercer, now the Marchioness of Edgeware, and I were wed this afternoon in a private ceremony. I hope you'll join me in taking a drink to my bride's quick recovery and our future happiness."

A delicate crystal goblet dropped to the table, shattering. The amber liquid soaked into the lace tablecloth.

Nigel lowered his hand and met Charlie's burning glare.

After a rather awkward supper and an even longer couple of hours in the drawing room listening to the disappointed young women entertain the guests with performances on the pianoforte, Nigel was finally able to escape into the cool night air on the terrace. Each and every mama in the drawing room watched his departure, frowning deeply and their eyes angry.

"A hunter's stray bullet?" George asked from the darkness.

Nigel started at the voice, but quickly regained his composure. He leaned against a marble column. "The hunting party was traipsing through my open fields . . . on the opposite side of the estate. If this were a hunter, it was human prey he was after."

"Our villain becomes more bold, Edgeware."

Nigel tightened his fist, not able to stop himself from imagining the terrible fate that had nearly befallen his Elsbeth. "These attempts on my life must be linked back to the smugglers who used my beach the other night. Perhaps I'm a damned inconvenience to them, so the blackguards feel justified in resorting to murder. What a lucrative business they must have."

"I'm not at all convinced that local smugglers are involved with this treachery."

"You don't need to be convinced." He threw his arms up in frustration. "You aren't the one they are trying to kill. Your wife wasn't shot this morning. I have a plan to trap those outlaws, to smoke them out. And I intend to personally witness the hanging of every single person involved."

"Be reasonable, Edgeware."

"They will hang. I vow it."

"And what if the people you hope to entrap are your villagers? The men and women who have grown up with you? What if they are only trying to make a living during tough times?"

"What do you know of this?" So George *had* been holding back information. Nigel should have pressed him harder in London when his friend's reluctance to speak on the matter first arose. If he had, Elsbeth's life might have never been endangered.

"Nothing . . . nothing of import, Edgeware. A rumor here and there, is all." George withdrew back into the shadows of the terrace. "I feel the need to scold you, though. I thought you were my friend."

"I am. What the devil does our friendship have to do with anything?"

"I would have thought you'd want a friend to stand up with you at your marriage . . ."

"Oh, the marriage." That was the last thing he wanted to discuss.

"According to Lady Olivia, your bride had been given a healthy draught of laudanum and was quite insensible all day. I wonder, does the new marchioness yet know of her elevated position?"

How was Elsbeth going to respond to the news of their hasty nuptials? Nigel had no clue. And though that singular worry had been gnawing at him all evening, it wasn't something he was willing to admit to anyone. Not even to George.

With a shrug filled with aristocratic arrogance, he turned on his heel and walked away.

Perhaps he needed to find a new friend, one with a lesser ability to scour out details. But, in truth, he would never wish to trade George for some mindless dolt.

"I can imagine any woman's ire when she discovers she was duped into a marriage, no matter how favorable the terms may be for her." George chuckled. "Do you desire to have a second stand up with you when you tell her? The duel that will most assuredly occur promises to be terribly dangerous . . . for you, Edgeware."

Chapter Seventeen

The next morning Elsbeth sat up groggily in bed. Her side, stiff and angry, punished her for the movement.

"Will you be needin' another draught o' the laudanum?" Molly, who was fussing by the bedside, was quick to inquire.

"No, please, no." Her mouth tasted as if she'd swallowed a down-filled pillow during the night. "Plain water, if you please."

Molly crossed the room to where a silver pitcher of water sat ready on a tray. "Brings back un'appy memories, this does." She clicked her tongue.

Elsbeth agreed. Too many distressing memories were stirring, triggered by all too familiar twinges of pain and helplessness. At least she no longer had a husband to contend with. At least she was free to tend to her injury in peace.

"The ladies Olivia and Lauretta 'ave been pesterin' me all morning to see you," Molly said after she pressed a glass of cool water into Elsbeth's fingers. She helped Elsbeth lift the drink to her lips.

"I think I would like my hair braided first." She savored the tiny swallow of water and was ready for more when an even greater need suddenly plagued her. "Um, I believe I require a hand getting out of bed, as well." She gave a meaningful glance toward the screened area in the corner where the chamber pot was hidden.

"Just like old times, milady," Molly clucked sadly as she helped her mistress cross the room. Her eyes darkened. "That reminds me. That dastardly Lord Edgeware demands to have a word wit' you as well."

My, Molly had certainly taken a quick dislike to the dark lord. "You don't approve of the Marquess?" Elsbeth asked after settling back into the bed.

" 'E's a bleedin' *man*, ain't 'e?"

Elsbeth's first instinct was to agree, but Lord Edgeware was so different from any man she'd ever known. She rather liked him—a realization that threatened to suck all the air from her chest.

"You better let my exuberant cousins in to see me now," Elsbeth said as she fought to steady her breath.

Molly nodded to her mistress, and opened the door.

Olivia pushed her way in the room first with Lauretta not far behind.

"Oh Elly, we were so very worried," Olivia cried. Fat tears dripped down her rosy cheeks. "You will live, though? Despite what everyone is saying?"

"Yes, my dear, I believe I will live. Who is saying I am dying?" She took Olivia's hand and squeezed it.

"La, all the guests are saying you must surely be dying." Lauretta rushed forward. "They are saying that is the only reason Lord Edgeware would marry you."

"Beautiful girls." She caressed her cousins' bright cheeks. They were dears to worry after her so. "I am firm on my conviction. I will not marry Edgeware. I will not leave you."

Olivia and Lauretta shared a silent frown.

"But-but Elly—"

"No, Olivia, my mind is set."

"How could she not know?" Lauretta asked.

Olivia shrugged prettily and then drew Elsbeth's hands into her own. "Elly, Lord Edgeware and you were married yesterday."

Married? Ice ran through Elsbeth's blood.

The golden band encircling her ring finger served as proof. How could he do this to her? Without her consent? Without a license?

Devils and demons, she was plagued. She was doomed to be unhappy.

Molly pulled the curtains open. The light crimson color of the morning sky was darkening thanks to a line of encroaching storm clouds. Lord Mercer had once given her a painting that had captured such a sky.

"You will enjoy the colors," he had said when he'd handed her the carefully wrapped package. That had been years ago when she still believed he was the artist. Foolish, blind child, she had once been, she had believed that a heartless man could create such wondrous works of art.

"You will enjoy the colors," he had said. The colors in the landscape were indeed beautiful. But the brushstrokes were quick slashes of frustration. An ancient ruin sat on a distant hill, awash in a bath of golden sunlight. The ruin's stone walls crumbling into the lush grasses. A tree, its pale bark scarred and its branches twisted from years of enduring storms, dominated the forefront. Only a few branches still supported life. A rocky creek frothed as it forced its way through countryside and threatened the roots of the dying tree.

When she'd seen the painting for the first time, tears had sprung to her eyes.

She should have known the truth right there and then. For all her husband saw in the painting was a collection of colors. While she had seen into the artist's soul and loved him all the more for his ability to share his beautiful soul with the world.

And yet Edgeware . . . Edgeware, so different from her Lord Mercer, had merely thought the painting in his drawing room was no more than a "pretty splattering of colors".

Dionysus . . . *Dionysus* . . . whoever he was, she needed to

know why he would dupe her into yet another loveless marriage. Why did he need her to be the subject in yet another
heartrending scene?

Why did he hate her so? What did she ever do to him to earn
his scorn?

"Elsbeth?" Edgeware's voice startled her. "You are crying?"

She tore her gaze from the window and glanced around the
room. Her cousins were gone. Even Molly had slipped away,
leaving her alone with him. It was now proper. According to her
cousins, he was her husband now.

"No, my lord," she said with a sniffle.

"No?" He dried her cheeks with a soft handkerchief anyhow.
"It would please me if you would call me by my given name,
Elsbeth. I am Nigel, if you recall." He settled into a chair beside
the bed. "I will not insist, though."

Molly had propped Elsbeth up in the bed with several pillows
and fixed her hair into a loose braid that neither pulled nor
pinched. But even so, she was uncomfortable.

"Was it legal, my lord?" she asked, not ready to speak with
him with the familiarity and intimacy that should be shared
between a husband and wife. She didn't trust him yet. And
worse, she didn't trust herself.

Edgeware frowned as he studied his nails. They were buffed
and well cared for.

"I mean, my lord, there were no banns read. I cannot imagine
there had been time to secure a special license."

"Does it matter?" he asked, still not turning his attentions
from those utterly clean nails.

Does it matter? She couldn't believe he'd ask such a question.
Of course it mattered. It mattered to God, to society, to
herself . . . she snuffed the angry response that was ready to fly
out of her mouth. She would do well to remember this man was
now her husband, and required to be treated accordingly.

"I ask," he said, "simply because I want you to know that it doesn't matter to me. If the vicar is unable to convince the bishop for special consideration in this matter, I am willing to repeat the ceremony . . . a hundred times if need be." He turned to her then. "My only desire is to have you as my wife, Elsbeth."

The heat of his gaze made her feel all the more trapped. Lord Mercer had wanted her like that, too. Like a possession. That was all she had been to him. A pretty possession. If not for the paintings . . .

"You didn't wish for this marriage," he said.

She turned away, unable to bear gazing into his black eyes while thinking of Dionysus. Instead, she stared out the window again and at the lightly tinted sky that reminded her of the artist she'd fallen in love with, the same artist who'd sought to destroy her.

The storm clouds had blown closer.

"Why the silence? Why don't you scold me?" Edgeware asked. "Why don't you blister my ears for acting against your wishes? Why do you hold back the anger I see dancing behind your eyes?"

"No," she whispered, closing those same betraying eyes. His tone had grown sharper, bitter almost. The pretty, loving words he'd spoken to her only yesterday were now gone. They'd faded away just as they had with Lord Mercer.

"Is it because you're afraid of me? Afraid I will fly into a rage and hurt you like that damnable Lord Mercer?"

She shook her head from side to side, all the while tears spilled from behind her tightly sealed eyelids.

"Are you afraid I won't wish to ever hear a cross word leave your lips? Afraid I will punish you on a whim?"

She attempted to fight a sob. Failing, she hid her face in her hands and cried in earnest.

"Men like Lord Mercer are cowards. Sniveling, worthless cowards." He pried her hands away from her face and caressed her cheeks again with that soft handkerchief of his. "Cry, scream, curse me. You may chase me from the room. You may wound my heart. But you will never so prick my anger that I would raise a hand to harm you. *Never.*"

Words. How many earnest-sounding words had Lord Mercer plied her with? How many lies had he freely given her?

"I cannot give you a child," she said with a sob in her voice. She pushed his hands away, not able to bear the sensual feel of his touch and not remember the heaven he'd introduced her to the other night. She needed to be strong against him, for no other option was palatable. "Nor can I give you love. I have no fortune. I have no property. I have nothing for you. Nothing. We aren't even properly married."

His lips pulled into a strained smile. "I see."

"Begging your pardon, I do not think you do. No matter how you badger me or weave your seductive charm, I do not want you. I will not have you. I will not let this marriage stand."

He drew a deep breath and rose from the dainty bedside chair. There was anguish, pure Dionysus-styled anguish in the way his shoulders sagged against the weight of her anger. He gave her a shallow bow and, without another word, left her alone in the bedchamber.

Nigel longed to have a paintbrush in his hand, to create in stains and dark pigments a solid image of the fresh torment cutting into his soul. This need, this unquenchable desire to paint was intruding into his daily life, something that had never happened before. And quite frankly, it shocked him to the core. His stormy relationship with Elsbeth was beginning to unravel the barriers he'd spent years constructing between Dionysus and himself.

For his sanity and hers, he should leave her alone. He shouldn't press his company upon her.

A lump rose in his throat.

He would do anything, anything short of letting the marriage dissolve, to return a bit of happiness to Elsbeth's life.

"Lord Edgeware," someone called out to him as he went briskly through the hall. "Lord Edgeware! I must have a word!"

Nigel ignored the call. He didn't have the energy to deal with the guests anymore. He should send them all home. The party was over.

But if he ordered them to leave, would Elsbeth find a way to escape with them? No banns had been read, no special license procured. If she were to contest the wedding, she would win. But in winning, she would be forever ruined in the eyes of the *ton*. What with the nude painting and having being caught in an indiscretion, her reputation couldn't survive another scandal. The guests would simply have to stay to act as a buffer until she accepted that.

He threw open the front doors and headed toward the stables. A storm was rising. A sharp wind rushed toward the dark clouds approaching from the south.

Elsbeth would have her way. Though he couldn't let her go, she would not suffer from his wicked presence. He would suffer alone. And apart.

Dionysus would bear the pain, not the Marquess of Edgeware. Never would he allow that powerful and important figure the luxury of suffering again.

He stiffened his shoulders and picked up the pace as he rounded the corner of the manor.

A sharp pain jolted him.

He stumbled to his knees.

"Elsbeth," he cried, as his face hit a paving stone.

★ ★ ★ ★ ★

"Edgeware." A hand slapped his cheek.

Nigel moaned.

"Edgeware." A second slap followed.

"What is this? What are you doing to the Marquess?" A new voice demanded. One he recognized.

"George?"

"A man attacked Edgeware. Hit him on the head," said the man who'd been slapping him. "I frightened him away before he could do more." That was Severin. Nigel recognized his voice now.

"And who was this phantom?" George demanded.

Nigel pried open one eye, a hellishly difficult task.

"I don't know. A kerchief covered his face," Severin said. "Thank God, Edgeware, you are revived."

Nigel blinked, forcing both eyes open. "Which way did he run?" he at least had enough wits to ask.

"That way," Severin pointed toward a path that followed the foundation of the manor house around to the back. "Did you see anyone, George? You came from that direction."

"No, there was no one on the path."

"Help me stand," Nigel said. His blood was beginning to boil over the villain's boldness. His anger quickly cleared his head, leaving only a dull ache.

Severin offered his hand and pulled Nigel to his feet. All three men started off down the trail.

"This is foolish," George was quick to say. "We won't find the villain hiding in the bushes."

"Then where is he?" Severin stopped in the middle of the path and poked his finger against George's chest. "You should have seen him."

"*I* should have seen him? Tell me, Lord Ames, why were you stalking Edgeware in the first place?"

Nigel crossed his arms and stayed out of the argument. It was quite possible that one of his friends was lying. Which meant, either Severin or George could be involved in the plot against him and also possibly responsible for Elsbeth's injury. But the very idea that someone he trusted and cared for would betray him was unthinkable.

Damn his throbbing head. It was keeping him from being able to think straight.

"Well, Severin?" George pressed.

Severin's jaw tightened. He hesitated for far too long before quickly saying, "I was trying to catch a moment alone with Edgeware." He cursed under his breath. "I spent the morning with Lady Lauretta—all in innocence, Edgeware, I swear. She is worried. Lady Mercer . . . um . . . um . . . her cousin . . . your wife, oh hell, Lady Lauretta doesn't believe her cousin wished to marry you. She called out to you in the hall. But she was in no state to be speaking with you."

"In no state?" Nigel asked.

"She . . . um . . . she said she wanted to bash you in the head like you did to me." Severin smiled sheepishly rubbing his bruised eye. "I told her I would give you a . . . um . . . a nobber for her myself."

"Ah-ha! He admits it." George rounded on Severin. "He admits that he was planning to ambush you."

"Were you?" Nigel tentatively touched the sore lump on the base of his neck. *"Did you?"*

"No! I was planning to talk with you while giving Lady Lauretta time to compose herself."

Nigel continued a few steps down the path, not sure what to think. If not Severin, then he'd be forced to return his suspicions back to George.

He rolled his eyes heavenward. That's when he saw, quite by happenstance, that one of the glass doors leading into his study was open. "Our villain's escape route, I suspect," he said with a nod to the door.

Neither George nor Severin seemed satisfied by the discovery. Both still eyed the other with suspicion.

"M'lord! M'lord!" Joshua came sprinting up. The groom's face was stark and pale, his breathing erratic.

What now? He had enough troubles to tend to; he certainly didn't need any more.

"M'lord, you must come to the stables," Joshua shouted. *"He-he's dead!"*

Chapter Eighteen

A few hours after sunset, Guthrie, the large footman who still longed after the gold sovereign Elsbeth had offered him earlier, volunteered to carry her to the small and generally ignored parlor at front of the manor house—a house Elsbeth still had a difficult time thinking of as her new home.

The bullet wound seemed so trivial, so minor when compared to how her body would ache after one of Lord Mercer's rages. Compared to the past, she barely noticed the biting sting in her side. And lying abed all day while contemplating her future was threatening her sanity. She needed a change in scenery to take her mind off the dangerously handsome Lord Edgeware, if only for a little while.

Even though Molly had begrudgingly given her approval, she remained in the small parlor, fussing like a nervous nursemaid with a newborn, until Lauretta arrived and sent Molly away. Elsbeth's young cousin appeared to be in a black mood. Once they were alone, she slumped on a small settee near the fireplace and cradled her chin in her hands. "He's a monster!" Lauretta wailed.

"Who is?" she demanded, with a measure of alarm. Had Lauretta fallen prey to Lord Ames again? Elsbeth was half out of the royal blue velvet chaise lounge Guthrie had placed her on and fully prepared to confront Lord Ames. He had no right to push his attentions on a young, innocent—

"Lord Edgeware, of course. Who else could I mean?" Lauretta said with an unladylike groan.

"Oh! Edgeware." Elsbeth settled back onto the chaise. Her stitches burned from moving too quickly. *"My husband."* Those two words got stuck in the back of her throat and threatened to choke her. She coughed. Like the marriage ceremony she couldn't remember, she couldn't seem to free herself from the lump that formed every time she happened to think about the dark lord—*her* dark lord. Her pulse sped and her cheeks heated as a memory of their wicked encounter in his study rose unbidden in her mind.

The memory felt as foreign to her as the bullet wound. Had she really touched him so brazenly? She seemed to recall trying to tear his shirt from his firm chest. But no, that couldn't be right. She would never be so—so—*hungry* for a man's attentions.

He was a man, a man with her future nestled in the palm of his hands, after all. She shouldn't be spending her time wishing for his return. But blast it, for the life of her she couldn't seem to think of much else.

Much to Elsbeth's relief, Lauretta helped to take her mind off the tempting Lord Edgeware. Her cousin spent most of the evening sharing her opinion of the house's décor—too dark and gloomy for her tastes—imparting gossip, and detailing the excitements of the day. Some of the guests had apparently decided to stay until the end of the week. A few had even confessed to harboring morbid hopes being part of the dangerous drama that was unfolding. Most of the gentlemen had spent the day hunting, while the ladies played cards in the parlor. Lady Dashborough had caused somewhat of a stir after Olivia had accused the lady of cheating. Despite everything, Lady Waver was still an unflappable hostess. Elsbeth was grateful to hear it. She didn't think she was up to taking responsibility for the household or its guests so quickly.

But the topic soon returned to Edgeware. Anger sharpened Lauretta's tongue when she recounted how the dark lord had punched Lord Ames in the face shortly after he'd been discovered alone with Lauretta in the portrait gallery. "Honestly, Elsbeth, Lord Ames was a perfect gentleman. And yet, your Lord Edgeware attacked him. The man is a brute, a monster. Papa will surely assist you in gaining an annulment. Imagine, trapping you into marriage like he did. He is a scoundrel, naught more than a common scoundrel."

Her cousin's venom should have fed Elsbeth's dark feelings toward the man who had forced her into a marriage she would have never agreed to, but it didn't. All she could think of was the honest, open way he had pursued her, how he'd asked to hold her hand, how he'd asked to be granted that first kiss, how he'd even warned her that he'd planned to seduce her.

He was different from any man she had ever met. For one thing, he was careful around her. He acted as if he cherished her feelings. At least that was until they were married yesterday.

Oh bugger, not that she cared, but after his brief morning visit, he hadn't given her the consideration of his company. He'd not even asked after her welfare. So much like Lord Mercer, he'd snagged the prize, and now it appeared he was quickly losing interest.

"Perhaps an annulment would be possible," Elsbeth said, but saying it aloud only made her feel all the more miserable.

Edgeware was a villain, a rake, a cad, a scoundrel . . . a man. What woman in her right mind would wish to be saddled to such a combination of ill manners? She *was not* lonely for him. She *did not* miss his company. Truly, she didn't. Damn the demon to hell. Damn him. Damn him. Damn—

"*Lauretta?* What did you say?"

"This afternoon, after Lord Ames frightened off the fiend who'd hit Lord Edgeware from behind with a sack of rocks,"

Lauretta repeated. "I said, Mr. Waver had the audacity to accuse Lord Ames of plotting to stick Edgeware's spoon in the wall."

"Someone attacked Edgeware this afternoon?" Guilt. Pure, uncomfortable guilt buzzed in Elsbeth's head. What had she done? She'd cursed a man whose life was in mortal peril. What kind of woman had she become?

Damn him for turning her into a shrew. No, no, forget that prayer. Protect him from harm, instead. Curses, how could she continue protecting her heart from him when his life was in constant danger?

"Indeed," Lauretta said, "it happened right outside the manor's front entranceway. Knocked over the head with a sack of rocks and would have been done in if Lord Ames hadn't happened upon the villain, too! And the Marquess's butler—" Lauretta shook her head slowly. "They found him dead in the stables. Strangled, I heard someone say. I shiver at the thought."

Strangled?

Poor Edgeware. He must be devastated over the death of his butler. Unlike Lord Mercer, Edgeware seemed to truly care about his servant's welfare.

Dionysus must have gone mad. For who else could be behind this plot against Lord Edgeware? And where did Charlie fit in all this? Did she still believe he was Dionysus?

Her heart said no. But if not Charlie, who?

Action. That was what was needed. She needed to act. She needed to stop Dionysus from further endangering either of them. She was struggling to get out of the chaise again when the parlor's pocket door slid open.

"I beg your pardon, Lady Lauretta. I need to have a word in private with my wife."

Careful of her wound, Elsbeth twisted toward the door until her gaze met Edgeware's. Shadows haunted his onyx eyes.

She was surprised to see him. It was late. The sun had set hours ago. He was still dressed for dinner and entertaining guests, in a fine black coat and contrasting snowy-white cravat. Her heart skipped a beat at the sight of him, giving her cause to curse that tender organ for being so easily won over.

He lingered at the door, waiting for her permission to enter even though this was his home, not hers.

Lauretta stood. "Please, do excuse me," she said sharply and made a quick retreat, passing by Edgeware without even a nod of recognition.

With a look of amusement, Lord Edgeware watched Lauretta flounce down the hall with a bouncing, angry stride. He shrugged and stepped into the room. "May I join you?"

Elsbeth stared at him, standing so straight and noble just a step inside the door. He seemed colder, more distant. More like she expected a husband to act. But not at all how she wished *him* to act.

"Of course, my lord. This is your home," she said with a sigh. "However, I pray you have not come expecting to claim your marital rights," she added, feeling her irritation surge.

A brow rose at that. "Ah . . . is that what you believe?" He tilted his head slightly as he studied her. His intense gaze lapped at her body like flames from a fire. "And how are your injuries faring today, my lady wife?"

Did he care, or had he come to her truly expecting to consummate the marriage tonight?

She couldn't help but wonder what it would be like to lie with Edgeware in his bed. Surely, the enjoyment she felt from their passionate encounter in his study was nothing more than an aberration, a fantastic deviation from reality. She still couldn't convince herself that what she'd felt at his hands was nothing more than a heated dream. She knew she shouldn't hope that she would ever forget herself so completely again. She wasn't comfortable with her body. According to Lord Mercer, her hips were too thin and her breasts too small. And she was impossibly cold. Hers wasn't a body that could give pleasure to a man.

"I believe I will live, my lord," she said sharply. "However, I do not believe I am up to any strenuous exertions to my person."

"I see."

She closed her eyes and tried to slow her erratic breathing. Prickly nerves were leading her into dangerous territory. She needed to calm down. But she was finding it nearly impossible to do so while a war was waging within her heart. She wanted him to touch her, to caress her, to *love* her. She wanted everything he could possibly give her. She wanted to feel him move over her and press her deep into his thick mattress.

But no . . .

She didn't think she was strong enough to endure the look of disappointment she'd find in his eyes after bedding her. Her frigid body would inevitably disappoint him. And that disappointment would eventually lead to loathing and resentment.

The situation was impossible! Why had he married her? He barely even knew her.

"Lauretta told me about your butler. I am truly sorry," she said carefully, hoping to turn the subject to a more pressing— and safer—topic.

Edgeware ground his jaw, clearly upset. "His death will be avenged." She felt the danger in his voice. It made the hair on the back of her neck rise. Her husband would make a formidable enemy.

"She also told me that you were attacked today. I pray you are well."

"Well enough." He rubbed the back of his neck as he took a half step toward her. They were still yards apart, not quite having to yell across a great expanse, but close. When he spoke, his voice was icy. "There is no reason for you to worry. I have the situation well in hand. In fact, I will be posting a footman at your chamber door."

"To keep me in or others out, my lord?"

Her sharp tone seemed to break through his icy demeanor. He heaved a long, audible sigh and took another step toward her chair by the fire. "Could you perhaps use my given name when you wish to curse me to the devil?"

"I cannot possibly know what you mean, *my lord.*"

He took another step toward her. Her heart rate quickened.

"I mean: the tone you use with me would be more palatable if you softened the blow by using my given name. It is Nigel, need I remind you? Not a terrible chore to trip up the tongue." He took yet another step toward her. He was standing nearly on top of her now. "I will not insist, though."

"Thank you—" she hesitated, unsure "—Lord Edgeware."

Fire flashed behind his eyes. "Elsbeth—" he bit off and stopped to heave another deep sigh. "I had come to apprise you of the situation and to assure you that you are in no danger. However, I see Lady Lauretta has already done so. Apparently, there is no other purpose for this meeting, so I will wish you a good night."

He turned. She'd thought he'd at least brush her cheek with a kiss. But he had not. Instead, he'd left her cold and more alone than before.

"My lord," she called out before he reached the door.

He stopped. Her heart counted the number of beats it took before he turned to face her again. "Yes?"

How could this sham of a marriage have any hope of working? The promise of long, miserable days appeared before her. This was not the future she had dreamed of when praying for her first husband's death, God forgive her.

But *this was* the future she was being offered.

Lord Edgeware was watching her. His dark expressive eyes mirrored her distress, her confusion. But there was also something else in that look he was giving her, something she wasn't yet ready to recognize. Deep in her heart she longed to believe that illusive *something* she was seeing might mean that there could be a safe, comfortable future waiting for her. A future where she could be happy. But to try and reach for it would mean she'd have to risk a heart she'd long protected. And yet, she had to try.

She wanted him to kiss her. *To love her.* But she didn't know how to ask for those things.

"*Nigel,*" she whispered.

She struggled to wrench the words she needed to say from deep within her heart, but they refused to come. She shook her head and waved him away. Her voice tightened again. "I am glad you came to talk with me. Good evening, my lord."

He stared at her, his brows furrowed. He just stood there, refusing to leave.

Her heart beat wildly in her chest, and she couldn't seem to catch her breath. She didn't know him, didn't understand his silent moods. Was he angry? Was he plotting to punish her? Or was his silence a kind of punishment?

Without a word of warning he stalked back over to where she was reclining. And before she could protest or pull away, he leaned down and brushed his lips across hers. His mouth tasted of brandy and spice. She sighed and leaned forward, seeking more, silently pleading for everything she couldn't find the courage to ask of him. His was a flavor she craved.

He cupped his hand at the nape of her neck and deepened the kiss. When she parted her lips, their tongues touched. He made love to her mouth with such exquisite care tears sprang to her eyes. She reached around his neck, pulling him closer, wanting everything he was willing to offer. And still, she was unsure how to ask—no, *demand*—that he give up his heart to her.

She barely kept herself from crying out when he slowly peeled his lips away. His jaw tightened and he looked so serious as he reached under her and carefully scooped her up into his arms, lifting her from her comfortable spot on the chaise lounge.

"What are you doing?" she gasped.

"Taking you to bed, my lady wife."

CHAPTER NINETEEN

Wind whipped up from the shore. Another storm was approaching, and this one promised to be worse than the one that had battered the coast only a few days earlier. Nigel stood for a moment at the edge of the cliff, watching the interplay of the billowy black clouds against the early morning sky.

"No smuggler will be foolish enough to brave the waters tonight. You can give your men a rest, Edgeware. All will be quiet," George said, as he approached the cliff's edge.

George, George. A sharp pain ripped into Nigel's chest.

Late last night he'd personally delivered Elsbeth to her bed, the narrow bed she'd been using all week. He'd been tempted to carry her away to his own chamber. But he doubted she would have allowed it. By the time he'd finished settling her beneath her bed's quilted counterpane, his whole body had ached to stay with her, to make love to her. But she was injured and weak. She needed her rest. She needed time to grow accustomed to the thought of being married to him.

Even so, he'd lingered just inside the door, wanting to crawl into her bed and sleep at her side. To rest, knowing she was in the same room as him, knowing that she was safe and well. He'd waited longer than he knew he should, hoping she'd invite him to stay. She didn't. Instead, she had called for her maid. With a heavy heart, he'd left.

And that was where Charlie had found him, just outside Elsbeth's chamber. His cousin had taken one look at him and pushed a bottle of French wine into his hands. *Smuggled* French wine.

"What the hell are you doing with this?" Nigel had demanded right before he'd herded his cousin into his study before anyone could see them. "Do you know what this looks like?" he demanded once they were alone.

"Nige, the bottle doesn't belong to me." A black look had darkened Charlie's normally jovial blue eyes. "I did a little poking around after Jenkins's body was discovered. I found this bottle, along with several more crates of illegal goods on George's estate."

Not willing to take his cousin at his word—not for this— Nigel went skulking through George's property. And like Charlie had said, he'd found crate after crate of smuggled goods in one of George's storerooms. The discovery struck him more sharply than a mortal blow to the chest.

Could it be true? Could George, one of the few men he trusted with his life, be behind the smuggling operation . . . and the attempts on his life . . . and the attempt on Elsbeth's life . . . and his butler's murder? He'd sat up all night trying to figure out what he should do, how he should approach George. And still, he had no answers. Friend or not, the men responsible for those crimes would hang.

"This wind is ruining my cravat," Charlie said as he joined them. He seemed to have no interest in the sky, the cliff, or the conversation. He found a stump and, after cleaning away the dirt and debris with a handkerchief, plopped down onto it and began poking at the soft ground with a twig.

Nigel wished Charlie and George would both just vanish for a while. Neither man was looking much like a hero this morning. Last night, after presenting Nigel with George's smuggled bottle of wine, Charlie had once again resumed his begging for money. He'd claimed he needed close to thirty thousand pounds for a solid investment. An investment whose details he had refused to disclose.

Nigel dug his fingers into his palm. The last time he'd declined to pay Charlie a large sum to pay for some supposedly *solid* investment, the money had disappeared from his accounts all the same.

That Charlie, his harmless cousin, would stoop low enough to rob him to pay off what was more likely a reckless gambling debt than some thought-out investment—and was no doubt plotting to do so again—only pricked his already ravaged nerves.

I'm overrun by betrayals!

Tonight.

Tonight, according to Charlie, the villagers were saying that the smugglers were planning to land again with their booty. "You will see then, Nige, who your true friends are," he'd said.

Nigel flexed his hand, his need for the relief only a paintbrush could provide him, growing urgent. Images of George being led to the gallows for murder—for brutally killing his butler, an innocent man who'd deserved better, he'd lead the bastard up the roughhewn stairs himself—and images of Charlie flirting shamelessly with Elsbeth while frittering away the Edgeware fortune joined the storm-whipped wind, echoing accusations in his ear.

"Enough!" he shouted.

George and Charlie, who'd been silent for quite some time, both jumped.

"Edgeware?"

"Are you quite cracked, Nige?"

Nigel turned to the two men he'd once trusted with his life and felt a strong urge to do murder. Whose? He couldn't say.

Logic dictated he wait for tonight and catch the smugglers in the act. He needed proof. And, thanks to his uncle's tutelage, Nigel was a ruthlessly logical man except when it came to his wife.

"Elsbeth," he said and abruptly turned back toward the house. This was too much for him to handle on his own. Whether she welcomed his company or not, he needed her.

After winning another heated argument with Molly, Elsbeth had risen from bed, and despite the pulling pain in her side, donned a light yellow morning gown and made her way to the breakfast room. A footman brought her a plate of toast and jams as she eased into a chair in the empty room. From where she sat at the small table, next to a series of large windows that looked out into the estate's gardens, she could see the sham ruin dedicated to the goddess Athena where Lord Edgeware— no, he was to be Nigel to her now—where Nigel had first looked upon her with that wolfish gleam.

And kissed her.

It hadn't been just a gentle brush of the lips, as he had promised. She pressed the tips of her fingers to her lips, remembering.

That kiss, and all the others that followed, demanded very little and had been like a series of silent pleas. Like his mouth was inviting her to return his passion with the same intensity— offering, instead of taking.

Gracious, she'd allowed her caution to be lulled by his subtle appeal. His seduction had appeared so seemingly harmless. In his study she'd given him her body and look what that had won her, an unwanted marriage with a man who was a bigger danger to her than her first husband.

It was true that Lord Mercer was a beast, but at least she'd realized early on in their marriage that he was not Dionysus— and not a man whom she could ever love. No matter how he had tormented her or tortured her—her heart had always been safe.

With Nigel, that layer of safety was slipping away. He was as different from the late Lord Mercer as day was from night. When angered, he might not throw her to the mercy of his friends like a master would toss a piece of meat to his hounds. It was worse. When she gazed into Nigel's expressive eyes she could almost feel his soul and a deep sense of loneliness. She could almost hear in his clipped voice the grieving, confused boy who'd lost his mother at birth and his father at the tender age of three or four.

This was a man who could rival Dionysus in his depths of feeling. This was a man who could tempt her heart. Such a man had the power to destroy her, for like Dionysus, she felt herself tumbling into love.

"Elsbeth!" Nigel's sharp voice carried down the halls shattering her thoughts. "Elsbeth!" She turned toward the door in time to see the servants fleeing the room.

"Lord Edge—Nigel," she said. Her heart raced at the sight of him. "What urgency has you shouting my name through the halls of your estate like a madman, or is this how you plan to call for your wife . . . my lord?"

He eased the door closed behind him and started toward her. With each step the coiled tension in him appeared to melt away. His hunched shoulders began to relax.

"Elsbeth," he said her name without heat this time. "Things are—I need—uh, we need to talk."

She set the toast she was holding back on the plate in front of her. "Yes, I suppose we should."

He settled into a chair next to hers and took his time drawing off his gloves. With a sigh, he reached out to touch her hand. "Dionysus," he said and paused. "There is something I need to confess."

He was going to reveal Dionysus's identity at last. But she wasn't ready to hear it, not when she was nearly convinced Dionysus was Charlie. Her heart wasn't ready to face that sad

211

truth, not this morning when her injuries had left her feeling weak and her feelings muddled. "I don't want to hear his name. Please, not now. He's a bounder who has threatened your life and coldly murdered your butler. As long as you recognize him for the villain that he is, that is all I need to know."

"But—"

"No," she said and sandwiched his hand between her own. "I will not give him the power to hurt me again. From now on, I will decide my own future . . . and with whom I intend to spend it. Edgewa—Nigel, you have been kind to me."

"Kind?" he sounded hurt by the charge.

"You have given me a great gift. You make me feel almost loveable. But, still, I do not know what kind of wife I will make you."

"Do not worry about the future, dove. I will make everything right, I promise I will. And I will make you happy." He sounded so confoundingly sure of himself. "You will love me. And after tonight, everything will be—"

"No, it won't," she said not letting him finish. She didn't want to love him. It would be safer not to love him, not to open her heart up for rejection or pain. It would be safer to give him no hope for the future. Perhaps then he would release her from this spell he was weaving around her.

"Please, Elsbeth, let me explain what's—"

"Lord Mercer was a difficult man," she said, looking away. That much was true. And the lie that followed came easily to her lips. "I don't know if my heart survived the encounter. I don't know if I am able to feel the feelings I should feel toward a husband. It simply doesn't seem possible." She drew an unsteady breath. "I beg you reconsider our marriage."

"No." He stood with a rush, almost knocking his chair over backwards. Pain flashed in his eyes, but he quickly concealed it. His voice hardened. "My marriage to you, though shabbily executed, is a decision I will never regret. If it takes a lifetime, I will make you understand that."

There was something about his determination that set her heart throbbing again. And it frightened her.

"Please," her voice cracked with emotion. "Please, I beg you. Leave me alone."

He lowered his head and turned away. He had the door open and was nearly in the hallway by the time she found her voice again.

"The bullet the other day," she asked. "Are you certain it was meant for you?" She no longer was. It was becoming more and more clear that Charlie viewed her relationship with Nigel as a roadblock to his riches.

"The danger will soon be gone." His voice was hard, clipped. "I have a plan to trap the villain."

"And Charlie?" she pressed. "You still trust him?"

Nigel waved his hand angrily as he retreated down the hall. "Charlie's harmless."

No, blast it! She had to bite her tongue to keep herself from shouting. *Charlie has never been harmless!*

Charlie was the one who had always found the liquor cabinet key whenever she would hide it from Lord Mercer. And he was the one who'd often provoked the worst of Lord Mercer's violent rages, especially when he knew the drunken lord would take his frustrations out on her. Charlie seemed to enjoy watching her torment, seemed to enjoy watching the events unfold like a drama at the theater. And once he'd almost . . . No, she wasn't going to think about that. He was a danger she needed to stop, for Nigel's sake and her own. Which meant, she needed to go to him.

To confront him.

Her breakfast forgotten, she found a footman in the front hall where a confusion of activity was occurring. A group of guests, anxious to return to London to personally spread the news of Nigel's surprise marriage, were leaving that morning. Several of the rooms in the sprawling house were soon going to be vacant. Elsbeth knew she shouldn't be surprised. If she hadn't been shot or entangled in marriage, she would have fled days ago.

She considered sending her cousins home. She had no right to keep them here with a murderous artist on the loose. But the thought of being alone with her husband was too much to bear. Much to her relief, not everyone was leaving Purbeck Manor. Lady Dashborough and her daughters, Mister George Waver, Lord Ames, and *Charlie* with his motley group of friends had all announced their intentions of staying until the end of the week, which was just two days away.

Gracious, there was so much that needed to be done.

"Can you tell me where Mister Charles Purbeck could be found?" she asked the startled footman.

He eyed her cautiously, seeming uncertain about how to approach the new marchioness. "In the library I believe, m'lady," he drawled after a long pause. He bowed deeply before returning to his duties.

She was still watching the nervous footman when she turned and slammed into Sir Donald's side. He'd been rushing toward the stairs and, like her, apparently had his mind on other matters. He seemed to shake himself out of his thoughts as he turned his gaze toward her.

He was a handsome young man. His features had all the aristocratic angles that often caught the attention of the ladies in the London parlors. She couldn't remember ever seeing him not dressed in the height of fashion. He was tall and muscular and very much in command of himself. But there was something about his all-too steady gaze this morning that made her shudder.

"Lady Edgeware." He stomped his boot on the hardwood

floor as he turned to regard her more closely. "You look exceedingly healthy considering the . . . um . . . circumstances." He
fingered that rather large watch fob he always wore. "Charlie
has been most distressed over the shooting, you must know. He
believes the mishap has pushed his cousin into a foolish decision. Many of us cannot help but agree. None of this would
have happened, do you not think, if you and Edgeware had
been standing out in the open?"

His question sounded chillingly like a threat. An icy dread
tiptoed down her spine.

"I feel fairly confident that I understand Mr. Purbeck's feelings and his intentions only too well, sir." She raised her chin
and stared down her nose at Sir Donald as if he were nothing
more to her than an unschooled child in need of a healthy dose
of discipline. "In the future, you should not feel obligated to
keep me apprised of his moods. Good day."

Without giving him a second thought, she started out in
search of the manor's library.

"You better watch yourself," she heard him hiss. But she
didn't need or welcome his warning. She already knew the
dangers facing her and Nigel.

Her side was burning furiously and her head felt rather light
by the time she reached the library door. Molly had been right,
of course; she should have spent another day abed.

She promised her various aches and pains that she would go
straight up to her chamber after confronting Charlie. There was
no possible way she would get a moment's rest until she'd
completed this task. Though she was as terrified as a cornered
rabbit, and shaking in her slippers by the time she reached the
library door, she steeled her courage and pressed forward.

Even if Charlie was Dionysus, this was something she needed
to do.

When she pushed on the heavy door she heard Nigel growl,

"She *is* my wife, damn it."

"That, I intend to challenge!" Lord Charles Purbeck shouted.
She saw the elder Purbeck clearly through the cracked door. He
raised his fist and shook it. The footman had been mistaken. It
was *Lord* Charles Purbeck, not Mister Charles Purbeck, who
was in the library.

She backed away, not wishing to hear more.

"If you're not careful, she will destroy you financially just as
she destroyed Lord Mercer," Charlie said as he passed by the
library door, pushing it closed again.

What was Charlie up to?

She had nothing to do with Lord Mercer's missing fortune.
Gambling had done away with Lord Mercer's money and when
the money was gone, it had created a pile of debts rivaling the
highest of mountain peaks.

Curiosity eating at her, she pressed her ear to the door.

"Don't speak to me of that . . . that bloody monster," she
heard Nigel sputter. A glass shattered within. "No one is permitted to speak against my wife."

"Nige, Nige," Charlie soothed. "We are on your side. Are we
not, Father?"

Lord Charles Purbeck grunted.

"Charlie, this matter is not open for discussion."

"How about the attempts on your life, Nige?" Charlie
pressed. "What will you do when you discover your beloved
wife's involvement in the affair?"

"She didn't even know me when the first attempt occurred."

"No? Are you certain? Perhaps she edged her way into
Dionysus's life in order to get close to you. Perhaps she is after
your fortune."

There was silence in the room.

"Has she yet lied to you, Nige?" Charlie asked smoothly.
"She lies beautifully, you know. Remember, I have known her

longer than you have."

Elsbeth's shoulders tightened in the growing silence.

"Tonight you plan to spring your trap? Tonight you will capture your smugglers. I pray your heart will not also be broken."

"I trust Elsbeth with my life," Nigel said, his voice low, rigid . . . almost uncertain. She wished she hadn't pushed him away. She wished she had listened to what Nigel had wanted to say to her that morning, because Charlie was doing it again. He was cleverly putting a wedge between her and her husband. She hadn't been able to stop him when he plotted against her marriage with Lord Mercer. Why did she think she could do anything now? Nigel trusted Charlie while he barely knew her. And Charlie was right about one thing—she was able to lie well.

Early that evening, Elsbeth posted a letter to her uncle, explaining matters and her plans to accompany her cousins home in two days' time. Not that news of her marriage would come as a surprise to him. Just that morning she had received a rather stunned note of congratulations from her aunt and uncle.

"Shouldn't you transfer your belongings to the marchioness's chamber?" Olivia asked when she returned to the apartment shortly before supper. "It doesn't seem proper that you remain put up in one of his guest chambers."

"She needs to be a watchin' you gels an' mendin' 'er aches," Molly answered sharply. "She's not needin' to be taking up her duties as marchioness or bothered by a man's whims."

There was a knock on the bedchamber door. Molly opened the door and took a large covered tray that Guthrie had carried up.

Lauretta appeared from the adjoining room. She was dressed in a pale yellow gown with a flowing train sparkling with crystals. Her cheeks were flushed and bright. "You won't be joining us for supper, will you?" Lauretta sounded a bit too hopeful, which made Elsbeth itch to shout, "Stay away from that bastard Lord Ames!" They were all bastards though, weren't they? All except for Nigel.

But even he wasn't perfect. No doubt he now believed any number of vicious things about her, all thanks to Charlie. And the variety of horrid things Charlie could tell Nigel might all be true. She wasn't the paragon Nigel believed her to be. Far from it.

Remembering her responsibility to her cousins, she pulled herself together.

"Molly," she said, forcing her aching body to rise from the bed. "I intended to take supper with the guests."

Molly "tsked" and shook her head. "Guthrie says your lordship ordered you to take your meal in this room."

"He didn't say anything about this to me. In fact, I haven't seen him since—" She felt suddenly flush, remembering the uncertainty in his voice as he'd defended her. If he felt doubts about her or her involvement in the murder attempts against him, she would do well to avoid him.

So she ate her meal after giving both Olivia and Lauretta several admonitions to behave themselves and having secured promises from their hostess, Lady Waver, to act as chaperone.

Taking her meal in the room was a good idea, Elsbeth thought with a yawn. Her eyelids grew heavy even before she finished half the food on her plate. And she barely landed on the bed before sinking into a heavy slumber.

"Been drugged, we 'ave," she thought she heard Molly say. But her maid's voice was so soft, so distant. "Your lordship's done an' drugged us."

CHAPTER TWENTY

Elsbeth slowly awoke to the sound of a gale force wind howling. The not-so-distant waves broke against the shore with thunderous crashes. And a driving rain was stinging the side of her face.

She shivered. One arm was pinched under her body at an awkward angle. She couldn't seem to move it. Nor could she imagine why she'd be sleeping curled up on the rocky ground. Never had she felt so cold or miserable. What a horrid, horrid dream. She tried to wake up, but couldn't seem to manage the task.

"Are you sure it's safe?" a man asked in the darkness.

"Aye, sir. The captain can handle any storm. Says he prefers 'em to running from harbor patrols," another man answered.

"Even so, the men down on the beach could be swept away in this squall."

"Better to risk the storm, than a hangman's noose."

Hangman? Elsbeth struggled to sit up. Her limbs didn't seem to be working. She really needed to wake up.

One of the two men passed beside her. She heard the footfalls. Though in all this wet and darkness, she couldn't see a blasted thing. A few moments later the second man approached. His boots sloshed in the mud. The freezing rain was coming down even harder.

"Please, help me." She reached out to the man. Her hand brushed his slick boot.

He stopped.

A flash of lightning glinted off the blade of the dagger in his hand. She held her breath as he bent over her, blocking the worst of the rain. He was dressed all in black, no wonder she'd had trouble making out his features. Even his shirt and oilskin cape were black. A black kerchief covered his nose and mouth. A large hat, designed to disguise, hid the rest of his face. A horn, carved from bone, hung from a strap across his chest.

"God's teeth! What in bloody hell are you doing out here?" the shadowy man demanded gruffly. He knelt down beside her and pressed his fingers to her neck. "At least you're alive," he muttered and then uttered a string of colorful curses.

She knew him, knew that voice. She blinked several times, trying to get her blurry vision to focus. It wouldn't. Her head hurt from the effort, and the world was beginning to spin back into soft gray nothingness.

She had to be dreaming again. Why else would a flickering light be dancing among a grove of trees? The dancing light was drawing nearer. The man kneeling beside her must have seen it, too. He cursed again, then put the curved horn to his lips, and blew a long deep note that was loud enough to carry about the roaring storm.

The sound seemed to upset the distant firelight. It swung wildly as it drew even closer. Shadows emerged from the darkness.

"Damnation, I'm not going to let you be the cause of my men getting caught or hung." The man whipped off his oilskin cape. His hands moved swiftly as he wrapped it around her shoulders. He then scooped Elsbeth into his arms and scurried to his feet. His quick movement jolted her buzzying head. Pain shot through the straining stitches in her injured side.

She heard a shout. Felt another sharp jolt.

And then, blissfully, nothing.

★   ★   ★   ★   ★

Elsbeth shivered uncontrollably. She awoke, still miserably cold and wet. A sharp slap on her face added insult to her unhappy condition.

"Leave off, sir," she mumbled groggily and batted the offending hand away.

"Wake up. Do as I say."

She was slapped again. It was amazing how impolite some people could be.

"Leave off!" she howled. Her eyes fluttered open. "I am quite awake!"

She had to blink several times before her vision cleared. And after it had, she blinked again, hoping to improve things. She was inside a small abandoned one-room cottage. The room, if it could be called that, was bare, the roof mostly gone, the walls crumbling in the strong gale, and the dirt floor muddy.

She shivered—this time from fear—and hugged a dripping cape to her chest that had been wrapped about her shoulders.

Nigel's friend hovered over her. "M-mister W-waver?" The words chattered with her teeth. "Y-you have abducted m-me? Why—?" She sat up, overcome with a fit of sneezing.

"Damnation!" He peeled off his leather gloves and shoved them into her hands.

His gloves, though large, were fur-lined and warm. "Thank you," she said just before pulling herself to her feet. The pulling pain in her side felt much sharper now than it had all day. And the room was becoming blurry again. He swore again and then reached out to catch her when she stumbled.

She pushed his anxious hands away. "I have a bullet wound in my side that hurts like the devil. I am soaked to the bone . . . and cold." She stifled a sneeze. "And I am foggy in the head, no thanks to you, sir." She took a step away from him, which she instantly regretted since it put her into the path of the driving rain coming in through where the roof was absent. She returned to his side where she could find at least the illusion of dryness.

"I did not do this!" He waved his hand in her direction. "Good Lord, Edgeware will surely kill me when he finds us." He began to pace, not seeming to mind that he'd wandered into the rainy part of the hut.

"You're one of the smugglers?"

"What do you know about that business?"

"I listen to conversations I oughtn't." She paused, eying Mr. Waver carefully. "You *are* a smuggler." Of course he was. Why else would he be dressed like the very devil? "And Lord Edgeware has found you out."

Her heart thundered a beat. "You—you are Dionysus?"

She stumbled back a step, overwhelmed by the thought of finally standing face to face with the artist, the madman. "You're trying to *kill* Nigel?" She just barely eked out the strangled question.

"No!" he shouted. His gaze sailed wildly around the room, seemingly startled by his outburst. "No," he said more sedately. "But that is how *he* wants it to look."

"Who?" Elsbeth could not help but ask.

"Who the bloody hell knows! Dionysus is as good a guess as any!" He gulped. "Forgive my language, my lady." He tossed off his hat and wiped a puddle of rain from his brow. "Wait a blessed moment." He stopped pacing and turned suddenly to stare at her. "You truly don't know Dionysus? But how can that be? That painting was so . . . so lifelike."

"I have never met the bounder, sir. I have no idea why he is determined to be my tormentor."

He stared at her for a moment longer. "We should join forces on that front, but there is no time to discuss that now. You believe this Dionysus is trying to kill Edgeware? That is an interesting thought . . . I must think about that . . . but not now . . ."

He closed the distance between them. The menace in his eyes left her quivering all the way down to her toes.

He grabbed her arms so tightly she yelped.

"You cannot tell Edgeware about this, my lady. I am trying to protect him. I swear I am."

"Y-you are not a-a smuggler?"

"Yes! I am that!"

The sound of distant voices carrying on the wind alerted the both of them.

"Yes," he whispered, "I smuggle goods. Just like my father and his father before him. My work helps support the whole village."

"B-but you d-denied—"

"I am not trying to kill Edgeware!" His gaze darted to the door. "I am as anxious as you are to uncover who is. In fact I have recently discovered a piece of evidence that will help lead me to the murderer. There has been talk in the village that Guthrie, one of Edgeware's footmen, has bragged about how much money he'd been paid to put a metal burr in Edgeware's saddle, a metal burr that nearly sent Edgeware to his death."

"Nigel is convinced that the smugglers are the ones trying to kill him though," she said, trying to put the pieces together in her fuzzy head.

"Yes, I know." He turned away.

"I cannot keep this from him." She shivered, wondering what Mr. Waver would be forced to do to her now that she'd refused to cooperate with him.

"Please, my lady," he said. "Please, give me a chance to plead my case to Edgeware myself. Give me a chance to tell him by the morrow."

If she didn't . . . well, Nigel had said it himself that morning:

He planned to kill the smuggler, which now appeared to be Mr. Waver.

"Very well," she said with a sigh. "Till the morrow. I will not wait a moment longer. I will not put him in further danger." Truly, she didn't wish her husband dead. Nor did she wish to see him kill Mr. Waver. Quite possibly with his own hands.

The voices outside had grown very close. "They will search the hut," she said. "They will capture you in a few moments."

The thought of being captured along with the man her husband was hunting sent a shiver of dread down her spine. Would he believe, as Charlie intimated, that she was a criminal too? Or unfaithful?

She closed her eyes remembering only too well Lord Mercer's punishments. His actions were always more vicious, more violent whenever Charlie had stirred his anger.

Would Nigel, after listening to Charlie and finding her with the smugglers, lose his temper in the same way? She closed her eyes, praying he was different but afraid her instincts about him were wrong. When it came to men, her instincts rarely led her in the right direction.

But Nigel? Not Nigel. He was different. Safer. He was a man who could steal away her heart.

She didn't think her heart could survive if he were to physically harm her.

But, considering the damning circumstances, why shouldn't he?

"I will need my gloves back, my lady." Mr. Waver didn't wait for her to offer them. He snatched the warm fur-lined leather gloves from her hands himself.

The voices were loud, nearly at the door.

"If Edgeware finds me out here, he might believe me guilty of conspiring against him," she said in a panic.

How could Mr. Waver escape Nigel's wrath? How could she?

"Ah . . . that might be true." His eyes were alight with new danger. "But you, Lady Edgeware, must be my diversion." He pushed her into the raging storm. At least he had let her keep his oilskin cape. "Do not worry overmuch, my lady. He does love you."

She stumbled across the clearing toward the search party with nothing more than Mr. Waver's assurances that Nigel loved her ringing in her head. The sharp pelting rain helped clear the last bits of fogginess from her head.

"Over here, m'lord!" she heard someone shout.

Nigel appeared at the head of the crowd of footmen like a forlorn figure in one of Dionysus's paintings. His dark features were as hard as solid stone.

She froze. How would he choose to punish her for her unexpected appearance in the middle of this crime? Would he beat her, not letting up with his fists until she lacked the strength to move or even cry? Would he lock her in the cellar with the rats and leave her to starve until one of the servants in the manor grew weary of listening to her cries for help? She swallowed hard and tried to ignore the pressure of her heart pounding painfully against her chest as she stumbled toward him.

What would he do to her?

Nothing.

Mr. Waver was right. Her gaze met Nigel's and her worries vanished. She suddenly realized she wasn't afraid of Nigel. Instead, she was afraid *for* him and *for* their future. What he thought of her mattered. She couldn't figure out when it had happened, but his trust in her mattered enough for her to want to fight for it.

CHAPTER TWENTY-ONE

Just as Charlie had predicted, Nigel found Elsbeth standing in the middle of this tempest.

She stumbled as she plodded a path toward him through the violent weather. The cape she wore whipped about her slender body, tossed by the wind. Her soaked nightclothes clung to her body shamelessly. Her golden hair was wet and tangled.

His chest clenched. She looked like a besieged princess fleeing her captors and returning to a country now laying in ruin.

Hell, her feet were bare.

This wasn't a woman who had willingly wandered out into a storm.

He ran forward and clasped her against his chest, protecting her from the driving rain by enfolding her into his voluminous cloak.

"You silly, silly dove," he said, very aware his lips were a mere whisper from hers. Her orange blossom scent made him long to taste her. "When will you learn there is nothing but mischief to be found in the rainy weather?"

Elsbeth sneezed. It was a dainty sound that made him smile and worry at the same time. "I was stuck in the rain when I first met you," she said gravely. "I suppose I should be more careful. Look how much of a muddle you've made of my life."

A smile curled her brave lips. Giving into desire, he brushed his lips across hers.

Deuce it. She was as cold as death. He swept her into his

arms. "Keep searching for another hour," he called to the army of footmen he'd assembled.

Both Nigel and Elsbeth were soaked to the bone by the time he reached the front stoop. He kissed her forehead while struggling with the door handle. "Don't worry. I'll find some place dry and warm for you, my lady wife," he said as he stepped inside.

He marched through the darkened house, up the grand stairs, down the hall, past her room, and kicked open the door to the master bedchamber. A healthy fire burned behind the grate of the fireplace, filling the room with healing warmth.

"M-my lord," she stammered after he returned her to her feet. She hugged the dripping oilskin cape close to her body. "Perhaps I should return to my chamber."

"We are both soaked and cold. There is no need to disturb the entire household. We can dry each other." He didn't need to glance in Elsbeth's direction to know she shuddered. "And then you can tell me how you found yourself to be out in that deadly weather."

After a search of his wardrobe, he found the shelves where his valet stored his heavy dressing gowns and a stash of towels. He grabbed up a fistful of towels and two gowns and tossed them onto the bed.

He then reached for Elsbeth.

She squealed and jumped away, tripping over the hem of her cape, a cape much too long to be her own.

Nigel didn't have time to wonder about that now. If he didn't want to lose Elsbeth to illness from the wet and cold, he'd have to get her out of those soaked garments.

"I am healthy as a stoat. I assure you, my lord." She dashed across the room. "I have no need of your assistance."

Foolish woman, she would hasten her own death if she continued to fight him. "Like it or not, I am your husband. I feel a definite responsibility after your health." He picked up a towel and crossed the room with a purposeful stride. "Tell me, Elsbeth. How did you come to be outside in the middle of this storm?"

She crossed her arms across her chest. "I-I woke up outside, my lord." Her gaze narrowed and she appeared to fight off a moment of confusion. "After you drugged me."

"Drugged you?" He took her arms and peeled them away from her chest. "Why in blazes would I wish to drug you?" The cloak fell easily to the floor.

"Charlie made you believe I was plotting against you with Dionysus."

"So you believed I drugged you in retaliation?"

Her pink tongue ran lightly over her lips as she nodded with uncertainty.

"I did not drug you." He kissed her nose, wanting instead to cover her lips with his. "And I don't believe you are conspiring with Dionysus against me. But if you feel you must, you can be sure I will not harm you for it."

Her thin nightrail was indeed soaked through and through. The fabric clung to her taut, rosy nipples and puddled between her long, creamy legs. He drew a ragged breath. And was suddenly as hard as the stones of Purbeck Cliff.

"Wife." His voice was strained. "We must get you out of these sodden clothes." The thought of peeling her ruined nightgown from her creamy body threatened his ironclad control. Yet the alternative, turning his back and giving her privacy, would surely put him in his grave.

"Close your eyes. I don't wish to embarrass you, but I do need to remove your nightrail."

Her cheeks flamed. "No. No. No. I can take care of myself, Edgeware." The fear that had flared in her eyes melted away as she ran her hand down his chest. Her fingers trailed a path from his shoulder blade to the flat of his belly. She tilted her head and moved closer to him. She reminded him of a curious kitten straying too close to the hounds.

"So, I am Edgeware again?" He lightly touched her cheek. Lord, if she kept looking at him that way, he would soon be doing much more than simply caressing her.

She batted his hands away, but with less vigor than before. "I am not injured. I assure you."

"That is not why I wish to remove your clothes." He dipped his head and traced the contour of her lips with his tongue. She trembled, yet her eyes slipped closed, just as he had asked.

Heartened, he grew bolder and teased her lips apart and eased his tongue deep inside her welcoming mouth.

Nigel's scorching kiss chased away the death-knelling chill that had settled in Elsbeth's bones. Like the other night in his study, this welling of need completely wiped away her caution. His gentle hands slowly moved over her body as he lifted her night-rail over her head. Not long after, a warm soft towel touched her damp skin.

She opened her eyes and peered curiously at him, trying to guess his thoughts.

"There is a bed nearby this time, love," he said. His cheeks were warmed by his rakish smile. And all of the sudden she didn't care that he was looking at her . . . all of her. Not while the soft towel and his warm hands stroked her body.

Hmmm . . . she sighed and peeled open his soaked shirt, rediscovering his rippling muscles.

Who was this man? Why did the soft glow in his eyes remind her of Dionysus's lonely landscapes? How could he touch her heart so easily even while she fought to protect it?

With the towel he teased her nipples until they were taut and tingling. The sensation snaked down to her belly and lower.

This time when he put his lips to hers, she parted her mouth at his touch.

He stroked her body all the way down to the damp curls between her legs. His touch awakened her body until a tingling, sinfully erotic warmth radiated out from that delicate place between her legs, spreading throughout her body. Like a fresh new day, she was gradually coming alive. Finally, she was taking her first slow breaths of life.

He swept her into his arms. With great care he lowered her onto the bed's exotic indigo blue counterpane. She snuggled into its warmth. His spicy, erotic scent lingered on the soft fabric. She wrapped it around her while she watched him peel his wet shirt off over his head. He tugged on one of his drenched leather boots. It refused to budge. With a growl he left them on and crawled onto the bed with her. He didn't seem to care that his boots were muddy and his fawn colored trousers were dripping. She helped him pull off his boots. He tossed them to the floor. Their gazes both followed up trousers to the straining buttoned flap at the front. Embarrassed, she quickly turned her head away.

She gasped when he touched her bare thigh and tugged her toward him. His skin felt damp and cool against her warm body. The contrast made her want him to rub his chilled, rain soaked body over hers. As if reading her mind, he kissed a path up her leg. She parted her legs as his caressing kisses moved closer to the heat between her thighs, a heat that was still throbbing from his deep strokes.

Their eyes met. His were hazy and filled with warmth. Biting his bottom lip he smiled at her. His gaze, deep and hot, raked her body over and over. "You are beautiful, Elsbeth. You're a dream come to life, a miracle of art. Everything I have ever desired."

He dipped his head between her legs and touched his lips to

her sensitive flesh. Elsbeth gasped with surprise and tried to pull away. "This is very embarrassing," she whispered as she buried her face into a pillow.

His tongue answered her, teasing her, creating a moist heat that bloomed and traveled up her body until even the tips of her fingers shivered with excitement. Her embarrassment, quickly forgotten, was replaced with a growing urge she couldn't quite name. She was dying, and he was pulling her apart. Ah, such a way to die. Wondrous sensations flooded her till she could no longer think. She could no longer do anything other than squirm against the building pressure between her legs.

She arched her back and pressed her lips together to keep from crying out. His mouth was on her nether lips, deeply kissing her, suckling her until she did cry out her pleasure. He seemed pleased by her response and rewarded her by easing his hot tongue inside of her. His fingers dug into her hips. She laced hers through his hair. He pulsed his tongue in and out, mimicking the movements of lovemaking until her body felt like it was about to come apart. Her hips came off the bed as her tender flesh tightened and then throbbed, spreading throughout her body until she was nothing more than a puddle of tingling delight.

Nigel kissed the soft inside of her thigh, setting off a fresh tremor of pleasure. Elsbeth couldn't seem to catch her breath, but it didn't matter. She smiled and squirmed within the soft cocoon of the bed's counterpane as he made his way up her body, peeling away the heavy bedcovering inch by lovely inch while kissing the top of her thigh, her hip, her stomach . . .

He wasn't even close to being finished with her yet. And surprisingly, she wasn't done with him either. She felt as sensual and confident as the woman portrayed in the nude painting Dionysus had created of her.

Perhaps a happy ending was finally within her grasp.

"Nigel," she whispered. Her heart thundered under the weight of what she planned to confess. Though she'd fought against her feelings every step of the way. He had refused to let her deny her passions, her need to be loved. And, whether she wanted to or not, she loved him. After all those lies about not being able to love, not being able to love *him,* he needed to know the truth. It was within her grasp to give herself the happiness she knew she deserved. And she was willing to take the risk.

"Nigel, I-I think I'm falling—"

"Good God!" he gasped and pulled sharply away.

Like a wanton she tried to draw him back. She missed his lips on her and the erotic heat his touch sparked throughout her body.

"No." He pushed her hands away.

Cold and embarrassed to have him staring at her so, nude and exposed—almost like that . . . that cursed portrait—she covered her breasts with her hands and tried to roll from the bed.

"Lie still," he ordered, his voice no longer honeyed. His wicked grin faded, so too did the hunger from his onyx gaze. "You told me you weren't injured," he said. It sounded painfully like an accusation.

"I'm not—I-I wasn't hurt." She gathered up one of his dressing gowns that was still lying in a crumpled heap on the bed. Feeling vulnerable, she started to cover herself. She should have never believed she could somehow transform herself into that beautiful, desirable woman in Dionysus's painting. She should have never tried to reach for something so out of her depth. She was a cold woman—so she'd been told many times over—and she shouldn't expect anyone to ever love her.

"Lie still," he ordered.

Terrified, she obeyed.

He pressed a towel to her side. She nearly leapt off the bed from the sharp pain.

Nigel muttered a string of oaths before drawing a long, slow breath. "You are bleeding. Damnation, what happened out there?"

Elsbeth lifted the towel and saw a few smudges of blood encircling the bullet wound in her side and a deep red mark where a stitch had been torn loose. No wonder her side was hurting more fiercely now. Seeing the blood, though only a slight trickle, triggered ugly memories, memories where she felt all too helpless . . . all too vulnerable. *Never again.*

She couldn't let down her defenses. Not yet. Not even with Nigel. He was still practically a stranger. His actions were often unpredictable. And her own were becoming more and more predictable. His appearance in the middle of the storm like some modern-day St. George had her falling into his arms, and into his bed.

Alarmed, she covered herself with the dressing gown and hugged her legs to her chest. "My lord," she said, her voice sharp. "I am more than capable of taking care of myself. I don't need you for a nursemaid."

He reached for her. She scooted across the bed "I-I—" She took a deep breath. "Please, do not touch me."

She held her breath, wondering what Nigel would do. He looked so very upset. His hands curled into fists at his side. Lord Mercer would have laughed at her, and would have touched her all he wanted. But then again, Lord Mercer wouldn't have cared that she was bleeding. Nigel did.

He dragged a shaky hand through his hair. "Let me help you. Doctor Pryor—" he started to say when the door flew open and crashed against the wall.

Molly stood in the doorway, her eyes wild. She clutched a

pistol with both hands.

"Stand away from my ladyship, you devil," Molly said, her English spoken carefully.

"Molly, no!" Elsbeth leapt from the bed and charged forward, still hugging the dressing gown to her chest.

Nigel pushed her aside, putting himself directly in front of the barrel of the pistol. "Let's all stay calm," he said. His voice sounded surprisingly steady. Much more steady than it had been a moment before. She wasn't feeling nearly as composed. She felt ready to pounce on Molly and rip the gun from her maid's hands.

"Molly!" she shouted, trying to get around Nigel. "Molly! Put that pistol down right now! You are only making matters worse!"

"Elsbeth," Nigel said quietly, "do not shout at her." With his arms spread, dressed only in his sodden trousers, he took a step toward Molly.

The pistol wavered. "I will no' be lettin' any man 'arm my ladyship. You 'ear me? No man will be 'arming 'er again."

"Trust me, Molly. I have no desire to harm your lady." He braved another step toward the maid. Elsbeth latched onto his arms, trying to pull him back.

"Please, Molly! Don't hurt him. I beg you, Molly!"

" 'E drugged us, milady. 'E drugged us but good with that dinner 'e sent to us. 'E was wantin' you docile so 'e could 'arm you. And I 'eard you crying out. I won't 'ave it. I will be puttin' a bullet in 'is gullet first."

"No Molly," Nigel said as he retreated a step. "There's no need to be putting a bullet anywhere. Elsbeth is unharmed."

"She's been stripped nude as a babe." Molly stared at the ruined nightrail on the ground. " 'Er clothes been ripped away, you brute!"

"Look at your lady," he said though he didn't step aside to

expose Elsbeth. "Does she look as if she's been abused?"

"Please, Nigel," Elsbeth whispered as she tugged on his arm, praying she could get him out of the way. Molly was still staring at the ruined nightrail. A murderous look was twisting on her lips.

"Molly! Look at me." He pried Elsbeth's hands from his biceps. "That's a good girl, Molly. No one is going to get hurt. Hand me the gun."

His hand shot out as quick as lightening and latched onto the barrel.

"You bleedin' bastard!" Molly shouted.

"No!" Elsbeth screamed.

The pistol fired just as Nigel twisted Molly's hand and pulled her up against his chest.

"So much for not waking the entire household," he muttered. A spray of plaster peppered their faces, and the spent weapon clattered to the hardwood floor.

Chapter Twenty-Two

Nigel's master chamber swiftly became overrun with the few remaining guests, all of them gawking. One glance at Elsbeth, still clutching that damned dressing gown to her chest as if her life depended on it, told him she was completely humiliated. Nigel was feeling quite the fool himself. He shoved Elsbeth's maid into Severin's arms.

"Lock her away somewhere," he said, giving Severin a nudge toward the door. "Everyone else, out! I'll be down in the drawing room in twenty minutes to explain what happened." He herded the other guests, his uncle included, out the bedroom door.

He pushed the door closed and turned the key in the lock.

Elsbeth stood in the middle of the room, pale and still as Purbeck marble.

"Right." He approached her as cautiously as he had Molly. "Let's get you dry and into your own bed. I'll have Joshua fetch Doctor Pryor. He will take care of your wound."

He pried the dressing gown from her fingers, quickly slipped it over her shoulders, and tied the belt at her waist.

"What will you do to Molly?" she whispered.

The question made him pause. The gun had fired wildly, putting a hole in the middle of a painting of his great-grandparents standing hand and hand in the middle of a pasture while dressed in finery as though they were ready to visit the king.

Had he been in danger from the maid? Probably. But in the

end no one had been hurt. "I don't know. What do you suggest?"

The question must have taken her aback. She studied him, her eyes filled with wariness. "Are you testing me, my lord? Are you testing my loyalty to you?"

"No." He sighed. What did he have to do to win her trust? His heart heavy, he scooped her up into his arms. Her hair was still damp. She needed to sit by a fire. "I won't abide by your falling ill. You need to get warm and to rest. We will talk further on this in the morning."

But when he lowered her to her feet in her chamber and turned to leave, her grip held firm on his arm. "Please, my lord."

Her return to her cold, hard formality cut him to the quick. His disappointment must have shown on his face, for she quailed. Her hand slipped from his arm.

"N-Nigel," she quickly corrected, which pained him even more. He didn't want to force affection from his wife. How in the hell could he convince her to give her love freely outside of the bed? "Please, you are going down to the drawing room to explain what happened. I wish to be there." She paused. "My place is at your side."

He wanted to refuse her. He wouldn't be able to breathe easy until she was safely tucked up in her bed with a footman standing guard at her door, and the doctor on his way.

A footman standing guard? Where in blazes was Guthrie? He should have been standing guard at her door all night. He should have protected her from abduction.

Elsbeth's hand, so perfectly formed, touched his bare arm again. "Please, Nigel. I'm strong and quite stubborn. A pulled stitch doesn't hurt me in the least. Let me accompany you downstairs." With betrayals blooming all around them, he couldn't be assured of her safety unless he personally saw to her protection, which meant he couldn't leave her alone.

"Do you require assistance dressing?"

"Of course not. I can be ready in a few minutes."

"Very well. I need to put on some clothes." He looked down at his ruined trousers. Nearly the entire household had just seen him barely dressed. He smiled wryly, imagining the shocking picture they must have made. "I will return to escort you to the drawing room in a few minutes, then. Together, perhaps we can figure this all out."

She smiled. Her rosy lips beckoned him as he pictured just how nude Elsbeth was under that ridiculously large dressing gown. "Ri-ight," he drawled, for a sudden lack of words. He gave her a quick kiss and fled.

Elsbeth pulled a sturdy gown from the wardrobe and slipped it on over her head. The bleeding from the gunshot wound had nearly stopped. But still she despaired that the chemise she wore underneath the gown was going to be ruined. She hated the thought of asking her uncle to purchase anything more for her. And then she remembered . . .

If Nigel refused to release her from this sham of a marriage, she would now have to apply to him, or his man-of-affairs, for money. She wouldn't even have the small quarterly stipend her uncle paid her. The realization hit her hard. She sank onto the bed and cradled her head. Her hopes for self-sufficiency were gone, again.

A small knock on the door alerted her to Nigel's return. She took a moment to drag a brush through her hopelessly tangled hair and secured the strands with a ribbon before opening the door. Nigel looked the part of the dashing lord of the manor as he stood at her bedroom door, dressed in a white shirt and buff pantaloons. A red velvet dressing gown was belted at his waist.

"Are you ready for this?" he asked.

"Of course I am," she said before he changed his mind and insisted she stay in bed like a blooming invalid.

"I'm glad one of us is prepared to take on those dragons circling in my drawing room. They're waiting to sink their teeth into this latest scandal, you must know. I, for one, would much rather run the other way."

He looked as vulnerable as the day he had stood outside the drawing room and confessed his dread at the thought of entering. She still found it hard to believe. He was well-respected and so wonderfully skilled at winning the affection of others. Lord, look at what his charm had done to her. He shouldn't need her support in facing the guests to explain what had happened. The fact that he sought it made her heart ache for him all the more.

With her permission, he lifted her into his arms and carried her to the drawing room where the rest of the household, in all manner of dress, were busy speculating on what had happened.

"I daresay she put that shoddy maid up to it," Lady Dashborough's voice carried across the room. "Her first husband left her penniless. She must be determined to have this one off before he can fritter away his fortune."

Nigel shifted Elsbeth in his arms. His expression tightened and his gaze narrowed. She feared his control teetered on a sharp edge. But unlike Lord Mercer, he didn't explode into a fit of rage. Instead, he cleared his throat as he forged into the drawing room.

"Lady Edgeware, though not well," he said, a tremor of anger in his voice, "insisted on joining in the discussion." He lowered Elsbeth to the sofa closest to the fire and piled several blankets on top of her. She welcomed the heat of the fire and the comfort of the blankets.

"Pardon me a moment, dove," he said, and kissed the top of her head. "I need to speak to a servant right outside the door. I won't be far or gone long." Without even a nod to his uncle, he left the room.

Olivia and Lauretta, both wearing their wrappers and frilly nightcaps rushed over to Elsbeth.

"What is going on?" Lauretta asked. Tears had brightened her eyes. "When we went to bed you were fast asleep. What were you doing in Lord Edgeware's room? Why is your hair wet? And what had happened to your nightgown?"

Olivia gave Lauretta a hard stare and shook her head. But it was Lord Ames who jumped up and guided Lauretta away. "Lord and Lady Edgeware are married now," he said softly. "A young unmarried lady such as yourself shouldn't be asking such questions."

"But I don't understand what is going on," Lauretta persisted.

Lord Ames blushed deeply. "Ask your mama," he choked out.

"Has Molly gone mad?" Olivia whispered.

"I don't know." She dearly wished Molly hadn't charged into the room with a pistol. What would she do without her trusted maid? Who would serve as her buffer and her confidant in *this* marriage?

Her gaze strayed to the large painting over the sofa on the other side of the room. The deep purples appeared much lonelier and the crimsons more sinister in the dim light. Lightening flashed. The isolated man in the painting, the man standing on the rock outcropping looking out over into an endless abyss, appeared to flinch. Elsbeth shivered.

"We can talk about the rest later, Elly." Olivia smoothed a hand over Elsbeth's brow, pushing a damp tendril of hair from her face. "You don't need to be afraid."

Nigel returned then with Charlie not more than a pace behind, his young friends curiously absent.

"I'd thought Mr. Purbeck had returned to London," Olivia

whispered. Her nose wrinkled as she watched the young man with a look of undisguised distaste.

"Don't delay any longer, boy," Lord Charles Purbeck shouted from an overstuffed chair. He had raised his leg onto an embroidered ottoman and appeared to be in some considerable pain. "Tell us what in blazes is going on." He slammed his fists against the arms of the chairs. "A servant tried to kill you, what? What?"

"Please don't get yourself riled up, Uncle."

"Not get riled up? You haven't presented our family with an heir. You've married yourself to a barren woman." The guests in the room gasped. "And, now, you're toying around with dangers that will get you killed. What should I be feeling, boy? What? Pride?"

Nigel closed his eyes. Elsbeth couldn't help but hold her breath. Even she was on the verge of jumping off the sofa to defend Nigel against Lord Purbeck. He'd embarrassed *her* husband in front of a room filled with guests. An explosion of wills was inevitable.

"Uncle," Nigel said, his voice unnaturally sedate. "You will not speak against my wife. Nor should you worry yourself over the future of the family title or family name. I am the head of this household and have all these matters well in hand."

"Bah! You are a fool and a damned dreamer. Just like your father."

Nigel's fingers tightened into fists.

"I had to raise you, provide for you because my fool brother went and got himself killed. Don't you ever forget that."

Everyone in the room was as still as death, waiting. Not even Lady Dashborough said a thing.

Charlie had taken a step back and appeared mortified.

This was it, Elsbeth thought. Her husband was about to

explode. The muscles in her shoulders wrenched into painful knots.

"There were smugglers using my beach," he announced to the room, turning his back on his uncle. "I believe the bullet that injured Lady Edgeware the other day was fired by one of them." He paused and turned to give his uncle another meaningful stare. "I believe I was the intended victim. I had planned to entrap the criminals tonight."

"Well?" Charlie spoke up. "Well? Did you capture *him?*"

"No. Every single man on the beach has escaped."

"I find that hard to believe," Charlie countered.

Nigel nodded in agreement. He then crouched down beside Elsbeth. "A servant has located Guthrie, the footman who'd been guarding your door tonight. He'd been knocked over the head and stuffed into a closet." He took a moment then to explain to everyone else how Elsbeth had been drugged and left out in the middle of the storm.

His onyx gaze was sharp, assessing, and there was something sparkling in them that made her heart race and her cheeks warm.

"I've also sent Joshua for Doctor Pryor." His voice was as gentle as a caress. "There is no need to worry. I'll make sure you remain safe, dove."

She wanted to reach out to him and brush away the tension straining his jaw. But old fears were hard to forget. Despite how she was growing fond Nigel, the thought of marriage *to anyone* still chilled her. Her hands in her lap, she let her gaze wander again to the lonely man standing at the edge of a precipice in Dionysus's painting hanging on the wall. Perhaps the painting wasn't a self-portrait, as she'd originally thought, but a portrait of Nigel. He kept himself apart. Even at this house party, he seemed to keep a wall around him, not fully including himself in any of the activities, not truly enjoying himself . . . except when the activity involved her.

"But what about that bloody crazed maid? It was *her* maid, was it not?" Lord Purbeck shook a crooked finger at Elsbeth. "I don't trust the situation, boy. I don't trust *her.*"

"I have already told you, Uncle Charles, that topic is not open for discussion." Nigel took Elsbeth's hand in his warm, strong grasp in an obvious show of affection. Elsbeth welcomed it. "Besides, we have a murderer to find."

"You already know who he is," Charlie said.

"Perhaps . . ." Nigel appeared uncertain. Was Charlie thinking of George Waver?

Mr. Waver had seemed genuinely afraid for his life at Nigel's hands. And he'd mentioned that Nigel was already growing suspicious of his actions. But Mr. Waver had appeared truly surprised when she'd insisted that she didn't know Dionysus's identity. And if *he* wasn't Dionysus, he wasn't the killer. Thanks to her recent investigations, she was beginning to know something about the smuggling going on at the estate . . . and the murder attempts.

"Guthrie, your footman," she said. Mr. Waver had suspected Guthrie was an accomplice. And it did make sense. He had been the one guarding her door. It would be easy for him to slip in sometime during the night and carry her away. "I wish to speak with him."

"What? Speak to—? No, Elsbeth, I don't want you involved any more than you already have been. This affair has nothing to do with you." Nigel paused. "Not really. The men who attacked you did it in an attempt to hurt me. I won't allow you to get further involved. I cannot."

"My lord," she said, her voice sharp enough to slice glass, "perhaps I didn't make myself clear. I am sure the confusion is entirely my fault." She drew a long breath. "I wasn't asking for your permission. I was asking for you to arrange for me to speak with Guthrie. If you don't, I will arrange it myself."

The room fell into a shocked silence. Olivia's jaw dropped open. So had Lord Purbeck's. Lady Dashborogh was sputtering. Elsbeth was feeling fairly surprised herself. Never, not in all the years she'd been married to Lord Mercer, had she stood up to her husband quite so forcefully. Doing so should have left her quaking in her slippers. But Nigel had promised that he would never hurt her. And, despite all her efforts not to, she was learning to trust him.

However, confronting him in such a public manner probably wasn't going to help their relationship. Hoping to soften the blow, she flashed Nigel a quick smile, one filled with challenge and a touch of an apology. She felt slightly lightheaded by her boldness, and by her body's reaction to him. More often than not, when they verbally sparred, he usually ended up kissing her. She leaned forward, her lips more than a little hungry for his touch.

"I am but your servant, my lady wife," he said. He rose from his crouched position beside the sofa. He didn't look happy. No, he looked as if he was on the verge of strangling someone. Surprisingly, she refused to back down or let his dark mood cow her. She tilted her chin up and matched his hard glare. Again, her cheeks felt flushed and butterflies danced happily in her belly as she thought about kissing him.

After a long, heart-pounding moment, he sketched a stiff bow and left the room for a second time to speak with the servant stationed outside the door. He returned in short order with Guthrie. The burly footman was grumbling, moaning, and holding his head as he stumbled toward the sofa a few steps behind Nigel.

"Guthrie," Elsbeth said sternly. She'd been trained to manage servants from a very young age and had honed those skills during her marriage. Lord Mercer had rarely taken the time to deal with such matters himself. "What has happened to your head?"

"What is the meaning of this?" Lord Purbeck barked.

The footman growled and turned a pleading eye to Nigel who only said, "Answer Lady Edgeware."

"I got knocked but good on me noggin, m'lady."

"You did?" While most servants were honest almost to a fault, there were always a few who could spin a yarn so tangled the truth never had even a flicker of a chance of seeing the light of day. She suspected that Guthrie, with his intense interest in gold sovereigns, fell short of being trustworthy.

She struggled to sit up straight on the sofa. Her side burned as if hot coals had been pressed there. The exertions that evening must have put a terrible strain on the wound, not that she would have changed anything that had happened with Nigel in the master suite. That was a memory, she suspected, she'd remember for a lifetime . . . even if their sham of a marriage ended in the next couple of days.

"Come over here, Guthrie."

The footman hesitated until Nigel gave him a none too gentle shove.

"Bend down and let me take a look. Head wounds can be tricky, you see. They should never be left unattended." All of which was true. If he were telling the truth, Dr. Pryor would be tending two patients instead of just one.

"M'lady, this is not—"

"Guthrie." Her voice was sharp, though not quite sharp enough to cut through glass this time. "Do as I say."

With Nigel's hand pressing on the footman's shoulder, Guthrie had no choice but to kneel down in front of her and lower his head.

She pushed aside his greasy hair and felt his scalp for bumps and tender areas. At first she was exceedingly gentle. Guthrie moaned and groaned and cried with pain even before she'd touched him.

"Where were you struck?" she asked him.

"Outside your chamber's door, m'lady" he drawled.

"No, Guthrie, where on your head?"

He pointed to the top of his skull. She skimmed her fingers over the spot he'd indicated. Guthrie yelped at the lightest touch.

Elsbeth frowned. In her experience, head injuries swelled up rather quickly. Considering the amount of pain he purported to be feeling, she should be able to find at least the beginnings of a bump or a knot. She was beginning to believe that she was examining an exceptionally healthy skull.

"You may stand now." She wiped her hands on the blanket and took a moment to consider what she should do next. She glanced at Nigel. He shrugged.

Guthrie rose. Anger filled the large man's eyes when his gaze met hers.

"There is nothing wrong with your head, Guthrie, except for a rather unfortunate case of lice. Do you care to tell us who paid you to drug me and then abandon out in the middle of a storm?" She glanced toward Charlie, hoping to prompt Guthrie into loosening his tongue. "Was this the same man who paid you to put a burr underneath Lord Edgeware's saddle, nearly killing him?"

" 'E never said anyone would be killed, m'lady! I never killed anyone!" Guthrie shouted and then made a dash for the door.

"Just give us a name!" Elsbeth called after him.

Nigel, Charlie, and Lord Ames all dove for the footman. But he evaded their hands and the hands of the servants that charged into the room roused by the commotion. With a shout, Guthrie disappeared out the door. The men in the room, except for Lord Purbeck, ran after him.

Soon after, the sound of a gun's shot ricocheted through the silent room. A man screamed. Another shouted "no."

Lauretta covered her mouth with her hands and darted to the window. Lady Dashborough's daughters, pale with shock, followed.

"Oh my," Olivia whispered, "poor, Elly."

No one else spoke.

Charlie ran back into the drawing room. "The footman's been shot! He's dead!"

Lady Dashborough fainted.

Over an hour passed before the guests settled down. No one seemed interested in seeking out their beds. The drawing room remained crowded. Several guests sank into comfortable chairs, some meandered around the room, staring quietly at each other.

"There's no sign of the man who fired the weapon," Elsbeth overheard Nigel whisper to Charlie upon his return.

"You already know who did this," Charlie replied.

Slowly, the talk returned to the subject of the smugglers. Elsbeth seemed to be the only one who believed them innocent of the killings. And since she didn't want to talk about what had happened to her out in the storm, not until Mr. Waver had a chance to explain himself, she decided to keep her thoughts to herself.

"What do you need us to do?" Lord Ames asked. "I, like Charlie, find it difficult to believe that your army of footmen couldn't catch even one person out of what had to have been more than two dozen men unloading a boatload of smuggled goods. Could it be possible that your smugglers are local town's people? Possibly relations of your footmen?"

"That's exactly what I think," Nigel said. "Which makes the thought of them wanting me dead even more chilling."

"The smugglers aren't trying to kill you," Elsbeth said before she could stop herself. She slammed her hand over her mouth and hoped no one had heard her.

"What did you say?" Nigel crouched down beside her and gently pried her hand from her mouth.

"See, Nige, I told you." Charlie said. Like his father had done earlier, he wagged a sharp finger in Elsbeth's direction. "Let me have twenty minutes alone with *your wife*. I know how to twist the truth from her."

The room erupted with excited chatter. Elsbeth sat as dead as a statue awash in dread. In a fit of rage Lord Mercer had once handed her over to Charlie for an entire evening. Charlie, parroting her husband's behavior, had slapped her across the face, knocking her to the floor. And when she'd tried to defend herself, he'd kicked her until she was huddled in a corner, fearing for her life. That's when he'd grabbed the front of her gown and ripped it. He'd pressed his vile lips to hers and Mercer had allowed it. Her husband had actually laughed when she'd tried, and failed, to push Charlie away. That was the night Lord Ames had tried to defend her. The foolish man's gallant attempt to rescue her had only made her husband's rage that night turn all the more violent. She shuddered to remember more . . . She would kill herself before willingly let anything like that happen again.

"Silence!" Nigel shouted. He turned back to her. "Elsbeth, I'm sure you understand why I need to know what's going on." His voice was frighteningly steady, but his eyes were alive with a look of ruthless determination. "What do you know about these smugglers?"

The man responsible will not live much longer, he had vowed. And she was fairly certain from the way he had said it that he intended to personally see that the punishment for their crimes were carried out. As the highest ranking landholder in the area, he would of course have say over the proceedings.

What to do? What to do? She couldn't tell him what she little knew, for she knew only one name. And Nigel was liable to kill Mr. Waver if she told what little she knew about his involvement with the smuggling operation. Circumstances did make him appear horribly guilty. And although she felt fairly certain he wasn't a murderer, she had no proof. But she needed to say *something* to Nigel. He might never trust her again otherwise, and she needed him to trust her as she was beginning to trust him. She pinched her eyes closed and wished herself invisible.

"Elsbeth," Nigel said. She flinched when his hand cupped her chin. "Elsbeth, look at me."

She refused, knowing what her refusal meant. His trust. Her happiness. Their marriage.

"Let me have time alone with her, Nige," Charlie said again, sounding hungry for the opportunity. "I know how to deal with her."

"No, I can handle this." Nigel took her hand and pressed it against his cheek. "Elsbeth, it is important that you tell me everything you know. It may mean my life, my dove."

To tell Nigel might bring about an innocent man's death. But to hold back the truth, she was likely going to destroy her future and her chance at finding happiness with a man she was beginning to love. She fiddled with her locket. She knew so little of love, so little of life. But she did know about honor. She wouldn't let Nigel kill an innocent man.

"I gave the man my word," she said with frightful ease. "I cannot give you his name."

CHAPTER TWENTY-THREE

Damn, he was a fool. Apparently all his efforts to win Elsbeth's heart had completely failed. She seemed more willing to protect a murderer's identity than to preserve her own husband's life.

Nigel let her hand slip from his fingers. He spoke not a word. He simply rose and walked out of the room. He needed to get away from this hell and just paint. It had been too damn long.

"Nige," Charlie called from down the hall.

"Don't you dare touch her," he said without breaking his stride.

He needed to find some canvas to paint on. Hell, even a roughly cut board would do.

"Nige! Someone is trying to kill you. What should we do?"

What should he do? He wasn't sure anymore. He'd hosted this blasted house party and put up with having all these blasted guests in his home in order to restore Elsbeth's reputation. Then, after his hasty marriage, which had caused most to rush back to London, he'd let the few remaining guests stay. He'd known Elsbeth would be uncomfortable dealing with him on an intimate level. And had hoped the guests would serve as a buffer, giving her time to learn to trust him.

His plan had failed miserably. He now feared he'd never find a way to win her trust, or her heart.

Which meant the guests were no longer needed or wanted. He'd personally arrange for Elsbeth's cousin's to be safely escorted back to their father. Everyone else, though, could do whatever the hell they wanted . . . as long as they did it outside the walls of Purbeck Manor.

As for him, he needed to get away. There hadn't been either paint or brushes at Purbeck since his uncle had tossed all of his art supplies into the fireplace's flames all those years ago. Dioynsus's domain was restricted to the dark, dank cellar in his town house. And that's where he needed to be. He'd hire a Bow Street Runner from London to investigate his butler's murder and tract down the smugglers. It was something he should have done days ago.

"Well, Nige? What do you want me to do?" Charlie asked.

"Send everyone home. I'm returning to London."

For two silent days Nigel rode in the carriage with his wife. He sat on the bench opposite her—a stranger to him—a woman who'd turned his heart inside out. She kept her lips so tightly pressed together that they had long lost their rosy hue.

He had no idea how to please her, or how to win back even one of her glowing smiles. Where was that giddy young imp who'd so firmly captured Dionysus's heart when she'd darted across that dewy field so many years ago? She certainly wasn't sitting across from him, wiling away endless hours watching the countryside. This woman was a mystery, a damned sullen mystery he feared he alone had created.

Love hadn't been enough to keep her safe, at least not his love. But, then again, when had it ever been? His love hadn't kept his parents from leaving him. And it sure as hell had fallen short of winning his uncle's respect and affection. He wasn't good enough. He'd never been good enough. That was why he had to keep that dark corner of his heart—the sensitive part of him that was Dionysus—hidden away.

He wanted to love her the way she needed to be loved. He *needed* to love her. He longed to make her giggle and blush and do all the things with her young lovers should be doing. But, with Elsbeth, he didn't know where to start.

Taking away her maid had been a step in the wrong direction. He'd left Molly at the estate locked in an attic room with a footman to guard the door. Elsbeth hadn't asked after her, but he could guess by the way her eyes sometimes grew misty that she might be thinking about her.

She, no doubt was thinking about a goodly number of things. She just had no desire to share any of them with him . . . her husband.

He cursed aloud. It was a long, colorful oath.

She didn't even blink.

Evening had blanketed the sky and the lamplighters had completed their tasks by the time the carriage pulled to a stop in front of Nigel's town house near Regent's Park. The area had been newly developed and the houses on the street reflected the neoclassical architecture so popular among the elite. Many of the homes resembled Greek temples. All contained highly imaginative elements such as large stone acanthus leaves topping Corinthian columns and imposing triangular eaves supporting the roofs.

The houses in the neighborhood were all very much alike, all except for the one Nigel's carriage had stopped in front of. The façade was brick, not marble or stone, its roof constructed from plain slate. The house was impressive in its sheer bulk and in its bold contrast to its neighbors.

"Come, my lady." Nigel hopped down from the carriage. He stuck his hand back into the door, offering to help her down. "We are home."

Home. Unlike the other homes in the neighborhood, no welcoming whimsy graced this building. The sight of it left Elsbeth very cold, in fact.

She accepted Nigel's hand. Her side pulled and burned with every little movement. The long journey had sorely irritated her injury.

"Should I call a doctor?" he asked when she leaned heavily on his arm as they ascended the steps to the front door.

"No." She straightened and made a grand effort to walk without assistance. "I am tired. Will you please have a maid show me to my room?"

He frowned and studied her for several long moments. Elsbeth expected him to insist on immediately sending for a doctor, but he didn't. After giving her a tense nod, he accompanied a grinning Gainsford, the house's butler, down a shadowy corridor.

"She is an uncommon beauty, my lord," she heard Gainsford say to his lordship. "My felicitations."

Nigel grunted.

A maid arrived a few moments later and led Elsbeth to her room, staying to help her get settled. "Milord will hire a proper lady's maid in the morning," the young maid said, sending Elsbeth's mood to a new low. Being reminded of how she'd lost Molly made her feel even more alone than before.

She didn't feel she had the right to turn to Nigel for company or for anything else. She certainly didn't feel she had the right to plead for Molly's freedom. Molly had threatened to kill him, and she'd . . . well . . . After she'd so soundly refused to tell him what she knew about the smugglers, she doubted he wanted anything to do with her.

She knew she needed to tell Nigel the truth about Mr. Waver. But what if Nigel, in a fit of rage, killed his long-time friend? He'd promised to do just that. And she had no reason to doubt him. So she kept silent. And stayed miserable.

That night she laid on her back on the rather large bed in what she supposed was now her room and stared at the adjoining door to Nigel's chamber. She listened to the creaking of the floorboards and the regular footfalls coming from his room. Her forefinger rubbed the cool gold cover on her locket as her ears strained in the darkness.

Nigel was pacing.

She had turned the key in the lock, but she still couldn't stop herself from keeping a fixed glare on the curved brass handle. Candlelight from his room leaked out under the door.

He never tested the handle.

Some time late into the night the light was snuffed.

Tears pooled in her eyes, blurring the darkness. She wanted him in her bed. Despite the chilling tension keeping them apart, her body still burned for him. She ached to learn more about the carnal pleasures of marriage. But Nigel hadn't even tested the handle to see if she'd locked the door against him.

Her tears spilled over her cheek, which only irritated her more.

If he'd tried to come to her, would she have opened the door?

Oh botheration! She roughly wiped her tears away. How could she expect Nigel to know how to act around her when she didn't even know what she wanted from him herself? And why had she spent her life waiting for some knight-in-shining-armor to come rescue her when she was more than capable of rescuing herself?

She slipped from the bed and padded her way to the adjoining door between hers and Nigel's bedroom. It was time she rescued herself.

Someone was in the room with him, moving quietly as if not wanting to disturb his sleep. Only Nigel hadn't been asleep. He hadn't found a sound night's sleep since his hasty marriage. And the string of long, frustrating nights had put him in one tiger of a mood. He tightened his hand on the revolver he'd taken with him into his bed. And waited, listening as the intruder moved closer. Well, he wasn't going to let the bastard win so easily. One more step and Nigel would roll over and pull the trigger.

The light scent of lilacs and orange blossoms caressed his senses, filling him with images of fields of wildflowers and a certain lovely woman who'd stolen his heart.

Elsbeth?

He kept his hand on his revolver. There was no reason to believe she would come to him. Not in the dark of night. Not to his bedroom. Not like this.

The brush of fabric—soft womanly fabric—whispered in his ear. Slowly, carefully, with the revolver still held at the ready, he rolled over. Her nightrail, a pale creamy white with just a touch of lavender shadows, almost appeared to glow in the dim light as she took another step toward the bed. Her creamy smooth hands were clasped beneath her chin. The pale texture of her skin with a touch of peach highlights begged to be touched . . . stroked . . . loved. Even in the faint moonlight seeping through the floor-to-ceiling windows, the rose in her cheeks appeared nearly luminescent. She was an artistic vision. A glorious, beautiful phantasm.

Perfection.

He slid the revolver under his pillow when she lifted the heavy, quilted counterpane. As silently as a dream, she slipped into the bed with him. She hesitated when her hand inadvertently brushed his naked hip. He slept in the nude, but of course she had no way of knowing that. Though they were married, they hadn't spent a proper night together as husband and wife. He held his breath, wondering if she was about to lose whatever courage had carried her into his room.

With a breathless sigh, she settled in next to him. Her delicate fingers lightly touched his cheeks. And with trembling lips, she kissed him.

He kissed her back. Of course he did. He moved slowly, tentatively. At first she pulled away, as if she didn't expect to find him so awake or so pleased to find his wife in his bed. Or perhaps her courage was faltering. The reason didn't matter. He kept a tight reign on his desires, not wanting to frighten her. Pleading with his lips, he let her know how much he wanted her kisses. He wanted Elsbeth and her love almost more than he wanted life itself. He wanted to celebrate her presence in his room as a victory for their marriage. But he couldn't shake the wariness that was drumming slowly against his chest.

She'd spurned him. She'd told him more than once that she could never love him. And now, she'd willingly come to his bed. She was making his head spin . . . and throb.

He grabbed hold of her wrists and pulled her questing fingers from his naked chest, though doing so was the worst kind of torture.

"Wh-what is this?" he had just enough wits to grumble.

He hated to be twisted about. And that was just what she seemed to be doing.

He searched her eyes, eyes that appeared nearly a deep purple in the darkness. "Why are you here? What do you mean to do with me?"

A nervous smile turned up one corner of her orange-scented lips. "If a husband needs to ask, I must be doing something horribly wrong." She wriggled against his hips. He groaned, his control slipping.

"Do not tease me," he said through a painfully clenched jaw. His grip tightened on her wrists. "I know what you're doing. What I don't know is why."

The smile faded. Her eyes turned up to the ceiling. And her teasing body suddenly became still as marble. "I want you, Nigel. I-I want to be in your bed. Tonight and every night."

Ignited by her words, he kissed her deeply . . . passionately . . .

thoroughly. And when he pulled away, breathless and near mad with desire, he placed her hand on his throbbing arousal. "I want you here in my bed, too."

With her lips forming a small moue, she stroked the full length of him. Her eyes widened. She ran her petal pink tongue over her full lips.

Though he didn't understand why she'd come to him, it was clear that she truly wanted to be with him . . . that she wanted him to act like a husband should with a wife. With exquisite care, he undressed her. His hands trembled slightly as he did. Removing her nightrail was like peeling away the protective paper from a newly purchased masterpiece, revealing a delicate beauty hidden beneath.

And her body was perfection. He caressed her as he would a beloved work of art. The soft curves of her hips contrasted against the slender plains of her stomach. Her skin was as silky as a mink's down.

The only flaw was where the bullet had nipped her side, an imperfection she wouldn't have if not for his own carelessness. He traced the line of stitches. The wound was still red and angry. He would send for a doctor to take another look in the morning.

"Does it hurt?"

She shook her head.

He gently slipped his hand between her legs. He stroked her, urging her body to open up to him.

"Please," she squeaked. "Love me."

It was all the encouragement he needed. With his mouth making love to her velvety soft lips, he slowly filled her. Her legs wrapped around his waist and he reveled in the most satisfying embrace he'd ever experienced.

I love you, Elsbeth. I love you like I've never loved anyone before. He couldn't quite find the strength to make that confession for her out loud. But the words were there . . . on his lips . . . waiting . . .

And every beat of his heart beat with the love he was feeling for her, his wife.

His beloved wife.

A wife who was *unwilling* to tell him what had happened that night in the storm. A wife who was *unwilling* to give him the information that might save his life.

Lord help him.

But still he loved her.

Sometime in the first gray light of morning, Elsbeth woke disoriented and drowsy. Her stomach and legs were pressed against something hard and warm. She shifted in the tumble of sheets, slowly remembering.

She'd not spent the night in her own bed.

The realization should have unsettled her. But the arms wrapped around her middle, the legs following the contours of her hips felt much too comforting, much too safe to worry her.

She twisted around, careful not to wake Nigel, and watched him as he slept. He was smiling, but she could tell by his deep, steady breathing he was sleeping soundly. With a featherlight touch, she caressed his stubbly cheek.

"Are you the knight-in-shining-armor I have been waiting for? Have you finally come for me?" she whispered the question.

His smile broadened though his breathing remained slow and deep. His slumber remained unbroken.

"I love you, Nigel," she whispered. And then, she too smiled, and drifted back to sleep.

CHAPTER TWENTY-FOUR

Later that morning when Elsbeth woke up again she discovered she was alone in Nigel's bed. She quickly returned to the adjoining chamber, dressed with help from an inexperienced maid, and set out to find him. She arrived at a small, shadowy breakfast room where a footman stood waiting to serve her. There was no sign of Nigel. And the footmen didn't know of his whereabouts.

Since she was hungry, she decided to sit at the table and wait for him. She nibbled on her toast and stared at the bare walls. Odd, she thought. There didn't seem to be any paintings in the house. A sunny landscape would help lighten the deeply shadowed, somewhat grim breakfast room. The next time she saw her husband, she would ask him about that.

She had other important things to talk about with him as well. Their marriage, for one. And their relationship. But the thought of opening the door to those topics terrified her. She'd much rather talk about the house's lack of paintings.

Though last night was one of the most glorious nights in her life—and something she wouldn't mind repeating—it settled nothing between them. She was still withholding Mr. Waver's name. They needed to trust each other with their secrets. But that was a step she didn't feel ready to take, which only made her feel as gloomy as the breakfast room.

She was picking at the eggs on her plate when Gainsford, Nigel's butler, came into the room. He cheerfully reintroduced himself and offered to give her a tour of the household whenever she was ready. He, too, couldn't tell her where she could find her husband.

"We are all ever so happy you have arrived at last, my lady," he said just before he left her to finish what was left of her breakfast. "We have been ever so worried after his lordship. He would lock himself away for days and refuse to see anyone. That will surely all change now."

She took a sip of her tea and wondered how Gainsford expected her to change Nigel's life. Lord Mercer hadn't changed a single thing about his life in all the years she was married to him. It was *she* who had radically changed her ways.

And here she was, sitting at another man's table, being forced to change yet again.

She knew she needed to trust Nigel with her secrets, with *all* her secrets. Especially with what she knew about the smugglers. They had left Dorset before dawn three days ago and before Mr. Waver could have had a chance to prove whether he would appear at the estate to confess his involvement in the smuggling operations. For two long days, she'd held her tongue. If Nigel came to any harm, her mortal soul would be damned. She knew that, but she still kept silent.

You will be his murderess if he dies. You will be no better than your late husband . . . or Charlie.

She dropped her half-eaten toast onto the bone china plate, no longer hungry.

She'd personally seen one attempt against Nigel when the boulder crashed onto the beach frighteningly close to where he'd been standing. Mr. Waver and Guthrie had both spoken of a burr in a saddle. And there had been the bullet that had struck her and the bag of stones that had hit Nigel in the head.

There may have been even more attempts.

"Dionysus." The name sounded like a curse beating on her

ears. If not for him, she would have never married Lord Mercer; she would have never met Charlie Purbeck or Nigel. Her life would have been so different.

Happy, perhaps.

Not that she'd been unhappy last night. Remembering how she'd spent the night in Nigel's bed brought a rush of heat to her cheeks and made her ache for her husband all over again. She'd never felt so sensual . . . so desirable . . . so loveable . . .

But why had he left his bed without waking her this morning?

"My lady," Gainsford said softly from the door. "The Earl of Baneshire is asking to see you. I have shown him to the front parlor."

"My uncle? He is here?" Elsbeth rose gingerly from the chair. After her late night excursion, even her softest chemise chaffed the puffy skin around the bullet wound. But for last night, she happily endured the discomfort.

Gainsford, a man well into his fifties but in better shape than most of the younger footmen, led her to a light and airy room decorated with pale blue colors and again, curiously, no paintings. Lord Baneshire stood in the middle of a blue and white Axminster rug. He was scowling.

"Uncle." She held out her hands and crossed the room to him.

He wrapped her in his arms, holding her tightly against his chest. "Elsbeth, Elsbeth," he whispered. "Olivia and Lauretta told me it all. Every detail. I heard how Lord Edgeware tricked you, that bounder. He has no right to you. You don't have to stay here. You don't have to worry about anything. I've come to take you home."

Home. A place of her own. A place where she felt safe. A place where she belonged. Lately, she didn't feel as if she belonged anywhere.

Lord Mercer's estate had never been a home for her. It had been a prison. A hell. And although her family had always been kind to her, she never felt like she truly belonged at her uncle's town house. A few nights ago she had hoped she could find a home with Nigel. But because of the secrets wedged between them, that hope was fading and the realization shattered her.

She collapsed in her uncle's arms, sobbing.

He petted her hair as he soothed her with nonsensical words and soft sounds. "I will make everything right again," he vowed, which only made her cry harder. "I swear I will."

She didn't know what made her open her eyes or turn her head. Perhaps she'd sensed him there. Her teary gaze met Nigel's as he stood in the parlor doorway. His jaw dropped slightly. A raw expression of pain sliced through his dark, glassy eyes. Never had she seen such naked torment. But she understood it. She felt it herself in her own heart.

"Shush now, Elsbeth," her uncle whispered, patting her head. "You don't need to worry any longer. I will free you from this disaster of a marriage."

She tried to call out to Nigel, but tears clogged her throat and she couldn't find her voice. By the time she could speak, the entranceway to the parlor was empty. She started to go after him. She needed to talk to him. Needed to tell him that she was hurting, too.

She needed to know if there was any hope left for her. She needed to know if she could build a home, here, with Nigel.

"Come." Her uncle took her arm, not letting her break away. "We need to talk." He led her to a powder blue sofa.

Her thoughts trailed back to that empty doorway. Nigel had looked as forlorn as one of Dionysus's paintings as he'd stood there, watching.

"Sit." Her uncle patted the cushion.

"I-I should—" she started to say.

"You should sit," her uncle commanded with such force her legs immediately obeyed. "Now then, I've already contacted my solicitor. He questions the very legality of the marriage since no banns were read nor special license secured. He doesn't believe you will even need to seek an annulment." He crossed the room and pulled a pretty ceramic knob to call a servant. "And I will demand reparations."

"Nigel has never acted maliciously against me or tried to harm me. In fact, he—"

"But you are damaged nonetheless. This dastardly deed will not go unpunished."

"You rang the bell, my lady?" Gainsford asked gleefully when he entered the room a short time later.

"No, *I* rang for you." Lord Baneshire said, leaving no room to doubt who was in charge. "Have all of Lady Mercer's belongings packed. I'll send a man over this afternoon to pick them up."

"Lady Mercer, my lord?"

"Yes. Lady Mercer." He swung his arm in Elsbeth's direction. "My niece."

"My lady?" Gainsford's cheerful expression fell. "I do not understand. You are leaving? But you have only just arrived."

"This marriage is a sham," her uncle said before she had a chance to answer Gainsford. "I'm taking her home where she belongs *and* before a full scandal erupts."

"A sham?" Gainsford frowned at that. "That cannot be true, my lord. The Marquess is a very cautious man. He would not bring a woman into the house as his wife if it were not true. He simply would not dishonor a woman in such a way, especially one he loved. My lady, I beg you . . . Do not leave."

"This isn't her decision to make. And stop talking such nonsense of love, my good man, and do as I bid!"

Gainsford stepped swiftly back into a bow. "Very good, my lord."

"Wait." Elsbeth rose from the sofa. She'd been a passive participant in her life for far too long. "Uncle, I appreciate what you have done for me. And for what you are doing now. I truly do. Your affection touches me deeply." She drew a long shuddering breath. She was tired of living her life while waiting— longing for a home, longing for a knight on a white charger to come rescue her. Despite her family's kindness, she didn't belong at her uncle's town house. Her life up until now hadn't been living. It had been nothing more than a long string of years of waiting . . . desperately waiting . . . for something special to happen to her . . .

She drew off her locket. She'd taken the first step last night. She was taking control of her life. Be it happy or painful, she needed to give herself the chance to truly try and live her own life, to make her own decisions.

"Gainsford." She held out the locket. "Please take this up to my room and have it placed with the rest of my jewelry."

"Very good." Gainsford tried a tentative grin. "And, Lady Edgeware, you will not be needing your belongings packed?"

"No. You may go. I need to have a few words with my uncle in private."

"I don't understand," Lord Baneshire said after Gainsford had left.

"I don't completely understand everything myself." She held up her hand, not letting her uncle interrupt. "Yet I do know Nigel needs me."

"But Elsbeth, I've been told that your life has been placed in danger at least twice. What kind of provider can he be if he allows this? And you cannot deny how you sobbed when I first arrived."

"You are right. I cannot deny that I cried." She slashed her hand through the air. Her heart felt more confused than unhappy. "Perhaps I simply do not know how to be happy."

"You talk nonsense, child. You sound just as flighty as Olivia. And that girl certainly doesn't know her mind."

Elsbeth smiled at that. "She knows her mind better than you might think, Uncle. That is precisely why she has yet to agree to marry."

"Women!" He threw his hands in the air. "What are you waiting for? Do you wish to remain with this man who trapped you into marriage or not?"

"Do I wish to—?" She didn't know the answer to that question. True, Nigel had married her without her permission. The marriage wasn't even valid. But to leave him . . . ? "I believe I have a duty to stay. I don't expect you to understand when I, myself, don't fully understand my own feelings regarding him, or this marriage. But I believe I have a responsibility to him. His life is in danger, and I fear I'm the only one who can save him."

CHAPTER TWENTY-FIVE

After escaping to the cellar, Dionysus took up the brush. He'd not sketched a plan nor did he have any idea what he should paint. He only knew the pain tearing at his heart. Elsbeth had sought her uncle for comfort, not him. Even after last night, she refused to share herself with him. He didn't know how he could convince her to offer not only her body, but also her heart.

Dark colors—blacks, deep greens, midnight blues—made for a mournful backdrop. His paints created a bleak landscape that faded into a deeply shadowed forest. He dropped his brush and turned to his worktable. With a mortar and pestle he ground vermilion mixed with a few drops of oil into a brilliant scarlet red paste. The paint lying insensate in the bottom of the marble mortar might as well have been his own blood.

She spurned his company as surely as she would turn her lips away from an inferior piece of fruit. She wouldn't even share with him the one piece of information vital for his own protection. She'd rather see him dead than to suffer, forced to share her life with him. What could he do to win her favor? He'd tried to offer her the truth about Dionysus—the one thing he knew she wanted—and she'd refused to hear it. And he hadn't insisted. She clearly loathed the artist who had so wronged her. Confessing the truth, telling her that he was Dionysus would only push her further away. She might even strike out against him. So what else could he do? What else could he offer? What did he have to give her besides the protection of his title, his family's name?

And his love . . . ?

Three days later he slashed his brush against the canvas. He'd spent most of his days hidden away in his dank cellar, ruining his eyesight while working in near darkness on his latest painting. For three days his brush moved with a force beyond his control. The bristles pulled along the fabric, as it smoothed the edge of a delicately curved neck. He knew she would have surfaced as the central figure of this work. Had it not always been that way? Her willowy figure gradually appeared in the middle of his desolate landscape. Dressed all in white, she huddled on the ground, her face hidden from view. She was crying. Of that, he was certain.

He'd caused her pain. From the first time he'd seen her, he'd brought her nothing but pain. Their marriage hadn't healed those wounds. If anything, it had made them worse. She spent most of her time away from the house. She was visiting with friends, she'd told Gainsford. The way his butler quaked and twitched when he was questioned about Elsbeth's whereabouts, Nigel suspected his butler knew it to be a lie. More likely, she was avoiding him and his butler was covering for her.

All his servants appeared to be besotted with Elsbeth and more than a little protective of her. He couldn't blame them. But it did complicate their relationship. Whenever he tried to confront her and demand that she tell him why she'd been spending so much time away from the house, a servant would burst into the room and interrupt him with some pressing household matter. When they did spend time alone together at dinner, she rarely looked at him. And his attempts to engage her in conversation were sharply rebuked.

If he tried to touch her hand, she'd flinch and pull away. When he'd discuss the Bow Street Runner's progress in trapping the smugglers, trying to involve her as if she were an equal partner—which he hoped she'd one day become—she'd swiftly cut him off. When he'd ask her about her daily activities, she'd pale.

She was up to something . . . but what?

Did she want to be free of him? Did she wish him dead? She'd certainly made it clear that she wasn't pleased to have been tricked into marriage. And, even though he'd questioned her about it several times, she remained stonily silent about what had happened to her out in the storm. Still, he held out hope that one day he would be able to win over her heart. And her trust.

The tension growing between them was eating at his soul. It would have driven him completely mad if not for the miracles that occurred in the small hours of the night. Like a beautiful phantom, she'd steal into his bedroom and in the silence of the darkness they'd make love until dawn.

Yet possessing her body alone wasn't enough. He wanted— *needed*—more. But how did he demand she love him without pushing her farther away?

He bit into his lip and dabbed his brush against the canvas. This was a painting his soul needed to do as a penance.

She didn't love him. Couldn't love him. Like the worst sort of beast, he'd trapped her into a marriage against her will.

He didn't deserve her. Perhaps would never deserve her. And yet he wasn't willing to let her go. He dipped the brush into a shimmering white paste, a color he hoped could capture the ethereal glow of the sheer nightrail she always wore to his bed.

A light knock on the door broke his concentration.

"My lord," Gainsford called out. The butler's voice wavered, a sure sign of nervousness . . . or guilt. "My lord, your uncle is demanding to see you." Gainsford paused. "He says he will search the house if I tell him again that you are away from home."

"I spoke with Lord Baneshire last evening," Uncle Charles said. He was sitting like a king in the drawing room, his pudgy fingers digging into a golden snuffbox. Nasty habit, snuff. One Nigel never could find a liking for. Uncle Charles sniffed loudly. "Unless you release Lady Mercer, he plans to expose you in a most undignified and public manner for your immoral behavior. Your marriage wasn't exactly legal, now was it, boy?"

"I intend to make it legal."

Uncle Charles sniffed again. "That chit is of no value to you as your wife. She is barren and a tainted widow. Everyone knows how her husband was a perverted monster. Even my boy Charlie, supposedly one of Lord Mercer's closest friends, admits to being horrified by his demented behaviors."

"She is wounded, not tainted."

"In your position, there is no difference." Uncle Charles sniffed again. "Set her up with a stipend and put her in a pleasant cottage that is convenient to you. Society will laugh off your outrageous behavior and call you a scamp, a rogue, and invite you to all their insufferable balls."

"No, Uncle."

"She is young and pretty. She'll make a fine mistress."

"She *will not* be my mistress." Uncle Charles was not listening to him.

"A man who has gone too long without a mistress is bound to make a mistake when choosing a wife. The wrong parts start guiding his decisions." Still ignoring Nigel, he reached into his box for another pinch of snuff. "I've seen it happen all too often, boy. Now, about the attempts against your life. That is why I've come. We *must* see that they are stopped." Uncle Charles slammed his fist into the arm of the chair, the snuff between his fingers flying. "I will not allow you to die young like your father! Damn you, boy. You should have told me about them earlier. Your horse-riding accident, it wasn't an accident, was it?"

"No."

"Of course it wasn't. I should have known. Unlike Charlie, you are a natural horseman."

"I have the matter well in hand." He simply needed to figure out how to win Elsbeth's trust and convince her to tell him everything she knew.

"So you say . . . no matter, I have hired several Bow Street Runners to thwart the villain." He pushed heavily against the chair and rose. "They're tracking down that George Waver. Charlie's idea, I know. But the boy seems to be gaining some sense as he ages, thank the good Lord."

There was no stopping Uncle Charles once he had set a course. Besides, the addition of a few more Bow Street Runners wasn't unwelcome.

This might actually be a good thing. With Uncle Charles distracted with chasing after the man responsible for the murder attempts, it would give Nigel time to make his marriage legal.

Elsbeth may not yet love him, but he wasn't willing to give her up.

Not a chance.

His uncle's visit had made that much clear to him. He needed to act, and act soon, to make it near to impossible for anyone to tear his Elsbeth away from him. Devil take it, he would have to suffer through another social event. It was the only way.

"Gainsford!" he called out through the halls of his empty house soon after his uncle had left. "Gainsford!"

The cheerful butler appeared from around a corner. "Yes, my lord?"

"Begin what needs to be done to plan a ball. As grand as you can imagine. I wish to celebrate my marriage in the most visible and crowded manner."

Gainsford's face paled. "A ball, my lord? With-with *people?* Are you certain?"

"Yes, Gainsford. The more the better." Nigel began pacing.

"And when shall this ball be held?"

Soon. Tonight would be impossible. It would take at least a few days to prepare for such an ordeal. To order the food. To send out invitations. "Friday should do."

"F-Friday, my lord?"

"Yes, Friday." He was adament.

"Very good, my lord," Gainsford gave a deep bow and hurried down the hall.

Elsbeth returned from a long, trying day of visiting a string of residences to find the Edgeware household in chaos. The servants were running this way and that while speaking far too loudly and apparently accomplishing nothing. After pulling off her gloves she grabbed hold of Gainsford's arm as he rushed by her. He nearly dropped the three-stemmed candelabra he was carrying toward the dining room.

"I beg your pardon, my lady. I didn't see you there, my lady," he stammered. "There is so much to be done."

"For what purpose?" she asked, a brow raised and her voice purposefully stern.

"For the ball, of course. He wants it held on Friday. Friday! And it has to be a grand affair with over half of England in attendance."

"I see," she said, wondering what her husband was up to. Though she had some stern words for him, it had nothing to do with this ball. Knowing well her duty as marchioness, she gathered the servants around and took the matter of planning the ball well in hand. She assigned each servant several specific tasks and had taken it upon her self to handle the most important details personally. After Friday evening, there would be no question that she was simply Nigel's *latest piece of baggage,* or *a grasping mishap.* His mistress. Indeed!

She may have been hidden away throughout her marriage to Lord Mercer, as if she were nothing more than an embarrassment or a failure. But she wasn't going to hide any longer. She had every right to take her hard-earned place in society. And she intended to do just that.

But it wasn't those whispering town tabbies who had made tears spring to her eyes. No, it was something that had been carelessly said to her by a lady whose reputation was far more tattered than her own. In fact, the very beautiful Mademoiselle Dukard wasn't a lady at all. She'd made her fortune from selling her favor to rich gentleman.

Gentlemen like Lord Mercer and—she wiped away a tear—Nigel.

Nigel.

"Even your Lord Edgeware keeps a mistress," Mademoiselle Dukard had leaned forward in her velvet chair, which was the exact shade as her lovely crimson gown. She'd said it in defense of her own profession. But the words hurt just the same. "He visits her several times a week, you should know. I hear he was with her yesterday."

Elsbeth had had to swallow down a sudden stab of pain.

"I've not come to discuss my husband," she'd said crisply. "It is his cousin, Mr. Purbeck who interests me. Do you know if his financial affairs have taken a turn for the worst recently? Is he in danger of coming to a bad end if he doesn't pay off an unsavory moneylender?"

Mademoiselle Dukard had given a deep throaty laugh. "I know of nothing so dramatic."

She told Elsbeth how Charlie was down on his luck, but that

was nothing new for him. And there were others in the *ton* who were much worse off. There had been a horserace at Newmarket whose outcome was supposedly guaranteed. But it didn't turn out how the young bucks who'd laid down a fortune in funds had expected. Charlie, the mademoiselle had heard, had placed the largest of those bets, though most of that money was not his own. Several of his friends lost small fortunes after being lured by Charlie into putting up their own funds on what he'd promised to be easy money.

"Of course your Edgeware is more careful with his fortune," Mademoiselle Dukard had said. "He spends more time with his beautiful mistress than at the horse races."

Elsbeth tried to steer the conversation back to finding the evidence she needed to prove to Nigel that Charlie was plotting to do him harm, but the mademoiselle resisted. Desperate to talk about anything but Nigel's mistress, Elsbeth had even tried to question her about Dionysus. What did she know about him? While Mademoiselle Dukard seemed genuinely interested in finding Dionysus for herself—it would make her a fortune in blackmail—she knew very little that was helpful.

Undaunted, Elsbeth had pressed on, all the while her heart breaking over the news of Nigel visiting his mistress even after Elsbeth had spent the last several nights in his bed. Perhaps she hadn't pleased him. Perhaps Lord Mercer had been right. Perhaps she *was* too cold for a man to enjoy.

"I don't know if you are aware," Elsbeth had said, while fighting off tears, "but several attempts have been made against the Marquess's life. Do you know if Mr. Purbeck or Dionysus or anyone else for that matter would have a reason to want him dead?"

Mademoiselle Dukard had pursed her glossy, full lips. "No, no, not Charlie. He's more like a vulture, circling the dead. He wouldn't kill. He'd only plunder." She waved her hand in the air. "As for Dionysus or the others in the Marquess's life?" She shrugged. "I cannot say."

No amount of prodding could get Mademoiselle Dukard to change her mind on that matter, and eventually she'd left the woman's parlor. Like Nigel, the mademoiselle firmly believed Charlie to be nothing worse than a swindler. Elsbeth knew better. Yet she didn't know how to convince anyone that he was a danger . . . to her . . . and to Nigel.

Nigel.

She swiped at another troublesome tear.

The thought of him going to a mistress . . .

Anger and anguish pounded in equal measure against her breast.

"Where is his lordship?" she asked Gainsford before sending him off to take inventory of the wine cellar. Lord Mercer had never been faithful. Apparently it was a flaw common to all men. No matter, she planned to take a strip off Nigel's sorry hide. He'd tricked her into a marriage she hadn't wanted and yet continued to see his mistress? The cad. The bounder.

"Why he's in his study, my lady. Do you need me to show you the way?"

Twisting her gloves with ruthless determination, she let Gainsford lead her to Nigel's study. He sat at his desk. His man-of-affairs, a smart looking man with thick glasses, sat in a chair across from him. He appeared to be working on a long list.

Nigel glanced up and gave her a smile.

Was he thinking of his mistress now while he smiled at her, his wife? Her heart shrank away from the thought.

After dismissing his man-of-affairs, he crossed the room and placed a kiss on her cheek that left her cold. He'd made love to her. His hands had moved across her body, making her feel more than she had ever dreamed possible. Had he been thinking of his mistress *then?*

"My lord," she said, curtly. She made a conscious effort to lay her twisted gloves aside and to not reach for the locket she'd stopped wearing several days ago.

He gave a long sigh. "Elsbeth."

Eyes dark as the midnight sky stared into her soul until she found it nearly impossible not to fidget. Surely, he didn't plan on just standing there . . . staring.

"My lord," she said again, feeling suddenly confused. When she was around him lately she found it hard to think, which only confused her more.

How could he make love with such passion every night and still pay visits to a mistress? How could he be so cruel?

She was about to demand an answer when she saw it.

Above the fireplace hung the town house's only work of art—a tempest ripping a delicate rainbow to shreds. The painting sharply reminded her of what he was doing to her heart.

Nigel cursed. He should have never allowed her entrance into this, his private domain. Her lips parted slightly as she stood transfixed by the painting.

That damned painting, a raging tempest that violently tossed about the waves at sea. The sea and the wind tore at the canvas. The purples, blues, and blacks created an ominous image of Dionysus's soul . . . of Nigel's soul.

No hope, no joy, nothing of beauty had been created by pushing those paints around that canvas.

"You loved Dionysus," he said at long last.

"Yes," she said.

"I see." He saw only too well what was occurring in her troubled mind. He should tell her the truth or set her free. He had no right to keep her close when she deserved peace.

Why couldn't he say the words? Why couldn't he tell her the truth? About Dionysus? Why was he so afraid of her reaction?

"Come to my bed tonight."

She blushed deeply. "I-I—" Her hands fluttered before landing squarely on his chest.

"Come to my bed, Elsbeth, not as a thief would sneak into a room but as my wife. Come to my bed when we retire."

Her sapphire eyes sparkled with a heat that curled his toes. Perhaps she was remembering last night. Remembering that he'd been a little extra daring while they'd made love. Elsbeth had arched her graceful back and purred like a kitten in response. And then as they cuddled within the cocoon of the sheets she'd kissed him with such tenderness that his heart had nearly burst.

If he kissed her now she would no doubt melt into his embrace and they would be repeating the events of that wondrous night in his study at his country estate here and now in this stogy London study. But he didn't want to take her that way. Nor did he wish her to continue to be a silent phantom sneaking into his bedroom in the middle of the night while a chilly wall remained between them in the light of day. She deserved to be wooed.

And damn it, he swore he would simply have to learn how.

"Please Elsbeth," he said, feeling like a beggar. "Come to my bed tonight. Be my wife." He swept up her hand and kissed her knuckle while seductive images flooded his body. The arch of a bare toe, the curve of an elegant neck, the shimmer of her golden tresses . . . an evening that was far too many hours away. "Let me prove to you that I can be the husband you deserve."

Not long afterwards, Nigel left the house on foot. With a jaunty stride he made his way toward Oxford Street.

"Where is the Marquess going?" Elsbeth asked Gainsford as he moved to close the door. She'd nearly convinced herself that Mademoiselle Dukard had been lying about Nigel. How could he turn her knees to jelly with one heated look and not be totally devoted to her? It was impossible. He may have had a mistress in the past, but no more. She refused to believe it.

Gainsford moved slowly, latching the lock before turning around to answer her. "I cannot say, my lady."

The butler's eyes danced a nervous jig.

No, it couldn't be true. Certainly Nigel wouldn't seek out his mistress shortly after imploring Elsbeth to make their marriage real. Certainly he wouldn't do that to her . . . would he?

"Fetch my pelisse." If she hurried she would be able to catch up with him. Confront him.

"And where will you be going, my lady?" Gainsford asked, his nervous eyes still dancing.

"I believe I will join Edgeware in his walk."

"Oh dear." Gainsford slumped against the door.

"Gainsford!" Her voice rose to make his name a command. She was determined to see this other woman with her own eyes.

"I will fetch your pelisse, my lady." He scurried away.

Catching up to Nigel was no easy task. He kept a brisk pace and only spared acquaintances he met on the street the courtesy of a tip of his shiny beaver hat.

She trailed several yards behind, hiding her face in the shadow of her straw bonnet. All the while, she kept a keen eye out for attackers. On such a crowded street anyone could stroll up to Nigel and stick him with the sharp end of a knife. It didn't appear that he was being the least bit cautious, either. He should have a footman with him or perhaps a friend watching his back. Well, even though he didn't realize it, he had her. And she'd fight for him.

At Oxford Street Nigel turned toward Hyde Park. Several blocks later he darted down a small alleyway. She waited, wringing her hands before following.

She was a ninny, the worst sort of ninny, too. Why, Nigel

could be visiting a friend, going to a gaming hell, or attending to any manner of pressing business a man of his position must surely be plagued. She should have never followed him.

And now she couldn't turn back. Not without first seeing that he arrived safely at his destination.

Thankfully, the alleyway was not the frightening den of filth she'd feared it would be. The apartments were tidy, albeit a bit cramped, and the street swept clean.

Nigel had stopped in front of an ancient two-story cottage tucked between the apartments near the end of the alley. Vegetables were growing in a miniature garden on either side of the short path that led up to the front door. Without hesitation he knocked.

Elsbeth's heart stopped when the door swung open. A voluptuous woman with the most glorious head of amber curls stepped out. She gave Nigel an easy smile and, swinging the door wide, welcomed him into her home. Of course the woman would welcome him with a smile. He, no doubt, paid the rent.

But his affairs didn't matter, did they? Elsbeth did not—could not—love Nigel. True, she had confessed her love for him while he was sleeping. But surely she'd been lying to herself. Surely, she'd known better than to fall into such a honeyed trap again.

A peel of laughter rose from the house.

She was fond of him, true.

The laughter grew louder.

She had believed him honorable. Perhaps her heart did hurt just a bit. She stepped closer to peer shamelessly into a window. The room, a small parlor, was filled with furniture that was quite old but well cared for. Nigel was seated in a wooden chair near the fireplace. A small boy, no more than five years old, squirmed and giggled on his lap.

The lad's eyes were dark like midnight . . . just like Nigel's.

His aristocratic nose and strong chin were delicate copies of the man holding him. The boy gave Nigel's ear a tug.

Both father and son laughed.

CHAPTER TWENTY-SIX

This was worse than Elsbeth could have ever imaged. Far worse. She backed away from the window heedless of the vegetables she crushed under her kid boots. How could she hope to compete when this woman had already given Nigel a gift she could never give?

Here, in this little cottage on a dingy back alleyway, lay Nigel's heart.

"Lady Edgeware?" Much to her horror, Nigel's mistress appeared at the door with a shawl over her shoulders and a woven basket on her arm. After a quick glance back inside, the woman stepped closed the door behind her. "Please, take my handkerchief."

Elsbeth dabbed at the tears she hadn't realized she'd let fall.

"You are very beautiful, Lady Edgeware." Nigel's mistress smiled just as warmly at Elsbeth as she had with Nigel. "It torments him, you know. He doesn't quite know what to do with you. Come." She stepped into the alleyway. "Walk with me."

"What about Nigel? Will he not miss you?"

The mistress laughed. "No, this is his time with Michael. My time with Edgeware ended years ago." She gave a wistful sigh. "I am Bess, my lady. Please, do not worry overmuch, I will not tell him that you followed him."

Bess accompanied Elsbeth back to Oxford Street. The two women walked in silence past the small shops and residences lining the road.

"Have you truly no questions?" Bess asked after they had stopped to peer into an upholsterer's shop window. Elsbeth shook her head, unable to think.

Bess put her hand on Elsbeth's sleeve and they began walking again. "I have a question then, my lady."

Elsbeth steeled her nerves. Clearly, this woman was in love with Nigel and had every right to be sorely jealous.

"Are you the one?" Bess asked and laughed before Elsbeth had a chance to be puzzled by the question. "Of course you are. It's foolish of me to ask, isn't it? He wouldn't have married you otherwise. He's loved you for nearly a decade, hasn't he?"

"We have only just met," Elsbeth countered.

Bess shook her head. The hand on Elsbeth's sleeve tightened. "*You* may have only met him, my lady. But I daresay *he* has known you for many years."

Dionysus. Nigel was his keeper. And Dionysus had plagued her for nearly a decade. What Bess claimed could be true.

"And now Nigel's life is in danger," Bess said. "I worry for him, though he's laughed off my concern."

"I fear his cousin is after his fortune and title. I'm doing all I can to stop him."

"Yes, I have heard that you've been making inquiries," Bess said. "Do not look so shocked. Living as I do gives me access to all manner of information. *All* manner." She lifted her brows. "Charlie Purbeck is a blackguard. I wouldn't trust him for even a moment. But, I believe you are looking in the wrong direction with that one."

"What do you mean?"

"I mean, my lady, Charlie does not have enough of a backbone to be a killer."

"But if not Charlie . . . who would want my husband dead?"

Evening came with Gainsford fidgeting even more than usual

and Elsbeth more rigid. If only she would smile when Nigel entered a room.

The dinner table was set for two with Nigel's best china. The servants were obviously trying to make a favorable impression on their new mistress. That was good. The more comfortable she felt in his home, the less she would feel the need to run back to her uncle.

Elsbeth, dressed in a plain gray gown that appeared to be a size too large, stood behind her place setting. Her hands curled about the back of her chair when he entered.

"You look lovely this evening," he said, and gave her a quick kiss on the cheek. He pulled out her chair and helped her to sit.

Her hand fiercely gripped his arm as she sank to the seat.

"You are in pain." Alarm shot through him. Infection. The doctor told them they had to watch out for infection.

"I am fine," she protested.

"I will have a physician come round tomorrow."

"Really, my lord, that isn't necessary."

"So, we are back to 'my lord' again."

Gainsford entered with a footman and a maid each carrying trays of food. The cook had outdone herself once again. The fare was better than anything he could remember tasting. Perhaps it was the company that made the food so sweet since, truly, he would not have been able to describe even one dish served that evening.

They ate in silence. Elsbeth kept glancing up at him, her eyes filled with questions, but she held her tongue. Nigel kept his peace as well until the last plate was removed and Gainsford had left the room.

"We are hosting a ball this Friday." He dabbed his mouth with a napkin. "In celebration of our wedding. You should meet with Gainsford in the morning to discuss the details."

She nodded and drew several agitated breaths.

"I pray you will be available to attend?" Had he been too imperial in his manner? Had he presumed too much by deciding to hold the ball without discussing it first with her? With Elsbeth so careful to keep her anger in check, he found it difficult to tell. Sometimes he dearly wished she would simply shout at him so he could know what was on her mind. Lord Mercer had taught her to hold her tongue too well, damn his black soul.

She carefully folded her linen napkin and placed it on the table to smooth out the edges. "Tell me about Bess and Michael," she said at last.

The hard edges of the chair's wooded back bit into his spine. "What-what do you wish to know?"

"Bess, she is lovely." Her chin was stiffly held, her gaze, naturally, unreadable. "And so is your son."

A glimmer of pain darkened her sapphire glare.

"Michael will be six years old this June. I plan to send him to Eton when he is old enough." Had he betrayed Elsbeth by lying with Bess six years ago? Oh hell, even if what he'd done was wrong, he wasn't going to apologize for the birth of his son. "I won't deny his existence to anyone."

Elsbeth began to tap on the table with the tip of her slender forefinger. She turned her gaze down to watch her own repeated movement.

"I would never ask you to." Her finger kept tapping. "Do you love her?"

Now there was a question. Six years ago Nigel believed himself in love with Bess. She smiled for him and always welcomed him into her bed. Her brand of erotic affection was like a soothing balm.

"Bess let me forget. Uncle Charles has never approved of the man I became. I am a dreamer like my father, he says. And he is right." She continued to tap her finger on the table. "I've

283

always struggled to please my uncle. When I was with Bess, she let me forget my responsibilities, my title, my name. When I was with her I was able to control my obsession to—"

Her hand stilled, and she glanced up.

He'd been on the verge of admitting to her that being with Bess quieted his obsession with painting. Bess had given him a glimpse of what peace must feel like.

Was that love? No, she'd simply given him an escape from his life.

"After Michael was born I came to realize I wasn't prepared for the responsibilities that come with illicit relationships. Like so many of the gentry, I cannot ignore a bastard child. A child is a child no matter which side of the blanket he is born."

When he saw his words were having no effect on Elsbeth, he stood. "Bess is Michael's mother. For the past six years, that is all she has been to me."

"Where are you going?" she demanded. For the first time since their marriage he heard a note of true anger in her voice. But since he was embarrassed by having to answer for an indiscretion that had happened six years ago, he didn't realize that her anger was a step in the right direction.

Instead of sweeping her into his arms and kissing her until she was breathless with need, he slammed his fist against the table. "That, my prickly wife, is none of your concern."

"Is it not?" Fire leapt from her heated gaze. "Is it not?" she repeated louder this time.

"You've made yourself clear from the first day of our marriage. You don't want to have anything to do with me. So why should I feel the least bit obligated to answer to you?"

"Because—!" she shouted. Tears glistened in her eyes, but she swiftly blinked them away.

"Because . . . ?" he whispered in the long silence that followed.

"In case you have forgotten, my lord," she said, her voice crisp enough to frost the crystals hanging from the chandelier, "your life is in constant danger. Yet you walk the streets with no apparent concern for your own welfare."

"Careful there, sweet, you sound almost as if you care."

"I do care, damn you!" She gave a little scream and pushed past him as she fled from the dining room. Shortly afterwards, a door somewhere in the house was slammed shut in a most unladylike manner.

I do care . . . Her words—words that had sounded as if they'd been ripped from the deepest depths of despair—echoed in Nigel's head as he disappeared into the cellar to paint . . . to do what he knew best.

Alone and apart. Life was easier that way. He didn't wish to cause her any more pain. Yet everything he did seemed to hurt her.

He didn't know what to do. So, for Elsbeth's sake and his own, he stayed in the cellar all night. He was too much of a coward to see if she would come to his bed, if she would still let him make love to her body even though it was her soul he yearned to touch.

The next day Elsbeth's cousins, Olivia and Lauretta along with their elderly maiden aunt, Violet, spent hours sequestered behind the parlor doors laughing and enjoying themselves. What they discussed, Nigel could only wonder.

As soon as her family left, he sought her out.

His senses alert, he quickly found Elsbeth in the small gold parlor in the back of the house. She was sitting next to Gainsford and, by the looks of it, in the middle of reviewing a complicated menu.

Gainsford took one look at Nigel and jumped to his feet. He stuttered some nonsense about needing to check on the butter and then rushed from the room.

"Good afternoon, my lord," Elsbeth said. She looked as fresh and clean as a new day after a week of heavy rain. She was dressed in a simple yellow and white striped gingham gown, and with her hair pulled back and tied up with a wide lavender ribbon.

"Please," he said. He might as well been that awkward, lanky boy painting flowers and a certain young maiden in Oxford. "Please, sit with me for a moment."

She pursed her dewy lips and tilted her head as she paused to consider the request. With the grace of a queen she glided over to the settee he stood beside and lowered herself onto the cushion. She sat with her back gently arched and her head slightly bowed.

He settled in beside her with considerably less grace. "I wish to hold your hand."

He uncurled his fist, ungloved and chilled, and waited to see if she would touch him in the bright light of day. "Remember that day at your uncle's?" he said while he bided his time. "I was so certain you would refuse to touch my hand. And that, my dove, made me even more eager to win your favor."

He was beginning to feel foolish sitting there with his empty hand raised. She had turned her head and was staring at his palm, wide-eyed.

With sad resignation, he closed his hand and pressed his knuckles into the plush cushion.

"You've been trained too well to hold your tongue, Elsbeth. My darkest wish is for your Lord Mercer to be alive again so I could kill him."

She recoiled from the violence of his words.

"What was your life with him like?" He'd not wanted to ask that question. He feared the answer. But Lord Mercer and the life Elsbeth had with him seemed to hang between them like a leaden curtain.

"I'd rather not talk about him." She reached for the locket that had curiously disappeared from her neck. Finding it gone she clasped her hands in her lap.

"For the sake of our marriage, I need to know more about the ghosts that haunt those lovely eyes of yours. You told me once that Mercer was a monster, and I don't wish to cause you any more pain by asking you to remember, but you have to talk about this. The torment was evident in your eyes even before you met me. I know, I'd noticed you and your troubled eyes at your uncle's ball. Let me try to take on some of that burden for you. Let me in, Elsbeth. Even if it's just a little."

"I-I don't know that I can. I don't know that I should. You have to understand, I was disloyal to my marriage vows. I was disloyal to him." She smiled painfully. "I was not a very good wife. I don't know if I can be one."

Her admission broke his heart. "You wrongly put the blame on yourself. From what you and Molly have told me . . . and from what I've heard about Mercer from other sources, it sounds as if he was the worst sort of husband. By being cruel to you, he was the first to break the marriage vow. And once that vow was broken, you were no longer under any kind of obligation to him."

"He was an angry man," she conceded. "It started soon after the wedding. He'd been boasting to his friends how he'd married the most beautiful woman in all of England. And—" she hesitated.

Nigel waited in silence.

She squeezed her hands together and then cleared her throat. "You probably need to know this. Your cousin, Charlie was visiting at the time. I had met him once before, but only briefly. He'd flirted shamelessly with me that first time we met, vowing that we'd marry. But I was already in love with . . . with . . .

Well, I put Charlie off, and I don't think he forgave me for it.

"And then at that cursed dinner party, where Mercer was boasting how he'd married the most beautiful woman in all England—much to my mortification—Charlie listed at least a half dozen ladies whom he believed more lovely. Some of the other men at the table had nodded in agreement. That night—"

She looked away suddenly. Her voice turned rough. "That one comment put Mercer in a black mood for the rest of the evening. He kept glaring at me. I puzzled over his odd mood, naturally. It was really quite embarrassing. That evening, after we retired, I confronted him. He struck me across the face. I remember falling to the floor." She fell silent again. "He pulled me back up and hit me again . . . and again . . . and again . . . and . . ." Her voice trailed off.

"*Oh dear God,*" Nigel whispered.

"By the next morning, no one would think me lovely looking like that, which only made him more cross." She turned back to Nigel, her gaze searching his. "Learning that I was barren only made him hate me more. And yet he was the one who had pushed so hard for our marriage. He was the one who had given me those paintings, claiming that he had created them. He was the one who'd claimed that the paintings had been made for my eyes, and my eyes alone."

That last part had been true. Nigel always thought of her when he painted. Ever since he'd first seen her as she'd danced across the field, his paintings were for her. Only for her.

"But I quickly learned he wasn't an artist. He didn't even *like* art." She sighed and closed her eyes as if remembering something that had once brought her pleasure. "For many years into my marriage I foolishly held onto a fantasy, hoping that there might be a knight-in-shining-armor lurking in the home wood and planning to rush the gates to save me."

She lifted her head. Her blue eyes shivered. "You knew me,

before my marriage? Bess says that you knew me even then." She swallowed hard. "Loved me. Because of Dionysus?"

He searched for the words to tell her the truth.

Her shoulders fell and she lowered her head again. "Of course that couldn't be true. You are a good man. You would have never allowed me to suffer at Lord Mercer's cruel hands. I waited for someone like you to come along . . . for Dionysus to find me. Surely, if you had known about my situation, you would have stormed the gates. You would have saved me."

"If only I had known . . . If I had it all to do over again I would have been a better man. I would have sought you out. I would have protected you."

Elsbeth did an amazing thing then. She reached out and took his hand, uncurling his fingers, smoothing out his tightly held fist.

"Your fingers are cold," she said. With both hands she vigorously rubbed away the chill. She then took his other hand within her palm and began rubbing. "Gainsford and I have decided to serve chicken for the ball, if that will suit. He tells me that Cook does wonders with some exotic spices and the chicken. I cannot remember the name of the dish."

"Khorma."

Elsbeth nodded as she continued to massage his hand and wrist. She seemed quite unconscious of her actions. He closed his eyes and imagined that they were alone and in the master suite. In the middle of the night she often touched him this tenderly. Under the cover of darkness she was a different woman, a sensual woman unafraid of her husband. In those late night hours he was grateful for what she'd given him. And yet, even though he was afraid of hurting her again, he wanted to be intimate with her in more ways than just the physical.

"Cook spent several years preparing meals for a general in India. She picked up several recipes." With nimble fingertips she worked to relax the sinews crisscrossing the back of his hand. Did she know what she was doing to him?

It was amazing how intuitive her movements were in finding the tension buried beneath his skin.

"Will that suit?" she asked, pressing quite hard on a particularly sore spot.

"What? Yes, yes, of course. The chicken dish will be fine. Elsbeth, do you truly find marriage to me distasteful?"

She dropped his hand and jumped up from the settee. "Oh, you are a vexing man, my lord!"

"Vexing, Elsbeth?"

"Terribly, horribly, so. And you know it well. So, please, don't pretend to not know that you're able to twist my head around." Her pretty little fists were pressed against the most exquisite hips he could ever hope to encounter.

"Twist your head—? How so?" He rose and stood directly in front of her. She was trembling like a small bird longing for the freedom of the vast sky. Her wide eyes remained riveted to his. Her stare fed the fire burning in his chest.

"You continually confound me, my lord."

"Nigel," he said. "My name is Nigel. I insist you use it."

He held out his empty palm. "Place your hand in mine." When she hesitated, he said, "I insist."

She was quick to comply.

He was acting the part of bastard, he knew. But if she'd only give him the chance, he knew he could make her happy.

"Good." He led her back to the settee. They sat side-by-side holding hands like a pair of naïve youngsters. "Now tell me, Elsbeth, specifically how do I vex you?"

"Specifically?" She chewed her bottom lip. It was an excruciatingly erotic act. "I do not wish to be fond of you, my lord."

"Nigel," he corrected.

"I do not wish to be fond of you, Nigel."

"And you *are* fond of me?" He could only hope.

"Yes." She tore her gaze away.

"A certain degree of fondness for each other is beneficial in a marriage." With a gentle caress of her cheek, he coaxed her gaze back to his. "I am more than a little fond of you, Elsbeth. I do love you, you know."

"No, do not say that." She pulled from him and fluttered her hands in the air. "Do not say that."

"But it's true. Perhaps you will never be able to return my affection. But Elsbeth, believe me when I tell you my love is genuine."

"*No . . . no . . . no,*" she said, shaking her head. "*You cannot.*"

He caught her fluttering hands in his. "Kiss me, Elsbeth. Let your heart hear what your ears refuse."

"But I refused to tell you the name of the smuggler."

"I know."

"You have a mistress—"

"I *had* a mistress."

"And a child. I-I cannot give you a child."

"Yes, I love my son. But I also love you. Kiss me, Elsbeth. Just one small kiss."

She stared deep into his eyes. Her throat tightened as she swallowed hard. "Just one kiss."

It took all of his control not to pull her into his arms and kiss her. But no, this was something she had to do for herself.

She leaned forward. She closed her eyes just as her lips brushed his. It was a chaste kiss not unlike one he would give an aunt. Her lips were hard and firmly sealed.

He despaired at his failure to reignite the passion he knew lay buried deep within her. He had seen that passion come alive several times now and had witnessed the miracle of her pleasure. He groaned deep in his throat from the memory.

She responded. Her lips parted as she heaved a tender sigh and sought his with a hunger he'd not dared to hope for in the light of day.

She clasped her hands at the base of his neck and clung to him while she deepened the kiss, swirling her tongue in his mouth with a courtesan's skill. Gradually, she pulled back. Her sapphire eyes were darkened with a lusty haze. A rosy glow colored her finely formed cheeks.

She kept her fingers clasped around his neck.

"So, where do we go from here?" she whispered.

"Hmmm." His mind filled with thoughts a gentleman should not share with the gentler sex. "I suppose you should tell me, Elsbeth, do you truly find marriage to me so distasteful?"

A sparkle brightened her eyes. Her lips curled into a delightfully wry smile. "I think I shall have to kiss you again."

CHAPTER TWENTY-SEVEN

She didn't want to love him, but it seemed the harder she fought against it, the deeper she fell. He'd woven a spell around her, one that made her heart pound heavily in her chest every time he was around.

When she kissed him, she tasted what she'd missed in her life for far too many years—a home. Not just a roof over her head but a safe place where she could rediscover herself, where she could live and grow. And love. A life with a man she could trust. Oh, she so dearly wanted to trust.

He traced his finger along her tear-dampened cheek. "I love you," he whispered. "Let that be enough. Let me love you."

With her mouth she told him how she was willing to share her life with him. She wanted—no, needed—the confidence he gave her more than she needed to breathe. Nigel touched her, caressed her, encouraged her while their tongues played a prelude to how their bodies would touch.

He eased the bodice of her gown off her shoulders and freed her breasts so he could put his mouth to its swollen bud, suckling and teasing her until her whole body was throbbing with desire. His hands roamed lower and he parted her thighs.

Ah . . . this was the way life should be. She prayed that this wasn't just another illusion as she lost herself to the moment . . . to the feel of his mouth on her body . . . to his love . . .

"Edgeware!" The gold parlor's narrow door swung open and cracked against a marble top cabinet. An expensive Wedgwood jasper and ivory colored vase plunged to the plush gold-tinged Persian rug. The vase bounced but didn't break.

Mr. George Waver, his clothes rumpled, his face smudged with black soot, charged into the room. Gainsford trailed close on his heel, wringing his hands in a helpless gesture.

"Oh my," she heard Gainsford mutter. He was no longer looking fretfully at Mr. Waver, but he was now looking at her and Nigel and the erotic positions of their bodies on the sofa. A shocked expression quickly turned to one of satisfaction, softening his furrowed brows while bright spots of color stained his cheeks.

Nigel sprang to his feet and with his arms spread wide to put himself physically between her and Mr. Waver. "Whatever quarrel you have with me, George, I demand you leave Elsbeth out of it. I will never forgive you for dragging my wife out into the middle of a storm and nearly killing her."

"Is that what she told you?" Mr. Waver charged.

She tugged on her gown's bodice, desperately trying to get the crumpled material up around her torso, to cover her breasts that were displayed for all in the room to see. It had been so easy for Nigel to get the cursed gown off her shoulders, she couldn't figure out why it should be so difficult to set herself to right again.

"She told me nothing. Damn you!" Nigel grabbed Mr. Waver by the cravat and shook him. "You bloody bastard! You coerced a vow out of her! You turned my own wife against me!" He shook Mr. Waver again.

Elsbeth had just gotten her sleeves back into place when she realized Nigel had finally cracked. His shell of control was gone, and if she didn't act quickly, he might actually kill his friend. She certainly wasn't going to let that happen. She rose quickly from the sofa.

"Nigel!" she shouted and sharply clapped her hands. "I

demand you stop this right now! Honor your bonds of friendship with Mr. Waver. Listen to what he has to say before you kill him!"

Nigel dropped Mr. Waver and rounded on her. His dark gaze glittered with fury. Amazingly, she stood her ground. Amazingly, she didn't fear that he might raise his hand against her.

"You know I am right," she said much quieter. "Ask him, why is he here? If it is to kill you, where is his weapon?"

"Gainsford." Nigel's voice was deadly smooth. "Escort my wife from the room."

"No, Gainsford," she countered and matched her husband's determined glare with one of her own. "I will not leave."

Gainsford appeared too mortified to move from his spot in the doorway.

"Elsbeth, what do you think you are doing?" Nigel whispered.

"Protecting you from yourself. You will not kill Mr. Waver."

"Kill him?"

"I will not permit it. You will listen to him."

"Kill *George?*"

"You will listen to me." She leaned in closer; her nose nearly touching his. "You will listen to me."

"I say, Edgeware, are you planning to kill me?" Mr. Waver drawled. He sounded . . . *amused?*

What was going on?

"I was planning to beat your bloody head into the bloody ground," Nigel answered without releasing Elsbeth from his heated gaze. "If you did indeed try to kill me, it would put a terrible strain on our friendship. I trusted you. And if I learn you harmed even a hair on my wife's head, I will have to put a bullet through you."

"Gainsford," Elsbeth said, her head spinning, "please fetch a pot of tea. I believe Mr. Waver, Edgeware, and I shall sit down and discuss this matter in a civilized manner."

"Civilized," Mr. Waver said with a light chuckle. "Now there's a thought that makes me shiver."

"Take a seat, George." Nigel ordered and then took Elsbeth's hand in his. He pressed her open palm to his lips . . . in front of a grinning Mr. Waver. Elsbeth's cheeks flamed. "Though I might not always agree with you, I will always listen to you, dove." He smiled then, his dimples deepening. "And please don't look as if you think I might eat you. It'll scare George."

Gainsford returned with a piping hot pot of tea and three delicately painted floral patterned cups. Elsbeth served.

"So tell me, George," Nigel said after making a show of sipping his tea. "Why have you overset my butler and forced your way into my home after hiding from me for nearly a week?" Where he sat, so close to her, his leg brushed up against Elsbeth's.

This closeness made her very aware of his body. She could feel his movements, no matter how small. Listening to the conversation, really hearing what Nigel was saying, was turning into a chore as her thoughts kept straying back to the moments before Mr. Waver had burst into the room and to how her body had been even closer to her husband's. Someone should open a window. The room was surely overly warm.

"A thousand pardons, Edgeware," Mr. Waver said. Laughter was still brightening his eyes. "Gainsford had told me you were away from home. But I knew he was lying, and I needed to speak with you without delay." He did have the decency to blush and murmur his next words. "I hadn't paused to consider the common behavior of newly wed couples."

Elsbeth squirmed with embarrassment. It didn't matter that they were married.

Nigel must have sensed her discomfort. He gave her hand a gentle squeeze. "You have better say what you need to say, George, before I call for a constable to haul you to Newgate."

"I suppose you are in the right if you wish to do something so drastic. It is true, I have been running the family smuggling operation from your beach. The whole village has been doing so for generations. But I swear, I have never tried to hurt you or your lady wife." Mr. Waver sipped his tea. "And I bloody well didn't kill your butler or that deceiving footman of yours." The beverage did have a civilizing effect on society. He very carefully set down the cup on a highly polished side table. "What I do know is that someone tried to kill Lord Purbeck this morning. If I hadn't been following him and if I hadn't had the opportunity to intervene, I'm certain your uncle would be dead right now."

"And why were you following my uncle?" Nigel asked calmly. He still held Elsbeth's hand, though it was very improper for him to continue such a blatant display of affection in front of guests. Perhaps it wasn't affection he was seeking in her contact, but strength. He had sought her strength before, though the very idea still astounded her.

"I'd believed Lord Purbeck was trying to kill you."

"Uncle Charles?"

"He is the heir apparent," Mr. Waver pointed out.

"Uncle Charles raised me as if I was his son."

"You aren't his son, though. But apparently he isn't the one we are after. His life is in as much danger as yours."

"With Nigel and Lord Purbeck out of the way," Elsbeth said, "Mr. Charlie Purbeck would stand to inherit the title, the fortune . . . and the power." It was the power Charlie craved most. Elsbeth was certain of that.

"Charlie wouldn't want to hurt me," Nigel was quick to say.

"I wouldn't be too sure," Mr. Waver said. "Lady Edgeware, you know Charlie from his acquaintance with your late husband. Tell me, what makes you believe he is capable of such treachery?"

"Lord Mercer and Mr. Purbeck were gamblers of the worst sort. They gambled with money they could ill-afford to lose." She drew a deep breath. "I believe Mr. Purbeck has somehow gotten himself into trouble by betting a fortune on a single horserace."

"I see," Nigel said.

"The cove was foolish enough to put all of his money on one horse?" Mr. Waver asked.

"No." She pulled her hand from Nigel's grasp and clasped her hands tightly over her knees. She bent slightly forward, well aware of her unladylike posture as she explained what Mademoiselle Dukard had told her. "I have learned that he didn't use his own money but had borrowed deeply from friends, telling them that they would all come out rich."

"This is unbelievable." Mr. Waver leaned back in his chair.

"So that is why he has been pressing me for the thirty thousand pounds," Nigel said. "But he's gotten himself deep into debt before and has never tried to kill me, or anyone else for that matter. I cannot believe he would do so now."

"Within the last week I have interviewed several women." She paused remembering the string of paramours she had encountered. "With their help I have compiled a list of gentlemen who gave Mr. Purbeck money for that bet."

"With whom have you been meeting?" Nigel asked.

She closed her eyes and shook her head. He wouldn't approve. What man would wish his wife to be consorting with women of that sort? But she needed to start being honest with him. She needed to trust him to be strong enough to hear what she had to say and to not punish her for it. "I met with Mademoiselle Dukard first."

Mr. Waver drew back with a gasp of surprise.

"It is dangerous to go after a killer alone and even more dangerous for a gentle woman such as yourself to go to the places where women such as Mademoiselle Dukard reside." There was a touch of anger in Nigel's voice, but it was similar to the kind-hearted scolding he had given Lauretta at the ball. "I don't want your life put into danger. Seeing you harmed shortens my life. You should have sent me in your place."

The mademoiselle had only provided Elsbeth with the most rudimentary of details. It was Nigel's own Bess who'd introduced her to the other women involved. She'd accompanied Elsbeth on the visits and they had been quite safe.

"Who I met with and how I was introduced to them is not important. What is important is that someone appears to be very interested in having you dead . . . someone who could make use of your money."

Nigel sprang to his feet. "Not Charlie. He is like my brother. He would never do anything to harm me."

Bess also didn't believe Charlie capable of murder. But neither of them knew Charlie's true nature. If only Nigel knew . . . yet Elsbeth could never tell him the full truth about that horrible night, or of how he seemed to relish watching as Lord Mercer tormented her. She could never tell him the pain, the humiliation she suffered when Charlie had joined her husband in the abuse.

"I still haven't ruled you out, George." Nigel shot an accusing finger in the direction of the chair where Mr. Waver was currently lounging.

"Are you back to that? I suppose I do owe you an explanation. Like I'd said, Edgeware, I have been using your shore to smuggle goods into the country."

"Yes? And you lied to me about it. Why? Why not tell me the truth when I asked you?"

"Why?" Mr. Waver lurched forward. "Because you are so damned innocent. You don't understand going to bed at night with a burning hunger in your belly. My family is respectable, yes. But there is no money behind that *respectable* name. My mother and father did the best they could to hold the estate together, mortgaging it several times over just so we would have a place to live, an illusion to preserve."

"You could have told me."

"I wasn't looking for a handout, dammit!"

The two men stared at each other seemingly deadlocked. The calming effect of the tea seemed to be wearing thin.

"Will you turn me in?" Mr. Waver asked quietly. "If you do, all I ask is that you try not to involve the rest of my family or the villagers."

Nigel clasped his hands behind his back and began pacing again. "Did you drug my wife?"

Mr. Waver's jaw dropped as he stared at Nigel, dumbfounded.

"Did you drug my wife and put her out in the storm to die?"

"He saved me from the drenching cold, Nigel. He didn't put me in it."

"Is this true?" Nigel asked Mr. Waver.

"Yes, Edgeware. I am insulted that you have to ask."

Nigel gave a small growl and tugged at his hair. The black strands all stood on end giving him a tousled look that Elsbeth thought adorable.

"Dammit, I no longer know who I can trust. Until this is over, the only person I will trust will be you, Elsbeth."

"*Me?*"

CHAPTER TWENTY-EIGHT

At three o'clock, the fashionable hour for riding, Severin turned his well cared-for but woefully old-fashioned phaeton pulled by two horses instead of the usual four onto the busy social circuit in Hyde Park. At least his two horses were prime specimens of horseflesh. Nothing at all to be ashamed of in front of the lovely Lady Lauretta.

This was the first time he'd ridden through Hyde Park for the sheer pleasure of a lady's company. Lady Lauretta spun an open parasol in her hand, her large hazel eyes never sat still. She appeared to be searching the faces in the park, perhaps searching for someone in particular. Severin worried her heart still clung to that milksop, Sir Donald Gilforth.

"Oooo," Lady Lauretta cried. "There's Elsbeth. And she is with *him*. She's smiling at *him*."

Severin turned his head after tipping his hat in passing to an acquaintance who had smiled a bit too lewdly up at Lady Lauretta for Severin's liking and caught sight of Edgeware riding in a sparkling curricle with the new Lady Edgeware seated beside him. Miracle of miracles, the severe lady was indeed smiling.

She looked quite beautiful.

"The Marquess appears to have a positive influence on your cousin," Severin pointed out.

"Papa says there is naught but trickery and deception under Lord Edgeware's roof. Poor Elsbeth." Lady Lauretta spun her parasol even faster. "Papa says she's been hoodwinked. She actually told Papa that only *she* could protect that bounder from the dangerous situation he's gotten himself into."

"You don't say," Severin said thoughtfully.

"She's been investigating the matter on her own. Can you believe such nonsense? I told her just the other day that I have never known her to act in a foolish manner, but look at her. I told her this myself, she is acting the fool now. And still, she refused to come home with Olivia and me."

"I say," Severin chuckled at the thought of the mild Lady Lauretta trying to face down the formable Lady Edgeware. It was a wonder that Lauretta didn't appear singed after such a harrowing experience.

"You are laughing at me!"

"No, my lady, not at you."

"You are! Olivia laughed the same way, telling me I was a silly innocent."

Severin tucked her hand into his large palm. "I am not laughing at you, my lady." He brushed a quick kiss across her knuckle. "I am merely amazed at your bravery. I once stood up to Lady Edgeware years ago and was presented with the most harrowing set-down I have ever been handed in all my life."

Lady Lauretta turned sharply and stared down her pretty little nose at him. Severin laughed again. She was so different from the jaded widows whose company offered him nothing long-lasting.

The fact that Lady Lauretta was also an heiress strangely did not matter one whit. It wasn't her money but her mind that attracted him. She had an uncanny ability to recognize not only visible talent but also the potential talent of budding artists. Just the other day he'd taken her to both Sotheby's Auction House and Christie's to discuss the various artworks offered for sale. With her sharp eye and his slick business sense, they could develop quite a lucrative business.

"I simply do not trust him." Lady Lauretta's gaze had returned to Edgeware's curricle. The Marquess's pair of perfectly matched blacks pranced alongside Lord Charles Purbeck's landau.

"Edgeware is a fine gentleman, my dear. I owe much to him."

Lady Lauretta tipped her head back so he could clearly see her entire face below the rim of her wide bonnet. "How so?"

Now that wasn't something a gentleman certainly shared with a lady.

A little over a year ago, Severin had slinked out the back way of a stinking gaming hell after losing a bundle of blunt he could ill afford to lose. He was following a path his father had taken, a path that led straight to ruin.

"Ho there," Edgeware had called to him.

Severin had stumbled, having imbibed far too much while losing hand after hand in cards. "Leave off, sir. Leave a man to his honorable fate."

Severin winced as he remembered. This was definitely not a story for genteel ears, for he had pressed a pistol to his own temple, fully intending to end his miserable life before he could drag his family even further into debt.

"You shouldn't play with such toys," Edgeware had said and pinched the pistol from Severin's grasp, pocketing the weapon before Severin could slur a drunken protest. "They could inadvertently hurt a man."

That was when Edgeware had begged Severin for his help. He had a pile of paintings he wished displayed and sold.

Severin now knew that Edgeware had no need to sell his paintings. He didn't benefit from fame; he shied away from it, in fact. And he certainly didn't need the money.

"Edgeware made a great sacrifice to save my life. Let's just leave it at that," Severin said to Lady Lauretta. He steered his phaeton off the social circuit and onto a shady tree-lined side path hoping to steal a kiss. He'd not had a moment alone with her since Edgeware's house party and he rather enjoyed exposing Lauretta to such shocking adventures as stolen kisses and hidden embraces.

"I told you no! I will not!" A woman's voice echoed through the leaves in the canopy above Severin and Lady Lauretta's heads. Severin drew the phaeton to a halt.

"What do you think that was about?" Lady Lauretta whispered.

Whatever it was, it wasn't at all a thing a respectable lady needed to be a witness to. "I have no idea." He jumped down from the landau and then took Lady Lauretta around the waist and swung her down to the ground.

"Wait here." He tied the reins to a tree. "But don't stand too close to the carriage in case the horses decide to bolt."

"No! I will not agree to help you!" The woman's shrill voice carried through the air and assaulted their ears.

Severin sprinted toward the woman's cries, following a narrow footpath, and then stopped mid-stride. Within a blink, he made his way back to Lady Lauretta. He took her by the shoulders, pulling her close. "I will be right back," he whispered before he gave her a thorough kiss on the lips.

"Oh my!" Lady Lauretta cried. A full blush bloomed on her cheeks when he set her back down.

"Won't be but a moment," Severin called, as he ran again down the narrow trail on a quest to rescue the distressed lady hidden somewhere in the park.

He drew to a halt when he reached a small clearing. A man and woman, both dressed in the unmistakable flare demanded by the *haut ton,* stood toe-to-toe arguing. The gentleman, if one cared to call him that, was twisting the lady's arm.

"No!" the woman cried.

Severin stepped into the clearing. "I would abide by the lady's wishes if you know what is good for you, sir," Severin said. He stripped off his riding gloves.

"You?" the man growled, still squeezing the poor woman's arm. "Get out of here, Lord Ames. This is none of your affair."

It took a moment for Severin to recognize Sir Donald Gilforth. The fop wore a high guillotine collar with an overdone strangling cravat. The combination of the two nearly swallowed the bottom half of Sir Donald's face. His highly polished beaver hat was pulled low on his brow. Perhaps Sir Donald didn't wish to be immediately recognized.

"Ducky," Severin gave a deferential bow and quick smile to the lovely courtesan. Recognition of the seductive lady dressed in a high-waisted gown of the sheerest silver muslin had been almost instant. "Is this matter truly none of my affair? Am I simply an old prude intruding on a romantic liaison?"

Ducky twisted away from Sir Donald and sauntered over to Severin. She pressed her hands against his chest. "Are you prepared to offer me a better deal, my lord?" In a slow, smooth motion, she moistened her lips.

Severin mutely stared at her slender fingers stroking his superfine navy coat. Not a glimmer of interest sparked, not even a quickening of his steady heart rate. In fact, his thoughts strayed back down the trail to where Lady Lauretta had been left stranded in the middle of the path. He really should return to her.

Ducky reached up and was poised to demonstrate her seductive skills on his lips when Severin took a step back. "I was merely looking to be of assistance to a lady in distress." He sketched a bow. "I see now I am indeed intruding. My pardon." He turned on his heel and made haste back down the darkened forest path.

"What do you suppose that was all about?" a soft voice whispered from behind him.

What in the world?

Severin spun around and planted his hands on his hips as he stared down at Lady Lauretta. She was pouting. Her dark brown ringlets bounced in the warm spring breeze.

"I am beginning to believe Sir Donald is naught but a rogue. Here he is found flirting shamelessly with that lady while openly courting Lady Constance. Shame." A smile sneaked into her expression. "I am thrilled, however, that I am not in Lady Constance's position."

"You-you followed me?" Severin sputtered, still not quite believing that the innocent Lady Lauretta had just witnessed Ducky's outlandish behavior. The Cyprian had nearly kissed him!

"Yes, I followed you. I wasn't about to be left all alone alongside that deserted roadway. Do you think I'm daft? I knew very well why you turned the carriage off the social circuit. Lord Ames, *you* were looking to kiss me again . . . like you did in the picture gallery."

Severin shook his head and started back toward his phaeton. Lady Lauretta looked much too pleased with herself. She should be scandalized at the very least.

"You were planning to kiss me?" She sounded much less certain now.

Did she really wish to know the answer to that question?

"I say." He heard her stomp her foot in the dry dirt. "I will not return to the phaeton until you answer me."

Severin smiled as he slowed his step. "Perhaps a little," he said.

"Perhaps a little? What kind of answer is that? What does *perhaps a little* mean? *Perhaps a little,* indeed!"

Severin turned around then. Lady Lauretta's cheeks glowed. The chit was enjoying herself. He suspected she hid an adventurous nature behind that veil of innocence she wore.

Perhaps it was time someone helped her discover the extent of that delightful character trait.

"Why don't you come here and find out what I mean?"

Lady Lauretta considered Severin, her expression grave. "I should think it is the gentleman's duty to come to the woman," she murmured before slowly crossing the distance between them. "Shall I place my hands on your chest? That lady with Sir Donald, she was going to kiss you, was she not? She placed her hands on your chest."

Severin could feel the heat of a blush rising to his face. Lady Lauretta should not have witnessed that. She should not even know such women exist.

"Yes," he said, and had to quickly clear his throat. "Yes, do brace your hands against my chest."

"Like this?" She had also risen up on to the tips of her toes and tilted her head.

"Yes, like that," he said, sounding a mite strangled. He drew the pad of his thumb over her gentle brow. This woman was everything he desired.

"Sweetest Lauretta, I will kiss you now."

What kicked in his chest when his lips touched her full mouth was not raw lust but something much worse, much more final. Slowly he drew back.

Lady Lauretta protested with the most endearing little cry.

Severin swallowed hard. His hands, he was amazed to find, were trembling. "Lady Lauretta," he said, "I believe I must call upon your papa in the morning and make this all very formal."

Her smile faded a degree. "What ever do you mean?"

Severin sunk down to one knee. "Marry me, Lauretta. With your keen artistic eye and depth of knowledge combined with my salesmanship, we will make quite a pair, you and I."

"We will?" Her frown deepened.

"I am not a rich man. Like your Sir Donald I am up to my

ears in debt, though I am slowly making headway on that front. I am not one to waste my funds, I will have you know."

"Sir Donald is in debt? But he dresses in all the latest fashions."

"So do I." The ground was becoming uncomfortable. A pebble was jabbing into his knee. "It is an illusion, living on credit, a grand illusion. Will you consider marriage to me?"

"I don't know . . ."

"Do you enjoy kissing me?" he shamelessly asked.

"Oh, yes," she glowed as she answered.

"And do you find me pleasant to look at?"

"More than pleasant."

"Do I bore you? Does my conversation put you to sleep? Do you think I am an awful dullard?"

"Oh, yes, terrible." Her smile returned.

"Would you mind being a partner in my enterprise? We could find young artists and help them to develop their talents."

"Oh, I would enjoy that." She paused while pursing her lips thoughtfully. "Partners, you say?"

"Partners."

"In that case, I think you should call on Papa this evening. There is no reason to dally, my lord." She sprung herself into his arms. And gave him an enthusiastic kiss that upset Severin's balance, sending them both tumbling to the ground.

Chapter Twenty-Nine

Elsbeth looked content as she ascended the wide, curving stairs to the suites that evening with Nigel at her side. The damning tension that had been keeping her from talking with him had apparently thawed. For the first time since their marriage, they'd spent the afternoon together. And had talked about important matters, picking apart every detail for Friday's upcoming ball. They'd also spent time discussing the smugglers and Charlie and even—very briefly—Dionysus. But that wasn't what was making him smile. It was that they'd talked about how the frail clouds that brushed across the sunny sky made them both feel wistful or how sneaking a treat from the kitchen made them both feel like a giddy child again. And they'd laughed.

Nigel had discovered that his pragmatic Elsbeth had a cunning sense of humor. Like him, she found the high sticklers in society amusing. However, she was distressed that some powerful members of society believed their marriage was a sham and their living together as one of the worst scandals to ever befall London. He promised that no one would question his devotion to her or to their marriage vows after Friday's ball.

Amazingly, after a day of sharing each other's company, they only disagreed once. She had mentioned that the seamstress had made a terrible mistake when cutting the bodices.

"You have to agree," she said as they neared the second floor landing. She put her hands just below her breasts, drawing Nigel's gaze to the gentle swells that had the power to make his body come immediately to life. "All my gowns are cut shamelessly low."

"Shamelessly?" he said with a laugh. "Your body is an artistic masterpiece, especially certain lovely parts that deserve to be worshiped. It would be a sin to cover them up any more than you already have."

"Worship? Is that what you call what you did two nights ago?" she asked playfully. A bright blush stained her cheeks.

Feeling suddenly serious, he caressed the length of her silky arm. "You are a treasure I intend to cherish with every breath I'm given."

"You are too pretty with your words," she said, and swatted his arm.

"Then let me use my lips in a different pursuit."

She gave a little squeal as he chased her up the last couple of steps to the landing. And then they stopped in front of his bedchamber's door. Her smile faded as she seemed to realize where he'd led her. She reached for the locket she no longer wore.

"Your locket," he asked. "Did you lose it?"

"No." She sighed deeply. "I chose not to wear it anymore."

She did? "You did?" What secret had she kept hidden in that locket? "Why?"

"I grew tired of the trinket." It was a lie. He was beginning to recognize the signs. He was learning how to read her body as clearly as he could hear her voice. When he reached for her, she tried to pull away from him, which didn't make any sense. They'd been getting along so well today. He wasn't ready to let it come to an end.

"The ball is tomorrow, Nigel. We should get a full night's sleep. Do you not agree?"

Of course, he agreed. They'd plotted together in order to come up with a plan to draw out the killer. The ball could prove to be a very dangerous affair. They should rest and keep their minds firmly on the situation at hand.

"Come to my bed," he said.

"I don't think I should," she said and dug her pearly white teeth into her bottom lip.

"I don't believe you," he said with a smile.

She blinked.

"Come to my bed, love."

She shook her head and looked a trifle confused as her pretty blush deepened. "It's a great leap of faith is it not, Nigel?"

"What is?"

"Trusting another person with your body and with your . . ."

Damn Lord Mercer. "I will never abuse your trust, Elsbeth. I love you. I truly love you. You trust that I'm telling you the truth about my feelings, don't you?"

He realized then that his poor, broken-hearted Elsbeth needed him to reach out to her. She needed him to love her and make her feel safe, secure. She needed a place where she could let her heart heal. She needed his love as fiercely as he yearned for hers.

Not wishing to continue this conversation in the middle of the hallway where a passing servant could disturb them, he took her hand and led her to his bedchamber, kicking the door closed behind him. He pushed aside the draperies surrounding his bed so he could sit at the edge of the bedding.

"Why did you say earlier today that you would trust me, and no one but me?" she asked as she wandered to the far end of the room. "Why me? I keep asking myself that question. And yet, I have no answer. I haven't given you a good reason to trust me. What made you take that leap of faith?"

"You are my wife." He could see right away that answer wouldn't do. He could only imagine how living with a bastard like Lord Mercer would make the sacred bonds of marriage feel like the bars of a prison.

She paused from her study of knickknacks scattered on top of a dresser and peered over her shoulder at him.

"A man *should* trust his wife," he said. "Just as a woman should be able to trust her husband."

"But I haven't proven trustworthy. I didn't tell you about Mr. Waver or the information I discovered about Mr. Purbeck until this afternoon. Do you not wonder if I'm keeping any other secrets?" She picked up a comb from the dresser top and turned it over in her hand.

"If you are, I trust you have a good reason."

"Even if that reason is to wish you dead?"

"Do you wish me dead, Elsbeth?" he said with emotion.

"I prayed for Lord Mercer's death. My prayers were answered . . . eventually." She dropped the comb and turned around.

"I would have prayed for his death if I were in your position, too. I don't see that praying for release from an undeserved hell is so great a sin." He steadied himself for an answer he might not want to hear. "Do *you* wish me dead?"

Her searching sapphire gaze pressed against his soul. "Not yet."

He laughed and patted the quilted counterpane. "I suppose only a fool would hope a wife never wished her husband to the devil. Come, sit beside me. I'm bored of all this peacefulness between us. I think I would like you to kiss me again."

When she hesitated, he added, "I am not at all like Lord Mercer. Do you not agree?"

She frowned as she considered the question. "I feel like I am perhaps a different woman with you."

It was one thing to sneak willingly into Nigel's bedroom in the dead of night. But to be lured to his bed like a rabbit to a fox's den made her knees wobble. A man had a right to demand his wife's submission in the bedroom.

Even though she loved Nigel, how could she ever feel safe? How could she know that he wouldn't ever demand what she wasn't prepared to give?

"I'm not Lord Mercer. Perhaps our marriage could be different from your first one? Perhaps it could be better?" he asked, speaking the words her heart longed to believe.

And it was true what she had said. He did make her feel like a different woman. He caressed her cheek and kissed her with such fierce desire, she felt as at ease with herself as the nude woman Dionysus had portrayed her to be.

Elsbeth turned so Nigel could unfasten the line of buttons down the back of her gown. This was what marriage could and should be like, safe and comfortable. She slipped her gown from her shoulders and let it fall to the floor.

"I will never demand you do anything that you don't want, dove."

"I want this," she whispered between kisses. "I want you."

This was the moment her heart had been waiting for all her life. She sought his kisses, his caresses, following his lead and boldly touching him in ways she knew excited a man. Soon, they were both in his bed. Soon they were both naked.

Nigel's breathing quickened. His arousal throbbed in her hand. She willingly gave him this pleasure. It pleased her to touch him, to know she was the cause of the glazed look in his eyes and the reason his head fell back on his pillows. The realization fed her own budding hunger.

She lowered her mouth to him. Nigel sucked in his breath when her lips touched him *there*. He groaned her name and she made love to him with her mouth. With a frustrated cry, he grabbed her shoulders. "Tonight is for you, my sweet dove," he whispered into her mouth. "Only for you."

His gaze, deep and hot, raked her body over and over. "You

are beautiful, Elsbeth. You are a dream come to life, a miracle of art. Everything I have ever desired." He touched her with his hands, running fingertips gently over her arms, ribcage, and hips. When he began showering her with kisses, she was lost . . .

They'd made love with a roomful of lit candles. She'd shouted his name. And after a short rest, they'd made love again.

The love of his life had drifted off to sleep after finding satisfaction for a second time.

Nigel traced the line of stitches on her side. The bullet wound was still angry and raw. He would send for the doctor to take yet another look at it in the morning. And he would be more careful when he took her again. But for now, he planned to let her sleep.

She shifted in the bed and moaned. Nigel, still aroused and uncomfortable, fought the urge to give into his desires a third time. He had meant it when he had said that this night was for her and her alone. He would let her sleep. She needed her rest.

She'd given him a wondrous gift tonight. She'd let him love her not as a man might love a dream, but as a husband might love a wife. For the first time in a long time, he felt at peace with himself.

Throughout the hectic day that followed, thoughts of that magical night stayed with Elsbeth. Nigel's gentle words, his coaxing her to trust him with her heart, made her smile at the oddest moments. She found herself smiling at the cloth in her hand early that morning while supervising a team of footmen as they polished the silver in the dinning room. It was a task she had trouble concentrating on, not just because of last night but also because tonight's ball promised to flush out the man trying to kill both Nigel and his uncle.

It was Charlie, she was certain. But Nigel had to learn for

himself the difficult truth.

"My ladyship!" Gainsford rushed into the room. She hadn't seen the butler at all that morning. Each had been busily preparing for the ball. And there was still much to be done. But he seemed to have forgotten that, as well as his place. He tossed his arms around her and gave her a most improper hug.

"Gainsford!"

The butler quickly regained his composure. He stepped a proper distance away and blushed as he waved away the curious stares of the young footmen. "Forgive me, my lady." He dipped a bow. "Just-just, I am ever so happy you . . . that you've come to this household, that you—" Gainsford cleared his throat and blushed.

Did the whole household know that she'd spent the entire night in her husband's bed? She lifted her chin and did her best to hold onto her composure. "Yes, Gainsford?"

"Lord Edgeware was *happy* when I spoke to him, my lady." He said this as if Nigel had never experienced a happy morning in his life, which was an idiotic notion.

"I am sure the Marquess is anticipating the excitement of this evening's festivities. And if we don't wish for him to be disappointed, I suggest we returned to our preparations."

The footmen all hastily returned their attentions to the silver. But Gainsford's lopsided grin was not to be so easily deterred. "You don't understand, my lady." Gainsford spoke softly now. "I bless the day his lordship finally found you. And I thank you."

Slightly shaken, she gave Gainsford a curt nod. She had so many more things to do and no time to be embarrassed by the servants. Evening would arrive soon enough and though the house was nearly ready, she would still have to prepare herself for the ball, a ball that would send a signal to all of London that she accepted her marriage to Nigel. Surprisingly, she *had* accepted her marriage to Nigel. And for the first time in a long time, she felt content.

By the time evening arrived, most of the tasks on Elsbeth's list had been ticked off. Many of the servants had disappeared belowstairs, and the house was quiet. Elsbeth fussed with a flower arrangement in the drawing room and caught herself smiling again. Despite fighting him every step of the way, she was now hopelessly in love with her husband. Did he know that she loved him? Had she told him yet? She couldn't remember.

"Elly, whatever are you doing fussing with those flowers? You should be upstairs dressing." Olivia flounced into the drawing room like a happy wren. Her stunning pale pink evening gown was cut daringly low in the bodice so that the flimsy material just barely kept her breasts contained.

Lauretta and Aunt Violet followed in Olivia's wake at a much more sedate pace. Elsbeth greeted her cousins and aunt warmly, giving each a kiss on the cheek.

Aunt Violet patted Elsbeth's cheek firmly. "At least one of you girls knows how to marry a man. You may not do it well, but at least you have accomplished the final deed . . . oh my, twice."

Lauretta appeared ready to burst into tears.

Olivia caught Elsbeth's arm and gave it a tug. "Let us retire upstairs and tuck you into your gown before the guests arrive."

Aunt Violet stamped her cane on the hardwood floor since the carpet had been rolled back to allow for dancing. "I have no desire to watch you girls twitter about. Show me to a comfortable parlor. And warm, mind you. I cannot abide with the drafts in this place."

Her voice must have carried to the far corners of the house, for Gainsford appeared suddenly in the room. "This way, my lady," he said very slowly, very loudly. He took Aunt Violet's arm. "I have a pot of tea heating up."

"Nice boy," she said, and gave Gainsford's arm an indulgent pat as she allowed him to lead her away.

Elsbeth led the way upstairs with her cousins following closely behind. Portia, her new lady's maid, was waiting in Elsbeth's chamber to assist her in preparing for the ball. Though Portia styled her long blond tresses into a mass of ringlets with a great deal of skill, Elsbeth missed Molly dearly. Molly had been more than a lady's maid. She'd been a friend.

Elsbeth decided right then and there that she'd speak to Nigel on Molly's behalf. She'd held her tongue too long about the things that were important to her. But no more. She'd make certain Nigel understood how important Molly was to her life.

Her newfound confidence didn't last long, though. As she listened to Olivia's musings on the coming evening, her heart began to pound.

Tonight they would catch the killer. Tomorrow she would wake up, and perhaps, start a normal day with a husband who cherished her. She needed to tell him how happy he'd made her. Perhaps she would make a grand announcement in front of everyone at the ball. Yes, then no one would doubt that their marriage was real.

"Lauretta, do sit up straight," Olivia scolded her younger sister, giving her a sharp poke in the back. "You've been slumping all day."

"I have a perfectly good reason to slump, as you well know. Papa has said I am not even permitted to dance with him tonight."

"Who?" Elsbeth asked absently as she took a final look at herself in the mirror. The sapphire silk gown had hundreds of tiny crystals sewn into the bodice. They sparkled in the room's lamplight as she turned.

"Lord Ames," Olivia answered for her sister. "He is a money grabber, Papa says."

"Indeed?" Elsbeth asked.

"He loves me," Lauretta wailed.

"He asked Papa for permission to marry Lauretta last evening," Olivia explained.

"And was summarily dismissed, I suppose?"

"Papa is ever so unfair! He refused to listen. Sir Donald is as poor as Lord Ames and he wasn't considered a money grabber."

"Your Sir Donald doesn't also have a reputation for being a rake," Olivia said with a laugh. "And he never steered you unescorted to one of the more deserted paths in Hyde Park in full view of half the *ton*'s tabbies."

"That's unfair." Lauretta jumped to her feet and pressed her fists to her hips. "Just yesterday I saw Sir Donald arguing with a woman of questionable morals. The same woman then threw herself at Lord Ames, who politely refused her advances. What do you think of that, *dear sister?*"

A sharp knock at the door brought the argument to an abrupt end. At Elsbeth's nod of approval, Portia opened the door. Gainsford handed the maid a small package. "His lordship requests Lady Edgeware wear this tonight," he said formally. " 'Tis a gift."

Nigel must have returned for the evening. Elsbeth fought a giddy urge to rush downstairs and greet him. But there was still much to be done, and she wanted to be ready and downstairs when the first guests arrived.

Portia bobbed a curtsy as she handed over the box. " 'Tis a gift, m'lady."

"Ooo," Olivia crooned while peering over Elsbeth's shoulder. "I wager he has given you some fantastic jewel."

Elsbeth held her breath as she untied the golden ribbon. The velvet cloth covering the box fell away.

"Diamonds," Lauretta said wistfully. "It has to be diamonds.

How utterly romantic."

Elsbeth lifted the lid. The excited breaths of Olivia and Lauretta brushed her neck. Like her cousins, she half expected to see the sparkle of diamonds or glimmer of jewels when she peered into the box.

No such fantastic sight greeted her.

"A plain locket?" Olivia cried. "It looks exactly like that old one you finally stopped wearing."

"How romantic," Lauretta said. "He misses your battered old locket, so he gave you another one."

Elsbeth felt faintly ill. She'd abandoned the locket and this one did look hauntingly similar. Had Nigel found it? Had he discovered what she'd hidden inside it?

Clutching the new locket in her hand, she searched the bottom of her jewelry box for the original one. It was there, precisely where she had directed Gainsford to leave it.

"Well? Open it." Olivia bounced, waiting.

A lever released the catch and the front of the locket sprang open. Inside, two tiny portraits painted on porcelain stared lovingly at each other. One was an uncanny likeness of her, the other of Nigel.

"Lovely," Lauretta whispered.

Elsbeth held the portraits up to the light. The brushstrokes were dainty and so carefully made. They weren't created by Dionysus's hand. Still, she shivered as she looked at it.

"The guests will be arriving soon," she said, and dropped the locket's chain on over her head. "And do not fret so, Lauretta, I will ask Nigel to speak with your father on Lord Ames's behalf."

"Oh, thank you!" Lauretta cried and hugged her. "I know Severin will be the perfect husband for me! He wants me to be his partner . . . in business!"

Partner? Before meeting Nigel, she would have never thought such a thing could be possible. But in the past few days she'd learned quite a bit about how having a man around could be pleasant, welcome. A man and woman could share common goals, and yes, even become partners.

And right now she had a great desire to go greet her husband and thank him for the unusual, but thoughtful, gift.

As soon as she'd finished dressing, she hurried down the stairs in search of him. She found Nigel in the front entranceway, pacing. Or, more to the point, wringing his hands and pacing. The fashionable dove gray suit he wore fit like a stylish glove. That magical warm glow, she'd been holding onto all day bloomed into a deep, stinging blush as she remembered the pleasures he'd brought her long into the previous night.

He must have heard the rustle of skirts, for he stopped midstep and turned to gaze up the staircase. His onyx eyes grew wide and his mouth dropped slightly open.

How she got the rest of the way down the stairs, she could not say. Perhaps she floated. Regardless, she stood mesmerized in front of *her husband,* staring deeply into his expressive gaze.

"Is everything ready?" she managed to ask.

"Yes." He took her hand and kissed it. "You look lovely," he said. There was a stern edge in his voice. If he indeed thought she looked lovely, his deepening frown certainly didn't support the notion. "I don't want you here tonight. I should have sent you away."

"My absence would raise far too many questions. This is our wedding ball."

Her cousins and Lord Purbeck were all standing around pretending not to be listening to what would no doubt be considered a most peculiar conversation.

"Damn fool boy," Elsbeth very clearly heard Lord Purbeck mutter.

Nigel ignored his uncle, if he had heard him at all. "If anything starts to happen," he said taking Elsbeth's hands in his, "I want you to get yourself to safety. You understand me?"

"What's going on, Elly?" Olivia asked.

"Someone is planning to kill Lord Edgeware tonight," Lauretta said. "Lord Ames told me all about it."

"And my life is in danger too, blasted bother," Lord Purbeck added.

"Oh, that." Olivia nodded.

"Does everyone in London know my business?" Nigel asked looking quite adorably harassed.

"Of course they do." Aunt Violet thumped her cane on the floor as she emerged from the front parlor. "It is the *ton*'s profession to *know*."

And that was where the discussion ended, since the guests had begun to arrive. Nigel kept a tight hold on Elsbeth's hand as he politely greeted each and every guest while a six-piece orchestra played softly upstairs in the drawing room.

As much as she wished it, Elsbeth wasn't able to stay by Nigel's side for long. It was considered quite unfashionable for a husband and wife to linger in each other's company at such an event despite their newlywed status. And it seemed that the guests at the party were determined to keep them apart.

"Promise me one waltz," Nigel said, and quickly kissed her cheek before being led away into a circle of men.

She watched him from a distance. The last time their eyes met from across the ballroom, he graced her with a smile. Such a simple gesture warmed her like a comforting cup of hot tea . . . or like a Dionysus painting of wildflowers.

Her heart twisted. No matter how she tried to let her love for Dionysus fade, she always seemed to fail. She feared the rogue artist would plague her heart until the day it stopped beating.

Who was he? And why did she still harbor soft feelings for him?

She had a mind to march over to her husband and tell him

that she was ready to hear the truth about Dionysus when Charlie caught her arm. A quadrille had begun to play, but instead of leading her to the dance floor, he steered her toward a quiet corner of the balcony. There, she stared at the demon lazily. No, she thought to herself, Charlie couldn't be Dionysus. He simply couldn't.

"I don't know how you managed it, Elly," he whispered bitterly, "but it seems you have quite completely won my cousin's affection. No matter how much I try to show him your true character, he still pictures you with a honeyed gaze."

She jerked her head away when Charlie tried to caress her cheek.

"Still cold, Elly?" Charlie chuckled lightly. "Do you even let Nige into your bed?"

"I don't wish to cause a scene, so I will pretend instead I didn't hear you." In place of the fear she would have expected to feel, she experienced an empowering sense of calm as she realized *she* could trust her husband. No matter what mischief Charlie tried to cause, she knew Nigel was watching out for her and would protect her. He would trust her word above Charlie's. "Please excuse me," she said frostily, and turned to return to the ballroom.

"Wait, please. We do both care about Nige. If you don't wish to see him harmed, you will listen to me. I beg you."

The note of desperation in his voice stopped her where she stood. A shallow bob of her head was her only indication that she was willing to hear what he had to say.

"George Waver has Nige in his pocket. I know you don't believe me, but I have proof that he is trying to kill Nige. If you care for my cousin, even just a little, you will use the power you have over Nige to convince him to stay away from George."

"Mr. Waver has explained himself, his actions. He would have been killed that day on the beach along with Nigel. He is not a murderer . . . you are."

"George is playing a very deep game, Elly. He is trying to make me look guilty, but I assure you I am not."

"I won't listen to another word. Good evening, Mr. Purbeck."

Elsbeth returned to the crowded ballroom where she was drawn into a circle of gossipy women. Yet, even though she had extracted herself from Charlie, his warning repeated itself in her head and she had trouble paying attention to the ladies around her.

Charlie had sounded truly worried.

And if Dionysus wasn't Charlie . . . and he wasn't George Waver, who in the devil was he? She needed to find out before the night was over. Nigel's life could very well depend on her uncovering Dionysus's identity. She couldn't wait a moment longer.

She glanced over and saw that Nigel was surrounded by an even tighter group of men than before. Even though she longed to hear the truth from his ears, she suspected that there was another in the house who would be just as able to help her.

Elsbeth excused herself from the bevy of women who were engaged in a heated discussion on whether ladies should indulge in reading novels. "Rots the brain," a lady declared as Elsbeth went in search for the man from whom she was determined to wrench the truth. She spotted him lurking beside a potted palm just outside the drawing room.

"My lady?" Gainsford inquired as she approached. She directed him into a private alcove near the top of the stairs.

"Gainsford," she said, jamming a finger against his chest. "You are the most inquisitive butler I have ever known. So tell me the truth. Who is Dionysus?"

"I-I cannot tell—"

"Gainsford! We are talking about the Marquess's life! I must know the answer now. Who is Dionysus?"

The poor man dabbed at his brow with a handkerchief. "We are running low on wine. Perhaps you could select a few bottles to serve with dinner?"

"You are changing the subject, Gainsford. Besides, shouldn't you handle—?"

"Oh no, my lady, his lordship *never* entertains. I wouldn't know where to begin." Gainsford pulled a large key from his pocket and pressed it into her hand before she could object. "At the back of the house. The door just past the kitchens leads down to the cellar, my lady." He gave her a pressing look. *"I daresay you will find everything you are looking for in the cellar."*

"The cellar?"

Gainsford shook his head vigorously. "Yes, my lady. *The cellar.*"

"Very well," she said. Her fingers were quaking by the time she hurried through the doors to the busy kitchens. She didn't spare the startled servants a passing glance as she marched toward her destination. The hallway past the kitchens was eerily silent.

She pulled a candle down from a sconce on the unadorned brick wall and held it above the rusty keyhole. The key turned easily in the lock, but the door held firm in the jam. She kicked it several times with her slippered foot before it opened.

Her answer was only steps away. She swung the door wide and rushed into the dark depths, stopping on the last step as she raised the candle higher.

A neat row of paintbrushes sat on a large wooden table just to the right of her. An easel with a medium sized canvas stood barely three feet away.

And suddenly she *knew.*

She stepped gingerly around the easel and gazed upon the unfinished painting. The broad brushwork was even more hectic

The Nude

and filled with more wild energy than any of his other works. That wildness that had once thrilled her now frightened her to her very soul. She was the subject of this latest work.

How could she not have known?

Everything Nigel did, his very scent made her think she'd just stepped into one of Dionysus's paintings. Of course the two men were one and the same.

The figure in the painting, which looked startlingly like her, was collapsed beside a pond. A painting, ripped into shreds, floated in the water just out of reach of her fingertips. The leafy vegetation in the forefront drooped, wilting, dying from the burden of her pain.

He should have told her. He should have insisted she listen to the truth. He should have insisted she understood exactly what he'd done to her. Like the woman in the painting, she felt like weeping. He should have told her.

Nigel was Dionysus. He was the one who'd trapped her in that horrid marriage with Lord Mercer. He was the one who'd painted that scandalously nude painting of her. And he was the one who had left her with an aching heart for all these years, a heart that suddenly felt like breaking.

Why? Why? Why did he do those things to her?

And why did he tell her that he loved her?

She reached up to the locket hanging like a burden around her neck and snapped the chain.

"Damn him," she cursed, feeling her bones ache from the years of repressed anger. "Damn him to hell and back! Why would he do this to me?"

CHAPTER THIRTY

Nigel glanced around the room. He'd last seen Elsbeth talking with Charlie, but now she had slipped away. As hostess she had many demands on her time, he knew that. But still, he felt uneasy.

"George would have been killed by that boulder. He's not trying to kill me, Charlie." Nigel said, but he couldn't keep his mind on the conversation. Where the devil was Elsbeth?

Every damned man at the party had come up with a list of names for Nigel to consider. Some, such as suggesting Beau Brummell was jealous of Nigel's connections with the Regent, were laughable.

"How about Dionysus? Artists tend to have a nasty streak," Charlie said.

Uncle Charles harrumphed. Severin chuckled.

"How can you think this is funny, Severin? Someone tried to kill Nige and my father."

Nigel merely shrugged and kept his gaze focused on the crush in his drawing room. There was barely enough room to dance, though the guests made do. Many were dancing with quite a lively gait, in fact.

"I heard Lord Baneshire has rejected your bid for Lady Lauretta's hand, Severin," Nigel said absently. "It appears your rakish ways are catching up to you."

"Damned nuisance, this lack of money. It has turned me into a man I despise." Severin pulled Nigel away from the crowd of men and lowered his voice. "Surely, Lady Edgeware has told you what I witnessed several years ago at Mercer's estate. I apologize for not doing more. That one time I'd stepped in, she gave me such a blistering set-down I never attempted to assist her again."

At that, Nigel quirked a brow. "What do you mean?"

"She is a strong lady. You are lucky to have found her." Severin frowned as he watched Charlie saunter away. Severin then swallowed a healthy dose of his drink, a strong whiskey. "If I were in her place, I wouldn't be able to abide to be in the same room as Charlie, much less speak civilly with him."

"Charlie?" Nigel asked. "He's harmless."

"Harmless?" Severin snorted and nearly choked. "Charlie encouraged that brute Mercer whenever he started to make sport of Elsbeth. I was there to witness one dreadful evening. Charlie and Mercer were deep in their cups and vicious. Thought I would die from shame, knowing what they were doing to a lady. I had to step in even though I'd probably only made things worse for Elsbeth, the poor thing. Men like that don't stop. They never stop."

"Mercer and Charlie raped her?" Nigel asked, quite unable to believe it.

"Charlie didn't. At least not that night. I made damn sure he wouldn't be in a position to touch a woman for several days, in fact. As for that bastard Mercer, I don't know. I didn't stay long enough to find out. I am sorry, Edgeware. I ended my friendship with them the very next day, but I now wish I had done more. At least with you she has a chance to heal and perhaps find some happiness."

Nigel was quaking with impotent rage. She should have told him. He would have kept Charlie away from her, protected her from his constant taunts. Thank God Severin had finally confessed what he knew.

"I'll have a word with Lord Baneshire this evening on your behalf, Severin. You're still a rakish young man, but I believe you will turn out well in the end."

"Thank you, Edgeware. You-you don't know what that means to me." Severin pumped Nigel's hand.

"Do you think you'll be able to handle it? Marriage, I mean?" Nigel asked. "I believe Lady Lauretta will expect a faithful husband."

"And she'll have one. My current lifestyle has long lost its luster. I'm looking forward to quiet evenings by the fire. And children. Lots of children."

Nigel had to admit he'd never seen Severin look so happy. He hoped he'd be able to convince Baneshire to change his mind regarding Severin's motives for wanting to marry Lady Lauretta. Perhaps if Nigel provided Severin with a healthy sum of money—in appreciation for keeping Dionysus's secret— Baneshire might see the reformed rake in an entirely different light. Yes, that would be the right thing to do.

As for Charlie, Nigel wasn't sure what he planned to do. He watched as his cousin laughed boisterously with Sir Donald. With Nigel and Uncle Charles out of the way, Charlie would stand to inherit everything. He would have all the money he would ever need. Perhaps Elsbeth had been right all along. Perhaps—

"Nigel." A slender hand touched his sleeve. Nigel's body reacted immediately to her touch. He smiled down on that hand.

"I don't deserve you, love." He covered her hand with his.

"No." Elsbeth's eyes were hard, her lips drawn to a thin line. "You don't deserve me, you deceiving bounder."

Her voice wasn't much above a whisper. Anyone around them couldn't possibly suspect how her words wounded him.

"Elsbeth? What is wrong?"

She held out the locket, the chain broken.

"*You.* You are what is wrong. You've lied to me from the start." Her voice rose. A few heads turned toward them. "Did you think I would be grateful? You've played me no differently than an unruly child wrecking a toy. Trapping me into one painful scenario after another. The nude painting that was inspired. Everyone thought such nasty things about me after that. Where else was I to turn but into your waiting arms?"

"Elsbeth," Nigel scolded, too confused to do anything but chide her. She wasn't making a whit of sense. A crowd began gathering around them and the scene they were making.

"Edgeware has never wished to harm you." George pushed his way through the throng to stand at Nigel's side. "Surely you know that, my lady."

She glared at George for a moment before returning her killing gaze to Nigel.

"Perhaps the Lord Edgeware you know is honorable, Mr. Waver. But I assure you, Dionysus lacks even a grain of decency."

"Dionysus?" a murmur rose in the growing crowd.

"Boy!" Lord Purbeck stepped forward. "Put a stop to this."

But Nigel only held out his hands, helpless to do anything but allow her to unmask him in front of everyone. After all the pain she'd suffered because of him, she deserved to be the one to rip this façade away.

"Lord Edgeware is Dionysus," Elsbeth announced. "With his paintings he tricked me. He made me fall in love with a monster . . . twice."

The room fell silent. Someone had even told the orchestra to stop playing.

"Is this true?" George demanded.

"Yes." Nigel wouldn't deny what Elsbeth had said. He deserved the *ton*'s scorn, not her.

The locket in Elsbeth's hand clattered to the floor as the

crowd pushed her out of their way and closed ranks around him.

"I say, brilliant work," a gentleman boasted.

"This is all so exciting," a lady twittered.

"Bah!" Uncle Charles snorted.

They were proud of him, laughing and patting him on the back. Oh, what a lark! He'd pulled the wool over everyone's eyes. He was ever so clever, was he not?

The porcelain lovers staring lovingly at each other within the locket were crushed under the feet of excited guests. The sound of Nigel's gift being destroyed burned in Elsbeth's ears as she let herself be pushed away. She didn't wish to cry in front of the entire population of the *ton*. She didn't wish to cry at all, in fact.

Hiding somewhere, curling up into a tight ball, and dying felt like a promising option. Nigel had betrayed her trust. He had lured her into feeling soft emotions, had lured her into opening her heart just so he could rip it to shreds.

She loved Nigel as fiercely as she had loved Dionysus.

Oh la, why had she not learned her lesson the first time?

She stumbled blindly into a side table. A hand curled around her arm and gave her a tug. "Come with me."

"Elsbeth?" How could she disappear so quickly? The rest of the world could go hang themselves. She was the only one who mattered. Nigel pushed his way through the crowd, ignoring the tugs on his sleeve and pats on the back.

On the stair leading to the bedchambers, he finally found a moment's peace. Surely she'd escaped to her own room. Where else other than her personal chamber could a lady go to hide?

He raised his hand to knock on her door.

"She's not within," Gainsford said as he emerged from the

darkened chamber.

"Where is she then?"

"I don't know."

Well, he simply would have to find her.

"Sir?" Gainsford shifted from one foot to the next, looking damned guilty. "There is something in there you should see."

"Are you snooping again?" The nasty habit had been a real problem when Gainsford had first taken employment with Nigel.

"Lady Edgeware had asked me to put something away for her. It wasn't my fault the latch fell open."

"I don't have time for games. I must find Elsbeth."

Gainsford grabbed Nigel's arm. "You must see this first, my lord."

Not wanting to waste time arguing, he followed Gainsford into Elsbeth's bedchamber. It was empty and cold as if she had never really inhabited the room.

Gainsford went straight to her jewelry box and produced the original golden locket. "She stopped wearing this the day the Earl of Baneshire came to take her home, my lord." Gainsford fiddled with the latch. "She told her uncle she was choosing to stay with you of her own free will."

When the locket sprang open, Gainsford handed over the necklace. "I believe Lady Edgeware kept the memory of the man she loved close to her heart. But she was willing to set that love aside. She set that love aside for you."

Nigel ground his jaw as he stared at the small scrap of canvas tucked inside the locket. He recognized it immediately. Of course he recognized it.

Tears pricked the back of his throat. The tiny canvas had been lovingly cut from one of Dionysus's paintings—one of *his* paintings. His brush had flowed over this particular canvas only a few days after he had first seen Elsbeth, the lithe schoolgirl. Her image had already seeped deep into his soul.

Unlike many of his other paintings, he had added his image to this one, a tiny figure hardly visible. He stood off to the side, separate from the action in the scene.

Alone, completely alone.

But Elsbeth had seen him. Not only that, she had reached out to him by plucking him from his faraway position in the landscape and had placed him in the honored spot next to her heart.

What had he done?

She had always loved him, just as he had always loved her.

What had he done?

That devil, Hubert had taken that painting along with the others. He'd given them one by one to Elsbeth. He'd convinced Elsbeth that it was his passion that had created the paintings. Lord Mercer had tricked her into believing that it was his heart she loved.

But she had always loved Nigel, just as he had always loved her.

Yet his carelessness had destroyed that love.

He had destroyed the most important love of his life.

"Nige."

Nigel blinked back the threatening tears to find that he was alone in the room. Gainsworth had left but now Charlie stood in the doorway, a crooked grin on his lips.

"Leave me," he growled.

"Nige." Charlie took a step into the darkened room. "Return to the celebration. Elly's outburst is just her way of rebelling against you. She tried to do the same thing time and again with Mercer. I tried to warn you. I—"

Nigel slammed his fist into Charlie's square jaw. His cousin dropped like a stone. "That's just a taste of what I plan to do to you for what you and that bastard Mercer did to Elsbeth," he said, and rubbed his sore knuckles.

He stepped over his cousin and rushed off to find Elsbeth. He needed to tell her what he should have confessed to her all those years ago.

"Edgeware and Dionysus are one and the same?" Mr. Waver asked as if he couldn't quite believe it. "Incredible."

Elsbeth didn't say a word. She was grateful for the company, though. Mr. Waver had pulled her from the drawing room and had led her belowstairs and back to the locked doorway to Dionysus's workshop. Or had she led Mr. Waver here?

"I should have known." He shook his head. "I should have guessed it. His creative streak, something that quite obsessed him, disappeared one summer. I'd thought his uncle had finally beaten it out of him. It should have been obvious the desire had gone underground instead."

She listened to Mr. Waver with only half an ear. Her head still buzzed from the shock. She had loved Nigel . . .

The key turned easily in the lock. The door opened without hesitation this time.

"So, this is where he goes to create?" Mr. Waver asked, poking his head into the darkened cellar. "Is this how you found out?"

She nodded. She hadn't cried. She'd probably never cry over this. The hurt ran too deep.

"Show me." Mr. Waver took her hand and led her down into the cellar. "Show me how his paintings have intruded on your love for him."

She forced herself to descend the stairs and once again study the unfinished painting set up on the easel. Mr. Waver stood a step behind her, his arms crossed in front of his chest. He held his silence.

"He betrayed me," she said finally.

Mr. Waver was unmoved.

The wild brushstrokes created an image that promised to be hauntingly beautiful. The woman Nigel had created from exotic dyes and crushed precious stones had a broken heart. The plants in the forefront wept with her pain.

"Why do you think the woman on the canvas despairs?" Mr. Waver asked after what seemed like a lifetime of grief.

"She is unloved," was her quick answer. She stepped forward, raising the candle higher to study the scene more closely. The destroyed and discarded painting floating in the pond caught her attention. What did the painting within the painting mean? She ran her fingers over the textured brushstrokes.

"She loved," Elsbeth amended her answer. "The love was not returned."

"Ah," he said. "Do you truly believe yourself to be the woman portrayed there?"

To that she had no ready answer. But how could she not be that woman? For too many years she'd loved Dionysus without having that love returned. And now, just as she believed she finally found love, this had happened.

"I suppose," he said, "Edgeware painted this scene because he felt guilty. You loved him and he could not love you back?"

But that couldn't be right. The painter felt the woman's grief, actually felt it.

"You proved your love for Edgeware in so many ways. How could he not feel guilty?"

Guilt? Where was the guilt in the wilting ferns, in the dark background, or in the deadly still water in the pond? Mr. Waver must be blind. The painter didn't feel guilt.

He felt unloved.

From one moment to the next, her heart sank. She'd been the one withholding her love. She'd been the one inflicting pain on a wounded heart. She was the one who had become the monster . . .

"I need to find him," she said. "I need to tell him that I love him. I need to tell him that I've always loved him . . ."

CHAPTER THIRTY-ONE

Elsbeth searched the far corners of the house, and still she couldn't find Nigel. Though the band continued to play lively tunes, many of the guests had left, dispersed to spread the exciting news of Dionysus's identity to the other ballrooms and clubs in London.

Her family and Nigel's were closed up in a parlor located in the back of the house. Lauretta sat on a sofa next to Lord Ames, her hand tucked into his lap. Aunt Violet, sitting on a chair across the room, didn't seem to mind. In fact, her aunt appeared to be deeply engrossed in a conversation with Lord Purbeck.

No one had seen Nigel.

"Ask Charlie," Lord Purbeck suggested. "He went to talk with Nigel after that unseemly display in the drawing room."

"His lordship is not in the house, my lady," Gainsford confided a few minutes later. "Every member of the household staff has searched for him. No one knows when he left, but he is not within."

"Have you seen Mr. Charlie Purbeck?" Elsbeth asked hoarsely, her heart stuck in her throat. "Has anyone seen Mr. Purbeck?"

"No, my lady. There was such a commotion, what with you announcing his lordship's great secret. He could have left at anytime without notice."

Charlie. She provided the diversion and he took the opportunity to kidnap and—God help her—kill Nigel.

She drew a deep breath. He may still be alive. She refused to stand idly by and let Charlie win this battle without a royal fight on her part. "Fetch my cloak and have a carriage brought around."

Gainsford paled. "But-but, my lady."

"And have dinner served. I'll not have the remaining guests neglected."

Gainsford opened his mouth to protest again, but he must have seen her determination sparking in her eyes, for he shut his mouth and hurried away. A footman quickly arrived and handed Elsbeth her cloak.

"Where are you going?" Mr. Waver asked. He blocked her path to the front door.

"Stand aside, Mr. Waver. Charlie has Nigel. And I intend to save him."

Mr. Waver refused to move.

"Bah!" Lord Purbeck growled behind her. "Charlie may be a stupid boy, but he would never hurt his cousin."

"Stand aside, Mr. Waver," Elsbeth said again, pitching her voice low.

"But we all just want to help, Elsbeth," Lauretta said.

Elsbeth spun around and found Lord Ames helping Lauretta with her pelisse. Olivia, curiously without a male escort, already wore her pelisse and was fussing with her gloves. Aunt Violet, also ready to go out, had her arm securely wrapped around Lord Purbeck's.

"I have distracted Papa, Elly, though I think he would join us if he knew," Olivia said with an uncharacteristically determined grimace.

"Very well." Mr. Waver still hadn't moved out of the way.

"Where are you going?" he asked again. "We cannot rush into the night without a plan."

When she started to protest, Mr. Waver raised his hand and lowered a quelling glance in the direction of Lord Purbeck. "Charlie, if he is indeed the man we need to be wary of, will not hie Edgeware to his bachelor rooms on St. James's."

"I'm not a fool." She hesitated, not wishing to blurt out her plans in front of her innocent cousins and her husband's friends. But there was no hope for it. "Mademoiselle Dukard." A blush stung her cheeks. "I planned to speak with her to find out—"

"Ducky?" Lord Ames said.

"That horrid woman in Hyde Park, you mean?" Lauretta said. "I should think Sir Donald would know what *that* woman is up to."

"I don't have time for this. The carriage is waiting. I must go. Stand aside, Mr. Waver." She pushed Mr. Waver to the side and threw open the door before the footman could do it for her. With her skirts gathered up in her hand, she charged down the steps and jumped into Nigel's carriage while the hellish black steeds snorted at the lead.

Mr. Waver, Olivia, Lauretta, and Lord Ames followed, squeezing into the carriage, though it was not designed to carry more than four people. Lady Violet and Lord Purbeck both were intent on joining them, but there simply wasn't room. Lord Purbeck shouted for his carriage to be brought around and demanded that they wait for him. Yet there wasn't time to wait. Much to Elsbeth's relief Mr. Waver rapped on the roof. "Mademoiselle Dukard's cottage is a good place to start," he said as the carriage swayed into motion.

Elsbeth sat back, her heart beating a dizzying tattoo, and closed her eyes. *Please, let me find him alive,* she prayed. *Please, don't let him die.*

The carriage lurched as it came to a sudden halt.

"Stay with the women," Mr. Waver said to Lord Ames. He already had the door open and one foot out. "I will go in alone."

No one argued. Certainly not Elsbeth, who was feeling fairly certain that she was missing something very important.

Lauretta and Olivia were whispering. Vaguely, she thought they might be speaking to her, but she pushed the notion away.

She sighed. What was it that she was missing?

"I always thought Sir Donald was a milksop," Olivia said, speaking much louder now. "I do approve of your new choice of beau."

"Why thank you, Lady Olivia," Lord Ames replied.

"And to learn that Sir Donald is as buried in debt as you are truly puts you on an even keel, does it not? I heard his debts came from a single gambling bet. Lady Constance told me just this evening that two rather frightening gentlemen had threatened his life while they were taking ices together just this afternoon. Most ungentlemanly to expose a lady to such individuals," Olivia said. Elsbeth fought an urge to cover her ears with her hands. She needed to concentrate.

"Perhaps that was what he and Ducky were arguing about in the park?" Lauretta said. "Perhaps he was trying to get her to help him do something utterly wicked in order to keep the moneylenders from extracting payment in a more violent way."

"What?" Elsbeth said, blinking as she opened her eyes. "What did you just say, Lauretta?"

"I was just wondering if Sir Donald wasn't trying to get Ducky to—"

"Lord Ames!" Elsbeth leaned forward and grabbed his arm. "Go fetch Mr. Waver, now! I believe I know where Nigel has been taken, and I fear we don't have much time."

The horses pulled the carriage through the London streets at a harrowing pace as they raced toward the docks. A thick fog rolled in off the Thames and seeped through the windows of the carriage creating a damp chill Elsbeth could not seem to shake.

"This cannot be right," Mr. Waver said, though he had obeyed without argument when Elsbeth had ordered him to give the driver the direction to his own warehouse. "You don't still believe I am somehow involved, do you?"

"No, I don't. But just like the night of the storm, he wants you to take the blame, Mr. Waver. Charlie can't be blamed for his cousin's death. He wouldn't be able to inherit the estate if he were connected to either Lord Purbeck's or the Marquess's deaths." The conviction in Elsbeth's voice amazed even her. No one could wrest control from her. Not now, not when so much depended on her success. "Don't you see? Charlie had been so insistent on proving your guilt, because you had been set up to look guilty."

As soon as the carriage rolled to a stop, Elsbeth jumped down before the steps had been lowered. "I do hope you have a pistol hidden within the folds of that cloak, Mr. Waver."

"I do," Lord Ames offered as he produced a large weapon.

"Gracious," Lauretta breathed, growing pale as her gaze fixed on the gun.

"Steady," Lord Ames said, and supported her with his free hand.

"I, too, have a gun," Olivia said. She held out an equally menacing weapon.

"Oh no," Mr. Waver backed up. "I will not go in there with a woman waving a deadly weapon around."

"Give that to me," Elsbeth said, and snatched the gun away from Olivia. "You don't know how to use this."

"And you do?" Olivia protested.

"Yes." Elsbeth didn't explain how she and Molly had taught themselves the deadly art of gunmanship after a particularly brutal summer. She checked to make sure the pistol was indeed loaded before charging ahead. The creaking of ships rocking at the docks carried through the eerie fog. Whole ships and buildings had disappeared into the mists.

"This way," Mr. Waver whispered. He took her arm and led her in the opposite direction toward a small door on the side of the long warehouse building that had appeared out of nowhere in front of them. Mr. Waver must have taken possession of Lord Ames's gun. He dropped the pistol into a pocket and pulled out a key. Despite the dim light he had no trouble unlocking the door.

Elsbeth pushed the door open and stepped inside before Mr. Waver could dare protest.

"Drop your weapon." Sir Donald's distinctive voice echoed up through the rafters of the empty warehouse. His voice so startled Elsbeth that she nearly let the pistol clatter to the wooden floor.

"I said, drop the gun, Mr. Waver." Sir Donald had barely glanced in Elsbeth's direction. She pushed her hand into a fold of her cloak, concealing the pistol Sir Donald had obviously overlooked.

Sir Donald was standing on top of a wooden crate with Nigel motionless at his feet and Charlie bound up like Christmas goose on the floor beside them. A burly cutthroat stepped into view. A long knife balanced in one hand.

"Drop the gun!" Sir Donald bent down and dragged Nigel up from the floor. Nigel's eyes were barely open. His head flopped against Sir Donald's chest. Sir Donald pressed a jagged knife to Nigel's throat. A thin ribbon of blood, Nigel's blood, coated the length of the blade.

Mr. Waver gave Elsbeth a sidelong glance before letting his gun drop to the ground.

"Found these three wanderin' about outside," a second accomplice said. This one had a wicked scar bisecting the right side of his face. He shoved Lord Ames, Lauretta, and Olivia into the warehouse with one heavy thrust.

Lauretta and Olivia stumbled to their knees.

"We'll have to kill them all," Sir Donald said with a chilling calm. He dropped Nigel and leapt down from the crate. "Bloody, bloody nuisance. This isn't working out at all how I'd planned." He spun on his heel and glared down at Charlie. "I'll still be taking the Edgeware family money, mind you. I'm owed that money. I would have never placed that damned bet if you hadn't twisted my arm, telling me I couldn't possibly lose. Which means I won't be able to kill you. Damned bloody nuisance."

Charlie yelped when Sir Donald kicked him in his side.

"Tie the women up," Sir Donald said to his henchmen. "We will dispatch them last."

Elsbeth backed away before a rope could be lopped over her wrists. She couldn't let herself be bound. Not with so many lives at stake.

"You think you're so clever, don't you Sir Donald?" she said as she closed the distance between her and Sir Donald.

"Yes. I rather do."

Lauretta cried out as the scarred man dragged her to her feet.

"Unhand her," Elsbeth ordered. She whipped the pistol out from her cloak and pressed it against Sir Donald's chest. "Tell him to let my cousins go. Now, or I shall shoot you."

"Put that toy away," Sir Donald said.

Elsbeth cocked the pistol. "I don't believe I will miss. Not standing this close to you. What do you think?"

"Elsbeth, no," Nigel cried out weakly just as Sir Donald tried to snatch her gun away.

"You are naught but a woman. That's what I think," Sir Donald said with a laugh. He grabbed the pistol's metal shaft.

She pulled the trigger and fired. His eyes grew wide with disbelief as blood bloomed on his arm.

"You bloody whore! I should have killed you myself instead of letting that oaf Guthrie dump you out into the storm."

He lunged then, his icy fingers curling around her neck, squeezing the life from her. She struggled, ripping at his wrists as the dimly lit warehouse grew even dimmer.

"No!" she heard Nigel shout. A sickly pop followed. Sir Donald's tight grip around her throat almost immediately loosened.

Sucking in air, she watched Sir Donald crumple to the ground at her feet. Nigel was standing on the crate. Mr. Waver was next to him. The pistol in Nigel's hand still smoked.

Sir Donald was dead.

Elsbeth's heartbeat thundered in her chest. She barely noticed the two burly villains trying to escape into the night.

"Elsbeth?" She didn't know how he'd gotten there, but Nigel was suddenly standing directly in front of her. He had a tight hold on her shoulders. "Elsbeth?" he said again and gave her a gentle shake. "Elsbeth, dove, speak to me."

She blinked heavily.

"She's in shock," someone said.

Slowly, ever so slowly, the world all around her returned. "You're Dionysus," she muttered.

Nigel's gaze darkened. "Yes, I am."

Still too numb to react properly, she merely shook her head. Lauretta was screaming somewhere behind her. Her poor innocent cousins, they should have never witnessed such a wretched scene. Why had they been allowed to come along?

She fought free of Nigel's grasp and half-walked half-stumbled to where Lord Ames hugged Lauretta to his chest. Her cousin's screams had thankfully softened to soft whimpers.

It appeared that everyone in the dark warehouse was just standing around not doing much of anything. Which seemed odd. And Nigel, dear living, breathing Nigel, looked frozen in place.

Olivia touched her hand to Elsbeth's cheek. "How are you?" she whispered.

"I am quite fine, thank you," Elsbeth said tartly, and fainted dead away.

CHAPTER THIRTY-TWO

The candle sputtered and started to dim. If there had been windows in his dank cellar, Dionysus would have seen that morning was breaking, that the dense fog was dissipating.

He hadn't slept. There was no possible way he could have slept, not after the way Elsbeth had looked at him, not after seeing the confusion and hurt bubbling in her sapphire gaze. How could he seek out his bed, knowing that she wouldn't be in it? He'd lost her.

It was time to do the honorable thing.

It was time to let her go.

Sir Donald was dead, and there was no longer a threat.

He ground fresh vermilion and worked the dust into a paste, taking his time to get the consistency just right. He dipped the soft bristles of his brush into the scarlet paste. And then paused to study the unfinished painting. His brush poised, he prepared his heart to finish the task he had started.

Gainsford entered the breakfast parlor and cleared his throat. "My lady?"

Elsbeth put down her fork—she'd only been pushing the food around her plate anyhow. She gave a shallow nod. Nigel's butler looked grim, even grimmer than the night before when Nigel's life had been in peril.

"His lordship requests your presence in the study, my lady," he said.

She'd not seen Nigel since the warehouse. Lord Purbeck and Aunt Violet had arrived in Lord Purbeck's carriage shortly after the excitement had ended. Nigel had spoken quietly with his uncle before sending Elsbeth, her cousins, and Aunt Violet away with Lord Ames.

All night she'd waited for his return. The first rays of morning were breaking through the heavy clouds when she finally drifted off to sleep. If he had returned to the house, he never found his way to his bed. For that was where she had spent the night, in his bed.

Gainsford cleared his throat again. "I am sorry about what happened last evening."

"At least it is over now." She stood gingerly. The rough activities the night before had tugged at the stitches in her side. This morning she was stiff and uncomfortable.

And incredibly sad. Why hadn't Nigel come to her? She'd lingered in their suite of rooms, waiting until nearly morning's end. Still, he'd not come.

She went to the study and found Nigel sitting at his large oak desk. His cravat hung loose around his neck. A dark bloodstain stood out on the starched white material. He wasn't wearing a coat or waistcoat. His sleeves were rolled to his elbows, his shirt and hands flecked with paint.

He didn't look up when she entered the room but continued to study a document sitting on the desk. He looked rumpled and tired and harassed and wonderfully, wonderfully alive.

Her heart flipped in her chest.

With a wave of his hand he dismissed his man-of-affairs who, without meeting Elsbeth's gaze, scurried from the room.

Once they were alone, Nigel raised his head and sighed. Those dark eyes of his no longer looked as if they reflected the depths of hell. They shined with something deeper, darker. He gathered up the papers before him and circled around the desk to stand in front of her.

"I trust you're well this morning," he said.

"Yes. And yourself?"

"Never better." A lie. His tortured eyes spoke the truth for him.

He held out the sheave of papers. "This is a deed for one of my smaller estates. I put the property in your name. The land will provide you with a comfortable income. In addition, I will send you a quarterly allowance. It is all spelled out in the second document."

"All . . . spelled . . . out . . . ?" Her heart sank to her toes.

"My life is no longer in danger. I thank you for staying by my side, for saving my life." He stepped back, putting a distance between them that she feared she would never be able to breach. "I have seen Charlie shipped off to an estate my uncle owns in the Caribbean where he will work off the debts he has collected. I will make sure he will never bother you again."

"Thank you," she said. The world felt as if it was tipping on its end. She grabbed the edge of the desk to steady herself. Something must have happened after she'd left him last night. But what? He'd promised he loved her. But if that was true, why was he pushing her away?

"You stayed with me. Without you, none of this would have been sorted out." He took another step away from her. "I would have been killed last night if not for your quick thinking. For that, I'll be forever in your debt. However, as much as you may wish it, we cannot annul the marriage. You must understand that. In society's eyes we are already joined. In truth, we are joined, you and I. I will do everything in my power to make certain the bishop recognizes the union. You need not worry about your reputation."

"I don't understand." She crumpled the documents she was holding.

"It's simply, really. I'm releasing you from any obligations you might believe you have toward me. We will remain husband and wife in name only. I am giving you the freedom you crave. The freedom you deserve."

He turned away from her to stare into the fireplace. "Please. Go."

But she couldn't. She stood there, her gaze fixed on his broad shoulders, stunned. The documents slipped from her fingers and scattered on the ornate rug. She would be free, forever free. That had been what she'd wanted. So, why did she feel as if he'd just run a knife through her heart?

She stepped toward him.

The muscles in his neck stiffened. "Go." His voice was sharp, angry. "Go. Now."

But she couldn't leave. Not like this. Her gaze strayed to Dionysus's small, violent painting above the mantle. The colors were dark, yet there was a fragment of a rainbow—a sliver of light—struggling in the midst of a terrible storm that was whipping the sea into a brutal rage.

The painting troubled her.

And suddenly she knew why.

"Before I leave," she said, "answer me one question. Why did you create Dionysus? Why did you feel the need?"

After a long, tense silence, she gave up and moved toward the door.

"I couldn't," he said, just as her hand touched the knob. His face was still toward the fire. "You see it. Don't deny it. I've seen you shiver whenever you look at my work. You recognize it. I couldn't risk letting people know."

"What did you think you needed to hide?" she asked gently.

"The emptiness." He raised a fisted hand to his chest. "I'm flawed, unworthy of my lands, my fortune, my title. My paintings are as flighty and empty as the painter who created them.

How could I risk letting my colleagues or my family discover such a defect?"

Her gaze again strayed to the violent storm in the painting. She recognized pain, anger, frustration in the brush strokes, but not emptiness.

And the rainbow.

She'd been wrong about it. How could she have loved Nigel and still have mistaken the painting's meaning? The storm wasn't destroying the rainbow. No, without the furious spiraling maelstrom, there could be no beauty. The storm raging within Nigel had created the delicate miracle.

Beneath the pain, beneath the self-loathing his uncle had forced upon him, there was hope. She prayed she could reach it. Oh, how desperately she needed to reach it.

She returned to his side and carefully placed her hand on his shoulder. "How can you believe yourself empty when your love has filled me so completely?"

He jerked away from her, moving so close to the fire that he appeared to be in danger of being consumed by the licking flames. "No, I have done nothing."

"*Nothing?* You have reminded me how to love. Even when I fought you, spurned you, you didn't turn your back on me. You stood your ground and waited for me to come to you." She drew a deep breath, fighting back the tears that were threatening. "Your love has freed me from the hell I'd been cast into."

The fire crackled as the coals shifted behind the grate.

"I created that hell," he said.

"No." She realized that their relationship was in her hands. If she wanted it to continue, she was going to have to speak the words she'd once thought she'd never speak again. Her lips trembled. "You freed me, Nigel. Your coming into my life has made me whole." She drew a deep breath and trusted him with her heart. "I love you."

A tense silence weighed down the air in the room.

"What did you say?" he said at long last. He turned toward her.

She grabbed his hands. "I said that I love you, Nigel." The words came much easier now. "I love you. And there is nothing you can do to get rid of me. I can be quite stubborn, I'll have you know. Once my mind is set there really is very little that can be done to change it." She smiled despite her tear-dampened cheeks. "You, my dear husband, are good and stuck with me."

He wrapped his arms around her and held her tightly against his chest as he crowned her head with a halo of gentle kisses.

"Thank you," he whispered.

Nigel slept late the next day. When he finally woke he felt more refreshed, more relaxed than he could ever remember feeling. Though he was alone in the chamber at this late hour, Elsbeth had once again spent the entire night in his bed, a pleasure he fully intended to repeat for as long as he lived.

After dressing and eating a quick breakfast, he grew restless. He sat alone at the breakfast table while his fingers fidgeted and the bitter scent of paints called to him.

An overwhelming urge to paint struck him hard in the chest. This wasn't right. Years and years of training had honed his ability to push all his artistic longings into that pitiful creature Dionysus. Yet over the last few weeks, his barriers had slowly eroded away until he no longer could clearly tell where his personality ended and Dionysus's began.

He buried his face in his hands and groaned. Elsbeth was married to a madman. She deserved better, but no matter how hard he tried, he feared he would never be able to completely destroy the demon infecting his soul.

"You are a damned dreamer, boy. A weakling." How many times had he heard his uncle say those exact words to him?

How many times had his uncle failed to beat the demon from him?

With a silent curse, he returned to the dank cellar, back to his personal hell.

But when he got there he saw that the door to his workshop stood open.

He ran halfway down the steps to find that the room had been stripped bare. Only a rough wooden table and a scattering of discarded canvases remained.

"Gainsford!" Nigel bellowed.

Elsbeth wasn't sure what to expect. She had left Nigel's bed before sunrise and had set the servants immediately to work. This was something she needed to do. Her love for Nigel and Dionysus could not remain fractured.

Nigel deserved more. And so did she.

She waited for him in a bright parlor in the back of the house. The sun streamed into its windows for a goodly portion of the day. The view of the flower garden was sure to inspire.

She bit her lip and prayed she'd done the right thing. Nigel, she was discovering, had feelings as tender and fragile as her own. What she'd done, she'd done out of love.

She prayed he'd view it in the same way.

The commotion downstairs grew louder. Poor Nigel, he sounded so very upset. "Gainsford!" he cried out again. Gainsford—who'd warned her that she was making a grave mistake—must have gone into hiding.

"This isn't a mistake," she told herself firmly. She settled in a white brocade chair and waited. Not a minute later Nigel came rushing through the door. His face pale, he eyes wild with emotion.

"What is the meaning of this?" he demanded.

"I have done what you should have done years ago, Nigel. I—"

"What I should have done?" He pulled his hand through his already mussed hair. "Bloody hell," he muttered.

With the grace of a queen, she rose and selected a paintbrush from a set neatly spread out on a table. She crossed the room and closed his fingers around its long, wooden handle.

Nigel stared at the brush.

"I have brought you into the light." All the furniture, save for the one chair, had been removed to make room for his paints and supplies. She'd done everything she could to transform the room into a pleasant studio.

"There is no reason to hide anymore. I love you. And that love has always included Dionysus." She caressed his cheek.

He didn't speak, didn't breathe. His hand tightened around the ferrule of the brush. He couldn't seem to tear his gaze from it.

"Nigel?" She began to worry now.

He blinked.

"Please, don't be angry. We can have it all moved back." Perhaps Gainsford had been right. Perhaps he wasn't ready.

Nigel wandered to the window and stared down at the flowers in the garden below. "Don't you dare change a blessed thing, Elsbeth."

A smile grew on his lips. "This is all rather a shock, you know." He shook away his stricken look and drew a deep breath. "You were right, of course . . . to move my workshop up here, I mean. I couldn't expect you to pose for me for hours on end in that cellar." That hungry look flashed in his eyes. "It does get rather cold down there, love," he said wolfishly and swept her into his arms.

"I love you, Elsbeth."

EPILOGUE

Leaves rustled high in the trees as a gentle wind provided little relief to the warm summer air. Nigel and Elsbeth had decided to walk back to the Baneshire Estate from the quaint country church whose weathered stone walls had witnessed centuries of happy marriages between the Baneshire family and the other respected members of the *ton*. Today was no exception. The church had been filled with friends and family spilling out onto the grassy lawn in front.

"Everything was perfect, absolutely perfect," Elsbeth said with a sigh. A smile brightened her eyes as she slipped her hand into Nigel's.

Holding hands with Elsbeth felt natural now. It had been three months since their hasty marriage at his home in Dorset, and he was uncommonly happy. And he had Elsbeth to thank for that. Her gentle encouragement of his creative soul had healed him.

He felt secure in her love and was beginning to trust that she felt secure in his as well.

They passed over a small wooden bridge. Water gurgled in the creek below them. The Baneshire house, a modest brick manor, loomed just over the rise. Soon, they would have to join the hordes of guests. Soon, duties to family would keep them apart.

"I would like to paint a portrait of you," he said. "Here . . . now."

She tipped her head back to smile up at him from beneath the straw bonnet shading her face. "Would I be wearing anything in this portrait?" Her sapphire eyes darkened. He was beginning to learn that look. Desire.

He leaned forward and traced the outline of her lips with the pad of his finger. "Just that smile, I believe."

She took his finger into her mouth and bit the tip gently, making his pants suddenly feel tight and uncomfortable. He searched the landscape for a secluded spot where they could escape for an hour or so. If they were careful, they could both return to the manor house unrumpled.

"There is a small hunting box not too far away," she said. Over the past couple of months she'd blossomed into a wonderfully wicked and sensual woman. She tugged on his hand. "We won't be missed."

He gladly followed her lead.

"There you are," Olivia called out from the path in front of them. "I suspected you would try and disappear. Lauretta and Severin would be vastly disappointed if you were absent for the first toast. Especially considering that you, Edgeware, just stood up with Severin while he married my sister."

While he scowled at Olivia, Elsbeth, his gentle wife, laughed at his discomfort. "Later," she whispered as they dutifully followed Olivia to the house.

"Have you told him?" Olivia asked.

"No, now shush," Elsbeth answered far too quickly and then hurried on ahead.

"Told me what?" He stopped in the middle of the path.

"You should tell him. Mama says he has a right to know." Olivia and Elsbeth continued walking on ahead as if he didn't exist.

Elsbeth linked her arm with Olivia's. "I am not ready. I'm terrified, if truth be known. Molly only told me yesterday. She

said I should have known myself."

The day after Sir Donald had been killed, he'd sent for Molly who had still been confined to the servant's quarters in Dorset. He'd spoken with the feisty maid at length in the privacy of his study. Molly, a bit wary at first, had agreed to try not to shoot at him again. She'd seemed sincere enough at the time. But perhaps he'd been wrong to let her return to her former position.

What trickery was the woman up to now? Elsbeth was terrified to tell him something? He ran ahead and caught her arm. "You can tell me anything. I won't be angry with you. You must know that by now."

Olivia laughed. "I doubt she's terrified of your reaction, Edgeware."

Elsbeth fluttered her hands in the air.

"Oh, stop being such a ninny and tell him."

His mind filled with horrible possibilities. They had only just found each other. He couldn't lose her now. *"Please, Elsbeth."*

"Very well." She took her time removing her bonnet. "Molly believes I am—I am—" She turned a plaintive look toward Olivia. "It just seems impossible."

"You are, what?" He pressed.

She's dying. He should have known their happiness couldn't last.

"Molly believes I am with child," she said with a rush.

"With child?" The world began to spin.

"I haven't had my courses for at least two months. I am usually very regular, you see. And I have been ill. Just in the mornings, mind you. It is impossible, though. I'm barren." Her nervous fingers twisted the ribbon on her bonnet, crumpling it beyond repair.

"With child?" He felt as if he were being smothered.

"It's not impossible, Elly. Mama already explained all that."

"*With child?*" A great buzzing filled his ears.

"Why does he keep asking that?" Elsbeth asked.

"He's in shock." Olivia gave Elsbeth a shove in his direction. "I think he's going to faint."

Elsbeth wrapped her arms around his waist and hugged him tightly. "Please don't, Nigel. I need you to be strong. I, for one, am simply terrified."

"You can count on me, Elsbeth." He closed his eyes and breathed in her sweet fragrance. A beautiful toddler with the face of an angel danced merrily through his thoughts. "A baby . . . *your* baby."

He wrapped his arms around her, amazed at how astonishing the world could be.

ABOUT THE AUTHOR

For Regency and suspense author, **Dorothy McFalls,** happily-ever-after is more than just a fictional ending. She's enjoyed every day of marriage to her sexy sculptor husband who often exhibits the patience of a saint. They reside in an artsy beach community in South Carolina with their two loveable dogs. Formerly an environmental urban planner, she now writes full time. Dorothy loves to hear from her readers at Dorothy@dorothymcfalls.com or visit Dorothy's website at www.dorothymcfalls.com.